Also by Kathleen Shoop

Historical Fiction:

The Letter Series:
The Last Letter—Book One
The Road Home—Book Two
The Kitchen Mistress—Book Three
The Thief's Heart—Book Four
The River Jewel—A prequel

The Donora Story Collection
After the Fog—Book One
The Strongman and the Mermaid—Book Two
The Magician—Book Three

Romance:

Endless Love Series:
Home Again—Book One
Return to Love—Book Two
Tending Her Heart—Book Three

Women's Fiction:

Love and Other Subjects

Bridal Shop Series:
Puff of Silk—Book One

Holiday:

The Christmas Coat
The Tin Whistle

A Novel

The Strongman and the Mermaid

KATHLEEN SHOOP

The Strongman and the Mermaid is a work of fiction. Names, places, and events have been used fictitiously.

Cover Design: Jenny Q—historicalfictionbookcovers.com
Interior Design—Rachelle Ayala

The ancient, superstitious Candlemas Day saying included in *The Strongman and the Mermaid* was drawn from countless renditions that have survived in many forms over time.

To Brian Charlton, Mark Pawelec, and Charles E. Stacey. None of the stories in the Donora Collection would be as rich and layered without your generous insight, information, time and patience. Donora's past and present flows through the historical society and Smog Museum and is a treasure to all who stop by to see what exactly started it all. Thank you from the bottom of my heart.

Note:
In 1910 the word *baseball* was mostly written as two separate words. I chose to write the word with the "modern" spelling so readers wouldn't wonder if it was a repeated, uncorrected error. This story is fiction. I used biographies and articles about Stan Musial as well as his autobiography to create the characters of Lukasz and Mary. Research on immigrants, especially Polish and Slavic immigrants who clustered in towns like Donora, contributed greatly to shaping all the characters. The folks at the Donora Historical Society provided details about the town including how the influx of immigrants impacted the town's development. Any errors related to life in Donora are mine.

There's something amazing about people who leave their entire existence behind in order to make a better life. There's something magic about two people finding each other in a far-flung place, almost as though drawn together by an invisible force. The strength and courage it takes to immerse oneself in a unfamiliar world provides the backdrop for *The Strongman and The Mermaid.* Immigrant might and American acumen inform this tale of a time when America was built from materials that were sprung from inside the earth, cooked and shaped into something completely different—steel. The industry defined an entire Western Pennsylvania region and its people. Their stories are alive and well today.

Chapter 1

Patryk Rusek

2019
Donora, Pennsylvania

It happened like this for Patryk Rusek. They came for him, over and over, bossing him, coercing, bribing, tricking him, pretending it was for his own good. But this time, Patryk prepared for the invasion. This time, he hid away, knowing if he kept his yap shut, they'd give up and leave him be. The banging came loud and hard then faded away, allowing him to drift off to sleep.

Then voices lifted, trailed off, then lifted again. Feet pounded upstairs. They were searching. It was them. Wasn't it? He talked himself into calming down, told himself he was having auditory hallucinations again. That's what they had tried to tell him before, wasn't it? Dammit, he'd had enough of their lies and demands.

He lived in America, home of the free and the brave, and no one could make him leave his castle on the hill. No one.

Not even his own family. They'd have to haul him down, out the door, and over the stoop on a stretcher, dammit.

A door slammed, shaking him from his slumber again. The rafters in the attic shuddered, sifting dust over him. He pinched his nose and held his breath to suffocate a sneeze.

Success.

Quiet again. His breathing eased, his heart slowed. He fell asleep until the attic door whined open. They wouldn't come up; they were afraid of the attic, of anything old. A stream of light illuminated the paint-chipped wardrobe standing against the wall.

Don't move, don't blink, don't even breathe.

It was maddening what they did, raiding like winter mice, scampering up steps, taking, burrowing, consuming his things, demanding he leave the only home he'd ever known. Liars. As if it was for his own good.

Whoosh! Curtains were drawn back so hard the rod flew across the room. Bastards. Sunlight shot through the arched window and lit the dust in the attic. The particles swirled and dipped like stars shimmering in a night sky. The sun warmed his arms and his mind worked around who had come to call this time.

They still hadn't noticed him on the old cot he and two siblings had slept in as young boys.

Don't breathe, don't . . . Patryk's nose filled with dust again, the tingling building. He snaked one hand upward, the other clutching a book to his chest. Maybe they'd assume he went for coffee and a cigarette and leave. But when he scratched the end of his nose, he sneezed with the force of all his desperation.

Hands gripped Patryk by the arms, shaking him. He refused to respond.

"He's alive," she said.

"'Course he's alive. He just sneezed," the teen said.

She shook him. "Look at his lips. Too dry." Soft fingertips pressed Patryk's forehead and cheeks. "Hot as Hades," she said.

One of them yanked at the book Patryk gripped.

"He won't budge," the teen said. "You sure he's not in rigor?"

"Stop joking, Owen. He changed the locks yesterday. He was well enough to do that."

Someone tugged on the book again.

"My God, he's ninety years of piss and vinegar," she said. "What's this book?"

Patryk had had enough. He bolted up, growling, making Owen and his mother stumble backward. His white hair swirled above his head. "I'm ninety-one, goddammit."

The woman gripped her chest and the boy chuckled. "Alive and well, Mom."

"'Course I'm alive. What the hell are you two doing? Breaking, entering, and abusing? Get out."

The woman shook her head and smoothed her hair. "Grandpa." She waved her hand in front of her face. "The dust up here'll kill you with your asthma, never mind the stairs." She inhaled deeply.

"It's asbestos," he barked through a cough, hoping that information would make them run screaming from the house.

"And today's the day," she said.

Patryk swung his feet off the cot, still hugging the book. The day for what? He couldn't remember. But he wouldn't let them know that. He stared at the window, where sunlight shot through. The cot shifted and squealed as his granddaughter sat beside him. The scent of lavender and grass filled his nose and she slipped her arm around him, squeezing him tight. She'd always been affectionate. "Please, Grandpa. We need you safe."

She pulled at the book again. He yanked it back. He knew from her sigh she was drawing from her ten years as a nurse to decide how to handle him. Patryk did not want to be handled.

She grasped him tighter and kissed his cheek. "It's all right. You can take the book. Just come downstairs. I'll make tea."

He looked the other way. "That grassy hot water you tried to slip me last time?" He grunted. "Hell, no."

She shook her head. "Lipton tea. No more healthy green tea."

He looked at her, noting the same tiny nose and round face that had been looking at him for thirty-five years. Every time he studied her, it was as if he was taken back in time. He would have done anything for his grandchildren before they all turned on him.

"Please, Grandpa."

"Shot and a beer."

"Grandpa."

"Those are my conditions."

She patted his hand like he'd done to her a million times. "All right," she said. "Why not?"

Patryk nodded his approval. "And the boy—he gets one too."

She blew out her breath as if trying to cover up her objection to such a thing. But Patryk had had plenty of shots and beers by the time he was the teen's age, so he didn't think anything of it.

She stood, coaxing Patryk off the cot. "Let's just get you down to the kitchen in one piece. Owen'll carry your book. It's heavy as hell."

He hugged it tighter.

"Please," she said. "You can have it as soon as we're safely downstairs."

He stared at his feet. *Safely*. As if he were a one-year-old trying out new legs.

"Tea for me. Shot and beer for you." She whisked dust off of Patryk's shoulder.

He finally made eye contact. "And him."

She sighed again and brushed her fingers over Patryk's scruffy cheek. "And Owen."

The boy jumped into the air, pumping his fist. Patryk smiled for the first time in who-even-knew how long.

**

In the kitchen, Patryk sat at the head of the square Formica table where he always did, near the chipped radiator. He leaned his elbow on it. His granddaughter muttered something about lead paint.

"Lucy, you worry like you're paid to do it. I could eat lead paint for breakfast and be fine. My God, if you could have seen what the mills used to coat my insides with . . ." He pounded his chest. "Made me stronger. All that crud's holding me together."

She shook her head and placed a shot glass and thick beer mug straight from the freezer in front of Patryk. She poured amber liquids and set the bottle of Old Grand-Dad whiskey on the book.

He gestured at the bottle. "Off my book. Betty's book. Mine now."

Lucy moved the whiskey. Splotches of soot marked the dusty linen cover. An outline of another object that had scalloped edges revealed the cover's original taupe color. Patryk's fingers, folded into claws by swollen, knobby knuckles, worked at the edge of the cover. He slammed it open and swiped at the first page several times before turning it.

"What is this?" Owen asked as he and his mother leaned forward to get a better look.

Patryk dragged his hand under the lettering on the page. In blue cursive, it read *Story of Donora.* Underneath, an oxbow river, railroads, and mills alongside it had been drawn.

Owen straightened and squinted out the window. "That's down there, isn't it? Along the river."

Patryk laughed. "Get that kid a beer."

Owen shook his fist. "Yeah, get me a beer."

"Owen," Lucy said. "This is crazy."

"Can yinz guys make the old guy happy for once?" Patryk rubbed his palms together.

Lucy glanced from her son to her grandfather. "Then you'll go with us? We have to do this and we're—"

Patryk lifted a crooked finger at Lucy. "Yinz're the last resort."

Her shoulders dropped. She couldn't deny it.

Owen lifted his camera and snapped a few pictures of Patryk.

"Show us what's in that old book," Lucy said. Patryk knew she wanted to soothe his mood.

"You say that as though it's just a book."

"It is just a book," Lucy said.

"Bullshit." He snapped his twisted fingers the way he always had when barking orders. "Sit."

Lucy sat beside Patryk, with Owen bookending him.

Patryk turned the page, leaned in, absorbed into the artful writing and faded watercolors, silent.

The Big Ben clock above the stove sent thick ticking into the air. Eventually, Lucy shifted in her seat, feeling Patryk's head again. "Too early for sundowning, but—"

Patryk snapped up straight. "I know what that means, and I don't have it. I go up and down as I please. The sun has nothin' to do with it. Any damn time an elder statesman stops to consider his thoughts, yinz want to shuffle him off to the asylum. I'm just going back in my mind, is all. This book. Grandma's book. I forgot all about it. But now . . ."

He pulled it to him and tossed back a shot. "Donora used to be something. Why, most days I couldn't see halfway down our yard to the Sordillo house, it was so full of smoke."

Owen flinched. "Sounds awful."

Patryk turned his gaze on his great-grandson, his sight as clear as when he was a teenager like Owen, sitting in that very chair. Patryk's eyes filled, remembering.

Owen flinched. "I mean, it's beautiful now." He pointed out the window. "Look at the sun and the trees. We can see all the way across the river. I meant that it had to have been awful *before*. Not now."

Patryk shook his head and looked back at the book. "No, no, no." His voice was soft and nearly inaudible. "Yinz don't get it. It was beautiful *back then.* Now it's awful. Back then, it was alive. All of it. Like nothin' before or since."

Owen and his mother exchanged glances.

"The town, the mills, the people," Patryk said. He turned the page and gasped. Owen and his mother moved closer to see what had caused him to inhale so sharply.

"Stan Musial," Owen said. "I've heard of him."

Patryk leaned back in his chair and rubbed his chin, his fingertips making a scratching sound. "Damn well better know 'im if you call yourself a ballplayer. He was something, all right. The best. The best."

"You *knew* him?"

Patryk furrowed his brow. "Everybody knew 'im."

"What's wrong?" Lucy asked.

"Well, the stories about Stan. So much to say 'bout 'im, but really, there'd be nothin' to say 'bout Stan Musial if there weren't stories about his parents. Their stories were demolished with the mills an'at, crumpled up, hauled away, forgotten." He tapped the book. "When was that?" He shook his head. "Never mind. It's all here in this book. Still alive."

Owen and his mother gave each other looks. Patryk straightened and pointed at them. "I can see it on yinz guys' faces. Yinz got no idea who Lukasz and Mary are."

They admitted he was right.

Patryk turned through the book. Each section heavy with drawings, photos, and newspaper clippings, each page thumping down, releasing dust plumes. "See how Betty made this book? A treasure book, she used to say it was. Others called it a scrapbook, but she said scraps implied worthless, extra. Back then, every blessed thing we had was worth something. Should've seen when I called it a scrapbook once. Right hook in the shoulder." He rubbed it. "Damn, I can still feel it. But she was right; this book's different. Keeps everything inside that everyone else forgets. Treasure."

Owen's eyes lit up. Lucy reached across the book and squeezed Owen's hand. Patryk knew Lucy had brought Owen with her thinking it'd be good for him to help with the old man. Now Patryk could tell that Lucy was certain.

He licked his finger, turning thick pages quickly, giving Lucy and Owen a glimpse at each. "Mills closed, men displaced, 1948 Killing Smog, 1945 greatest football team in the country *ever* . . ." He kept turning and turning.

"The Magician," Lucy said, making out the title of a section before Patryk turned the page. There was more—Stan's batting stats, pitching stats, and then he stopped. Sophie and Nathaniel's Wedding. The Circus Dancer, The Undertaker. *Plop, plop, plop,* the pages fell.

The dust made Lucy sneeze and Owen's eyes water, yet they scooted closer to Patryk and his book. Finally, he stopped turning. The page had some faded black-and-white photos of the mills and people.

"Who're they?" Lucy asked.

He stared into space for a minute. "Short answer, they were Stan Musial's parents. But that's not who they really were. That's who folks decided they were later."

Patryk looked at Owen, then Lucy. "They were . . . well, I can't just label them like he was a stove and she was an umbrella." Patryk shook his finger. "He used to repair umbrellas at one time, if I remember right. I was told that. Haven't thought of that in ages."

"Well, now we need to know," Owen said.

Patryk looked up. Owen's eyes were warm as his lips pulled into a smile.

"Get 'im his beer, Lucy. Yinz are gonna need a minute for this here story."

Lucy rolled her eyes and Patryk turned another page. "The Strongman and the Mermaid," it said in faded teal-blue pencil, each letter its own little piece of art.

"What's that?" Owen asked.

Lucy grabbed for the book. "How 'bout we do this later, Grandpa? After your appointment?"

Patryk gripped the table edge and glared at Lucy. "Get the beer," he said through clenched teeth.

She cajoled, prodded, and tried to pry his fingers from the table. But his strength surprised him as much as her. Finally, he saw resignation in her face. He knew the exact moment something made her decide to let him stay. She got up. "Then *tomorrow*. No excuses. We aren't leaving until you're safely relocated."

He growled and threw his hand in the air. "Get the beer!"

She finally did. She splashed some Iron City into a cloudy 1979 commemorative Pittsburgh Pirates glass and slid it to her son. Owen took a swig and turned a little gray. He looked at his mother, conveying that he wouldn't be so exuberant with his next sip.

Patryk nodded and turned back to his book, tracing over the illustrations of mermaids, red birds, baseball gloves, and bats, circus animals and performers, and cemetery headstones, of all things.

Lucy left to make the call to reschedule the meeting at Blue Horizon Retirement Community.

Patryk brushed Owen's arm with crooked fingers. "If yinz could hear how Miss Mary told the story, none of us believed her, really. Oh, that laugh of hers. Bigger than life." He looked back at the book. "But my sister put it all here."

"I thought you said Grandma wrote it down?" Lucy asked, coming back into the room.

He looked up, squinting. "I forgot. Suppose it started out as my sister's book. Yeah. Betty and Karen were joined like the Siamese twins that came with the circus every year." He traced the illustrations with his finger before reading the words.

Lucy sat down. Owen took another sip of beer, his shoulders hunching at the bitterness.

"The girls told the story 'bout Mary first seeing Lukasz. Nineteen twelve, was it? No. Nineteen ten. At least that's how she always told the tale." Patryk looked at the words, tapping his finger across the page.

"It all began then, I think, if the recollection in the first place was right. This whole book was written backward through time."

Patryk scratched his chin again. "I suppose that's how we remember things, 'specially when the mind begins to forget." He stared into space, seeming to talk to himself more than to his family. "Unwinding . . ." He twirled his hand in front of him. "The memories come backward like pulling threads off a bobbin. Now yinz got me thinking. Boy, oh boy, there's stuff in here that no one should remember, it's so personal, but it was a long time back, so it should be told. Every little bit."

Chapter 2

Mary Lancos

January 1910
Donora, Pennsylvania

It always went this way. The fireplace embers released their last heat and a sharp plunge of cold loneliness would waken Mary before sunrise, bringing an alarming sadness familiar as her own skin. Winter infiltrated the room, rattling the windows, sinking into her pores, and pushing her fully to the last edge of slumber.

She rolled to her side, her knees tucked close to her belly, and pulled the quilt just above her nose, her breath providing heat. She stared at the navy-blue ribbon of night sky that peeked through the section of window not blocked by curtains. Sleet pinged and flashed against the pane. *Hail Mary, full of grace . . .*

This prayer loosened the loneliness that tried to root itself each morning. The holy words gave Mary hope for the day, for her future. She crossed herself, asking for forgiveness for secrets she kept, for God to understand why she must sew them tight inside until the time was right to let them out.

Her sister Ann's arm flopped over Mary's face, reminding her of the goals she'd set. One day, she'd own a home with just the right man—bear-like, like Papa, with strong arms to hold her tight and keep her warm. He'd be kind and brave and smart, and he'd earn the kind of money that allowed for a home with gas heat and indoor bathrooms.

She'd share her secrets with her family then. Then everyone would understand why she had kept them in the first place.

Kick, kick, kick. All night long. Ann's feet were always going even while in deep sleep. She shifted, then dragged her icy toes up Mary's legs, searching for heat. Mary flew out of bed, hopping from one foot to the other. She removed the lampshade, snapped a match across a stone, then lit the wick. Teeth chattering, she replaced the shade, turned up the flame, and rushed for her dress, sweater, and an extra pair of stockings. She dressed in record time.

Irritated that Ann and Victoria were still snug in bed, Mary shook them by their feet. "Get moving. It's warmer once you're up."

They groaned and burrowed deeper under the quilt, their separate forms congealing into one lump.

"You two are eleven and nine," Mary said. "I was keeping two houses at your ages."

"Goll-leeee," Ann hissed from under the quilt, dragging out the last syllable of the word like she always did to convey her endless consternation that she was required to do anything besides gaze at herself in the mirror. "You're a thirteen-year-old *grandma.* An awful bossy one."

"Light the fire, Mary," Victoria said. "Then we'll get up."

Mary drew deep breaths to keep from yelling. One time she had staged a strike, refusing to get up when her sisters didn't, and all it had gotten her was a smack from Matka and triple the work as her sisters had dashed off to school. "No strikes in the mills, no strikes at home," Matka had said, practically spitting at Mary.

Mary didn't have time for nonsense. She grabbed the edge of the quilt, took a few deep breaths as she reconsidered what she was about to do then ripped the quilt off the bed as if performing a magic trick. With the lantern in hand, she marched out of the room, her sisters screeching like trapped raccoons, causing the boarders down the hall to stir.

As she passed the room where the boarders and her brothers slept, the door opened and Mr. Cermak stepped out. Mary startled and sucked back her breath. He pressed against the wall, his plaid robe exposing his hairy chest. "Morning," she mumbled, cringing and picking up her pace. She looked over her shoulder to find him staring at her. She shook off her disgust, silently ordering him to leave their house and find another place to live. His presence always chilled her. She couldn't say why, but she kept as far away from him as two people living in a four-room house could.

**

At the back door, Mary hummed Christmas carols that had lodged in her mind. She pulled on her father's worn coat, the one she'd been told to wear when fetching coal from the backyard seam. Her fingernails caught weakened threads and pushed right through them. "Darn it." She readjusted and tugged the coat on, buttoning it to the top. She glanced at the lineup of black and gray wool coats and wished for a new pastel-hued winter coat cut for a girl. She examined the damaged shoulder seam. They hadn't had time to mend all the things that needed it. All the female Lancoses had been too busy, and she certainly didn't have time that morning.

She put on a knit hat that smelled of stale sweat and she was out the door, worming her fingers into gloves that had holes at the end of each finger to make her work easier. With her pail and lantern, she entered the outhouse. Balanced over the pot, she finished quickly, then it was back into the windy predawn air.

Mary reached the entrance into the hillside that had once been part of the Heslep family coal mines. She should have dug the coal the night before, but she'd been too tired after working at the Dunns' and rowing across the Monongahela River to fetch Papa from work.

It turned out he had stayed on for a second shift, so it was all a waste of Mary's energy. Except that she loved the water. The shy Donora moon was a close second. The night before, the sky had been unusually clear of smoke, clouds, and soot. She had stopped mid-river and lay back, bathing in the moon rays that washed her with silver light, making her think that the moon's appearance signaled good luck in the new year.

Inside the hillside, Mary's breath formed cottony clouds. Eighteen degrees? Twenty? It was too cold to matter. She shifted her lamp, identifying the coal seam she wanted to work. She dragged her fingertips along the craggy lines for just the right spot, hung the light on the hook, then hauled back with the pick. Her first swing struck the shale, the shattered rock plunking into the pail. She emptied it and hauled back again, this time plunging the pick with a thud in the soft black at just the right angle. Coal chunks sprung out, filling the pail.

And so her day began like any other, with rhythmic picking and plunking in the clasp of darkness. Her father had taught her to wield the pickax like the seasoned miner he was. Soon there'd be breakfast and her trek to the Dunns' gas-heated home. Oh, the warmth. Clean, even, constant.

But this day wouldn't end like every other. There was a dance for Mary to attend. Her humming of Christmas carols shifted to the ragtime tunes they'd hear that night.

And there was Samuel.

His handsome face formed in Mary's mind—happy eyes, mesmerizing gaze, his tallness that made her feel delicate, the way she imagined every girl of normal height felt every day. Thinking of the New Year's Dance made her chores feel like playtime. And that was the way she liked to see things. The want-tos in life came alongside the have-tos. They went hand in hand like dancers. She was old enough to understand that life might bring far more have-tos than want-tos, but there would be at least a few love-tos. And this dance was one of those.

**

Mary poked the wooden spoon at the half-frozen porridge and added a splash of condensed milk. She scrambled eggs for several boarders, got her sisters and Johnny off to school, dressed her young brother George, and fed two-year-old Rose. Mary set out the ironing board for Matka, added more coal to the stove, and laid the irons on top to heat. Finally, Matka appeared from the cellar with an overflowing basket of clean laundry. Mary cleaned the dishes before readying the lines for her mother to hang the freshly ironed clothes.

"Don't dawdle at the Dunns'," Matka said. "Lots to do and—"

Mary thrust her foot into her boot and wiggled her toes before looking at the sole. Worn nearly through. Might get her through winter. They'd have to. "The dance." Mary's breath caught at the thought of Matka not remembering. "Tonight."

Matka grumbled, drawing Mary's attention. Mary glimpsed her mother's disapproving headshake and her heart clenched. Nothing was ever enough. Mary yearned for one encouraging word, one shared moment over the exhilaration that she was old enough to frequent dances and that a boy who was taller than her wanted to go together. Was that too much?

Mary's strength and power stemmed from the work she did, but . . . She pressed her chest, each breath she took carrying the loneliness that wakened her every morning. Had Matka passed that along to Mary with brown eyes and long legs? Mary might not be able to fight against her never-ending height, but she didn't have to carry the same dour outlook.

She studied Matka, her grim-lipped expression as she pulled a man's shirt from the basket, shook it then scrutinized it for stubborn stains.

Just once Mary wished the two of them could share the delight of something exciting. She shrugged. Did Matka even know the meaning of delight? Had she ever felt it?

Mary sighed. No sense in wishing for someone else's view of the world to shift. Instead, Mary set her mind to finishing her chores and doing a day's work. That would be that. She'd go to the dance whether Matka was happy for her or not.

Mary finished with her boots and squirmed into her little-girl coat, the fabric binding across her shoulders and back as she struggled to button it. She tied her hat under her chin and wrapped her scarf tight, its fibers scratchy, making her sweat despite the cold seeping through the walls. "Bye, Matka," she said, light and airy as possible, sending a prayer up that her mother would have an easy, predictable day. It was the only thing that would smooth Mary's path to the dance.

No response.

"All right then." Mary glanced back one last time knowing Matka was submerged too deep in ironing to even notice she'd left the house.

**

For the second time that day, Mary burst into the frosty morning air. Striding down Marelda Street, she adjusted her hat against the obstinate wind and kept an eye out for ice patches. At Tenth Street, she headed down the hill and her gaze went to the orange sunrise-colored flash of flames shooting from the blast furnaces at the south end of town. The searing flare cut through the gunmetal sky. The sight startled her, even though she'd seen it a thousand times since the Lancos family had moved to Donora years before.

Mary made a mental list of the work she needed to complete. She'd wasted time the night before trying to fetch her father, who was sleeping a couple of hours at a friend's in Webster before taking the day shift. But on the way home, she stopped at Harvey Harrison's and got him to agree to fetch her father after work tonight so Mary could get ready for the dance.

There would be a final hurdle to leap at the end of the day. Matka's face would go red, no doubt, her forearms would tense, and she'd strangle whatever household tool was in her grip when Mary revealed that she'd promised to clean Harvey Harrison's mother's house after church free of charge and had paid him two pennies in exchange for retrieving her father.

She could imagine the sweat beading at her mother's hairline, the vein in her neck popping out as she listened. Mary was prepared for either a surge of anger or the restraint of it, her mother biting back resentment, the result looking like she was curbing a wild dog by wrapping her arms around it. It was the price for an evening of waltzing, polkaing, and chicken reeling the hours away.

Oh, she couldn't wait. Samuel's recent growth spurt had put him well above her five-foot-ten-inch height. The thought of dancing with a boy who towered over her was thrilling. Her mother insisted the other boys would grow taller, but Mary wasn't so sure. None of them showed any ambition in the height department as of yet.

Sirens blared and Mary stopped short. Something was wrong at the open hearth. She forced herself to breathe again, grateful her father was in the mines and not the mills. She looked into the sky at the sooty clouds that hung below the ones Mother Nature had made. Though she couldn't see it, she could feel the rising sun. The dark sky would yield a silver sunrise. Hints of celestial brightness drew her eye eastward, daylight emerging as shades of pewter and gray. People in other places saw daily sunrises the color of the blast-furnace flames and lived with clear blue skies every day, but in Donora, there were only rumors of sporadic blue skies.

Way back when, a long time before, the hills and valleys of Donora had been nothing but green with dark, fertile soil, home to just four families living under every color of blue sky. But once the men who'd bought up all the land had figured out the earth that grew the giant red oaks could turn out something even more valuable, the town called Donora was born and gave to the world like a mother to her children.

The trees were chopped and cleared. Massive machines were built, and the sheer size of the mills made them skinless, hulking, fire-breathing beasts that fed on everything the land and people could give. Mary still stopped to gape when she walked close to them.

The north-flowing Monongahela provided the perfect horseshoe of land to build it all. Donora's families and their homes came with the miles of mills. The original leading citizens had flooded the valley with the mills, scrambling to stake out prime property in 1901. The others who had come after set down a house anywhere they could, creating the spiderweb of crooked, slapped-down streets that wound around and up the hulking hills.

The poor lived next to the rich Irish and Scotch. The Italians lived next to the Poles, and the Czechs next to the Hungarians. It didn't matter as long as the mortgage or rent was paid and everyone worked his behind off. The homes were often slapped up fast to meet the ever-growing population. Houses were sometimes cobbled crooked, backed into old coal mines, or bent off hillsides like hunched old women keeping watch over McKean Avenue, the blast furnaces, open hearths, and wire mill, making sure it all worked and never stopped for anything. Maybe a pause for an injury. *Maybe.* Donora existed solely because of miles of hot, smoky, money-making, back-breaking mills.

Mary heard feet pounding before she saw who was coming. Through the fog the shape of Sally Mahue materialized—bolting, arms pumping, out of breath. Mary reached for her, knowing by the girl's expression it was her father who the siren had sounded for. Sally stopped, her eyes tearing. "Have to get my gram."

Mary nodded. There was nothing she could do or say that would help. She squeezed Sally's hand and the girl nodded and took off running again.

Mary knew Sally understood her clumsy silence. It was the way things worked. Until there were details, there was nothing anyone could do. Mary dug under her scarf and pulled her collar up to button the top, forcing her thoughts back to something pleasant. The silver sun.

Sometimes these mornings, layered in glimmering clouds and shimmering with metallic dust, gray fog, and black smoke made the most magnificent night skies. The metal was precious in so many ways. She wondered if Samuel might see it the same way, and she thought that might be just the thing she said to him as they walked to the dance together that night.

Chapter 3

Lukasz

Myscowa, Poland
A small village near the Wisloka River
January 1910

This was it. Lukasz Musial's last chance for a new life.

About the time Mary Lancos was cataloging the list of chores she had to complete before she went off to dance the night away, a young man named Lukasz Musial was living four thousand miles away in the Austrian-controlled Polish countryside in a village called Myscowa.

Poland wasn't even really Poland then. At least not according to the maps and such. On account of politics, wars, and settled deals with noblemen, Poland had been partitioned into sections and ruled by Russia, Prussia, and Austria. Poles who had some money hopped ocean liners, searching for more, eager to find everything their Polish land refused to yield.

But it was a high price to get to America. And for young, robust men like Lukasz, who lived in rural Myscowa with no land for them to work and no bustling industry to fund their passage, emigration plans stalled and left them idle, hungering in every way.

But on one fresh day in 1910, Lukasz stood big and bold, surveying the mountain walls that dropped into the farmland under his feet. Lukasz wasn't tall, but he had heart and was as strong as six oxen. Though just five foot five, no one ever considered Lukasz a small man. And so on that very day, he stood gazing into the horizon, knowing this contest to win passage to America was his last chance to change his life. He summoned every ounce of strength. He had to win.

There, in that rolling winter field, Lukasz ignored what he lacked and reveled in the sight of a rich golden sun, the miracle of its reliability. He squinted and shielded his eyes from the brightness bouncing off the snow. The gilded orb rose up the mountains, grazing the craggy edges with its morning ascent before rising high enough to drop its rays out of a pristine cornflower-blue sky. The rays warmed Lukasz's cheeks but didn't melt the packed snow.

He scratched his chin, plotting his strategy. His gaze swept over the field, where a little white farmhouse blended into the snow, only the smoke twisting out of the chimney and a bright blue door drawing attention to it. Someday, he'd paint his door blue just like that.

Off to the side and behind the house were two barns. One bore blackened planks with gaps that allowed shots of sunlight to shine through. The other barn was new and tinier than the first, thrown together after the fire. The brightness of sunlight and color invigorated Lukasz. He inhaled deeply, the cold fresh air stinging his lungs, reminding him he was alive, he was strong, and he was about to change the course of his life.

He straightened his shoulders. This time, he would triumph. He stood in half a foot of snow, his feet screaming as ice sliced through his worn soles and thin leather boots, the pain setting his determination. He started toward the competition site.

Movement caught his eye and he squinted toward the space between the house and burned barn. There they were.

He wiggled his toes and clenched his jaw. The figures marched toward him like an army regiment. The sun outlined Lukasz's rivals, obscuring faces. Lukasz widened his stance and crossed his arms, warming his hands in his armpits.

Though he couldn't see their faces, he knew every last one of the men lumbering toward him. Each of Lukasz's friends had matured into mighty oaks. Their strength measured far beyond their intake of food, as though nutrition wasn't needed to grow scraggly Polish boys into hulking men.

They knew each other like brothers, and because of that, Lukasz had already inventoried each man's talents and shortcomings as they pertained to this particular task. Only one person had a chance to beat him: Lukasz's lifelong nemesis, Waldemar Kowslawski. The prince, as Lukasz thought of him.

The group neared and Waldemar cast his shadow over Lukasz, standing in front of him, punching his fist against his palm.

Damn Waldemar. Always eclipsing, always menacing. Lukasz pushed his chest out and clenched his jaw, keeping every shred of nervousness below the surface, planning to use the energy when the time came. Lukasz shook out his hands, holding Waldemar's gaze.

Waldemar smirked. The tension between the two men coursed through Lukasz like waves on the Wisloka River. He rubbed his sore shoulder, then straightened to his full height, masking his discomfort from sleeping on a hard floor. This was it. Only one ticket to America left to win. With it came transport to Hamburg and lodging until it was time to embark on the ship, meals on the *USS President Grant*, then lodging with a sponsor family in America.

Freedom. Opportunity. Hope.

Lukasz's stomach growled as he thought of the pamphlet and postcard they'd read at the tavern the other night proclaiming the riches to be found in America, Donora specifically. The postcard, sent by the Kowalk family, showed a lavish brick home with a large porch, white picket fence, and a tree-lined lane that swept through gentle green hills and led to other homes nearby.

It was the kind of house that a wealthy nobleman would own, but Lukasz and his friends had been told that any man willing to work hard could earn enough to purchase such a thing. A castle for the common man. Lukasz thought again of the barn floor he'd slept on the night before. His own castle was unimaginable, yet something told him it was attainable. He could feel the contest's promise deep in his bones.

The men pointed, murmuring to one another about the contest, practicing their technique for getting hay bales into the barn through the loft doors. The man to move the most in the allotted time would win. Lukasz kept to himself and shook out his legs, trying to work the icy chill out of his limbs. Once he got to America, it would be easy. All that his dream life required was hard work in a mill or a mine. Backbreaking work was all a Pole knew. But in America, determination bore a job, a home, a wife, and a full belly.

A brisk wind rose up, stinging Lukasz's cheeks. He shielded his eyes from the sun with his hand and stared again at the barn. The group of competitors splintered as the task drew near. Another burst of wind whistled over the land, obscuring what little murmuring was left between the men.

The loft doors heaved, burst open, and slammed into the sides of the barn, sending out a boom. Otto Bosko, farmer and owner of the final ticket to America, stood in the opening, his work pants and shirt dirty from earlier chores.

Otto had no desire to move from his home to America, and he opted instead to use his luck at having acquired the ticket to entice the village men to compete for it. By doing so, they would finish the work he had due without him paying a single one of them. Half of his remaining hay had survived the fire, and he needed it moved to the new barn before it grew wet with the next thaw and storm.

A wagon drove up to the barn, laden with hay bales. Lukasz's stomach flipped. He bounced and shook out his arms again, pacing, puffing out his air. It was nearly time.

Otto lifted his arms to the heavens. "This way, men!"

Feet crunching over snow and the occasional call of a crow too stubborn to have left for the winter were all that broke the hush of the day that would begin a new year and someone's new life. Lukasz inhaled deeply, the frozen air sparking his lungs with every breath. The scent of stale whiskey emanating from several competitors made Lukasz even more certain Waldemar was his only competition.

"Had a dream last night," Adam Dunajki said. "I won." He smacked his hands together. "I'm gonna win."

"Only in your dreams," Lukasz said.

"Samanta prayed six rosaries for me." Igor Raszminski crossed himself. "Gave me a magic kiss this morning too."

Lukasz snickered. "Strength is needed. Not magic kisses."

"*God-given* strength," Igor said.

"Pfft," Lukasz said.

"Believe a little more, Lukasz," Igor said. "Say a rosary, dream a good dream, summon Janosik or the firebird's brother or something. Maybe then your life will change."

Lukasz had heard these myths and had gone to church his whole life. None of it brought anything dependable. "Each of you"—he pointed at them—"believes in something different. Yet our lives are all the same. I believe in myself."

Adam shook his finger. "All the same? You've no woman anymore."

Lukasz pushed his friend's hand away, thinking of the mermaid he'd been dreaming of for months. If only a real woman came to him as often. "You either."

"Things are changing, Lukasz. I can feel it," Adam said. "The woman of my dreams is coming soon."

"The firebird came to me in a dream," Kacper Mazur said and told his story of why this signaled he'd be the winner.

Lukasz shook his head. He closed his eyes and envisioned how best to toss the bales of hay.

"Hurry, men!" Otto gestured toward the wagon as he stuck his thumbs into his waistband and sucked in his belly. "These are the rules. One by one, each man will be given the same two minutes to move as many bales from the wagon into the loft as possible."

The group nodded along. Feliks and Gabriel made the sign of the cross as they listened. Otto had tried to move the grappling hook from the old barn, but it had been long rusted, refusing to move a centimeter. So, the hay bales needed to be tossed by pitchfork into the loft.

Lukasz eyed his competition. None of them would challenge him aside from Waldemar. Waldemar, the lifelong blister on Lukasz's heel. *Przystojny misiu*, "handsome bear," all the girls called him. The village girls loved his protective size, dark wavy hair, strong jaw, and jewel-green eyes, which they claimed held them captive. All Lukasz saw was his arrogance.

Waldemar lifted his chin with his typical superiority, massaging his fingers, studying his opponents.

Adam was called first. Lukasz wished him well but knew there was no way he'd win. He was powerful but clumsy. Otto turned the hourglass and Adam began, his groans and grunts marking each toss. Each time, he fumbled his grip on the pitchfork and stabbed repeatedly before getting the bale into the air. Eleven, twelve, thirteen tumbled into the loft, the fourteenth brushing the lip of the opening before plummeting back and knocking Adam off his feet. With a hand up from Otto, Adam's turn was recorded and he was sent to watch the rest of the competition. Better than expected. Lukasz rubbed his churning stomach. Maybe he'd underestimated his rivals.

Lukasz and Waldemar watched the next thirteen men. Each displeased participant slunk past, resignation wrapping them like woolen underthings. For them it would be another winter in the village, dreaming of America, drinking to compensate for the loss. Only Nikodem Janos beat Adam's number, and only by one. When Nikodem made his last grumbling attempt, Waldemar scoffed, a wicked smile pulling just one side of his mouth upward. He grinned at Lukasz, who knew what he was thinking—the ticket was his.

But it wasn't. Not yet.

Lukasz made eye contact with Adam, who was putting up a good face for a bad game. Lukasz nodded, indicating he was sorry Adam had lost out. Adam gave Lukasz a friendly smack on his back and leaned close to whisper, "Waldemar stayed at Basia's, full of drink, welcoming the New Year for a second night in a row. The win is yours."

Lukasz looked at Adam. Was this true? Would Waldemar have spent the night before this contest so foolishly? Inside, Lukasz swelled with relief. The prince would have been a tough combatant, but now, with this news, Lukasz's blood surged, empowering him.

Otto stepped toward Lukasz and Waldemar, licked his lips, and smiled. "Let's make this more interesting."

Lukasz put a fist to his lips and blew to warm his fingers.

Otto tossed both men pitchforks. "Clear the rest of the bales. These ninnies know you both could easily best them, so you're going to compete one on one. Load the hay 'til it's gone. Whoever gets the most into the loft gets the ticket."

The men who'd lost their chance at America murmured then finally cheered. "Yes, yes, you can do this, Lukasz," Adam yelled. "This is yours!"

Lukasz shook his head. "Change in rules? That's not fair to the other men."

Waldemar snickered.

"You want Waldemar to finish up the bales and get the ticket?" Otto asked. "You want to lose that way? Crying foul?"

Lose? Lukasz's stomach flipped. What did the rules matter? He was as strong as Waldemar. If Waldemar really had spent the night drinking with Basia, it would limit his height advantage.

"All right." Lukasz stomped past the men, grabbed the side of the wagon with one hand, swung himself into the back, and stabbed the pitchfork into a bale. He turned to the men and spread his arms. "*Chodźmy.*"

Waldemar cracked his knuckles and sauntered toward the wagon. He climbed into the back and took his place near the bales closest to the loft across from Lukasz. "Any more rules?" he bellowed.

Otto waved him off. "Get on your damn mark."

Lukasz bent his knees and picked his spot to stab the bale.

"Get set," Adam added.

"Go!" all the men shouted. Lukasz was slightly behind Waldemar, both of them digging their forks into bales and heaving them into the loft. Lukasz kept silent, not wanting to let any of his strength escape with a useless grunt. But Waldemar's rhythmic groans filling the valley air punctuated the onlookers' cheers.

Each man had three bales into the loft when Waldemar figured out a way to use his height to shave off time and effort. He quickly pulled ahead of Lukasz by one bale.

Lukasz's mind worked on two tracks, focusing on the task before him and remembering that, more often than not, he'd tossed hay bales by hand into the loft. He threw his pitchfork aside and backed up in the wagon to stand at the perfect distance to throw at the best angle. He gripped a bale and heaved. The bale somersaulted into the loft. Lukasz launched the next into the air, squatting down for another before the one preceding it had landed. The next bale knocked Waldemar's clean out of the air.

Waldemar turned and growled at Lukasz.

Lukasz kept on track, his bales turning through the air, landing in the loft one after the other, surpassing Waldemar's number by two. Waldemar tossed his pitchfork aside and began to bend and toss using Lukasz's method. Nine more bales to go between them.

Waldemar was gaining ground, each of them having tossed twenty-three bales into the loft.

Three more to go. Heave, flip, flop into the loft. Each had twenty-four bales in.

One more to go.

They paused, eyes meeting. The cheering stopped, and the silence made it so Lukasz could hear the breaths of the men around the wagon.

The ticket!

Lukasz's mind clicked back on and he squatted, reaching for the bale at the same time that Waldemar did. They both yanked, the string holding the bale together digging into Lukasz's fingers and burning his skin. He ripped back again to loosen Waldemar's grip.

Waldemar stumbled toward Lukasz, and for a moment, he seemed to fight the momentum. But then his body went with the tugging and followed the bale as Lukasz yanked. Both the bale and Waldemar forced Lukasz onto his back, knocking his breath away like a candle snuffed by a wind gust.

Waldemar ground the bale into Lukasz's chest with a snarl. Lukasz's vision blurred and he tried to focus on the faces peering at him from over the side of the wagon, cheering for him to get back up. Lukasz tightened his grip on the bale, unable to breathe, unwilling to give up. Waldemar rose to his feet, increasing his leverage, and jerked the bale away.

The world slowed for Lukasz. Waldemar took his time, stopping below the loft and turning back, grinning through labored breath. Lukasz couldn't watch. He turned his head, fighting to regain his air, and rolled to his side as Waldemar's final grunt came with his victory toss. The bale whooshed as it landed into the loft, sealing the results. Chest thumping followed, more bellowing, and only half-hearted claps for the winner.

Lukasz covered his eyes as oxygen filled his blood again, his lungs expanding and contracting, and he wished that somehow he might not live to take the next breath. What was there to live for? What would he do for the rest of his awful, empty life?

Chapter 4

Mary

Even in the smoky morning haze, Mary reached the Irish house on Thompson Avenue in good time. The Dunns weren't the only Irish family in town, but they were the only Irish family she currently worked for. The home was stately, mysterious, and welcoming. It had three floors and a cellar. The first floor was four expansive square rooms with soaring ceilings, plus a cozy fifth area—the kitchen and a keeping room, which sprawled across the back. Mary guessed she could fit her entire house inside two of those rooms if she wedged it right. The exterior of the Dunns' house had originally been apple red, but the soot and smoke had stained the brick an angry black, leaving only slivers of crimson near the mottled mortar.

The leading citizens of Donora—the store owners, doctors, lawyers, and the higher-ups in the mills—had bought property and built their spacious homes all at once and quick as anything. The miners, like Mary's father, blast furnace helpers, wire-pullers, and even molders often built their homes one room at a time over the years, creating a ramshackle, haphazard look. But one thing unified every house—every single structure fell victim to the choking air that deposited filth as it swept through town.

Mary entered the Dunns' through the back door. Clean warmth swallowed her as she hung her coat and hat in the cloakroom. Mary tiptoed into the keeping room, where she mended and ironed. The older Dunn boys spent time there practicing their letters or resting when they were sick or bored with their massive bedroom and playroom upstairs.

Entering the kitchen, Mary inhaled the scent of lemon with her whole being. Oh, it was magnificent. "Lemony" was how girls like Mary described the homes where the town big shots lived. Mary and her friends' homes smelled like death's cabbage, week-old meat, and eggs.

Mrs. Dunn hobbled from the direction of the butler's pantry. She held little Peter on her hip. Strawberry patches spackled her ghostly skin, making Mary gasp.

"Watch Peter, won't you, Mary, darling?" Mrs. Dunn smoothed her son's hair back from his tear-drenched face and handed him to Mary.

Like always, Mary playfully pinched his cheek, hugging him close. It had always worked to calm her siblings, and Peter too. His shallow, stuttered gasps smoothed into even breaths.

Mrs. Dunn exhaled deeply and pressed both sides of her expectant belly, her eyes squeezed shut.

Mary stepped closer, fear sweeping through her. "You're too early."

Mrs. Dunn straightened and inhaled, nodding. "Six more weeks. Maybe," she said through her exhale. "Just this headache and now . . . I'm so tired." She grabbed Mary's wrist. "I need more help today. Please."

From all of Matka's pregnancies, Mary knew what Mrs. Dunn needed. Her mind flew to the dance and her plans to attend it with Samuel. "I can watch Peter while I clean," Mary said. "But I have chores at home too. And there's the dance tonight." Mary covered her mouth, scolding herself. The words were out, and she wanted them back. Mrs. Dunn was very generous, and Mary knew better than to complain. Still, the thought of missing the dance made her eyes sting with tears.

Mrs. Dunn gestured for Mary to follow her, then stalked away, pulling her shirtwaist loose. Mary gasped again. Her boss was far out of sorts, and she wasn't sure how to get her gathered back up.

"I know," Mrs. Dunn said. "Your Samuel asked you to go with him."

"Oh, he's not mine, but yes . . . the dance." Oh yes, oh yes. Mary could barely keep from floating every time she thought of him and the dance.

Mrs. Dunn headed back through the butler's pantry and into the foyer, Mary right on her heels, relieved that the woman had remembered Samuel had asked her, that it was important.

Mrs. Dunn stopped short, her large hazel eyes shifting wildly, conveying desperate pleading, something Mary wasn't used to seeing in her. In the room above them, four sets of feet clomped, the chandelier crystals clinking and shimmering, reminding Mary the boys had a day off from school due to building repairs. Mrs. Dunn put both hands over her ears, her perfectly coiffed hair sprouting from its pins, loose locks spiraling down her cheeks. Her despair seeped through her skin, changing her from a beauty to an ordinary lunatic Mary might see dragged off to Mayview after a night of carousing.

Mrs. Dunn clawed at her scalp. "This headache."

She looked as though she might press her ears right through her skull. Mary hated to see someone suffering. "I'll make tea."

Mrs. Dunn appeared childish, begging to be saved, wanting to be held as much as her son. "Tea? Oh yes. Please."

A bang came from the playroom above them. Mrs. Dunn drew a breath and let out a scream. Peter startled, his body stiff. Mary patted his back, bouncing him while cradling his head against her shoulder. She'd heard frustrated screams from many a mother, but not from Mrs. Dunn, not from mothers living in lemony houses.

Mrs. Dunn lifted her skirts and took off for the stairs, gripping the banister, leaning on it as she ascended. "Boys!" she bellowed.

Mary followed, juggling Peter in the crook of one arm.

Mrs. Dunn tripped on one of the treads. She stopped, heaving for breath, and Mary slipped her free arm around her waist. "Perhaps a rest after tea would help," she said. "There's more of that peppermint blend you loved so much at Christmas."

They plodded upward, Mary supporting her as they went. She'd never seen Mrs. Dunn raise her voice, chase after children, grow red in the face, or clench her fists. Even when one of her boys monkeyed on a priceless chandelier, she merely stood on her antique Louis XIV chair and quietly helped him down with a smile, light fixture and child intact. Countless times, Mary had come upon her with her passel of puppy boys gathered around her, the youngest in her lap as she read aloud and taught them their lettering, every hair in place.

When they reached the landing, the door to the playroom flew open, the knob crashing into the plaster. Mrs. Dunn flinched. "Enough!" They halted, one boy flying into the back of the next, their eyes wide with surprise, jostling into their mother and Mary.

Mrs. Dunn reached for Teddy, but his hand slipped out of hers, so she latched onto nine-year-old Michael's arm as he skirted by. She turned him into her body and swatted his bottom, hauling back twice, face in a grimace, every contact with his behind making him suck back his breath. Mary glanced at the other boys, whose jaws dropped. Mary'd seen and received many a smack—wallops to the bottom or cheeks, body blows, screaming fits that blew back a kid as much as an open hand. But the way Mrs. Dunn pulled her hand back, hesitating before hitting, made a gentle thwacking more than a painful hit, telling Mary that Michael was fine. Shocked, but fine. Mrs. Dunn released her son, covered her mouth, and headed toward her bedroom. Mary jerked her head to tell the boys to get back inside the room.

They froze for a moment, then scrambled away, the door closing as they examined Michael's bottom as if discovering fire for the first time.

Mrs. Dunn had been clear when she had hired Mary that she wanted calm and quiet in her home. She taught Mary not to manhandle the boys or bellow—like Mary'd been accustomed to doing—when she minded them. The habit had finally taken hold, even softening Mary's ways with her own siblings. A well-placed snarl was often more effective than a swat.

Mrs. Dunn grasped Mary's hand. "I can't believe I did that."

Mary averted her gaze so as to not embarrass her boss. "I forgot already," Mary said. They entered the bedroom and went through to Mrs. Dunn's dressing room.

"I swatted little Michael." Mrs. Dunn's voice was thin. "I'll never forgive myself."

Mary guided her to the chaise lounge. "That's nothing," Mary said. "He's fine." She adjusted Peter on her hip.

Mrs. Dunn kicked off her shoes, yanked up her dress, and released the ties on her stockings, rolling them down to her ankles. "I'm losing all sense."

Mary shushed her and covered her with a soft wool blanket, tucking it around her feet.

Mary backed away, rubbing Peter between the shoulders. "I'll put the baby down and the water on." She was sorry that Mrs. Dunn was ill but was pleased to help her, to know she was needed by a woman who normally didn't need anything at all.

Mary was walking out of the room when she heard a sob. She turned to see Mrs. Dunn covering her face. "Oh, Mary. He's not the baby anymore. The new one's almost here." She burrowed deeper into the chaise.

Calming silence wrapped around them. Peter buried his cheek in her shoulder, drifting into sleep, a bit of slobber wetting Mary's shirtwaist.

"Would you like to sleep before tea?" Mary asked.

"Yes, yes. And stay longer today. There's so much to do, and I can't get to it. Patty's coming later. Yinz two are all I have today."

Mary flinched. Yinz? Another indicator that Mrs. Dunn was unhinging. *Yinz* was just one word she'd been teaching Mary was a sign of being uneducated and lazy, the kind of word that Mrs. Dunn had left behind when she decided she wanted to marry a man like Mr. Dunn. "There'll be more dances. Promise."

Mary swallowed hard. She thought of the dance at Miller's Hall, of all the chores she needed to do for her mother before Samuel would arrive for her, of the shirtwaist with dotted cotton and the skirt she'd cleaned specifically to wear tonight.

Mrs. Dunn pushed upward and reached toward Mary. "Please. I'll pay extra. For the children, please."

Mary knew that Mrs. Dunn trusted her with the children and the house more than nearly any other of her help, all of whom were currently unavailable due to illness. Mrs. Dunn's weakened state softened Mary. Victoria and Ann could help their mother if Mary was late getting back. Once home, Mary could work fast and still get to the dance. She'd never seen Mrs. Dunn fragile, her typical dignity dissolving. Mary nodded.

Mrs. Dunn pulled the blanket up to her chin and turned onto her side. "Take the dog you like so much when you leave. Extra pay. You can add it to your hope chest." Mrs. Dunn mumbled into the arm of the lounge.

"Dog?"

"You know." Mrs. Dunn's voice came papery thin. "The Staffordshire."

Mary drew back. "Extra cash'll be fine."

"Nonsense. The spaniels. Take the teeny one and tuck it away. Mr. Dunn'll never notice. He hates those things," she said, falling into sleep, her breath slowing and deepening.

Never notice? Mary nearly fell into a laughing fit at that. When Mrs. Dunn had bought the set of twelve porcelain Staffordshire spaniel dogs, Mr. Dunn had said he'd have broken them all if they hadn't cost so much money. "*What* a waste." He tossed his hands over his head as he paced. "What *a* waste. What a *waste*!" He may have hated the dogs, but Mary was quite sure he'd notice one of them missing.

First things first. She would talk to Mrs. Dunn about cash payment when she was feeling stronger. Mary headed for the nursery but was stopped by another crash and yelling. The boys in the playroom again.

She threw open the door. "What's the ruckus?" She patted Peter. "The baby's finally asleep." Her voice was strong now that she was out of Mrs. Dunn's earshot.

The brothers lay clumped in the middle of the room, wrestling, faces Christmas red and sooty as though they'd been cleaning chimneys. Mary stomped her foot, and they unwound their limbs and sat cross-legged as she'd taught them. "Your mother needs her rest." She thought of her chores. "Your faces are black as night . . ." She considered what she was about to say. Would it cause even more trouble? No, they were plenty old enough. "You're going outside to play. Don't come back 'til the streetlamps come on."

"But—"

"But nothing."

"It's so cold," the eldest said.

"You've got the warmest coats in town."

"We're hungry."

"Take some bread."

They looked at each other for a moment. "Alone?" Michael asked.

She blew out her air, knowing that she couldn't follow them out to play and get the work done. Mrs. Dunn was a far more protective mother than Mary was accustomed to. Every kid Mary knew played outside from the time they were weaned, only half watched by a sibling or two.

Excitement spread over the boys' faces as they realized what Mary was saying. They filed out of the room, and Mary heard the sound of feet flying down the stairs. She knew that despite their initial whining, this was the chance they'd been waiting for—an adventure into town, out from under their mother's oppressive care.

Mary tucked Peter into his crib, and his legs curled up to his belly as he stuck his fingers into his mouth and fell deeper into sleep with a full-bodied sigh. Wanting him to get a solid sleep, Mary wouldn't pull his fingers out as she'd been instructed. She smoothed his hair, marveling at his sweetness. It'd become clear to her years before that motherhood was a stew of struggle and blessing—exhausting children hanging off hips, breasts, and chandeliers, if one had a chandelier like the Dunns'.

Then there was the love. Oh, the love, the milky, honeyed smell of baby skin. Stolen moments when little arms looped around a neck, a peaceful Dunn baby snuggled into arms for a rest. Mrs. Dunn's fatigue was obvious, but at least she had money. She had help. She had Mary. And except for what was transpiring that day, Mary viewed Mrs. Dunn's motherhood as an enormous blessing.

Mary backed out of the nursery, considering her mother's world. In order to feed Mary's ever-growing household, Mrs. Lancos took in boarders, men who stuffed themselves into their home to sleep between shifts, eat two meals a day, and have their laundry done once a week.

Most of them were fairly pleasant and, except for Mr. Cermak, they were disinterested in the Lancoses beyond lodging there until they could afford to buy houses or move in with the families of the women they found to marry. Mary's father insisted that in America, the pattern was clear—each and every child would do better than his parents. And so she looked forward to the day when she'd have her own home with a lemony, instead of cabbagy, scent. If there were going to be children on her hip, they would be as sweet and clean as Peter.

Chapter 5

Lukasz

Having lost the ticket, Lukasz found the urge to chase Waldemar down, tackle him, and stuff the ticket down his throat too strong to resist. He balled his fists and strode toward his foe. But three steps in, a circle of friends engulfed Lukasz, slapping his back and telling him to keep smiling. As though Lukasz smiled a lot. All but Waldemar filed past Lukasz with encouraging words, lamenting their futures, saying they were heading into town, where they'd spend the rest of the day with each other and bottles of vodka.

Adam came last. Lukasz looked past him, noting that Waldemar was nearly out of sight. Adam sighed and stuffed his hands deep into his coat pockets. "Sort of glad you lost, Lukasz."

Lukasz flinched.

Adam held up one hand. "No, no. It's that we'd rather *you* stayed than him. Waldemar takes everything from us on account of his bearing." Adam puffed up his chest, imitating Waldemar's arrogant, wide walk, arms bowed out at his side, pelvis pushed forward. "*Handsome bear,*" Adam said with a high-pitched feminine voice, making Lukasz finally smile. Adam was nearly as large as Waldemar, but he wasn't a jackass. Adam adjusted his hat. "The girls, the jobs, those dinners Basia brings him. Everything here is his. Good riddance."

Lukasz understood. "You tell it straight from the bridge." He stuck his hand out to shake Adam's. "I appreciate your honesty."

Adam bowed his head, humbled. Lukasz tried to force a chuckle at the thought that his compatriots preferred him, but found no humor.

Resignation. He felt that, good and thick.

Lukasz had never hoped so hard for something like this ticket. He wished he'd never heard of the Kowalks who lived in Donora, Pennsylvania, their letters bearing tales of warm homes overflowing with well-fed children, or their invitation to sponsor the winner. And the postcard—the gorgeous home that beckoned from across the Atlantic.

He wished he'd never seen the fliers depicting the riches afforded Americans. He should have blocked such expectations from his mind. He'd allowed them in again. The pain at losing, at knowing it would take him years to save for passage to America, wrenched his insides. The searing knowledge that he'd almost saved enough the year before rushed back at him as he recalled lending money to Prot Gwozdz, supposedly for his sick mother.

But Prot had promptly gambled it away, leaving Lukasz with nothing but the burden of being duped by a man who'd never pay him back, and ever-present, piercing despair. Prot's mother had died from lack of care. And so Lukasz was still in Myscowa, unable to make a meal of humiliation and loneliness, occasional odd jobs leaving mere crumbs to save, providing occasional blinks of hope, mirages gone in an instant.

Adam took Lukasz by the elbow. "Tavern. Fair maidens await." Adam eyed the rest of the men, who were disappearing into the village at the edge of the farm.

Lukasz stepped away. "Go on."

Adam's shoulders slumped. "If you're not there by midnight, I'm coming after you."

Lukasz adjusted his hat, knowing he'd eventually end up at the tavern. Nothing had changed. Nothing. "Sure."

Adam backed away. "Now you can forget your search for your fantasy life, your blue almonds that don't exist—"

"I just want to work, dammit."

Adam hit his hat against his leg, his eyes downcast. "I know. We all do." He broke into a jog to join the other men.

Lukasz exhaled, eyes stinging now that he was alone. He wasn't so sure he could go back to life as it was, though he had no choice. He stared at the loft, hands on his hips. One bale. Just one.

A shadow moved in the loft, catching Lukasz's attention. The figure moved toward the opening. "Lukasz! Come up."

Lukasz started to turn away, not wanting any more slaps on the back.

Otto knocked on the door to draw Lukasz's attention back. "I have a proposal."

A job? Curiosity tugged at him.

"Come on up!"

Lukasz squinted at Otto, not ready for another disappointment.

"Come on!" Otto gestured and disappeared into the loft.

Why not? He wasn't ready to drown himself in the tavern yet, anyway. He ran into the barn and up the stairs that led to the loft.

Otto pointed. "How about you finish stacking these bales for me?"

Lukasz rubbed his sore shoulder. Hadn't losing the competition been enough for one day? But perhaps Otto meant something more. With Waldemar leaving, perhaps it would be Lukasz who got first choice of the odd jobs that arose.

Lukasz stuck his hand out. "I can rebuild the old barn, feed the animals, anything. I'm good with my hands."

Otto waved him off. "I know. That's what I want to talk to you about. Besides stacking the bales, I mean. It's those wire animals you make."

Lukasz drew back. Had he mentioned them before?

"Old Ryszard showed me the dog and bear you made at his shed when I went to get the horseshoes fitted. Said all the wives he knew love them. Been letting you board for the cost of the animals he sold. I believe it's the rare man who's got money and loves his wife enough to buy her treasures."

Lukasz sighed.

"Listen. I know Ryszard's been like a father . . . his son left to marry and when your mother . . ." Otto cleared his throat. "Anyway, you stepped in to fill his spot."

Lukasz grimaced, not liking to think of his dead mother, to admit he and his father were at odds most of the time, or that he had never gotten along with his half-siblings or his father's wife. "I'm sorry Ryszard's dead. Since you've been on your own for a while . . . I could use something like that right about now. The wire animals, I mean."

Lukasz missed Ryszard deeply. He longed for when his mother was alive and his father had loved them both. Since her death, everything had changed. Life was difficult with an empty belly and a solitary path. Lukasz hadn't made a new animal in months, but he kept one in his coat pocket, unsure of who to give it to.

He reached into his pocket and pulled out a wire mermaid he'd originally made for Mr. Jamroz to give his daughter. She had died on the very day he had finished the work. "Made it for Urszula. The girl down the lane near the market."

Otto bent closer, studying the tail and moving the scales back and forth with his finger. They were strung together with thin wire, glistening with blue and green enamels. "Poor Urszula."

Otto straightened, rubbing his belly, staring at the wire form. "The beguiling Wisla Mermaid. Visits the Wisloka in the summer, they say." He nodded. "Perfect for Celina. She tells Teodora and Stefan her own version of the story every single night. A happy version. They dream better with a sweet, beautiful version. Celina claims she's even seen her at the river bend on St. John's Eve. Tells the older neighbor boys the scary version."

Lukasz nodded. Parents always told the tale according to the audience, and many made up their own account to teach lessons or inspire kids to behave well.

"It's perfect," Otto said, his voice revealing his wonder. "I'd heard about your work. Now I see. It's a beautiful thing."

Lukasz handed it over. The hammered metal created a lifelike form, the layered scales moving, capturing light and bringing the creation to life.

"Been dreaming of the mermaid myself since making this one." Lukasz had kept that secret from his competitors. He'd never mentioned that he believed his dreams might bring him luck. The other men would have chided him for his folly after he had teased them for so many years. Lukasz had been right to doubt. He had found no luck that day.

"The wife'll think I'm a king if I give this to her. Made me sleep on the floor last night. That barn fire was my fault, and she won't have it. Won't have me anymore. And I can't remember the last time . . ."

Lukasz already knew that story and was more concerned with where he would sleep than Otto's marital strife. "So if I give you this, I can board here and work for you and—"

"No." Otto's gaze snapped away from the mermaid to meet Lukasz's. "Can't afford you."

"But—"

"I can't. Wife'll never allow a boarder in the barn after the fire."

Lukasz snatched the mermaid back and put it into his pocket.

"Wait," Otto said. "Stack the hay and I'll give you bread and vodka. Fresh out of my wife's oven and my still. When I have other work, I'll hire you first. In exchange for the mermaid."

Lukasz looked away.

Otto kicked at loose hay. "Think about it?"

Lukasz leaned against the loft door, surveying the horizon, noticing the very point where the snow disappeared into the woods that led to the river bend. He often found peace and quiet at the edges of the Wisloka River and longed to hear the rushing north-flowing waters. The idea of his lost America flooded back, bringing familiar sorrow. He usually kept the sadness folded away inside. Now, unleashed, it expanded in his chest as he remembered his mother. His eyes closed. He struggled to recall the low, slow scratch of his father's spare words as he taught Lukasz to chop wood and carve a knife handle.

His longing brought to mind his mother's embrace, her soft cheek against his as she pulled him onto her lap and squeezed him tight when he was too big for her to do so. It was as if she'd known she'd be gone soon. As if she'd known she needed to infuse Lukasz with her affection so that when she died, he'd remember there was such a thing as a warm, loving touch in the world.

A thrust of wind stung his cheeks and he heard his mother telling him what she had cooked that night for dinner. "Thin broth this time. It'll be heartier tomorrow, Lukasz. *Mój słodki aniołku*, my sweet angel. Promise."

He could almost feel her hand stroking his head as he smiled at her from his seat on an overturned bucket. *Thunk, thunk, thunk.* The short leg on the pine table had jiggled with every swipe of his butter knife across the fresh bread. The image of his father—when he was warmer, kinder, gentler—came. He had braided Lukasz's mother's hair the last time she washed it, right before the cough had finished her. His father's thick fingers had worked three sections of her golden hair into neat plaits. Then he undid it, dissatisfied, even though his mother had been pleased. He braided her hair twice more, each time slower, Lukasz's mother's eyes closing as though the act of braiding was as soothing as a good medicine.

And now even the blacksmith, Ryszard, had passed away. The isolation, despite having friends, smothered Lukasz.

Snowflakes began to fall past the loft doors. No, they weren't falling—they burst into being. He moved toward the opening and gazed up, expecting to see dark, heavy snow clouds, but the sky was still blue, the sun shining. And yet, snowflakes. He studied them as they crystalized. Otto leaned out the door, palm extended. He looked upward too. "What the hell?"

Lukasz'd never seen snow do this, but there it was, diamond crystals hatching out of thin air. He tried to catch snowflakes as they snapped into existence. This world as he'd known it couldn't be all there was; the odd snow proved that. It reminded him that things didn't always stay the same. He thought of Otto's proposal and the mermaid he'd made. Maybe he should have given the mermaid to someone else when Mr. Jamroz had refused to take it after Urszula died. He'd even paid for it.

Lukasz dug into his pocket, running his thumb over the smooth scales. He thought of the mermaid dream that brought the beautiful, dark-haired half-fish who called to him each night and made him bolt upright out of sleep in a mix of joy and sorrow. Perhaps it was the sadness that came with this particular creation that kept him from sleeping soundly. Maybe getting rid of this precise mermaid would provide peaceful sleep and finally stop his search for "blue almonds," as Adam had called Lukasz's dreams of better things.

Lukasz pulled the mermaid from his pocket and looked at it.

Otto's special blend of vodka was sharp, bold, and punishing if he drank too much. Lukasz imagined the initial sting on his tongue, the spirit ripping down his throat. He looked at Otto grabbing at air, trying to catch the strange snowflakes. Lukasz shook his head. The vodka would allow him to lure the memories of happier times with his parents back into the chamber he locked tight in his chest. His mouth watered. The vodka.

He handed the mermaid to Otto, who held it in the streaming light.

"I'll pile the hay for the vodka and bread," Lukasz said.

A smile slowly spread across Otto's lips. He nodded and stuck his hand out to Lukasz. "You're good with your hands, Lukasz. Really is a waste it's not you headed for America. A real waste. You'd do well there, I know."

Lukasz didn't need to be told that. He felt it in his bones every single day.

**

Lukasz finished stacking the bales in the required configuration, and Otto came back to escort Lukasz into his home to dry his boots in the kitchen while they settled up. Lukasz stood near the fire, wiggling his toes as they started to thaw. Otto's wife, Celina, entered and narrowed her eyes at Lukasz, her lips curling back like an angry dog's. Otto handed her the mermaid, and she studied it with the same angry face. Lukasz worried her reaction meant he would not be paid his bread.

"Oh," she said, covering her mouth. She glanced at her husband, her expression softening, her eyes questioning as she held his gaze.

Lukasz wanted to leave as soon as he could.

She moved closer to the lamp on the table, turning the mermaid back and forth in the light. "It's the good mermaid. The one I tell about in my stories." She glanced at Lukasz, then Otto again. "How beautiful," she said, her voice barely above a whisper. She reached for Otto's hand, and he took it, winking at Lukasz.

Lukasz ballooned with pride. Celina gestured at the bread and bottle of vodka on the dry sink as she and Otto disappeared into the back room. Lukasz understood this as permission to take and an order to leave. He gobbled the bread and put his feet into his barely warmed boots, his mood heavy, his dreams lost.

Chapter 6

Mary

In Mrs. Dunn's cellar, Mary grabbed rags, the canister of rug freshener, and the sweeper, hoping to finish a good deal of her work before Peter woke up. She entered the Dunns' formal parlor with her rags and started around the room. Even inside the homes in Donora, there were several kinds of dirt to be addressed. There was red dust from the iron making, heavy white dust from the wireworks, and black soot that came from open hearths and the fireplace and stove in nearly every home in town. People like the Dunns used gas, coal, and wood depending on the room in the house. The gas helped cut down on the inside dirt. Not completely, but boy, it was nice to have cleaner heat in most of the house.

Mary dampened the rag with lemon oil and carefully slid it over the mahogany tables, revealing a shine as the soot adhered to the rag. She was especially careful with the little table where the Staffordshire dogs sat, sliding the dogs aside and dusting clean the blackened outlines they left. She picked up the tiniest porcelain dog and ran her finger over the brown and white enamel, her thumb caressing its head. It was little enough to fit into her apron pocket, small enough to secret away in the hidey-hole she'd made in the fireplace hearth at home to stash things she'd one day display in her own home. An Irish home like Samuel could provide.

She looked at the dog again, turning it back and forth in the light, wanting it so very much. She thought of Mrs. Dunn's offer, but she couldn't accept it. Not when she knew what would happen if Mr. Dunn ever found out she'd been given such a valuable gift for no reason, and not when she knew the fit her mother would throw when she wasn't given cash for her extra work.

She settled the dog back with its shiny pack and caught her reflection in the gilded mirror that hung in the foyer as she walked out of the parlor. Her shirtwaist was grayed with soot, and her once mulberry-red skirt was worn to dull pink. Mary straightened, studying herself. She imagined that this was her home, that she was mistress of the fine décor and mother of rambunctious boys. Samuel was the only boy she could imagine as her husband. She pictured him in his parents' house, one very much like the Dunns'. She opened her arms and spun around. It would be wonderful.

She walked toward the mirror, assessing her attractiveness. She drew her fingers along her dark hair. It waved along her hairline over her ears and was gathered in a bun at the nape of her neck. She was no fragile bloom. The men she knew preferred their homes to be substantial and their women delicate.

But Samuel, he liked Mary just fine.

"Sunflower tall," he'd said about her at the riverside the past summer, the first time she had realized he was interested in her. Before that, she'd had an inkling he liked her when he and his family had attended a party at the Dunns' and she had been hired to take coats and serve drinks and dessert.

Right in front of Samuel and his parents, Mrs. Dunn had complimented Mary. "A graceful server and a fine keeper of my home," she'd said to them. Mary repeated it the way Mrs. Dunn had said it; she shaped the words soft and gentle, each one distinct and clear. Mrs. Dunn sounded nothing like most of the people in Donora, who smashed old-country words into their new English, creating something unique and warm yet utterly unrefined, like iron ore before being heated into magnificent steel.

Samuel was older than Mary by two years. His intelligence, along with his father's influence, had earned him a place at the University of Pittsburgh at the age of fifteen. Younger than most of the college students, he came home as often as he could and spent time at local dances rather than those in Oakland with the older students.

At the time he'd left high school for Pitt, Mary stopped attending school to work full time. It was soon after that she'd had the chance to impress him with her domestic talents at the party. She held her hands up as though he were in front of her, ready to dance. She stepped into a waltz, imagining his arms around her, their lean bodies fitting perfectly together, a hint of his spicy cologne lingering afterward. She couldn't wait. Oh, the way Samuel had smiled that night she was serving! He had showered her with attention, heating her insides and making her hands quake, jiggling the whiskey-filled, cut-glass tumblers on the gleaming silver tray.

Right then, with the ice shivering in the tumblers, that was the moment Samuel had first seen her worth. He knew that even though she was a daughter of an immigrant, forced to quit school despite her achievement, she would make a fine wife. And he could provide everything needed for a lemon-scented life.

Still, something bothered her. Mary felt warm toward him, but she was fairly sure she wasn't experiencing the sensations that other girls had described when discussing the boys they liked. She assumed it wouldn't be long before she'd feel her stomach flutter when she thought of him kissing and holding her as they danced. Soon, surely.

Mary's practical nature ruled her. Mrs. Dunn had done her a great favor that night when she had amplified her talents for Samuel and his parents. Those moments had made Mary realize she was worthy of an Irishman, or she would be soon through the guidance of Mrs. Dunn. In the same way the mills took humble chunks of earth, brittle iron, and limestone and turned it all into exquisite, elegant, resilient steel, Mrs. Dunn was milling Mary, and she could feel her conversion from the inside out. From raw, immigrant daughter of a Czech miner with rough language and clumsy manners, her iron soul was being refined. She was *becoming.* As sure as Mary felt the sun rise even when hidden behind a cloak of smoke and fog and clouds, she felt her own transformation.

**

With the last swirl of the rag, push of the broom, and sweep of the vacuum, it was time to spritz the room with lemon water. She donned an apron, made peppermint tea, got Mrs. Dunn up and moving again, and prepared a supper of ham sandwiches and soup. She set the table in the keeping room for all the Dunns except for the mister, who'd be entertaining men from Pittsburgh at the Monongahela Country Club. She added dessert forks to the place settings since Mrs. Dunn liked them even when they weren't having fancy dessert. She liked to use her things, to see them every day no matter how humble the meal.

The boys tumbled back into the kitchen just as night fell. Mrs. Dunn stared at Mary. "They were out all this time?" She didn't just stare, she glared, and her eyes hardened in a way that Mary had never seen from her. The woman yanked a hanky out of her sleeve. She waved the boys to her, spit on the fabric, then rubbed at their dirt-covered cheeks, mumbling. Mary would have sworn on the Bible that Mrs. Dunn was quietly but most definitely cursing like a Slavic steelman, suddenly as Bohemian as half of Donora. Since letting them out earlier, Mary hadn't thought about them, that they were running the streets. They were old enough to be out but not experienced at independence. There, with the moon rising through the kitchen window, Mary fully realized she should've asked permission to send them out. Panic swept her.

"I'm sorry." Mary grabbed a cloth from the countertop to help wipe the boys clean. "I just wanted you to get some rest and for me to get my work done, and Peter needed to sleep."

Mrs. Dunn swiped at Michael's cheek with her hanky, making him flinch and whimper. She stopped and stared at Mary. "And you wanted to get out for your dance."

Mary stopped rubbing at Teddy's cheeks and released her grip. She smoothed his windblown hair. He smiled, his reddened cheeks making his eyes bright, and she knew they'd had a good day adventuring. She glanced at the clock over the doorway. Mrs. Dunn's gaze followed. Mary couldn't deny it. Her wanting to get to the dance was the exact reason she had sent the boys out alone.

"I'm sorry, Mrs. Dunn." Mary wanted to go to the dance but never wanted Mrs. Dunn mad at her, not for any reason.

Mrs. Dunn scoured Michael's chin harder. "They aren't heathens, you know, running amok like . . . mill hunkies." Mrs. Dunn froze, then released Michael's cheeks as well. "It's no use. They're filthy. It's a tubbing for each of you tonight. Hang your coats and wash your hands in the utility tub. That'll do until after dinner."

Mrs. Dunn tossed her rag into the sink and turned to Mary. "I shouldn't have said that. And now you're too late for the dance, aren't you?"

Mary sighed, relieved by the return of Mrs. Dunn's soft tone, but she was still frightened to lose her approval. She didn't like hearing Mrs. Dunn use the term "mill hunky," but Mary also knew, deep down, that Mrs. Dunn had the same immigrant blood she did, so she forgave it.

Mary smoothed her apron again, looking down at her disheveled outfit, nodding. She'd never be able to clean up and leave with Samuel for the dance, even if her sisters had completed her chores for her.

Mrs. Dunn touched Mary's shoulder. "There's no reason you can't go to the dance alone a little later. You've gone with your girlfriends a million times."

Mary looked up, considering this. It wasn't the way she wanted it to be this time, but it would still be worth it to go and dance with Samuel. She touched her hair and thought of the skirt and shirtwaist she'd already made sure were clean and pressed. "You're right. I can make it if I move fast enough."

Mary pointed out that the table was set and the serving dishes were loaded and ready on the buffet. She went over the duties she'd completed that day and sighed, running her hands down the front of the dark linen apron. It had a vibrant red design and reminded her of the few pieces of linen her mother had brought from Bohemia when she had immigrated to the United States.

Mary knew that Mrs. Dunn's family was Czech, too; she was sure that was why she'd taken such a strong liking to her, and yet Mrs. Dunn had no sign of a foreign accent, no immigrant anything except the apron. Mary often strained to hear the Czech or even a bit of rough shoving together of refugee words in Mrs. Dunn's voice, but other than this day—when Mrs. Dunn had pulled her shirtwaist free of her skirt, bellowed for the boys to stop their rumpus, smacked her son, and mumbled Slav obscenities—there wasn't a trace of old country.

She married a nice, Irish-American man who went to work in one white shirt that turned gray between home and mill and changed into another once he reached his office. Nearly every item in their house was brand-new or an expensive antique. Clean, new, good. That was the life Mary wanted.

She took off the apron and grabbed her coat as Mrs. Dunn shuffled her out the door, her voice back to its usual lightness. "Go on, Mary, go on. You can make it!"

Chapter 7

Lukasz

With a bottle of Otto's vodka in hand and a fistful of Celina's bread in his belly, Lukasz traipsed toward the Wisloka River, the place he found contentment since Ryszard died. Not normally in the dead of winter, but if his yearning was going to gnaw at him, he'd prefer to be alone in the place where the sound of rushing water gave him hope that things could always improve, that all bad things ultimately pass.

He pulled a woolen scarf from his coat pocket and wrapped it around his neck. He stepped into the tree line and stopped, taking a swig of vodka.

At first taste, it was like any other biting alcohol, but whatever it was that Otto put into his blend, there was a sweetness that lingered, demanding he take another swig. He chugged again and forced his feet toward the river bend. Adam's invitation to join them at the tavern came to mind and Lukasz turned in the direction of the village. No. He wasn't in the mood for jovial resignation, their acceptance of the end of their chance for America, like dogs happy for scraps.

Lukasz couldn't bear it. He wasn't exactly sure why it hit him so hard. Perhaps the others had never truly hoped for anything different, never sought the blue almonds Adam insisted didn't exist.

Lukasz uncorked the bottle and drank, the liquid flowing easily now that his throat had been numbed. He went on again in the direction of the Wisloka, working his way over the tree roots hidden under the snow. At the river bend, he brushed snow from a log near the bank and sat, the water lapping at the shore. The winter freeze tamped the river's scents, though he could easily call up the mud, water, fish, and the full bloom of oak trees and roses that would eventually burst to life again.

He looked toward the water. The setting sun turned the sky purplish orange. The frigid water sparkled like amethyst and amber, jewels in a queen's crown. His arms and back ached, matching the pulsing pain that came with thoughts of his family.

He rubbed the back of his neck and told himself not to drink anymore, to let the sips he'd taken settle in and do their work. He held the bottle close and inhaled with his whole body. Now he could smell it—the scent of water, the frozen earth, and his woolen scarf, always calling to mind his parents. The alcohol was doing the reverse of what he wanted.

His father's low rumbling laugh filled Lukasz's ears. Recalling his mother's firm grip when Lukasz had strayed too close to the thresher made him grab his own shoulder. His sadness grew heavier and he gave in to the enticing booze, the desire for it to stop the flow of sweet but smothering memories. The sun settled lower and the wind kicked up. He uncorked and drank again.

The urge to lie down overwhelmed him. Lukasz took another swallow and kicked at the snow in front of the log, revealing a dirt spot wide enough for him to curl on his side to rest. He lifted his head and took another drink, the jeweled river water turning gray with the slumbering sun. Twilight blackened patches of water streaming between ice jams.

One more drink. He pulled his scarf up around his mouth and ears, lay his head on his bent arm, and began to fall away.

**

Sometime later, a voice startled Lukasz out of sleep. He lifted his head, opening his eyes and listening for footfalls to go with the voice. Nothing. He lay his head back down, fading away with a rattling snore.

The voice came again, calling his name, floating past him as if on the river current. A woman. So clear. He opened his eyes but didn't move. The voice called again. It was the mermaid he'd been dreaming of for months. Or was someone really there? He shot upright and rubbed the hip that had dug into the frozen land. Insanity. No one else was there, least of all a woman, least of all a mermaid.

It was then he saw something move in the distance, out in the middle of the river, near the ice jam splitting the water in two. There was a clear outline of someone sitting on the ice, gazing downriver. The person got to his—no, *her*, definitely a her—knees. Long hair fell down her back and swirled around her waist in the cold breeze.

Lukasz squinted again, his fingernails digging into the ice-encrusted dirt. His mind went to the wire mermaid he'd made, all the stories from his youth about the Wisla Mermaid who appeared on the Wisloka in summer months. But those were just stories. It was impossible. He thought of his ridiculous friends, his own dreams that held firm. Nonsense. All of it.

Yet there she was, moon bathing on a bed of ice not far from shore. It had to be her. He rubbed his eyes with his fists, scolding himself for believing there was a mermaid alive and well right in front of him. *Only a dream, same as all the other nights.*

As though the woman had heard his thoughts, she turned, her gaze locked on Lukasz. He couldn't look away, and a shiver spiraled down the center of his back.

"Go on, Lukasz. You'll find your way. Go."

Lukasz jerked back, his breath knocked away for the second time that day. He rubbed his eyes again, then refocused on the ice as fog gathered. He gripped his chest. Fog rolled down the river. Fog. He exhaled deeply. *Of course.* Only fog. He sat back on his knees and groped for the vodka bottle, but when his fingers came up empty, he looked and saw it was on its side, cork tossed away. He glared.

Had he really drunk the whole thing? His throat went dry. He squeezed his eyes shut, then looked back toward the ice. The undulating fog lifted for a moment, and he knew. Otto's vodka had done its work. He was hallucinating. He was no different than all the other drunks. He lay back down, cradling his head on one arm, the alcohol still warming him from the inside out, and he stared into the fog.

He should have headed to the tavern right then, but he couldn't move, didn't want to. And as he fell toward sleep again, he thought he saw the woman on the ice slip into the water and reappear near the shore's edge, resting her chin on her arms, watching him, shushing him, stroking him, telling him all would be right in his world. *Come into the current, and you'll find your way.* The words came as though formed inside him rather than spoken by someone else.

"What?" He held his breath, straining to listen.

She beckoned, wiggling her fingers to coax him toward her, a small smile on her lips.

Come into the current. It'll do its work.

He squeezed his eyes closed. Had the mermaid known the depths of his sorrow, how hopeless the day had turned him? Maybe a swim into the river—an icy, watery death—would finally make all the bad go away.

Come closer. You can rest with me. Far, far away. Rest, then you'll go.

Something brushed the back of his head. He opened his eyes. It was a warm sensation, like when his mother last held him. It made him feel loved and the sense of it expanded inside him, making him obey.

He crawled nearer the river's edge, the water lapping at his hands, its icy bite numbing his fingertips. She took his hand, her soft, warm fingers laced with his, sending tingles through his body as she lured him forward. His eyes widened and she no longer pulled at him but simply held his hand, smiling. His eyes grew heavy all over again and he thought that dying right then would be just fine. He'd struggled enough.

Now he knew she existed. He only wished he could tell his friends it was so. The stories were true, and he did not mind being the next victim of the mermaid who coaxed men to their drowning deaths. Nothing else in life would be as amazing as being drawn to the bottom of the river by the lovely mermaid who'd come into his dreams every night for months.

Chapter 8

Lukasz

The pain rose to a crescendo in Lukasz's ears, churning like the Wisloka, compressing his brain, turning his stomach, forcing him to his knees to retch. All that vodka came splashing out of him. He fell forward, the river stones digging into his palms. He blew out his air, trying to order his thoughts. What had happened?

Otto's vodka.

He hadn't been drunk-sick since he had taken his first drink at the age of nine. Lukasz fell onto his back, the cold stone against his spine clearing his thoughts. He was at the river with his bottle and his lost future. Otto's recipe was legendary, yet everyone drank too much of it. No one stopped until it was too late. Wonderful going down, then it turned like a belly full of snakes. Now his thoughts were writhing, bundling up in his head.

Waldemar. Lukasz's last chance at America—Donora, Pennsylvania. He pictured the postcard he'd seen of the town, the stately home with the undulating leafy yard and wide porch. How beautiful Donora was. To have a house like that, an American castle, available to any man willing to work hard. That's all it required, and it'd nearly been possible.

The wind blew hard, forcing Lukasz to his feet. Another burst smacked his back. He stumbled forward. Bracing himself against the wind, he stared out to the ice jam in the middle of the river. The fog had fallen away to reveal the top of the ice.

The mermaid.

He looked at his hand, the one that he swore the woman had been holding. His teeth chattered. *Stupid man.* He rubbed the hip that had been jammed into the hard earth while he slept. She'd seemed so real, even more than his dreams had. Even with Otto's vodka, he was sure he'd seen a girl. Positive. Was the mermaid any less fantastic than a real live girl sitting on the rock in the middle of a winter river, swimming to him and luring him to the edge of the water? He'd taunted his friends for thoughts of mythological creatures coming to them in dreams.

Another ticket.

The voice exploded inside him, paralyzing his breath. The wind spiraled around him then pushed him from behind, and he stumbled and stepped into the waterline. He backed away, gripped his chest, and squinted into the churning fog. The shape of a woman rose up on the ice jam, and Lukasz's jaw dropped. He looked around and back. She was still there, gazing downriver. He looked at his feet. Was he awake or asleep? When he looked up, the fog was rising, swallowing what appeared to be the same woman he'd seen earlier. The Wisla Mermaid who summered in the Wisloka waters, right there, talking to him, repeating the same two words.

Another ticket.

He shifted his feet and kicked the bottle, and it clinked against a rock and broke. Was it possible? He looked up at the full moon, its edges blurred and shimmering, and a snowflake hit his nose. The stars were veiled with the same fog that climbed across the water. He searched the fog for the mermaid.

Gone.

The warmth she had brought when she'd held his hand, the words she said—to go, to find his way. Another ticket? He shook his head. The vodka. It had to be that holding him in its dreamy grip.

He exhaled and hugged himself, looking out into the river, squinting to see any sign of the mermaid or a real-live woman.

Nonsense. A dream. Otto's vodka had induced it. That was all.

Yet something made him believe there was another ticket, that there was one more chance. And he was alive. That much he knew. That made him turn from the temptation of the river and run for the tavern, for the comfort of the friends who'd be waiting to hear his story and assure him he hadn't lost his mind.

Chapter 9

Mary

Mary ran most of the way home, cresting Tenth Street, then turning up onto Marelda. Halfway up the hill, she stopped to adjust one of her stockings, which had loosened and formed a ball under the arch of her foot. In the dusky haze, she made out a large cluster of people walking just past her house, away from her. One of them carried a lantern, its light revealing their shapes. She'd know that lanky build anywhere. Samuel. Hands in his pockets, bent over to hear what his shorter friends were saying as he moved with the others beyond her house.

Even at a distance with just the lantern light, she knew most girls in his group would be dressed in fine coats, have pinked lips and Gibson girl hair, perfectly loose and secure at the same time, their hats pushed to one side. Maybe she'd misunderstood when she thought he'd asked to go with her to the dance. High-pitched giggles pierced the hush that came when the trains and tugboats paused for breath. The feminine laughter carried on the smoky wind like music. Cynthia. Always with a delicate twittering, always luring. The sight of them in the golden lamplight brought angels to Mary's mind, and she wanted to be with them more than ever.

Mary brushed the front of her coat to remove any dirt from the day and adjusted her dusty hat. She yelled for Samuel, but the train below shrieked, swallowing her voice inside it. She jogged to catch up, but the group disappeared over the crest. She stopped herself from chasing them. Even if she got Samuel's attention, she wouldn't have wanted him sitting in her house, waiting for her to get ready.

She sped to 1137 Marelda Avenue and burst through the boot room door, shook out of her coat, and surveyed the kitchen for unfinished chores.

She glanced into the dining area and gave Matka a peck on the cheek as she grabbed an apron. "Looks like Ann has the potatoes and cabbage on, and the table's set. I'll finish up and serve. Victoria can clean up before she does homework, so I can go to the dance."

Her mother pressed a fork into the boiling potatoes. "Some boy stopped by."

Mary's breath solidified in her chest.

Matka shrugged. "Told 'im yinz couldn't go together."

Couldn't go? Mary balled her fists, upset that Matka had said she couldn't go and petrified that she'd been rude. "He came into the house?"

Her mother continued to stab at the potatoes. "All of 'em did."

Mary scanned the kitchen, the smell of root vegetables and something sour hitting her as hard as the lemony scent of the Dunns' home. She looked into the next room, where they ate, which doubled as her parents' bedroom when they were full to the brim with boarders. "All of them?" She wasn't sure how embarrassed she should be.

She reminded herself that more kids lived like her family than like Samuel and Cynthia's. Still, she would have cleaned, spritzed the air with lemon water, or tossed lemon juice around at the very least if she'd have known a whole crowd was coming inside. If she'd been ready on time, she would have slipped out and met Samuel on the porch. She wanted him to remember her as she'd been at the Dunns' house, the sweet compliments she'd been given even if she'd been serving drinks at the time.

Matka stirred the vegetable soup and sampled it, holding the hot spoon over her hand. "The dance was all right when ya were gonna redd up the boys' room first. Damn pigsty. They need yinz girls' help."

Mary's throat tightened. "It's clean enough for a bunch of men. They all stink anyhow, and I'm not touching their underthings, no."

Matka grumbled into the pot. "Git home earlier next time."

"Mrs. Dunn was sick. Baby's nearly due. I was helping. I just—"

Matka looked over her shoulder. "She pay extra?"

Mary thought of Mrs. Dunn's offer of the Staffordshire dog and shook her head. "She will."

Matka stabbed at the potatoes again, splashing water. "Yinz're quite the pair. She's queen, and you're her lady-in-waiting—"

"Please," Mary said. "Just once, let Victoria do my work and let me leave. Abigail and Nellie and—"

"They're still in school, Mary. You've a different lot. That's a dance for a different crowd."

Mary shook her head. "Lidia and Natasza're going. They barely speak English. The dance's for everyone, not just . . . You're wrong." Mary held her breath as soon as the words were out of her mouth.

Matka gripped her arm. Mary braced for a slap. It wasn't the first time her sass would earn her one. She glanced down at Matka, who was glaring.

"Watch yer mouth." Matka released Mary and turned back to stirring.

Mary rubbed her arm, forcing herself to relax, willing her words to quiet as they came out. This once, she wanted this one thing. "Papa would say I should go. He thinks I'm fit to marry someone who owns things, an Irishman or . . . I'm not going to meet anyone like that in this kitchen."

Matka jerked around, brandishing her fork. "Oh, I know. Papa's damn dreaming, his damn wishing. Goddamn waste. Thinks 'cause yer born in America, no one'll notice yer parents have hunky accents, that you have to read the news to yer mother and scratch aht grocery lists for her. Hope don't pay bills. Eat today. That's how to survive."

Mary's eyes burned with tears. She worked so very hard, tirelessly, happily most of the time. She simply wanted one respite, one opportunity, one particular dance. "I can teach you to read, Matka. If you let me, you'll see how easy writing is."

"When? My work never ends. No."

Mary knew better than to push. She'd tried since she was small and excited to share what she had learned at school. "Samuel. The boy who came by. He likes me. His father's high up in the mill, and if I could just see him at the dance and—"

"Who?"

"Samuel Blake."

"Oh." Matka rolled her eyes. "Thought he looked familiar. Same block head as his father. Big manager at the blast furnaces. Asshole." Matka's words sliced, hot and pointed. She often harbored dislike for powerful men, men she saw as slighting her in some way, at some point in time, or by merely existing.

"They're a nice family," Mary said. "I met them once."

Matka's furrowed brow relaxed. She set the fork aside and took Mary by the arms. She studied her daughter, leaving Mary with the sense that something had turned, that suddenly her mother understood.

"Dear Mary. A man'll find ya, and I hope he ain't a miner. I *hope* yinz have a girl to slave the way you do for Mrs. Dunn. I can hope, Papa can wish, but yer job's to do the work because work makes hopes and dreams unnecessary. Me and Papa'll absorb all the disappointments the world lays at yer feet, and someday you'll do the same for yer children. You'll marry

Czech. A grocer. Somethin' like that. But now? Just help us feed the family. Always another dance down the road."

Mary looked away, disappointed that she'd been wrong about her mother understanding.

"Besides. Papa's waitin' on ya. Picture 'im sittin' riverside: 'Where's my Mary?' Then what? He'll pay to be ferried." She brushed her hands together as though wiping away dirt. "Money made, money gone. Wasted."

Mary pursed her lips to keep the angry words pushed back.

"Work," her mother said. "It'll bring what yinz girls need, knowing exactly what to expect. And if there's a surprise, a Scotch or Irishman? Well, I'll probably drop dead in the street and ya can sweep me aside and take my dress for yer hope chest you ain't got. So tonight, as usual, cross that damn river and fetch Papa 'fore he disappears into some bar."

Mary thought of the dance. Could she still make it if she hurried? "I got someone else to fetch Papa."

"What?" Matka flinched. "Who?"

"Harvey Harrison."

"Why'd that lazy ass lend a hand?"

Mary looked at her feet, steeling herself for what she knew was coming. She should have kept her yap shut.

Matka crossed her arms. "Young lady?"

Mary knew what her mother was asking. "I paid him."

Matka grimaced.

"Just a little."

Matka's eyes narrowed, then she turned back to the boiling cabbage. Sometimes being shunned was better than a slap, but it twisted Mary's insides more.

"Don't be angry. Please," Mary said, even as she was choking on her own ire at missing the dance, at Matka not caring a lick.

"Git yer money from Harvey 'I'll kiss a pig for a penny' Harrison and git Papa. Mortgage's late."

And so Mary did. She dashed to Harvey's house on Fayette Avenue and got the money back, mumbling all the way down to the river, marveling at how she'd started the day thinking she was in control of her life and was ending it reminded there's no such thing for her. Not yet, anyhow.

Chapter 10

Lukasz

Lukasz reached the tavern, heated by the sprint that took him there. The men drinking would know about another ticket. That's where all the news of the village was born and died.

He undid his scarf and entered, wiping his brow and nose with his coat sleeve. At the bar, he stepped between Adam and Kacper, looping his arm around their necks. "I saw *her*. I saw the mermaid. She said there's another ticket to America, my friends. Have you heard? Has this ticket been reported yet?"

Adam gaped at Lukasz and pulled away. "Oh my." He patted Lukasz's back. "You've been to the bottom of a bottle."

Lukasz raised his eyebrows. "Well, Otto—"

Adam and Kacper whooped and fell forward with belly laughs. "Otto's bottle? That explains it," Adam said.

Lukasz grabbed his friend's arm. "No, no. Well, yes. I did have Otto's bottle, but this, what I saw . . ." He couldn't believe he was saying it. "It was real."

Adam pulled up a stool and signaled the tavern owner. "Get this man your best pull of water." He helped Lukasz onto the seat and steadied him as he swayed.

"Sounds crazy," Lukasz said. "But I saw her. Told me to find my way. You believe me, Kacper? You saw a firebird in your dreams."

"Oh, so now you believe in our great Myscowa myths?"

"There's another ticket," Lukasz said, repeating the woman's words. He pressed his chest with one hand and guzzled the water before slamming the empty glass onto the bar. "Hand to God, hand to God, hand to *God.* I *saw* her. Heard her voice like it was inside me. And I'm alive. But I wanted to die and . . ." Lukasz shook his head, trying to make sense of his own story.

"Look who's praying to God now," Igor said.

Lukasz shrugged. "My heart stopped beating at the sight of her. I couldn't breathe. What I can't say is how on this snowy earth that mermaid reached inside me to stop my heart and I'm not dead." Lukasz took Adam by the shoulders and looked directly into his face. "I'm alive, right?"

Igor sprinkled some tobacco onto paper and rolled it. "Oh right, the Wisla Mermaid visits in winter and is interested in Lukasz. Tell me more, my little friend."

Lukasz shook his head, ignoring the shot at his height. He knew it sounded insane. He thought he might be crazy.

A barrel-bellied old man a few seats down raised his glass to Lukasz. "Ya sound like every man who's drunk Otto's przekląć vodka."

"Right you are, Toby," Kacper said. "Lukasz can't get Petra to look his way, but he can lure the Wisla Mermaid down from Warsaw and up from the depths of the Wisloka?"

"No one sees her until at least late May," Justyn Sas said.

The barkeep filled Lukasz's glass with amber liquid.

He downed it and stared at the thick golden-brown swirl left at the bottom. "America. Another ticket."

"Oh, Lukasz. You *lost.* We all lost. It's over," Justyn said. "You've always been mad at Waldemar for him being bigger, taking Petra, all of it. You've had a grudge from the moment you were both born on the same day, same time, forced to share the luck of that bright star that hung over you both."

Waldemar. It was true. He hated the sound of the man's name. He had carried resentment toward Waldemar, no doubt, but this wasn't that. "I think that's what she meant. Said for me to go, to find my way. In America."

Adam shook his head. "Lukasz . . ."

"Remember that place in the letter? Donora. The Kowalks there said they'd sponsor anyone who could make his way there."

Toby slid his empty tumbler down the bar to the keep, who caught it without even looking.

"The Kowalks paying your way?" Igor asked.

Lukasz shoved his glass down the bar like Toby had. The keep pushed it back without filling it. It stung Lukasz's palm as it smacked into it. He didn't have to reach into his pockets to know they were empty.

"Mermaid dreams," the tavern owner, Wolski, said. "Worth nothing."

"It wasn't a *dream*. And I think I'm going." Lukasz eyed the wall where they stored the bottles and kept track of the records held by various villagers for things like number of arm-wrestling matches won, handstand contests, number of backflips while drunk and sober, even records for breath holding. Lukasz was in the top five in all of them, champion in several. Waldemar currently topped him in two. Lukasz would have to look at that man's name for years to come even after he left for America.

"In a year, you could save enough. Maybe," Adam said. "If you can swing enough work and eat dirt for supper."

Lukasz spun his glass. That was true. He thought of the ticket he'd saved for, almost paying his own way before lending it.

The tavern door opened, sending a crisp gust of wind inside. Everyone cringed away while trying to keep their eyes on who was entering.

Waldemar Kowslawski stood in the doorway, snow swirling around him like a tornado.

"Shut the damn door!" Wiloski said.

Waldemar kicked it closed and sauntered toward the bar, pulling his gloves off one finger at a time. His clothing was new, his usual smirk in place. Lukasz turned away and went back to spinning his glass on its bottom edge.

A full glass of whiskey came flying down the bar, clinking into Lukasz's empty one. He knew who'd sent it without even looking.

"Drink up, friend," Waldemar said from a few stools down.

Lukasz fired the glass back. "No, thanks."

The glass came again, stopping against Lukasz's empty.

"Don't want it." Lukasz shoved it back.

"I'll take it," Toby stopped it midway back to Waldemar.

Waldemar swaggered toward him, grabbed the glass from Toby, and set it in front of Lukasz. He rested his foot on the rod that ran along the bottom of the bar and leaned on the wooden top. "Can't even accept a gift from an old pal? I'm leaving soon and wanted to say my goodbyes." He pushed the drink closer to Lukasz's fingers. "Too small a man, are you?"

Lukasz took the glass. "Big as I need to be." He put it to his lips, eager to have Waldemar get on with his journey, to never see him again.

Waldemar stared at him. "Ah. There we are. Drink up."

The superior taunting was too much. Rage burned in Lukasz's throat. He put it to his lips again, but then hurled it into the stone wall across from the bar, shattering it and two whiskey bottles that sat on a shelf.

The bar went silent.

"Big man," Waldemar said.

Lukasz glared, pulling himself up as tall as he could while sitting on a stool. "Big enough."

"Prove it," Waldemar said. "Every Pole is strong as an ox . . . you can't beat me, though. Never could. But if you can prove it, go ahead."

"Prove what?"

"Your size."

The men hooted and let out whistles. "Let him be. Lukasz's bested you plenty of times over the years," Adam said.

Waldemar scoffed.

"He's too drunk to do anything," Igor said.

Lukasz fumed. He wiped his lips with the back of his hand, got off the stool, and stood in front of Waldemar, his legs wide for stability. He balled his fists at his sides to keep from falling over.

Waldemar's expression didn't change. He didn't look angry, scared, or irritated; he only looked as though he needed something to keep him from being bored.

"I work like an ox," Lukasz said. "You live like a housecat, curling up at Basia's feet to be petted, eating midday meal with Petra. You're softer than you look. You won't work hard enough in America to earn one of those houses. You'll be back in a year."

Waldemar's mouth pulled up on one side. "Think so?"

He waited for Waldemar's fist to fly. When it didn't, Lukasz nodded and lifted his.

Waldemar pushed away from the bar, towering over Lukasz. "Not like that."

"Scared?"

Waldemar held his fists up and examined his ropy fingers. "You know better than that."

"Then what?" Lukasz asked.

"Feat of strength."

Lukasz glanced at the list on the wall again. This was what Waldemar wanted? Lukasz drew back, relaxing. It didn't make sense.

Waldemar scoffed then swayed, his eyes unfocused for a moment, and Lukasz's mind raced. Waldemar stumbled and caught himself on the bar before straightening and brushing off his clothes as though he hadn't just revealed his drunkenness. Waldemar had been able to hide it behind his swagger, but Lukasz saw it clearly. *Pijany.* His nemesis was ploughed.

Another ticket.

Now it was Lukasz who found a smirk on his lips. This was his chance. He glanced at the wall, the lists of records held by either him or Waldemar, and calculated his best chance for winning.

If Waldemar had drunk so much that he was swaying, he was inebriated. Lukasz had nineteen years' experience with him. Lukasz could lure Waldemar just close enough to the edge that the big ape would send himself right over the cliff. *Another ticket.* Lukasz didn't need another ticket. He could get *the* ticket.

Lukasz stepped closer, poking Waldemar's chest. "I bet you your passage to America that I can hold a handstand longer than you."

Waldemar shoved Lukasz's hand away. "I'll beat you, easy."

Lukasz spread his arms and raised his eyebrows. "Sure about that? I hold the record."

The men in the tavern didn't even wait for Waldemar to agree to the contest before they jumped up and cleared the tables from the center of the room so the two men had space to kick up to handstands.

"I'm due to win," Waldemar said.

Lukasz could win this, drunk or not. Waldemar was strong, but he had those long legs to keep in the air. This contest favored Lukasz no matter what condition he was in.

The barkeep set up a series of hourglasses to mark the final time as one of the men was sure to break a record. With a deep breath and big exhale, the two men kicked up. The others cheered them on, mostly rooting for Lukasz.

He saw the barkeep turn the second hourglass. The first five minutes were a breeze for Lukasz. His stomach was full of booze, but he figured Waldemar only had two more minutes in him at most. The stone floor was cold against Lukasz's palms, but at six minutes in, the floor felt flat. It was easy to stay up.

Seven, eight, nine, ten minutes. Lucasz couldn't believe it. Waldemar stayed upright. Eleven minutes. Perhaps Waldemar *hadn't* been drinking.

Lukasz shifted his hands, walking several paces forward, then back.

He glanced between his arms to see Waldemar turning circles on his hands.

"Keep that up, you'll be down in no time," Lukasz said.

"Says the man with the belly full of whiskey," Waldemar said through his arms, his face reddened.

"Not long now, *dupek*," Lukasz said.

"You've always been jealous, Musial."

"You're a *dupek*. That's all."

"A *dupek* with a good handstand. Surprise."

Lukasz walked his hands so that he couldn't see his rival any longer. He *was* surprised. He shouldn't have been. Lukasz had seen Waldemar do wondrous feats of strength through the years when he wasn't being lazy.

Lukasz closed his eyes. "Stay up, stay strong," he told himself. His shoulders started to burn. His fingers were starting to bend, no longer easily lying flat against the stone.

He stole a glance at Waldemar. His fingers were curling as well. His shoulders shook.

Waldemar looked up, met Lukasz's gaze, and sneered. Lukasz kept his shoulders locked, wanting to appear solid, not as shaky as he felt.

Twelve minutes.

His elbows ached. He shifted his weight to one hand to shake the other. He almost fell over but fought back, straightening. The crowd gasped and then cheered. He met Waldemar's gaze again.

Lukasz's shoulders quaked, his fingers curling into his palms. He closed his eyes. *Stay up, stay up.* His hands and shoulders tingled; his elbows locked. He wouldn't hold much longer, not with the alcohol working against him. And as he told himself it was just a little bit longer, his head grew heavy.

Another ticket.

The voice expanded his chest like it had at the river. This was it for him. He could not lose. He opened his eyes to better balance. *Stay up, stay up.*

Lukasz started to tip but caught himself. He dug his fingers into the stone, staying up. Spots gathered in front of his eyes, and he could no longer hear. Soon, his feet dragged further over, pulling him off-balance, sending him crashing to the stone floor, his dream for America falling away with his drunken handstand.

Chapter 11

Mary

Far, far away from Lukasz and that tavern, Mary reached Gilmore Docks, untethered the rowboat, and hopped in, careful not to slosh cold water over her feet. She shifted her bottom and gripped the oars, her woolen gloves warming her hands but making it hard to grasp the frigid wood. She glanced over her shoulder to check for barges or other boats before starting across the fifteen hundred feet of river that divided Donora from Webster.

She dug the oars into the water and heaved, slicing perpendicular across the dark water. The Monongahela, the river of work, was every bit as responsible for the coal and steel profits as earthen materials and manpower. Nearly every time Mary was on or in the river, it brought her peace. The grinding mill, groaning trains, and boats rumbled around her, but at least no one was yammering at her.

With long, even strokes, she waited for her anger at missing the dance to release its grip, waited for the moment when the motion relieved her of her troubles.

Anger never brought anyone anything good, so she focused on what she saw in front of her. Miles of wireworks and open hearth and blast furnaces hugged the horseshoe bend in the river. *Behold*, she thought every time she saw it from the river, *the power of the metal giants, churning out more steel.* The sheer strength of the machinery impressed her. Heat and purpose pulsed in her chest as she rowed, thinking of it. Each part of the mill did its job—cooking, combining, separating, reducing, stretching material, and shaping metals into the things that were building America. The operation was reliable; it was the heart and soul of the town itself, and nearly everyone worked there.

The blast furnaces shot flaming columns into the sky, where the heat licked at the stars. To Mary, the whole outfit was beautiful, alive. The mills provided jobs for the townspeople in one form or another, each part of the process feeding the next. Her father's position in the mines produced the coal that made the coke that started the process of making steel. Living in Donora was special. Living there, anything was possible. Most of the time.

Pull, release. *Pull*, release. *Pull*, release. The current was strong that night. Each stroke required her to adjust her movement to stay on course—straight across to Webster.

She made steady progress before pausing to readjust the angle of the boat. The movement and the power it took to row across allowed Mary to exorcise her anger toward her mother. Workhorse. That's what Mary was to her. Mary was proud of the amount of work she could do and the responsibility she managed, but she was equally irritated when her mother didn't appreciate it.

Mary had to admit she wasn't perfect. She swallowed the guilt that rose up in her throat every time she recognized the lies she told. She hid away small treasures in the fireplace hearth, gifts that people like Mrs. Dunn would have nested in a painted hope chest for a daughter Mary's age. Mary yearned for special things, yes, but didn't begrudge her mother for not providing sparkly gewgaws and silver mirrors and brushes; her mother didn't own extra things she could give to Mary like Mrs. Dunn did.

It simply made Mary work harder at being self-sufficient. She refused to let her disappointments shape her outlook. She'd seen ladies with dark, dissatisfied, scowly faces, every exchange encrusted with resentment that chased away every pleasant person they encountered. No, Mary felt her disenchantments, but she let them move past her like the Monongahela waters cut the valley, folding its black body around the land before rushing on.

**

At the Webster shoreline, Mary removed her gloves, lifted her skirt, and had begun to climb onto the dock when her papa surprised her by jumping into the boat. He coughed and wheezed, his body jerking, making the boat lurch, nearly tossing them into the water. Mary gripped the dock and her papa finally stilled, settling the boat.

"All right?" she asked.

He leaned over the side and spit into the water, then pulled his collar up to his chin and nodded. His face was blackened with coal dust, the whites of his eyes glowing against his skin and the smoky night.

Mary pushed one oar against the dock to move away and began to row.

Her papa crossed his arms and cleared his throat. "Berta Peskova's ruined."

Mary lifted the oars out of the water and leaned forward. Papa was often silent on their trips home, exhausted from his shift. She thought a double shift and his regular turn would've left him completely mute. The boat listed north, and Mary readjusted course. "Sick?"

"*Tehotna*," he said.

Mary put one oar in the river to angle the boat southward and started rowing again to stop the sadness for Berta's new lot from suffocating her.

"Cumet doblba."

"Papa, she's not dumb. She's first in class. Ahead of the boys."

"Didn't keep far enough ahead. Now she's in the rice. Ruined."

Mary knew what he meant. The girl was unmarried and with child. Mary pulled, her shoulders straining as she lengthened her strokes. "I feel so bad for her."

He scoffed. "She did it to herself."

Mary stretched forward and heaved back, drawing deep breaths.

He shook his finger. "You're strong. You're beautiful."

"Papa."

"You doubt? Stuff that away. You're very handsome."

She chuckled and dug one oar into the water to keep the boat straight, grateful she had something to do with her hands during this conversation, familiar with how it would go. "Handsome isn't beautiful."

"Did you see the photograph we had made of you children? Wide eyes, pretty pink cheeks. The picture of beauty, a body of strength. You've grace and resilience, like the steel they mold into every imaginable shape and size for every unimaginable thing. This is America, and someday you'll have yourself a prince. An Irishman? Scotch? Even a Czech store owner."

She groaned, knowing he meant Ralph, the boy he often said she should marry. Mary had no interest in him. Still, hearing Papa talk about her marital prospects this way salved her mother's harshness, her resignation that Mary might not fulfill her dreams.

Papa pulled his coat tighter around him. "Your mother prefers Ralph. Someone like us. He has as much chance to be an American prince as an Irishman. I tell you, your generation will be indistinguishable."

Mary shrugged. Ralph's house would still smell like cabbage soup. Mary thought of her earlier conversation with her mother. Her father held high dreams for her. Matka stomped them out. She almost explained that Matka had ruined her chance to go to a dance with Samuel, but she didn't want him to argue with Matka when they got home. Her parents' moods moved like wind—sometimes light, often dark and angry—and to pit one against the other would make things worse. Matka was heavy handed with Mary, but Mary was protective of her. She always kept things smooth between her parents when she could.

"Anyone in America," Papa said. "Any single man can grow to live the life of a royal. Not like back there." He pointed his thumb behind him as though his Czech motherland was just beyond the Webster side of the valley.

When Mary completed her stroke and the oars met, Papa clamped his hands over hers, stopping her from pulling again.

"You're American. You read and write English. You cook and clean and sew and row and make decent money—all with a smile. An Irishman, like Mr. Dunn, who came from stock that was once kicked in the face, now lives like a king in Donora. That's what's possible for you as wife of the right man. Ralph might be just that man. That's what's possible for your sisters and brothers too."

Her cheeks warmed at hearing her father gush in a way he never quite did. Still, Ralph was not her pick.

Papa took her chin in hand. "Don't look down when I say you're handsome, strong, and brave. Only up, only forward. That's where your eyes belong. You'll make your family a beautiful home someday."

Mary thought she might cry. Her heart swelled. Her father barely spoke nine words at a time most days.

He covered her hands with his again. "Know your worth. No more dusty outside games with the neighborhood boys. Time to be a lady—no more bats, no more balls."

The cold January wind raced over the water and stung her cheeks where hot tears moistened them. She pulled out of Papa's grip and wiped her eyes with the back of her hand. She loved playing ball with the Pizankys and the Carvellis, teaching her brothers how to catch and hit. Not that she had much time for it, but she couldn't imagine not playing every once in a while.

He took her hand back and squeezed it, his skin rough on hers. "See that?"

She shook her head.

"You flinched at the feel of my hand."

"I didn't."

"You did."

Had she? She shook her head, knowing what he was getting at. "No. Calluses show you work hard. I'm proud of you and your work."

Papa tilted his head and studied her. "I know you are. But for you, there's a man with calluses on his brain, a man who oversees the men on the floor of a steel mill. You want a man who can work his daylight hours and have the weekend at some club playing golf, enjoying the trees, away from the choking smoke and fire. You want a bedroom for every single child."

Mary's parents worked so hard. She never said aloud that she wished for any of that, and she wondered if he'd overheard her talking to Ann and Victoria. "I don't mean to—"

"I know. Matka is hard on you, and you don't complain, you don't whine or get sick or have a mood and take to your bed. You're a queen without a country, and that's what you must feel deep in your heart. You're worthy of a man who understands the value of a woman bearing as much strength inside her as the steel he makes. And someday your mother and I'll live with you in an enormous, sprawling home. *Obrovský*." He held his arms wide. "We're expecting it. Someone like us, like Ralph, can provide that. An Irishman would be lucky to have you, but he wouldn't understand *us*."

Mary chuckled. She knew how things went. She shared that dream—to have a fine home to share with her parents. Though Ralph wasn't part of her plans, Papa's belief in her was reassuring, different from the way her mother made her feel. Her heart pounded and her eyes filled, and she couldn't contain it any longer. She sprang across the boat and flung her arms around Papa's neck. He held her for a few breaths, and she thought maybe he recognized the specialness in this one instant. He patted her back, dismissing her.

"Get moving. Your matka will holler for days. Oh, her voice." He hunched his shoulders. "Like a knife."

Mary squeezed him harder. She knew what he meant. But he drove her mother crazy as well, and Mary herself had been at his mercy when the panic of taxes and mortgage set in. Papa worked far harder than his pay showed. Endless toiling and bad lungs forced him to miss an occasional day, and his unsympathetic boss used that as an excuse to withhold a full week's pay. Then her mother let him have it. Their screaming rattled the roof.

Though his pay came steady most of the time, he only made ninety cents a week, and that was the reason her mother took in the endless stream of boarders. Mary clung tighter to Papa. This moment would be precious to her through the years, but she knew better than to think it meant something more than it did. As gentle as her father was in this moment, she knew if she revealed her hidden fireplace treasures, they'd be taken from her and sold to pay the mortgage or taxes without a thought for Mary's plan to use them as a dowry.

"Now, now, Matka'll punish us both." He patted her back again and coaxed her to her seat.

She nodded, shifting and rowing again, smooth and fast. With every pull, she leaned back enough to see the clouds parting, revealing a sliver of moon.

Pull, pull, pull.

The next few minutes brought an even clearer sky. The stars pulsed like a thousand heartbeats before the orange and red of the blast furnaces whooshed upward, stealing their luster, absorbing it into the arrogant, supreme flame. Black smoke swallowed every flicker of the universe's light as though the mill fires had been put on earth to do just that.

Chapter 12

Lukasz

Way back in Myscowa, in the tavern on the edge of the village, Lukasz roused from sleep with a clamp-like grip on his shoulders. Somebody was shaking him to consciousness. The scent of stale beer mixed with a distant odor of piss turned his stomach. He groaned but squeezed his eyes closed, unable to fully waken. Next came a splash of ice water, forcing him upright. He swiped his face dry with his shirtsleeve.

"Up, *glupie*," a voice said.

Lukasz groaned again and rubbed his desert-dry eyes and focused on the face above him.

The tavern owner, Wolski, pulled Lukasz's hands. "*Rusz to*!"

Standing, Lukasz staggered toward the bar and steadied himself on the wooden slab. Was it his blurry vision or the whiskey tangling his thoughts? He tried to straighten and get his legs to work. Flashes of the night before reminded him what had put him in that bar that night . . . morning? Afternoon? He had no idea. A glass of water appeared in front of him. Wolski leaned in, resting on meaty forearms.

Lukasz guzzled the drink.

Wolski pulled out a bucket from behind the bar and placed it in front of Lukasz. His stomach churned and burned, and in seconds, he was reaching for the wooden pail, releasing everything left in his stomach. After several minutes of vomiting and then dry heaving, he finally settled, still hugging the bucket.

Wolski gestured. "Set it on the floor."

Lukasz did.

"You had Otto's bottle at the riverside. That'll do it." Wolski's tone softened, his eyes kind, searching. "I won't even sell the stuff. Better to have my customers back every day."

Lukasz nodded, embarrassed. He rubbed his forehead, trying to roll back through the events from the night before. Deep inside him, regret seeded itself along with worry and hopelessness, even though he couldn't remember what had prompted those feelings.

Wolski rubbed his bicep. "Listen up. I'll make this easy for you." He pressed one forefinger with the other. "First thing that happened, you showed up here distraught."

Vodka, the mermaid.

Wolski pressed his ring finger. "Then Waldemar showed up with a bet."

Lukasz groaned, closing his eyes, lowering his head onto his fists. "Handstands."

"Handstands," Wolski said.

The weight of defeat stirred his belly again.

Wolski backed away from the bar and opened a drawer that slid out of the back wall. He slipped a piece of paper across the bar. Lukasz's name was written on the front of an envelope. A bill for a night's sleep on a cold stone floor. He'd have to pay with work in the kitchen.

"I can work midday and night to pay you back."

"*Gulpie,*" Wolski said. "Open it."

Lukasz drew back and turned the envelope, tunneling his finger inside and removing the paper. He stared.

"Passage to Hamburg, then New York," Wolski said. "Then passage to . . ." He pulled the envelope back and studied what was written there. "Donora?"

Lukasz stared at the man. Confused, he pushed his hand through his hair, unable to call up the memory that matched this information.

Wolski gave him a postcard. "You won."

Lukasz drew back, trying to recall how that could be. The last thing he remembered was when he began to topple. Waldemar had still been upright.

Wolski let out a long whistle. "Must've blacked out as you crashed down."

Lukasz shrugged.

Wolski smacked his hands together. "Once the handsome bear began to fall, he went down like an old oak." Wolski came around the bar and took Lukasz by the shoulder, guiding him to a table. Mrs. Wolski came out from the back room.

"Breakfast," she said, holding plates high. She set a full dish in front of Lukasz. Buttery eggs, sausage, and potatoes. Normally he would have shoveled the entire bit down in two seconds flat, but all it did was turn his stomach. She returned with mugs of coffee.

She patted Lukasz's back. "*Tylko troche.*"

Lukasz turned to her. "Thank you, but I don't think I can get it down."

"Just a little," she repeated. "My cooking cures all."

"Eat," Wolski said. "Cooking's all that woman does. Deserves a little praise."

Lukasz nodded, knowing it would insult her if he didn't eat. He held his breath, trying to force away the nausea, and dug into his pockets for money. He shook his head. "Nothing."

She pulled something out of her apron and held it up. A wire animal. A deer. Lukasz had made it months before for Petra.

"Came to me by way of someone who didn't see its value." She patted her husband's shoulder. Wolski took her hand and gazed at her. "It's precious," she said.

"I made that," Lukasz said, staring in wonder at the wires and flattened metal enameled in shades of brown. Seeing it in someone else's possession made him proud he'd created it, that someone loved it. His cheeks burned.

"And it's payment for breakfast," Mrs. Wolski said.

Wolski winked at her and she winked back, their loving nature making Lukasz miss his parents when things had been better for them. She patted Lukasz's shoulder.

"Thank you," he said. She smiled and left. He stared at the plate full of wonderful foods, overwhelmed by the way his morning had turned. Was this really happening? *Another ticket?* The mermaid may not have been real, but Lukasz's dream was coming true. The thought thrilled and frightened him—something he wasn't expecting.

"Quite the spectacle last night," Wolski said.

"And I won." Lukasz couldn't believe what he was saying.

Wolski used his fork to push Lukasz's plate closer to him. "It's like you don't remember."

Lukasz's dream of the mermaid seemed more real to him than winning the contest. Fear overtook every other emotion. "I can't go."

"You've got passage to America. Freedom. You can be anybody, do anything. No more kings to tell you who you are."

"Yes, yes," Lukasz said. Fright cracked inside him like a whip. Now that he had the ticket, his big dreams dissolved.

Wolski shoveled a forkful into his mouth. "The Mermaid of Wisla even—"

Lukasz waved him off, then put his head in his hands, rubbing his temples. "I'll never drink again."

"*Co po trzeźwemu myśli, to po pijanemu powie,*" Wolski said.

"No, no, it was the booze talking, making things up. I don't really want to leave. I didn't see some mermaid. I don't believe in things like that."

"Sure made it sound as if America would be the answer to your prayers and that you nearly dove in the frigid water, summoned by our famous mermaid."

"Oh, that vodka."

"So. No? You stay?"

Lukasz thought of the letters from the Kowalks, the postcard of the American castle. Alexander and his family were happy, working, living in their own home. Lukasz knew it was where he'd find his opportunities.

Yet regret crept in. Had he tried hard enough to overcome the obstacles? Could he fulfill his dream for a better life without having to leave his homeland? He shook his head, knowing that fear was turning his thoughts inside out.

"You'll leave tomorrow."

Lukasz looked away. He thought of Ryszard's forge. "I could make a go of the forge. His son said no but—"

Wolski stabbed at his food. "*Lepszy wróbel w garści niż gołąb na dachu.*"

"I have the bird in hand, yes, but the nest is here."

Wolski licked a finger and dug back into his bacon. "Waldemar said that family who sent the postcard sponsors lots of people, that you were set to go at one point and you lent the money away. Your nest's no longer here. I'd leave if I were a young man. There's nothing here. No work, no fields for you, nothing. I'll leave this pub to my son. But that's it. This tavern survives by the lucky chance of selling the one thing you boys can't get enough of."

Lukasz thought of Petra.

Wolski pointed his fork at Lukasz. "And don't stay for some girl. She don't even want you. Plenty of girls in America."

It wasn't as though Lukasz wanted Petra. They barely spoke, but one day she had invited him into her father's barn, did things with him, then curled into his lap afterward, saying she'd see him the next day. Next thing Lukasz knew, Waldemar was at her supper table instead.

"And jobs," Wolski said. "The work you get in that Donora place might be backbreaking like here, but you'll get paid. No kings, no princes, no peasants. *Freedom.* A president, a vote. Paupers become rich, rich, rich. No greedy landowners."

Lukasz smiled. This was what he'd wanted. He rubbed his belly, working the fear away. He was hungry again. His stomach growled, the shock of having found out he had won the ticket finally wearing off.

America. It would finally be his.

**

Lukasz packed clothes, some wire, and tools into a suitcase and bag, then hitched a ride from Adam, who was making a delivery to a village upriver. It was Lukasz's one chance to say goodbye to his father. He didn't know what to expect, but as he drew closer to the tiny shack he shared with Lukasz's stepmother and their children, he debated whether he should have sought his father at all. His heart pounded, and he realized he'd be disappointed if his father demanded he stay in Poland, and he'd be angry if his father sent him on his way with a smile.

When Adam pulled the wagon up to their shack on the edge of the woods, Lukasz disembarked.

"I'll be back in a little while," Adam said.

Lukasz nodded, having already explained that he didn't need much time.

He found his father, Piotr, around the back of the shed, patching mortar in the stone barn. His father's square jaw and gray eyes were cold, and the sight of them stopped Lukasz's heart a little. He thought of when his father's eyes had been soft and warm, when he had braided his wife's hair with such care and love. Lukasz told himself this was for the best, that there hadn't been room for him in his father's second family when he took them on, and there wasn't really room for Lukasz in Poland, period.

He took off his hat and stepped closer to his father. "I'm going to America."

His father lifted his chin. "I heard."

Lukasz didn't know what to say next. He shouldn't have been surprised at his father's response, yet he was. It hurt, but it fit with how they'd lived since Lukasz's mother had died. "Looks like you've got this patch job under control."

Piotr Musial scoffed.

Lukasz yearned for the time when his father would tousle his hair or pat his shoulder as he worked his letters at the kitchen table after supper.

Lukasz's emotions spiraled, nauseating him. He almost bolted away. His father had severed his life from Lukasz's years before. A surge of anger came. He wouldn't let it control him. This was the last he'd see his father. The weight of that sat heavy like a hay bale to the gut. Lukasz grabbed him up and held him close, squeezing when the old man stiffened against the embrace. His father's staccato breath took Lukasz by surprise but told him so much.

He patted his father's back. *That was it.* The realization settled deep in Lukasz. His father had treated him like a stranger because he'd been unable to accept the loss of his wife and keep the presence of his son. It had broken Piotr in a way that Lukasz hadn't been able to feel until that moment. Now it shook him. His chest ached at the knowing. Their sorrow would tether them forever, no matter how far Lukasz went.

He gripped tighter, the scent of farm and hard work on a cold day filled Lukasz's nose. All the hurt from being pushed aside, having to search out friends and men like Ryszard to stand in as family, had kept Lukasz alive, allowing him to bury his loss and continue living. His father's marriage—the betrayal, as Lukasz had seen it—finally made sense. His father loved Lukasz best, loved his mother best, and had to let them go in order to live.

Lukasz patted his father again. "It's all right, my father. I understand."

His father nodded against Lukasz's shoulder, then pushed away, staring at the ground. Wind gusted by, making him notice the wet splotch on his collar, left by his father's tears.

Lukasz backed up. "Goodbye."

His father nodded and turned. Tears burned Lukasz's eyes and he rushed to the front of the shack where Adam was pulling up in the wagon.

Lukasz swallowed a rising sob. He hadn't cried like a child in a long time. He'd roughed up his heart, calloused his soul, and thickened his skin each and every day since losing his mother. This was good. Finished business. He vaulted into the wagon and nodded, but didn't look at Adam.

As they pulled away, Lukasz looked over his shoulder at the shack, keeping his eyes on it until it snapped out of sight, telling himself that no matter how scared he may be in the New World, it'd be better than anything he was leaving behind. His loneliness would travel, its grip around his midsection, but at least America meant a chance to make a life that would allow him to forget what he'd lost.

A new life would mean he'd make his own family. Somewhere a woman waited. One who'd see his worth and never know anything but the best of him, far beyond the reach of Waldemar's shadow.

They passed through Myscowa, and Lukasz said his goodbyes to his gathered friends. Adam drove Lukasz to catch the carriage that would take him to Hamburg. He'd stay there until it was time to board the *USS President Grant.*

With his suitcase and bag in the back of the vehicle, Lukasz grabbed the side of the carriage to steady his legs. He couldn't breathe, overcome with emotion again, unable to make eye contact with his friend.

"You'll need these more than I thought," Adam said.

Lukasz looked up to see Adam holding two hankies.

"Mama made them. Said she's sorry to have rushed them, that the back isn't pretty like she likes her threadwork to be. But she couldn't let you leave without them. Said the pattern's paisley. Made them in shades of blue and cream because she thought the colors would set off your 'gray, soulful eyes and blond hair.' As if you'd be wearing the hankies like shirts or something." Adam chuckled and shrugged.

Lukasz took them and ran his finger over the blue embroidered flourishes and curls that decorated the corners. "That's so . . . thank her. I know she couldn't leave Trudy to say goodbye. Thank her, please. It's the kindest thing she could have done."

Adam nodded. "One for you and one for your—"

"True love," Lukasz finished the sentence that he'd heard many times over the years when a man was too poor to offer his wife a ring to engage her for marriage.

Lukasz was struggling to tamp the urge to cry, but his body betrayed him. He dabbed his eyes with one of the handkerchiefs, knowing Adam understood the complex feelings rushing through him. "Sure hope there's true love for me," Lukasz said, forcing his breath to steady. "But if not, I'll take a nice home with a white wooden fence. That's all I need. I know I can count on earning that. That's the very least I can expect."

Adam slapped Lukasz on the back and guided him to the carriage door. "You were born under a lucky star, Lukasz. Only good things await you."

Lukasz had mocked the idea in the past. Waldemar had been born the very same day and moment, and until this point, all the good things had gone to him. Lukasz folded the hankies and tucked them into his pocket. "If I'm so fortunate to fall in love, I'll send word to your mama."

"That's more like it, friend." Adam gestured for Lukasz to climb into the vehicle. Lukasz did so then stuck his head through the window and waved.

"All good things, Lukasz," Adam said. "All good things. And if not, you can come back. The Silenskys came back, pockets full, just last year."

Lukasz smiled. He didn't know exactly what to expect when he arrived in Donora, but something told him he'd never return to Myscowa. That was not his lot.

They waved as the carriage drove away. Lukasz pulled the handkerchiefs out of his pocket and ran his finger over the embroidery again, feeling comforted that Adam's mother had been so kind. He turned them over to study the work on the back.

True. The threads crisscrossed, stretched back and forth like life's path sometimes did. But the back of each hanky was exactly the same, and no matter how Adam's mother saw the work, she'd made them with love, and Lukasz would cherish them.

He took a last look at the valley, the winter land draped in diamond snow turned blue by the clear sky and midday sun. His heart seized, but he resisted the pull of comfort that staying, as bad as it would be, would bring.

No.

His life was ahead, away, in America.

Chapter 13

Patryk, Owen, Lucy

2019

"A strongman," Patryk said, opening and closing his fatigued eyes. "Everyone in Poland was, but Lukasz was different. His height should have made him weaker, less sure of his prowess, but it didn't. He had expressive eyes, a quiet way most of the time, but when he needed strength, it was there like magic."

Patryk had barely finished speaking when Lucy and Owen ushered him to the couch in the front room. Lying down, Patryk shifted to his side, his eyes closed, and Lucy pulled a knitted afghan over him, tucking it under his chin.

"It's pretty hot for a blanket," Owen said.

Lucy cocked her head as they stared down on the old man. "He seems fine with it. The elderly are often cold."

Owen slung his arm around his mother's shoulder, startling her. Old Spice filled her nose. Her little boy was long gone. She couldn't remember the last time Owen had willingly been affectionate to anyone except his girlfriend.

The two looked at each other. Lucy knew better than to break the moment with words, so she draped her arm around him, squeezing his shoulder.

Owen moved in the direction of the kitchen, pulling his mother with him. "Let's see what the book says about Lukasz's ship ride to Donora. I mean, what about all that mythology stuff? Mermaids? Firebirds? They really believed that?"

Lucy could barely contain her excitement at seeing her son thrilled by something abstract, historical, or academic after paying attention to only baseball and girls for the last four years.

"Sounds crazy, doesn't it? Must've comforted them or something."

Owen nodded.

"Let me make some sandwiches," she said. "And put the coffee on."

"I'm gonna get me another beer, an *Arn City*."

She tousled his hair. "You've got the accent down all right. Read from Grandpa's book while I make lunch." She opened the fridge and groaned. "Oh my."

"What?"

Lucy pulled several plastic-wrapped bundles from inside and held them up. "Bologna, chipped ham, Velveeta." She set them on the counter and pulled out mayonnaise.

Owen got a loaf of white bread from the box. He looked closer. "Expired."

Lucy flinched, then smiled.

"What?" Owen asked.

"Nothing's expired until it's in somebody's belly."

Owen raised his eyebrows.

"Grandpa's favorite culinary saying."

"Yeah, he's got an *arn* stomach. *Arn City Beer* makes arn bellies, Gram used to always say." Owen opened the packaging and took a sniff of the meat inside.

"Amazing the man's lived this long. Used to just cut around rotten spots, yelling about how wasteful my generation was," Lucy said, bending farther into the refrigerator, weeding through it. "Here. This is still good." She pulled out identical bags of lunch meat. "Velveeta's fine. Thousand-year shelf life, at least."

Owen rubbed his arm. It had been sore from too much pitching. "Bologna and beer, what could be better?"

She laughed and fished a knife from a drawer. "Just don't tell your coach. He bit my head off when I let you have ice cream for your birthday. And it was locally sourced and organic!"

Owen turned in his chair to get a better view of his mother. "Just think."

"What?"

"All this work I do weight lifting, speed and agility training, strict diet, year-round hitting and fielding coach, but it never seems to be enough. And then there's this dude Lukasz Musial and all those other Poles, half-starved and working like beasts, tossing freaking hay bales into a loft like it's nothing. I mean, maybe we should eat more straw and bologna."

Lucy pulled the elastic off her wrist to secure her hair into a ponytail. "Yeah, well, keep that plan between us. Your father would never forgive you, never mind Coach Hoke."

"And booze," Owen said. "Definitely more booze."

"I'm drawing the line there, mister." She gestured at the book. "What's it say about Lukasz's trip to Donora?"

Owen sat and turned a page. "List of stuff—boarded in Hamburg, met Flora Kurtz and Michael Wagner on the ship, disembarked in New York, went separate ways, and arrived in Donora on February 2, 1910." He turned the book diagonally and squinted. "Says 'steerage, no sleep, sick to stomach whole time.' Next thing's all about the family he stayed with once he arrived. The Kowalks."

"Guess Lukasz wasn't blessed with an iron stomach," Lucy said.

A loud choking snore came from a room away. Lucy froze, mayonnaise dripping from the knife. Patryk's breath evened out, and she and Owen giggled. "Grandpa's got a lot of life left," she said.

Owen nodded.

"So go ahead," Lucy said. "Keep reading."

Owen turned back to the book, sneezing as he leafed to a heavy, dusty page. Lucy's eyes filled, staring at her son's back. She wiped the tears away, sniffling, thinking how lovely this moment was. She wanted to freeze it and etch it into her mind for when Owen was ornery and disinterested in anything family oriented, anything having to do with her. So when he snuck another swig of Iron City, she simply turned back to her sandwiches, pretending nothing else mattered right then except what was happening in her grandfather's house.

Chapter 14

Lukasz

Donora, Pennsylvania
February 2, 1910

It was Thursday when Lukasz's train pulled into the Pennsylvania Railroad Station in Donora, Pennsylvania. The squealing and lurching dragged him from slumber. He shifted in his seat and leaned his forehead against the window, the glass cooling his skin. He rubbed the kink in his neck. Outside, it was nearing dusk, or so he thought.

What time was it? He didn't have a timepiece. When he had last looked out the window, before being lulled back to sleep, the lemon sun was rising through emerald-green trees and cornflower-blue skies. He rubbed his temples, unable to recall the arrival time for Donora. He swore his stop had been scheduled for afternoon, but it looked like dusk.

He dug into his pocket and pulled the ticket out. *One p.m.* He squinted at the view—low-hanging black clouds obscuring blackened buildings and not much else. He rubbed the pane, trying to clean the soot away to let the light in. Still dark. Had he slept through his stop? Perhaps his mermaid had pulled him to his death and he was just now realizing?

Groggy and hungry, he stood and shuffled toward the exit, the sour stench of far-traveled bodies filling his nose. He pulled the postcard out of his pocket, studying the illustration featuring lush emerald hills, and pristine white fencing around a grand brick home with clean, painted trim. As the line of passengers bottlenecked, he bent to look out the window again. Nothing bore any resemblance to the postcard. He shrugged, dismissing his confusion, and pushed the card back into his pocket.

"Back in Donora!" A man shouted in Polish as he lifted his arms in victory and pushed through the doorway that led to the next car. Lukasz tried to shove ahead to ask the man if he knew the Kowalks, if this was indeed Donora, the place on the postcard, but couldn't get around the people blocking him.

Donora. This was it? He hadn't missed a stop? The part of Donora featured on the postcard must have been a distance from the train station.

He'd been given the Kowalks' address, and Adam had promised to send word to them regarding the date Lukasz would arrive. Adam swore that the family would send someone to meet him at the station; they never missed the chance to sponsor and welcome a new man from their old village. Lukasz would live with them until he found work and a place of his own.

The train door swept open and Lukasz craned to see outside. He inched forward, almost his turn to disembark. The man in front of him froze at the door before finally rushing into the crowd.

Screeching, puffing, pounding, clomping.

The cacophony knocked Lukasz back. His gaze shot around trying to match objects to the sounds they were making. The commotion filled him, shaking his insides. He clenched his lone suitcase and adjusted the bag strap across his body. A fat, smoky cloud pushed past him, the thick, grainy air coating his tongue. He cleared his throat, but an eggy taste turned his stomach. He'd been dragged into hell.

The air tickled his nose, making him cough and sputter. It was as if he'd been lowered down a chimney. Finally off the train, he bumped into one person after another as he progressed toward the ticket office to wait.

Lukasz's travel mates rushed past him, jostling and spinning him as they sprinted toward loved ones, filling him with caution and excitement at the same time. Shouted names and snippets of conversations he couldn't understand rushed by. He looked this way and that for someone familiar. Would the Kowalks look like they were from Myscowa? The earsplitting sound of grinding gears, like a thousand wagons' ungreased wheels, disoriented him.

Tuning into the voices, Lukasz recognized the predominant tongue—English. He'd already learned *please, thank you*, and *hello* on the trains from New York to Donora. He craned his neck, looking for anyone who might be looking for him.

He stood in the middle of the crowd, his ears honing in on the press of machinery noise again. It was a breakneck hammering, as if a million nails were being hammered into metal at once. He reached into his pocket for the postcard again but had to cover his cough. He rubbed his nose, finally sneezing, fully tasting the bitter air.

A hissing sound called his attention to his left, where great columns of fire exploded into the sky, shooting orange, red, and blue all at once. He drew back, clenching his chest, his heart pounding his ribs while at the same time giving him the sensation that it had stopped beating altogether.

What was that fire? He looked around to see that only a few others seemed to be stunned by the sights and sounds. Everyone else simply went about their shuffling, carrying, and greeting, unfazed by the assault on every one of their senses.

Under the blasting and whining of the machinery, he could hear the call of boats, a low groaning that came between train whistles and the chugging steam that drove them. New

York had met him with a crush of people, but there was nothing like this dark, suffocating sound of grinding metal that made him think he might be swallowed up by a great lumbering hell beast.

Bewildered, Lukasz hobbled back, the crowd pushing past him, pressing him against the brick walls of the station's head house. He'd been lonely, hungry, sad, beaten up, and much more back home, but this fear, like the day he was given the ticket, tasted like the bitter eggs that now burned his eyes and coated his insides. This twist of inhuman, otherworldly power stole his breath.

The postcard. He pulled it out, hand shaking, unable to make sense of the house in the picture and what was in front of him. Where were the postcard-pretty homes and fresh air?

A sharp, boyish voice cut through the ruckus. "Kowslawski! Waldemar Kowslawski!"

Lukasz was stunned at hearing something recognizable threaded into the braid of unfamiliar noise. Hell, even the sight of Waldemar would have been good at this point. Lukasz pushed away from the wall, looking for the burly, graceful handsome bear.

"Waldemar Kowslawski!"

Lukasz got onto his toes, looking between the masses, over the heads of people passing by. No sign of Waldemar.

"Waldemar Kowslawski."

Lukasz moved in the direction of the voice, stretching to see who was yelling this familiar name. Was it possible that Waldemar had found another ticket and was in Donora too?

"Kowslawski. Step right up! I'm looking for you!" the voice said with a half laugh.

This time, Lukasz found the source of the yelling. A scrawny boy. He looked like any boy from Myscowa. He tossed his hands in the air and shouted again.

Lukasz pushed forward. "*Szukam Waldemar Kowslawski?*"

The boy narrowed his eyes on Lukasz, then back at a paper, then back at Lukasz. He couldn't have been more than twelve. "*Jesteś nim?*"

Lukasz set his suitcase down and held his hand out. "Lukasz Musial. I won the contest for the ticket."

The boy shook his head and stepped back. "Kowslawski?"

Panic gripped Lukasz. He grabbed the boy's wrist. "Kowslawski won first. They sent word, but then I beat him at—well, I won the ticket. Adam sent word. He should have, anyway. *W porządku?*" He dug into his pocket, produced the ticket stub, and shook it at him.

The boy squinted at Lukasz, then looked back at his paper.

"Kowalk," Lukasz said. "Your father? I'm looking for Alexander."

The boy studied Lukasz again.

Lukasz's heart slammed so hard, it dizzied him. He dug in his pocket again and pulled out the postcard. "Here."

The boy took it, turned it over, and read the back.

Lukasz forced a swallow. *Please.*

The boy handed it back. "*Witamy!*" he said, removing his hat and giving Lukasz a little bow.

Lukasz exhaled. "Thank you, thank you. I'm so glad to be here," he said as they shook hands.

"*Jestum* Nathan," the boy said.

"*Syn* Alexander?"

"Number one son, yes. *Chodź tędy.*" Nathan jerked his head in the opposite direction, took Lukasz's suitcase, and started to weave between the people who were still finding their paths.

"Right behind you," Lukasz said.

They passed through the train station and exited onto Meldon Avenue. Lukasz coughed into his hand. People flooded past them, jostling, rushing.

"You'll get used to it, Lukasz."

Lukasz stared at the boy for a moment. "To what?"

"The air. The mills. The noise. The work. Smoke means work and money."

"And castles!" Lukasz patted Nathan's back. Nathan narrowed his eyes at Lukasz all over again, but something caused him to look away.

Lukasz followed Nathan's gaze upward. The fog and smoke were curling away, the clear air spreading as far up as the sun, revealing patches of blue sky.

Nathan gaped as though the sun hadn't risen every day of his life. "You brought the sun, Lukasz! *Przyniosłeś błękitne niebo.* Tonight, we celebrate."

Lukasz stared at the sun and the smoky-blue haze around it. "You act as though the sky isn't always blue."

The boy chuckled and pulled Lukasz's sleeve. *"Chodz.* Mama made you—well, she made Waldemar a late breakfast, but now it's for you."

Lukasz rubbed his growling belly. He hoped it wouldn't be a problem that he was not Waldemar, but he was too hungry to care. As they made their way along one street and then up steep, brown hillsides on stairs so steep he couldn't believe they didn't tumble down, he looked back, finally getting a wide view of where the train had left him off.

"Monongahela River," Nathan said.

Lukasz hadn't even realized he'd been standing near it earlier. The clouds parted farther, the sky growing bluer, and now he could see the expanse of the mills he'd heard about. They stretched along the river like a fire-breathing dragon he'd seen drawn in a storybook. The clanking and bursts of red flames rose again, startling him and making him grab the banister.

Nathan pointed. "You'll work there. Blast furnace, probably. Wireworks, maybe." Nathan raised his fists to show off his biceps. "Good work for Poles."

Lukasz stared, watching as the structures along the riverbank spewed fire and smoke. He was awed and confused, thinking of what Alexander Kowalk had written. He'd said they were making America in Donora, but all Lukasz could see were pipes and smoke. Nothing seemed to have been created, but rather this vision was the insides of something unimaginable, a beast's insides turned out. No white picket fences anywhere.

"Hurry," Nathan said.

Lukasz nodded and kept his questions to himself. Blast furnace? Wireworks? He thought of the thin wire he'd packed in his suitcase. The enormous buildings that snaked along the riverside made thin, graceful wire like Ryszard gave him to make his animals?

"Lukasz." Nathan's voice came from farther up the stairs. "Move it, friend."

Lukasz could hear the irritation in the boy's voice and didn't want to give the idea he would be a burden. He stepped upward, trying to imagine walking into the belly of the flaming creature below. What type of work could he do that would contribute to such a beast, a metallic animal alive as he, something that appeared to work on its own?

**

After they turned a corner, Nathan lifted his arms. "Welcome to Short Street." He pronounced it in English, then Polish.

"Krótki Ulica?"

Nathan nodded and pronounced "Short Street" in English again. "Our street."

Exhausted from traveling, Lukasz's eyes and throat burned, the smoke causing the stinging to worsen, and add to his disorientation. House after house was strung along with barely a breath between them, while others were wedged at awkward angles into the hillside, one home's foundation nearly on top of another's roof. Still others seemed to be carved from the rock itself. Lukasz hadn't spent much time in cities and could not fathom living shoulder to shoulder. He'd owned nothing in Myscowa, but there'd been space. He pulled out the postcard and held it up to Nathan, but he was already turning away, toward approaching voices.

Nathan lifted the suitcase. "There," he said. "There they are."

The voices neared and the bodies belonging to them began to take shape through the fog.

A woman about Lukasz's height came into view, with a passel of children fanning out behind her. She glanced at Nathan and took Lukasz by the shoulders. "Waldemar?"

"Lukasz Musial, Mama," Nathan said.

The woman drew back and squinted at Lukasz. Her pinched features conveyed hardness, coldness.

"Nie Waldemar?"

Two little ones squabbled behind the woman. She grabbed each one by his shirt, pulling them close and quieting them. This silenced the rest of them. The hammering machine noise was dulled with the distance up the hillside, but its permanence increased Lukasz's breath, his anxiety. He tried to will his worry away. He wanted to explain that he'd worked hard for the ticket and would be just as good a guest as Waldemar would have. A good American. This was his chance to be free of constraints that kept any peasant from owning land in Myscowa. He was finally free to craft a life, to make a home just like the ruling class in Poland always had, and he would not disappoint his sponsors.

Lukasz shook his head, but Nathan was already answering for him. "Waldemar won the ticket, then lost it to Lukasz, Mama. *This* is our guest. Lukasz Musial."

Nathan's mother shook her head, looking Lukasz up and down.

Nathan pointed up. "He brought the blue sky, Mama." He pushed Lukasz forward.

She exhaled and looked Lukasz over once more. The corners of her mouth twitched as though a smile was trying to bloom. She looked upward, shielding her eyes from the sun. Her expression, still sour but softer, conveyed a sense that perhaps what her son said was true. This stranger had brought the blue sky and a golden sun, and that changed everything. Finally, a full smile snapped to her lips, a smile that somehow pinched her face even further. Lukasz was cautious about her mood. Was she smiling?

"Candlemas Day," she said. "It's meant to be. *Witamy*, Lukasz Musial." She threw her arms open and enveloped him, kissing his one cheek and then the other. Lukasz stood in her warmth, unsettled but wanting her welcome to continue.

She wiped his cheeks with her thumbs in a way his mother used to do. He was swept by emotion, the sense of belonging.

"I'm Zofia."

Seven other children of varying ages from Nathan down to just a little one who could barely toddle on his own stared up at Lukasz. A little girl took his hand and dragged him toward a clapboard home.

"*Będziesz jeść,*" Zofia said. "Then you'll rest, and later we'll get our candles blessed at church. You'll feel good to sit in church tonight, Lukasz."

Nathan moaned and his mother smacked his bottom. "*Cicho, Bóg cię wysłucha.*"

Nathan rubbed his backside. "God can't hear me."

"He hears it all," she said.

"I'll pray extra," Nathan said.

"You better," she said starting down the way.

The group moved along, stopping just a few doors down. Lukasz expected them to continue on, but the kids pounded up the front stairs to one of the houses in the middle of the bunch. No white fence? No rolling green yard? This one had no fence and boasted a mud patch in front. He stopped himself from pulling the postcard from his pocket, from asking if there was a mistake.

The slim one-level gray house had two windows in the front, one on either side of the door. Lukasz followed the others up the wobbly, crooked stairs that led to the porch. The home was cobbled together with uneven boards, but a green wooden chair with boots under it near the front door lent the place a bit of warmth. The porch was sturdy, but close up, Lukasz could see it had once been white. Now black soot covered it from one end to the other.

Zofia opened the front door and it whined. She waved her hand to let them stream into the house. Inside, Lukasz's eyes adjusted to darkness.

"Get the lamps burning, Nathan," Zofia said as she took Lukasz's suitcase and set it on the floor. She hung his coat and hat on a rack inside the doorway. Lukasz followed Zofia into a kitchen with a tiny worktable, a dry sink full of pots and pans, and a cooktop. Beyond the kitchen area was a large table. Mismatched chairs surrounded it, with extras scattered around the room. At the back of the space, a long, worn settee sat under the windows. All of the furniture sat atop a dirt floor with carpet remnants flung about to cover as much of it as possible.

Lukasz inhaled. The scent of bacon filled the space, making his mouth water.

"Bedrooms off to the sides," Nathan said, pointing in both directions. "You'll share with us boys. Papa's adding another room soon. And flooring. Someday a second story." He kicked at the packed dirt. "Working on a deal for tile and wood."

Lukasz nodded as Zofia crossed herself and adjusted the flue at the stove. He wasn't so sure about all this church stuff since he didn't attend regularly, but he wouldn't say that. The last thing he wanted was to offend his sponsor family.

The Kowalks weren't related to Lukasz's family by blood, but in that moment, just being from the same village, he felt as if they were. His back to Nathan, he pulled out the postcard, traced his finger across the fence, imagined the hilly lawn, and inhaled the dirt floor of Zofia's home.

He folded the postcard and shoved it back into his pocket.

It'd been so long since he'd been welcomed into a home complete with a matriarch and other children. He sighed, not caring that the Kowalk home bore zero resemblance to the grand Donora home pictured on the postcard, that none of what he saw was what he'd expected.

Zofia led Lukasz to the table. Nathan introduced each of his siblings again, then they scattered to go fetch water and use the outhouse. Zofia brought Lukasz a glass of water. "Nathan, go to the pump one last time before food is served."

He nodded, took the bucket, and left.

Lukasz drank the water down. "Thank you. Thank you so very much."

She brought him a heaping plate of food. "Eggs, pancakes, bacon, and a mug of coffee."

His mouth watered as he reached for the fork, and she clasped her hand over his. "A beautiful day to arrive in Donora, isn't it? That sky," she said again.

He nodded. "Yes. Thank you again."

"Eat up. Sleep, and then we'll tell you our plans."

He took the first bite of egg and closed his eyes. It had been some time since he had eaten the breakfast at the tavern where he'd won the handstand contest. He had eaten little in Hamburg or on the ship, with his stomach churning most of the journey. It seemed as though he'd won the ticket just yesterday, yet his travels seemed to have taken a year, the four thousand ocean and train miles an unimaginable journey.

Zofia patted his hand. "Good?"

He nodded, barely breathing, he shoveled it in so fast. "Thank you, thank you."

She smiled, squeezed his hand, and went to the window near the sink. She pulled the curtain aside and plunked one hand on her hip. Lukasz tried to eat slowly and savor each morsel.

She shook her head. "Gone. *Niebieskie nieboare jeszcze raz szary.*"

Lukasz sipped coffee. "Pardon?"

She shrugged. "Sky is gray again." She snapped her fingers. "Just like that."

He thought she actually looked relieved that the gray sky had returned. He stood up and leaned to see the sky through the window, but couldn't from his angle. "*Feels* blue to me," he said, sitting again. "A great day."

"*Nie chwal dnia przed zachodem słońca,*" Zofia said.

Don't praise the day before sunset. Lukasz had heard the saying many times back home, but he was confused as to everyone's attention on the color of the sky. Surely it wasn't gray all the time. Being with Zofia and enjoying the scrumptious food lent him all the optimism he needed.

"Blue sky, gray sky. Same sun, same moon as Myscowa? No? Yes. I believe so. All's possible, isn't it? Your letters said as much, and we all believed it. I believe." Lukasz couldn't believe how easily the words fell off his tongue, how comfortable he felt in this unfamiliar, unexpected home.

Zofia turned and gave him that big smile that somehow pinched her face into an odd unattractiveness that did not match her warmth. "Ah, Lukasz. You're just the sunshine we need around here. Meant to be. And you're right. You'll love Donora and all its treasure. Wait and see." She glanced at his empty plate. "More?"

He nodded.

Zofia scraped the last of the eggs and bacon onto his plate. With the final morsel of egg in his belly, Lukasz sat back in his chair, full, pleased in a way he couldn't remember being since he was a tiny boy sitting at his mother's feet in front of a night fire while she sewed and his father read week-old news, grumbling but never saying just what was making him irritated.

And so, as had been said multiple times, he began to feel as though the sun had shone just for him that day to remind him that this journey was intended not for Waldemar, but for him. He liked how the Kowalks all said he brought the blue sky. Perhaps the sun itself had been Lukasz's lucky star all along, calling him to Donora since the day he'd been born.

The mermaid flashed to mind. He tried to push away the silly thought, the ridiculous dreams. This was a new world, and he was sure there wasn't room for senseless stories of a mermaid who pulled sailors and swimmers to their deaths, or surfaced on a riverbank to tell a young man his destiny was to cross the ocean and take his place in a home that sat atop a hillside overlooking a fiery beast.

He looked toward the kitchen window, where smoke and darkness, blue sky and sun had come and gone just in the time since he'd arrived. No matter. Here he was—handstand champion, strong immigrant, and future American, fulfilling a mermaid's wishes, imaginary or not.

Chapter 15

Mary

At the Sixth Street gate, Mary entered the wireworks to the sound of steel being molded into nails. Shots like gunfire mixed with the high-pitched grating of women sanding nail heads shook her insides. The heat emanating from the machinery and human activity should have made her baking hot, but it only made her feel the winter air more fully, shooting through the building like God himself was blowing on it.

Mary lifted the lunch pail for Mr. Dunn to her nose, inhaling the smell of chicken soup and bread, trying to block out the sulfur and oil odor. Mrs. Dunn always worried about Mr. Dunn's stomach, not wanting to give him any reason to eat a bad lunch at a hunky bar, get sick, and stay home underfoot and in her hair.

To someone who didn't know Mrs. Dunn, that might have sounded harsh, but Mary observed her daily. She would sweep into the kitchen and use her hip to playfully boot the cook, Mrs. Harper, aside so she could pack her husband's meal, humming as she did. She folded and tucked a linen cloth, napkin, and fresh embroidered hanky into the pail. Mary could still see Mrs. Dunn's long pale fingers and her clean, pink nails patting the bread then closing the lid as though sealing the meal with love.

Mary passed by the section of the mill that had several holes in the wall. The dark space lit up with blinding light. Sunshine shot through with golden rays. Mary stepped into the warmth. It was gentle and soft, not like the punishing machine heat.

She couldn't remember the last sunny day they'd had. Perhaps she'd been too busy to notice. No, everyone noticed the sun when it beamed like this, when the clouds curled back to reveal precious blue sky. Remembering the meal she had been sent to deliver, she ascended the stairs to the rooms that overlooked the operation below.

When Mr. Dunn's secretary opened his office door, he saw what Mary held and his smile lit the room like the sunrays that sprayed the mill floor. His phone rang and Mary began to exit, but he motioned to her to stay as he answered the phone. He turned his back, stiffening. "No," he said. His voice was tight and deep, making Mary recall how he had bellowed when he saw the sales ticket for the Staffordshire dogs his wife had purchased.

"Absolutely no." He shook his head. Mary could hear a voice coming through the receiver but not what was being said. Mr. Dunn rubbed the back of his neck with his thick fingers, avoiding his neat, slicked-back black hair. He was tall and graceful, his presence commanding respect, but not in a way that created constant fear. If people like Mary did their jobs well, he rewarded them.

Mr. Dunn stiffened again. "Fire him." He turned and slammed down the phone, looking up at Mary. He cleared his throat. "I apologize, Mary," he said, waving her toward his desk, his tone softer again. "Thank you."

"You're welcome," she said, her hands shaking slightly.

The softness in his voice, slow and welcoming, unnerved Mary more than if he was gruff all the time. His sudden pleasantness made her never want to be the subject of his anger. She hoped she never did anything to earn it. He cleared away papers and pencils and took the pail from her. She set the linens down and unwrapped the bread.

He waved her off. "No need for all that. I'll have this all down in a few seconds."

"But Mrs. Dunn—"

"Don't tell her."

He washed his hands at a small sink near the window looking over the river. He shook his hands dry. "Spoke to your father." His voice became serious.

Mary gasped. Had she done something wrong? Perhaps Mrs. Dunn had told him she had let the boys out to play all day on their own. Was she next to be fired?

She held her breath.

He smiled. "Don't be frightened."

She nodded.

"I'm hiring you onto a shift here."

Her eyes widened.

"As a nail girl. You'd be perfect. My wife trusts you implicitly, and I need someone with pure motives working around here."

A rush of excitement and confusion surged through Mary. "But Mrs. Dunn. I—"

He sat down and held up his hand. "This won't happen until you've turned fourteen. You'll still work for Mrs. Dunn on Wednesdays and whenever else you can. Your parents need the money. Mortgage, taxes, all of that."

What about rowing her father to work?

Mr. Dunn snapped the napkin into the air and let it fall into his lap.

"That's all," he said, leaving Mary with questions to be answered by someone else.

"Thank you, Mr. Dunn."

He blew on a spoonful of soup and nodded as he pulled the newspaper close enough to see. "Run along," he said, not looking up.

Back down on the floor, she passed Weira, a Polish girl who used to sit next to her when they both went to school, before Weira had become a nail girl. "Line's down," Weira said.

Mary nodded.

"Tonight . . . Candlemas at St. Mary's?" Weira mangled her English, gesturing to help communicate. Most of the time they understood each other, but when Weira—or anyone from the old country, for that matter—was tired or distracted, English words fell away.

Mary smiled, glad to hear Weira trying to use it, at least. "No. St. Dominic's."

The girl wiped her hands on her apron and shook her head. "*Przesączają się dach.*"

Mary shook her head, recognizing a Polish word. "Roof?" She gestured above them.

Weira nodded. "Water, roof."

Now it made sense. "Again," Mary said, thinking it was the second time the roof leaked that year.

February second, Candlemas Day, was one of her favorite Masses of the year. It was a celebration of the Blessed Virgin Mary and her purification forty days after having given birth to Jesus.

"Everyone's invited," Weira said.

Mary exhaled, relieved there was another church to go to that night. "I've got to get our candles ready," she said. "Yours ready?"

Weira held her hands apart about twelve inches. "Birthday candle, yes."

The sunrays coming through the holes in the sides of the mill brightened, filling the space even more. Weira turned into the warmth. "Sunshine today. Much winter still."

Mary thought of the ancient, superstitious saying all the old ladies in town recited each year.

If Candlemas Day be fair and bright,
Winter'll have another flight.

If Candlemas Day brings clouds and rain,
Winter hides and will not come again.

It had been dark until she had entered the mill and the sun had poured through the cracks in the building. "So what happens if it's sunny and cloudy? What then?" Mary liked her superstitions to be clear and concise.

Her friend shrugged again. "I guess we'll see."

The nail line jerked behind them, startling Weira. She waved to Mary and jogged back to work, the same job Mary would be doing in a few months' time. Mary's pride that Mr. Dunn had offered her a prized job did not stave off the emptiness that came with knowing she wouldn't see Mrs. Dunn each weekday. Perhaps the sun had brought the bad luck of six more weeks of winter. Perhaps it had brought misfortune altogether for Mary Lancos.

Chapter 16

Mary

Nail girl? No more work daily with Mrs. Dunn? Mary rushed back to get more information and finish her work for the day. Breathing heavily as she entered the kitchen, she asked Mrs. Harper where Mrs. Dunn was.

Mrs. Harper stalked toward Mary with a dish of mashed potatoes and gestured for her to sit. "Out to lunch." Mrs. Harper slopped food onto a plate. "Eat up. Lots of dusting to do."

Mrs. Harper pulled out a knife and began chopping celery at the speed of nails being molded at the mill. "Took the whole gang to see her friend at the club. That tall redhead with beady eyes."

Mary nodded and ate. "Mrs. Walsh."

"Yes, that one."

Mary completed her work and went home, all signs of the lemony sun gone, the bleak sky mirroring Mary's disappointment to have finished before Mrs. Dunn returned. When she reached home, she found a note written by Ann, saying Papa would sleep at the Mazals' over in Webster so Mary wouldn't have to fetch him.

It also said Matka was dropping a set of pressed linens at the rectory and a set at Mrs. Smith's house. The boys and little Rose were with Matka, and Victoria and Ann were who knows where. The boarders? If they were there, they were sleeping between shifts. Only the muffled sounds of the town below broke the silence.

Mary loved being alone in the house, accompanied only by the thick ticking of a castoff clock her father had found and repaired. The thought that she might not be able to work for Mrs. Dunn as much once she was a nail girl made her think of all the little things that Mrs. Dunn had given her and done for her over the years.

With the house to herself, Mary chanced to look at her special things, the items that would have gone into her hope chest if she'd had one, if her family didn't sell everything of value that they ever came across.

Mary moved quickly, going to her hidey-hole in the fireplace hearth. She lifted the basket that held wood and set it on the floor. She jiggled a brick, the metallic sound filling the room as she slid several out, scraping one over another. She removed a tin with a wired lid.

Inside was a fold of cotton fabric. She opened it on her lap as though setting a picnic. A circle of thick blue velvet ribbon sat at its center. Beside it was a thinner spool of quarter-inch blue cotton ribbon. She lifted the velvet and it unspooled, spilling through her fingers like water. Mrs. Dunn had given her the expensive trimming—a remnant, she told her—for something special. The thinner, inexpensive but new cotton ribbon would be perfect for Candlemas Mass. She would wrap her mother's candle with it, surprising her with something unexpectedly new and pretty.

Mary didn't think she'd ever have a need to eat if she could just be surrounded by lovely things. She exhaled as she replaced the items in the tin. She slid it back into the hole, checking that her other gifts were secure there too, then set the basket back. Mary wished she could share their existence with her family but was satisfied with her quiet moments alone for the time being.

Mrs. Dunn considered Mary the type of girl who needed a hope chest because she believed that someday Mary would be engaged to a man who expected his fiancée to come to the marriage with household items. Someday she would display the precious items proudly, touch them daily, and enjoy them like Mrs. Dunn did hers.

**

Mary gathered the family candles and a small basket of juniper she'd saved for Candlemas. In the kitchen, a simmering pot and the thick scent of sauerkraut reminded her she was home. She set her supplies on the table and stirred the soup that stood at the ready so the boarders could have a bowl between mill shifts if the timing didn't allow them to sit down with the Lancoses for dinner. She added coal to the stove and put the iron on top of it, hoping she could remove the wrinkles from the older ribbons.

Mary set a small ironing board on the table and spread out candles, juniper, old ribbon, and one special length of new ribbon for her mother's candle. She snipped off the frayed end of one tattered length and smoothed it, humming a dance tune.

The wooden floor creaked behind her.

Hair stood on the nape of her neck. Chills worked over her skin. Without even turning, she knew who was lurking.

Mary pressed her chest, turning around. She leaned forward, exhaling a held breath. "You scared me, Mr. Cermak."

He leaned against the doorjamb, one ankle crossed over the other, and lit a cigarette. "Mikulas. Told you that plenty of times." He sauntered to the stove, lifted the soup's lid, and ladled himself a bowl.

"Careful with your cigarette, Mr. Cermak," Mary said. "Matka'll pitch a fit if she sees ashes in the soup."

"Oh, I know. And it's Mikulas."

Mary tensed against the shiver working down her spine. She wound the new blue ribbon around the creamy-hued candle that was her mother's birth candle, then tucked the juniper into the ribbon.

"Not polite to use your first name," Mary said, wanting him to go. "Age dictates that."

He set the bowl on the table, then spun a ladder-back chair around and straddled it. "Rules, rules." He slid the ashtray over and set down his cigarette. He slurped the soup and cocked his head. "Seventh straight day for cabbage soup, and it still tastes all right."

Mary glanced at him, wondering if he was being sarcastic. She was certainly tired of bland soup, but bristled at his criticism.

He took a drag off his cigarette and set it on the side of the ashtray before finishing off his bowl. "Could use some bread, though. That fat man, Harley, eats more than his share."

Mary shrugged. "Baking's tomorrow." She hoped the frigid weather would ease up for using the oven outside.

He fingered one of the wrinkled blue ribbons waiting to be ironed. "Always at the ready, aren't ya, Mary?"

She cringed as though his mere touch was debasing the fabric, degrading her. Though the kitchen was rather chilly that afternoon, sweat pricked at Mary's hairline. She swiped at it with the back of her hand.

"Thunder candles," he said.

Mary exhaled, relieved for something to talk about instead of him adding to the silence with his quiet encroachment. "Protection and good luck for the year to come."

He picked up a piece of juniper and ran it under his nose, inhaling deeply. "Smells so good. Clean, lovely. I'll give you that. But nonsense to believe such things." He stared at Mary through half-closed lids.

She drew back. His actual insulting words were nothing compared to how they slipped out of his mouth, glomming onto her skin, turning her stomach. She went for the iron, palming it to test the heat. Only warm. She opened the flue to encourage the fire's heat.

She returned to the table, reorganizing the materials he'd disturbed. He extracted a tin from his shirt pocket and popped it open. He selected a cigarette, caressing its length with his forefinger, blackened from his work at the blast furnace. "Want one?"

Mary shook her head, focusing on her candles and pushing away her discomfort as best she could. There was something behind the offer of the cigarette that unnerved her. He slid his chair closer. She froze, and his gaze shifted from the cigarette to her lips.

Mr. Cermak pushed another cigarette toward Mary.

She reached for the scissors. "No. Thank you."

He grabbed her hand.

She wiggled free of his grip. "I need to finish this."

He clamped onto her hand again, but a door slammed and he let go.

"I'm sure you do." He took out his pocket watch and flipped it open. "Have to go. Can't be late." He stood and spun the chair back to its proper position. Mary snipped the ribbon and trimmed the others, pretending he wasn't there.

"See you later," he said.

She nodded, not meeting his gaze. When she heard her mother talking to him, the oxygen was restored in the kitchen. Finally, she breathed.

**

Matka entered the kitchen, her arms laden with grocery bags. Mary jumped up and took the load, setting it on the slim table under the window.

She was about to tell her mother how uncomfortable Mr. Cermak made her when Matka took a coughing fit. She covered her mouth with one hand and steadied herself on the countertop with the other.

Mary patted Matka's back until she stopped hacking, then put the kettle on and removed the honey and a canister of tea from their small pantry. "Your cold's back?"

Matka cleared her throat, nodding. She sat at the table.

Mary prepared tea and took it to her mother piping hot.

"I'm skipping Mass tonight," Matka said. "Too much to do. Took to bed for two hours today. Now look." She swung her arm outward. "Yinz got nothin' to eat. The place is a mess. I can't keep up. Lazy as a fat dead man. Hate today."

"Cabbage soup's fine, Matka." Mary pressed the back of her hand to her mother's forehead. "You don't have a fever. Come to church. You'll feel better for going. I'll help when we get home." She wanted Matka to enjoy Mass, to carry her candle with the most beautiful ribbon at the church.

"Ann's sick too," Matka said. "Coughing, sneezing rotten bad."

"Ann's always on the verge of death. Keeps me up all night with her hacking. Believe me, I know," Mary said, remembering they had to go to St. Mary's. "Another leak at St. Dominic's, so St. Mary's invited us there." Mary went back to ironing a piece of ribbon.

Matka rolled her eyes, making Mary want to change her mother's mood.

"How lovely is that? Mass at St. Mary's on the Blessed Mother's special day," Mary said.

Matka slumped, looking exhausted, and rubbed her temples. "Don't need to attend every single feast day. No one's keeping track."

Mary straightened. Of course people were keeping track. "Have to go. I'm *named* for Mary."

Matka stared at Mary, then dropped her face into her hands. "Dammit. Yer named for my *friend* Mary. From way back across that big Atlantic Ocean."

Mary frowned, knowing that was untrue. "I'm named for the Blessed Mother. You said so."

Matka's lips drew thin, her eyelids heavy, threatening to close. "*You* said ya were named for the Blessed One. Yer father and I just went along with it."

Mary stopped pressing the ribbon. "Not true."

"It is."

Mary drew back and studied Matka. Her eyes were the same molasses color, the knot of hair at the nape of her neck had loosened like always by the end of the day, her skin was light with a perfectly round dark spot at the corner of her right eye that disappeared into her crow's feet when she belly laughed. All of these conjured the image of Matka, yet her strange confession left Mary confused. It was as if she did not know the woman sitting across from her.

What other fables had her mother told? Mary ironed with a vengeance, slamming the iron onto the ribbon as if sheer force would ease the creases and erase her mother's statement. "I remember the very day you told me. We were at the coal seam." She thumbed over her shoulder to the tunnel in the backyard.

Matka shook her head, deflating Mary further. "Yinz girls're too old for storybook tales, and I'm too tired," she said. "Grow up."

Mary's face grew hot. Matka was practical and sometimes harsh, quick with a smack and often distant, but this? A lie? Mary could handle harshness, but lies about her very beginnings?

"Yer almost fourteen. I was married by yer age."

Mary remembered what Mr. Dunn had said that morning. "Did Papa get me hired on at the wireworks? Mr. Dunn said so."

Matka nodded.

Mary pursed her lips. Disappointment upon disenchantment. She didn't want to leave Mrs. Dunn. Working there once a week would not be enough, and Mrs. Dunn would find a girl to replace her.

"Nail girl gits more money," Matka said. "We need it."

"Mrs. Dunn pays me well, and it's steady."

"She'll take ya on Wednesdays. That'll do."

Mary laid her hand on the iron. Cold. She put it back on the stove and picked up the candle that she'd been given when she was born. "I like working at the Dunns' house."

Matka pointed to the clean blue ribbon hugging the juniper against the birth candle and glared at Mary. "Where'd this ribbon come from?"

Mary had the feeling she should lie. "Mrs. Dunn."

"Why'd she give it to ya?"

Mary replayed the September day that Mrs. Dunn had given it to her. "I stayed a little longer to help with baths."

"Was it painful for her to part with such a pretty ribbon?"

Mary jerked, not sure what her mother was getting at. "Course not. She's very generous."

"Ya hid this ribbon."

Mary nodded, feeling ashamed. So much easier if she had simply lied. No wonder her mother fibbed about Mary's name.

No, that was different.

"I just wanted something nice for you on Candlemas Day," Mary said. "It's for you, your candle."

Matka's expression relaxed as she rubbed her thumb over the ribbon. Mary noticed her mother admired it as much as she did. But when she met Matka's gaze, her expression had turned stony again.

"We need *money*, Mary, not ribbon. Mrs. Dunn's wrong to pay debt in *things* instead of money. She think we can eat this?"

"Matka, please don't—"

Matka shook the ribbon. "Always had an eye for shiny, beautiful things. Working for the Allens, now the Dunns. All those fancy . . . *everythings*. Sparkling homes with golden trinkets and wives lunching. None of 'em lift a pinky finger." Matka spat the words through clenched teeth. "You're a woman. Start using your head. The mill'll pay cash. Never useless ribbon."

Mary raised her shoulders. "The Dunns pay me." Wasn't as much as a nail girl made, but still.

Matka blew out her air, narrowing her eyes. "That woman threw good ribbon aside without a thought. She don't understand the value of a dollar. She don't understand *us*."

"She's Czech. She *is* us."

Matka pursed her lips. "The scent of lemons went to yer head. That woman's forgotten herself."

Mary's chest burned. "No. She says I have all the smarts and charm and work ethic to make a very fine wife to the kind of man like her husband. She believes in me." Mary wanted to blurt out all the little things she'd been squirreling away for the hope chest she didn't yet own, but she knew better than to flaunt Mrs. Dunn's life in front of her mother. She should have said she found the ribbon. Why couldn't her mother appreciate the little things, the fact that Mary had wrapped only her mother's candle in the gorgeous ribbon?

Matka sat back in her chair as though Mary was more taxing than her headache.

"I thought you'd like it," Mary said, her anger beginning to roil. "You *should* like it. Any other mother would." She sucked in her breath as if doing so would pull the words back in. She braced for a slap, but her mother sat frozen.

Matka rubbed her head again and leveled her gaze on Mary. "Ya look down on me, turn yer nose up at our plain things that smell of cabbage and—"

Mary shook her head. "No!"

Matka crossed her arms and stared again, crushing Mary with her heavy contemplation.

Yes, Mary wanted so many things, and she desired a better life that smelled clean—that *was* clean—but she had never meant to insult Matka.

Matka leaned forward. "I wanted life to be different too, Mary. I did. That's why we're in America. We all want wonderful things when we're girls. Look around." She spread her arms. "We own this. Understand? Mismatched wood, weak roof, boarders—doesn't matter. We *own* it. All the shiny things I wanted as a girl? Yinz girls'll see what happens to that. All that?" Matka snapped her fingers. "Gone."

"I understand, Matka. I do." She didn't agree with her, but she knew what she was saying. Why didn't Matka believe Mary could have all this and more? Why didn't she believe in Mary like Mrs. Dunn?

Matka looked away. "Someday you'll thank me for the truth, for opening yer eyes 'fore someone else does it, tearing yer heart out. That mortgage, much as I scream about it, much as it's a heavy weight, it's a gift. Reminds us that we own something, payments or no. We ain't strangled by a king's whims. Be practical, damn it."

"I already quit school for you, even with good grades."

"And now's time for the mill. Most girls ain't given that job. It's important, and the most valuable thing the Dunns gave ya yet."

"What about Ann and Victoria? They could work more. Once a week sweeping Mrs. Lamb's porch isn't enough for them. I was washing floors every day at eight years old."

Matka clenched her jaw. Mary hated conflict but couldn't keep her mouth shut. She looked at the candles she'd been decorating. "Can we just go to church?" Her voice was barely above a whisper. "We'll all feel better. I mean, it's almost lucky that the St. Dominic's roof leaked. Now we get to celebrate Candlemas at Blessed Virgin Mary."

Matka's eyes glistened. What was wrong with her mother? Was she going to cry? She was a passionate woman whose emotions swung from explosive tirades to the thick hush of silent aggression, interspersed with humor but never tears, never weakness.

Mary started to leave the room to give her mother privacy, but then she thought of how Mrs. Dunn soothed her children when they were sad, hurt, or even in a fit of anger. She loved them sweetly, gently. Maybe that's what Matka needed. Someone to care for her that way. Maybe she just didn't know *how* to be soft.

Mary reached for her mother's hand and brushed the back of it. Matka startled but didn't snatch her hand away. Mary squeezed it, and Matka squeezed back, forcing a smile.

"Father Kroupal'll give ya forty lashes for saying the leaky roof's lucky. Six weeks into the year, and it's stuffed full of bad luck."

Matka's humor relieved Mary, but she knew her mother was keeping secrets, something that made her emotional.

"Father Kroupal did take down the decorations too early," Mary said, wanting to further lighten the mood.

Matka turned away again and Mary thought she wiped a tear.

Matka chuckled, still letting Mary hold her hand. "Sanctuary Christmas tree was so dry, just about lit the whole place on fire. Farming superstitions don't go far when buildings start to burn."

Mary raised her eyebrows. "Far as the leaky roof, I suppose."

Matka cocked her head, studying her daughter again, but this time the distance was gone. "Yer a hopeful one. Smart." Matka finally pulled her hand away and brushed her fingers over Mary's birth candle. "Somehow this candle stays tall and graceful as if it ain't been lit two dozen times. One point, I figured you'd been buying new ones to replace it. Stately, like you. I guess we bought the right candle for ya. Lucky."

Mary smiled, touched by Matka's gentleness. She stopped herself from saying as much, not wanting to ruin the moment.

Matka took a length of the ribbon Mary had yet to iron and wrapped it around the candle, adding juniper. "Ya like to see the candle burning, but want it perfect and tall 'til the very end, don't ya? Somehow enjoyed but new."

"Yes," Mary said.

"I'm sure you'll have that. Both things. Somehow, if anyone in the world'll keep and spend at once, it'll be you."

Matka delivered the words with unusual softness, but the pointedness pained Mary as she absorbed the sadness tucked inside them.

Matka pushed away from the table, mood lighter. "Well, go on. Git your brothers and sisters. Yinz'll make us look bad if we slog into church late. Let's see if we can turn things around for the rest of the year."

Mary brightened. She hopped up and flung her arms around Matka's neck.

Matka stiffened and pushed away, taking Mary's chin. "Sorry I don't smell like her." Matka shrugged. "Like Mrs. Dunn. I know I ain't—"

Mary pulled her mother into her arms again, forcing the breath out of her. "You give me everything I need, Matka. Even she knows that. All that's good in me comes from you."

Matka flinched, making Mary let her go. "Thank ya, Mary," she whispered as she picked up the ashtray from the table. "Mr. Cermak's coming back for supper?"

Mary took the hot iron from the stove and put another length of ribbon on the ironing board. "No. And he makes me feel like . . ." She couldn't find the right words to describe her revulsion. He was her mother's favored boarder.

"Like what?"

Mary shrugged, searching for the words. "He's awful."

Matka sighed. "Pays on time, every time—"

The door slammed in the other room, and the boys' yelling and screaming drew Matka away before Mary could articulate what caused her hair to stand on end whenever Mr. Cermak was near.

Matka's voice rose in the other room. "In or out, dammit." Mary heard a smack, which must have landed on one of the boys' bottoms, and she braced for the wailing that would follow.

"How in the hell did yer clean sweater get covered in dirt? Head to toe, covered in—that's not mud. Ya rolled in dog shit?"

"Chicken shit," Johnny's voice came, timid and sweet.

Mary sighed. She'd have preferred dog crap.

More dirt—worse than dirt—to be cleaned. It was endless. Now wasn't the time to push a conversation about their boarder and his ways. Matka was exhausted and needed his boarding dollars. And getting rid of a boarder might give her mother another reason to get her into the mill even faster than planned. Mary didn't want to think about the awful way he made her feel so she pushed him out of mind, just like always.

She put the candles into the basket as Matka appeared in the kitchen, hauling Johnny by the collar, both their faces pulled into angry angles. Mary thought her mother was going to tell her to go to Mass alone.

"All these traditions and beliefs, *useless*. Learn that now, Mary."

Matka's frustration filled the kitchen the same way Papa's struggling breath rattled his chest, expanding into the air so that Mary experienced the cough as though it were hers, too. She was sure she'd never own such futility, the kind her mother carried. "It's all right," Mary said, forcing her voice to be light.

"It's always all right," Matka said. "Whatever trouble comes'll come no matter how much we pray to the Blessed Mother for something different. Yinz girls'll learn that the wishing and wanting is worse than whatever bad thing actually happens."

Mary disagreed. "We're not going?"

Matka glared at Mary, hesitating.

"Please."

Matka pursed her lips. "Fine. We'll go."

Mary believed what Mrs. Dunn had said about making her life work the way she wanted. The hope chest, the things Mary concealed in the fireplace—she knew she'd been right to do it. Her secrets made her feel guilty, but they were solid pieces of the good life that would come for her, and they showed that Mrs. Dunn saw her worth.

Matka was overrun by life. Mary shared the grind that pressed her daily. But there was nothing in Mary's young body that hinted she might ever be so hopeless, so angry. No, she was different from her mother and the other women around town. She had plans, she had high expectations, and she had the Blessed Mother on her side. And someday she'd share her treasures with her mother. Someday she'd ease the sharp knife from Matka's grip and alleviate the urge to stab herself with all that had gone wrong over the years. Her mother would then see that dreams were as reliable as any good job in the mill.

Chapter 17

Mary

Candlemas Day, 1910

Donora was barely a decade old, but it boasted fifteen churches. Each had been built on the foundation of traditions of the nationalities represented in town. Five of them were Catholic. Saint Mary's had been founded by Polish immigrants in 1902, and it sat on the corner of St. Mary's Drive and Second Street, perched above the mills.

As the Lancos family approached the church, the blast furnaces lit the night from below, the flames pushing through the smoky veil as if in celebration. Mary thought the establishment of the town with all its purifying fire was as much a nod to the Mother Mary as Candlemas Day itself.

Mary and her family entered the packed church, crossing themselves with holy water. The wetness against her forehead gave Mary immediate peace, the hush of ritual seeping into her skin. They slid into a pew a few rows from the back, squashing together to take up as little room as possible. Mary took each candle from her basket, passing it to its proper owner.

George yanked at the collar of his wool coat. "Tickles." He dragged out the word. "I'm hot."

Johnny added his own whining. Matka shot them a look and quieted them.

Mary inhaled the scent of candles burning all around the sanctuary. Johnny and George began to fuss again, elbowing and shouldering one another, grunting like pups wrestling over a bone.

Matka reached across Victoria and gripped George's arm. He dropped his candle, cracking it. The crash echoed and the family in front of the Lancoses stiffened, then turned with widened eyes. Matka forced a smile at the mother, who offered an understanding nod before glaring at her own children, issuing a warning. Matka dug her fingers into George's shoulder and whispered in tight words, "Settle yer ass. God's watching."

Mary scooped up the candle pieces and put them in the basket. They should have left George's candle at home. He was just too small to be trusted with it. Mary pretended it had never happened, telling herself that her candle, her mother's, and sisters' were the most important to be lit.

Ann leaned forward, making faces at Teddy Luineski. He put his fingers into the sides of his mouth and pulled his lips apart, crossing his eyes. Matka reached past Mary and glowered at Ann. "*Not* in the Lord's home."

Ann straightened right up. Teddy got a pinch from his mother.

At the altar, Father Burak crossed himself. "*In Nomine Patris, et Filii, et Spiritus Sancti.* Amen." He would cross himself fifty-two times during a Mass. Mary had counted when she was small, before she knew the Latin well enough to understand.

On one side of the priest was a marble statue of the Mother Mary lovingly gazing at Jesus. The stone was sculpted so finely, the swaddling and Mary's robes looked as if they were draped with fabric. On the other side of the priest was a statue of Jesus all grown up, arms open, palms upturned as though welcoming each of them into his home.

Mary closed her eyes. Sitting there, beside her family in the womb of the church, away from anything uncomfortable or unwanted, warmth filled her.

Victoria sneezed, loud as a man—as everyone in the Lancos family did. She dug into her sleeve for her handkerchief, but Mary could see she must have forgotten it. Mary passed hers to Victoria, who promptly emptied another sneeze into it. "Keep it," Mary said.

When the time came for the candles to be blessed, the congregation sang "Ave Maria," and Father Burak walked down the aisle, lighting the candle of each person sitting in an aisle seat, who lit the candle of the person seated next to them. In English or his best attempt at Hungarian or Bohemian, he welcomed the visitors from St. Dominic's with a smile.

Mary held the long thick beeswax candle that had been made for her upon her birth. It would be used over the years until she died, and then it would be buried with her, its protectiveness no longer needed when the soul rested.

Baby Rose sat in Matka's lap, dozing against her chest. Every so often, Matka kissed the top of Rose's head and rocked her gently. As irritating as the children could be, their mother loved a little one asleep against her chest, docile and unable to express displeasure or bark demands.

Ann and Victoria held their candles, and Johnny crawled onto Mary's lap with his. Three-year-old George slid onto Ann's lap, blocking her from smiling at Jeffery Vinski or making faces at Teddy. The sermon was delivered mostly in Polish with some clarification in English.

Father Burak's voice boomed, but it was light and hopeful instead of dire and foreboding like so many priests. "Halfway through winter, the Christmas season ends today. We celebrate our mother, Mary, who on this day took Jesus into public, forty days after his birth. We bless these candles, the light they send into our lives, protection from storms, from thunder, from all of life's losses. Whether it's from a leaking roof . . ." he paused for the laughter as the parishioners considered the plight of St. Dominic's, "or a strained relationship. Our celebration eases deep sadness that can flush through one's body with every heartbeat. Faith is like a candle flame, strong and bright, then nearly snuffed away. Believe in the light, in the Church, in our mother, Mary. *Ave Maria, gratia plena . . .*"

When it came time for offerings, Mary's mother put in a few coins from her kitchen tin. Mary pulled pennies from her pocket. Victoria and Ann eyed the change, and instead of Mary putting them all in at once, she doled her pennies out to her sisters.

With the offering, Matka's shoulders relaxed and the vein in her neck that popped when she was angry receded. Matka leaned into Mary, the unexpected softness enflaming Mary's constant, low burning guilt. The tears her mother had shed earlier and this quiet time in church told Mary she was unfair to her mother. *Please God, make me a better daughter*, she prayed.

She hated to hide things from her family. She told herself that she would follow her mother's orders and would ask Mrs. Dunn to give her money when she worked extra instead of the lovely gifts she hid away. She would be dutiful in giving the money to her mother from this point on.

She would still ferret things away for her hope chest, things she found or that she told her mother she was buying when she managed to save extra money, but when it came to Mrs. Dunn and her payment for extra work, Mary would try to be more honest.

Mary looked at Matka with her closed eyes, squeezing Rose close, rocking, embodying a peacefulness Mary rarely witnessed. The stillness reminded Mary of her mother's expression on the rare day she enjoyed a glass of lemonade on the porch or the sunset on clear days, like today when the sun had seemed gilded, when the sky was blue as Johnny's eyes. The Mass had been magic.

Father Burak went back to the altar, turned, and raised his arms. Victoria sniffling into the hanky was the only thing cutting through the silence until Father Burak continued with the Mass.

"In the name of the Father, Son, and Holy Ghost. *Orationis vade in pace.* Care for your neighbors, and goodness will come with the blessing of your *gromnica.* Take the renewal, the blessing, and go forth." He exhaled and dropped his hands. "And don't let those candles blow out, or all good fortune will disappear like boys on wash day."

This unusual casualness at Mass, even at the end of it, caused the silence to thicken. Someone hiccupped and Matka burst out laughing. The rest of the congregation joined her, the joviality emanating out like a wave from the Lancos family. The silliness of Father Burak's words and the idea that they all believed it in some way brought out the happiness in them.

Mary and her family shuffled down the aisle toward the exit. Ann played hide-and-seek using Mrs. Landowski and Mrs. Lisenski as shields between her and Teddy. Mary glanced at Matka, waiting for her to scold Ann, but she'd already launched into conversation with Mrs. Wojcik, each doing her best to bridge Mrs. Wojcik's Polish with her hobbled English.

Johnny edged his candle flame as close to the back of George's hair as he could without setting it on fire. Mary crossed herself and blew out Johnny's candle. She snatched it out of his hand and told God that this extinguished candle didn't count for bad luck since doing so meant the boys didn't light each other or anyone else on fire.

Still, she was determined that her candle and her sisters' would remain lit the entire way home.

Victoria sneezed toward Ann's candle, causing the flame to bend forward, nearly disappearing. Every person in gawking distance stared. Just seconds into the night, and Ann's candle was nearly out.

With all breath held in the vicinity and near miraculous power, the flame leapt back up straight and strong. The crowd whooped and laughed, issuing blessings on their own still-lit candles. No one was more relieved than Ann, who exhaled with relief so deeply that her breath snapped the flame out like it was on a switch.

Mary's heart stopped. She bent her candle toward Ann's and lit it, wax dripping over her hand.

Her sister jumped. "Hot!"

"You're fine," Mary said, already telling herself the candle had not just been blown out.

Victoria shook her head. "But your wax is uneven. Bad luck for sure."

Mary puffed her cheeks out and turned her candle to even out the dripping. "There. No more bad luck."

Her sisters rolled their eyes as they filed out of church. At the doors, Ann turned with her candle. "You carry it. The wind's whipping, and I'm not going to take the blame if the candle blows out before we're halfway home."

Mary groaned and took the candle, her sister skipping down the stairs, her hand in the air to greet her girlfriends gathered on the sidewalk. Mary looked behind her. Matka had stepped out of line, talking to her friends, their heads bent together as though sensitive or bad news was being passed. Her mother bit her lip like she did when she wanted to hold back emotion or certain words.

Victoria's friends dragged her away and Mary, getting bumped by passing people, stepped down from the sidewalk into the street and waited. Johnny and George dashed around, playing tag with other children. Mary called to them to stop, but they ignored her. She craned, searching for Weira or Kasandra to tell them how much she had enjoyed their Polish Mass.

"Mary!" her mother called, waving her daughter in the direction of home. Mary noticed her mother's tattered collar and told herself she would mend it the first spare minute she had.

Mary shuffled along the curb. Shots of wind came and threatened to snuff out the candlelight. She inhaled sharply. *No.* Time slowed, allowing Mary to feel each separate heartbeat, letting her come to the conclusion that the year's good luck would be extinguished just moments after Mass had ended.

But then someone stepped in front of her, blocking the gusts, allowing the flames to bounce upright again. She couldn't believe her eyes. The flames shimmied. She looked up at the person standing on the curb in front of her. "Thank you."

She didn't recognize the man, yet he looked somehow familiar. He had blond hair, light eyes, and a strong jaw. A tiny smile tugged one side of his mouth higher than the other. He stood on the curb, keeping her gaze.

Mary was sure she'd never seen him before because she would have remembered his eyes. Gray, with a hint of blue. She stared. The somber grayness obscured the blue like Donora hid its blue sky, only revealing it once in a while.

"Thank you," she said again.

A wagon drove past, causing the crowd to shift and nudge her from behind. She stepped closer to the sidewalk, but remained standing down in the street.

He tipped his hat. "*Moja przyjemnosc.*"

"Mary!" her mother yelled. "Rose needs a change!"

Mary lifted her candles to indicate she'd heard, and refocused on the man. Or was he a schoolboy? His face seemed knowing, but there was a glint in his eyes like any boy she knew. She understood when he'd said, "you're welcome" in Polish. She suspected he was newly arrived. He understood what she'd said, but he didn't reply in English.

"*Now*, Mary!" her mother yelled again.

Mary knew that tone. "Time to go." She started to step onto the sidewalk, but there were so many people clustered around the man that she walked along the curb toward home.

He tipped his hat again.

She smiled and bumped into the back of Mrs. Bucjac, nearly snuffing out her candles again. "Apologies," Mary mumbled as she stepped around the woman, her mother growing more irritated. Turning down Second Street, Mary looked over her shoulder, catching sight of the man again. He was waving at someone Mary couldn't see through the crowd.

When had he arrived? Where was he living? Why had he chosen Donora?

Another bit of wind swirled by, lifting the brim of her hat. She focused on getting home with the candles lit, to earn the proper protection from Mary, Mother of God's thunder candles. The idea the Lancoses might lose the protection that year was too much to bear.

Chapter 18

Lukasz

The mermaid broke through the surface of the dark water, crystal droplets falling from the tips of her lashes. Her full lips and bare shoulders beckoned, making Lukasz want to pull her close. She continued to rise, moving toward shore, toward Lukasz. He strained to see where her tail met her human form, but it was too dark. She offered him a crooked smile, and he returned it as they reached for each other. A clumsy, lurching motion propelled him forward. She leaned toward him, their fingertips touching, and Lukasz wanted her against him. But every step he took was jerky, her eyes widening, then narrowing as a confused look fell over her face. One final jerk toward her, and she was gone, and he was falling.

The crash to the rug-covered dirt floor woke him. He flew to his feet, as confused as the mermaid had looked before she had disappeared. He looked at the bed he'd been sharing with the Kowalk brothers. Michael's foot dangled over the edge. Lukasz massaged his kidney. Nothing like a good kick to wake him up.

He rubbed his eyes as the details of the mermaid came to him for the first time since leaving his homeland. It was like being back at the Wisloka riverside the night he saw her, the comforting caress of her fingers on his hand, her push for him to find his path—it was all back as though real, as though it had only ever been real in the first place.

He exhaled. So much had happened since that night—the trip across the ocean, the transport to Donora, meeting the Kowalks, attending Candlemas Mass, the intriguing young woman whose candle flame he'd saved from the blustery wind. All of it was new and stimulating in ways he'd never imagined. His body seemed to function even without proper sleep.

He glanced at the bed stuffed with Kowalks and figured it was better just to get some of the coffee he smelled wafting into the room rather than to try to go back to sleep. He pulled on his pants and changed his shirt, thinking of the Mass, the security and good luck the candle ceremony had promised. Hope coursed through him as he stood in the middle of the cramped room, the scent of shoes, dirty clothes, and sweaty bodies filling the space.

None of that mattered. Once he allowed the unexpected goodness of Mass to settle, a sense of rebirth stirred. The idea of candles—thunder candles blessed and tasked with protecting families and households from every manner of storm—was silly, yet in those moments, the positivity that was promised might as well have been made of cotton threads, as real as the clothes on his body.

**

"Lukasz!" Zofia said as he entered the kitchen. She took him by the shoulders, guiding him to a seat at the table. She set a plate of potatoes and eggs before him and filled his coffee mug and added a splash of white liquid from a can into it. "*Mleko.*" She held up the can of condensed milk to show him. "Special for you. Sweetened *mleko.*"

The thick richness made him close his eyes to savor it.

"You're a quiet one, Lukasz. Not like my Alexander," Zofia said, patting his shoulder.

He nodded, eager to meet Alexander when he was off work. "Thank you again. For everything."

She poured herself a cup of coffee and sat at the table's head. "At first, I nearly told Nathan to take you back where he found you. *Pech.* Never good luck when a guest's arrival doesn't match the letter that announced him." She tapped her temple with her finger. "But then I thought, *nie.* This is meant to be, you. Not Waldemar. I can feel it. You coming on Candlemas Day. That glorious blue sky and bright sun. All of it."

Lukasz laid his fork down. "Thank you."

Zofia patted his hand. "Alexander has arranged for Nathan to take you to the blast furnace today. There's a job."

Lukasz furrowed his brow, not understanding what a blast furnace was.

She fluttered her hands in the air, making a noise. "*Ogień.* Fire. They make iron, *gorący metal* before it can be steel," she said. "Each year, we add another room onto this house, and it's all because of the work in those furnaces."

Lukasz drank his coffee and nodded. He thought of the postcard again, the pristine white house and lush green grass. He pulled it out of his pocket and showed her. "I'd like to earn money for that."

She studied it and smiled as she tapped the picture. "It's a miracle, that mill. Makes everything possible." She continued to stare at the card. "They dig out the insides of the earth, heat it up, add just the right combination of ingredients to mix and separate slag from iron and well, like I cook. Everyone in Donora's making something in some way."

Lukasz raised his eyebrows, entranced with Zofia's description.

She looked up. "Can you imagine? Hour after hour, day after day?" She sipped her coffee before looking back at the card. "The iron's brittle and hard, too hard to build America. They have to do more to it to make the steel that bends and gives and holds the world up. All it takes is the exact order of smelting and melting and mining and . . . well, just know this—the mills are as dependable as your heartbeat." She pressed her chest. "Nothing in the world is so reliable as those mills. Be that reliable yourself. Show up, keep your trap shut—which you seem pretty good at doing—work harder than the guy beside you, behind you, in front of you. Do that and you'll make a life for yourself, Lukasz. You'll get that house." She held up the card. "Sure as you're sitting here drinking that coffee swirled with fine, sweet condensed milk. America can give you all of that. *Wszystko.*"

She handed the postcard back. He grinned, only partially understanding how all of what she said was possible, that down the hill in the hulking mill he had seen when he arrived, they were cooking the very earth they stood on. Yet, he believed. The rewards that would follow from working there were exactly what he'd been wanting—purpose, opportunity, and means to make a life.

Zofia leaned back in her chair, her arm strung across her belly as she sipped her coffee. "They love the Poles in the mill. Strong as the steel they make, machines themselves."

Again a surge of hope, the mere possibility of making a good life, flooded through Lukasz.

"Trick is getting them to hire you on."

He nodded. "I'm ready, Zofia. Just take me there."

**

Full bellied and shot with caffeine, Lukasz pushed into the cold morning with Nathan at his side. His parents had given him the day off from school to show Lukasz around town and get him to where he could meet the bosses and foremen friendly to Alexander Kowalk. "You'll meet my dad tonight," Nathan said. "You fell asleep before he came home last night, and he was gone before you woke this morning."

They walked straight down Fifth Street to the entrance gate to the mill. Nathan narrated and labeled everything they passed.

"Slag," Nathan lifted his voice over the grind and crunch of mechanical tools as they passed freight cars zipping back and forth carrying metal, coal, and thick glowing . . . something.

"It's waste. Extra. Sits on the iron, they tap it, take it away, dump it on the riverbank or in the woods down a ways."

Lukasz nodded, recognizing Nathan's Polish words but not grasping what it all meant.

Nathan gestured. "Mill hospital beyond there. Wireworks, there." They continued on, weaving in and out of the people going about their days.

Nathan pointed again. "Open hearths over there." As they reached the blast furnaces, their towering height caused Lukasz to stop midstride. He scanned the structure up and down, marveling, trying to imagine how many men standing on shoulders high they were. One hundred? Two?

"This is where you'll work. Hopefully," Nathan said.

Thick gray ash flitted through the air, held up by black soot that burned his eyes.

Nathan grabbed Lukasz's wrist. "Don't rub. You'll get the red eye and they'll swell shut."

Lukasz nodded and squeezed his eyes closed to rid himself of the irritant. But even as he did it, he knew it was fruitless. The air tasted like it looked, grainy. He smacked his tongue on the roof of his mouth, shuddering.

"The taste'll go away soon," Nathan said.

Lukasz looked into the sky, searching for the sun. East was over the river. He thought he saw an orb that glowed white through the ebony smoke.

"White sun?" Not like his lemon-yellow Myscowa sun, not like the one he had supposedly brought with him the day before.

Nathan lit a cigarette and then another, handing it to Lukasz. "It's good," Nathan said as though he knew exactly what Lukasz was thinking. "Smoke means money. That's how you'll get your house someday. Can't cut yellow sun and blue sky with a knife and fork, can we?" Nathan rubbed his thumb over his index and middle fingers to indicate money.

Lukasz took a drag from the cigarette. He was beginning to understand. No sapphire sky, but food, money. There were homes for all in smoky, steel-making Donora, a future. He thought of his arrival, when everyone had said he had brought the blue sky. Surely it returned daily, even for a bit.

Nathan waved Lukasz closer to talk in his ear. "Fat Danny owes my dad. Job should be yours if it's still open." He pulled Lukasz by the sleeve. They entered the mill and Lukasz covered his mouth, coughing, awed by the sights and sounds.

The groan of machinery without buffers and black air took his breath away. He stood in the shadow of the hulking metal machinery, big as mountains but made by man, making him as insignificant as an ant.

Tools, Lukasz reminded himself. They were nothing more than tools like he used to make his animals. He chuckled. These implements dwarfed him, looming overhead, unlike the wire, hammer, enamel, and pliers that fit into his palm. These were God-sized tools that used thousands of men to run them, to handle the product they made. The angles of the cross-hatched scaffolding, great ladles, and cranes moved quick, dumping loads and swinging back for more. He didn't know where to look first. He didn't even have the language to name what he saw.

They stood near three men driving a metal pole into the bottom of one of the brick sections, and thick liquid the color of hell rushed out. The men jumped aside, one of them catching some of the liquid on his pants. His co-workers batted the liquid away, screaming and laughing at the same time. The heat coming off the molten metal burned Lukasz's face even as the bitter winter air filled the rest of the space inside the mill. Nathan jerked his head in the other direction and pulled Lukasz by the arm.

They were moving away when a scream turned them back, making them look upward. A man dangled from a crane, his shriek cutting through the noise. Lukasz rushed toward the crane, not knowing what propelled him to do so. Nathan pulled him back just as wires the size of Lukasz's forearm crashed in front of them. The man hanging onto the crane lost his grip when the crane operator tried to turn it so that there was a platform under him. He fell to the ground, a heap of soot-covered flesh, barely moving but writhing all the same.

Lukasz started toward the man again. Nathan yanked him back with one hand, pointing in the direction of the tapped furnace with his other. Red sparks flew, landing on Lukasz's shirt, putting tiny holes in it. He brushed them away as molten liquid rushed out of the furnace, following a pathway right in front of them.

"Isn't anyone helping him?"

A siren sounded. "They're coming," Nathan said.

The work didn't stop, not for one moment. The writhing man rolled to his side, alone, in pain. Nathan pulled Lukasz again. "This might be your chance to hop in now that he's done."

A job due to the bad luck of another man's injury? Lukasz's belly roiled at the thought of it. He wanted to help. He wanted to at least tell the other men to stop and see to the injured worker. Nathan pulled him back again. Finally, a truck with several men carrying bags pulled up near the injured man. They vaulted out to help, allowing Lukasz to move as Nathan directed.

"He's all right now," Nathan said. Lukasz wasn't so sure but followed anyway.

As they passed men working, Lukasz heard languages he knew were Polish or English or Czech, but there were others he'd never heard. The languages came together, blending and spilling out like the hot metal that had been tapped right in front of his feet. The excitement of searching for a job was now edged with paralyzing sadness at seeing the injured man left alone, writhing in pain, like wolves might leave a wounded pack member behind, eventually scooped up like manure. Dark and lonesome. The words throbbed inside him.

They entered the small office where the hiring for the blast furnace and open hearth occurred. Nathan explained that he spoke and wrote fluent English and had composed a note to Fat Danny Burke from his father, Alexander, on Lukasz's behalf.

While they waited, Lukasz moved toward the bank of windows overlooking the mill floor. From that height, he saw the men lifting the injured worker onto a stretcher. He strained to see as far as he could in one direction, then the other. Not one bit of the mill paused in response to that man being injured.

A door slammed and Lukasz turned. A man entered, shirt so white it glowed against the blackened walls and dust-covered desk. His belly threatened to burst his shirt buttons right off. His thick, rolled neck was as wide as his shoulders. He waddled toward Nathan and Lukasz, face red, eyes yellow and watery.

As his fat fingers raked through his orange hair, he spoke English so quickly, Lukasz had no chance of understanding.

"Job's filled," Nathan translated. "Last shift."

Lukasz's face fell.

Nathan gestured toward the window, pulling the barrel-belly white shirt toward it. They all peered down to the floor, and Lukasz knew they were discussing the injured man and that there was now another open position. The thought of working in that part of the mill startled Lukasz. He was willing to do anything but decided right then he would not be the next man dangling from machinery while others went about their work, unable to stop and help.

Nathan pointed at the crane again.

The white shirt scowled and tapped his fat finger on the glass, drawing their attention to the crane. A man jogged across the raised walkway, heading toward the spot where he would work. The men left the office, and the white shirt gestured at someone Nathan said was a gang boss. The boss returned a signal and the white shirt headed back to the office.

"That job's filled already too," Nathan said, translating the gestures for Lukasz.

Nathan tapped the note in his hand, drawing Fat Danny's attention to it. Lukasz was having trouble even reading the meaning of what they said with their eyes.

The man shook his head and threw his fat sausage arms into the air. "Wireworks!" Lukasz recognized that word. "Tell Griffy to hire your man as a favor to me for '07. Summer, not winter. Be clear about that so I don't trade on the wrong favor."

Nathan translated and pulled a pencil from the long thin pocket of his trousers and made a note on his paper. Fat Danny brushed soot from his shirt, smearing it. "Goddamn it," he said, already turning his back to them. Nathan stalked after him and tapped his shoulder.

Lukasz held his breath, surprised that the young boy was so demanding, that this adult man in charge with a white shirt and clean hands actually listened to him. Nathan tapped his pencil on the paper. Fat Danny pushed the paper away. Nathan pushed it back, holding the pencil out too.

"Alexander Kowalk."

Nathan spoke his father's name as though it was a threat. Lukasz crossed his arms, unsure about this approach. Fat Danny exhaled, stomped away, then paced back, taking the pencil and paper, scribbling something as he rattled off what seemed like orders to Nathan. Nathan doffed his hat and broke into a jog, signaling Lukasz to follow.

"This way," Nathan said. Lukasz ran along with him while Nathan translated what had transpired with Fat Danny.

"He owes my papa. But, well, you saw what happened. Job's gone. And he heard there's an opening at the wireworks, but not for long. He just sent a fella down that way a few minutes ago. Fat Danny passed the favor to Griffy at the wireworks. But we need to get there before Jacob. I know 'em. He's lazy. He's probably only made it to the first rod mill. If we're lucky, he stopped off for a shot and a beer."

Lukasz didn't understand much of what was happening in Donora, but it was odd that a man who worked with his hands like Alexander should have sway over the white-shirted men in offices.

A passing railcar overflowing with red-hot cargo stopped their progress at the tracks.

"What kind of valuable thing did your father do to earn these favors?" Lukasz asked.

Nathan shrugged. "My father's the best molder in the mill, for one. Saves them money every single day he works. Makes Fat Danny look good for doing nothing but barking at people all day. And other things. People like to please my father."

Lukasz nodded, making a note to ask what exactly a molder did later. "And this Griffy?"

Nathan shook the paper at Lukasz. "This favor is for Fat Danny, not my dad."

Lukasz couldn't imagine how favors could be so plentiful that one would be spent on a Pole who had just set foot in town the day before. Though there weren't golden streets nor white homes with green grass and tiny, pretty fences, and the skies were pewter, not blue, this transaction reflected what he'd been told about America. This made his loneliness disappear.

Nathan pulled Lukasz's shirtsleeve. "Griffy owes Fat Danny, get this, for marrying his sister. This favor will stretch out for years and miles."

Lukasz laughed. That he understood. A peasant's answer to royal marriage.

"Like you," Nathan said. "Soon you'll have a wife."

He had much to do before taking a wife. He needed a home. Well, first he needed a job. Someday a wife.

The railcars passed. Nathan jogged with Luaksz at his side, picking up speed toward the furnace gate. "Hurry, before Jacob or someone else takes the job at the wire mill. This favor only works if we get there first," Nathan said.

Lukasz was pleased that if there were favors to get a newly arrived immigrant hired on so quickly, that his host family had the connections to make it happen.

But the idea of relying on favors unsettled him, too. He'd been told—the pamphlets written in Polish had promised—that a man's sturdy back was what brought a job, not favor, not a monarchy for peasants, trading women for power and crushing men who didn't play along. He hoped this wasn't the way of the mills, that this was just his fortunate chance to get his first job.

Chapter 19

Lukasz

Lukasz and Nathan sprinted out of the blast furnace gate, heading north, back toward the wireworks. They passed the number one and two rod mills. Nathan didn't break pace, panting and pointing as they went. "My papa works in number two." He picked up speed. "Hurry."

Lukasz was disoriented from the smoky darkness, but he sped up to keep pace with Nathan's long strides.

"We'll swim in the river in summer." Nathan gestured beyond the mills to the black water that collared Donora's flatlands like a horseshoe. "Hedderman's Grocery there, Newhouse Hardware there, Miller's Tavern—they make a melt-in-your-mouth sausage sandwich."

Lukasz kept pace, nodding along. He thought of what Zofia had said about how to prove he was worthy, to always show his best strength.

"Leo's Tavern there. Never go unless you're looking for a scuffle."

Lukasz wasn't looking for trouble of any sort.

They reached the third rod mill and rushed inside, panting. They stopped, hands on their knees. Slowly, Lukasz caught his breath and looked around. Hissing, writhing snakes shot out of a black hole, glowing red and spooling into circular bundles. The sight turned Lukasz breathless for the second time that day.

His eyes absorbed the sight while the rumble and full weight of the operation shook his insides.

Nathan leaned closer to Lukasz. "That's the wire."

Lukasz drew back and thought of the wire he'd brought with him from Poland to make his animals. The wire that was being made in front of his eyes was suited for a giant to shape into mountain-sized woodland animals and river-born mermaids. He was starting to wonder if he'd been dropped into a fairy story, and the giants simply hadn't shown themselves yet. He couldn't fathom how wires so thick and long could be used for anything. He'd worked plenty with molten iron in Ryszard's forge but never any that moved like an animal, half-liquid, half-solid. Maybe that's why the sun shone silver instead of yellow—all its rays were captured inside the walls of these great steel-making beasts.

Nathan pulled Lukasz into a room and closed the door, cutting the noise in half. His ears rang and he shook his head, trying to eliminate the vibration.

"Mr. Griffen," Nathan said, straightening, his tone crisp and respectful like the tone Lukasz had used when talking to the priests as a boy.

The man scowled, his square forehead crisscrossed with lines that conveyed a permanent sense of disgruntlement. "Yeah?" He barely moved his lips.

Nathan held out the note. Mr. Griffen scowled more deeply, refusing to take the paper, and Nathan began to explain. Lukasz recognized some of the words—Fat Danny, Kowalk, blast furnace.

Mr. Griffen snatched the note, spouting off in English. He read, flicked the note, and shook his head. "Jacob

Janowski. Gave him the rookie laborer job. Two seconds back."

Lukasz saw the disappointment in Nathan's face as his shoulders slumped. He translated for Lukasz, telling him that he would make a case for him for when something else opened up. Nathan stepped closer to Mr. Griffen and rattled on.

Mr. Griffen took Nathan's shoulder, moved him aside, and looked Lukasz up and down. "Small," Mr. Griffen grumbled, leaving Lukasz to wonder what the word meant but understanding it conveyed something negative.

Nathan balled up his fists and made the gesture for strong. It was then Lukasz realized they were discussing his qualifications.

Mr. Griffen looked at the paper again, mumbling. He threw on a coat and waved for them to follow him.

"He'll show you the works so if there's an opening, you'll be familiar," Nathan said.

Outside the office, the noise swamped them again. But Mr. Griffen still shouted things over the din, and Nathan translated, with Lukasz catching every other word at best. Mr. Griffen showed them the line where nails were separated. Platoons of women in grubby dresses glanced at the trio, then refocused on their work. They separated the nails, then ground the whiskers. Nathan rubbed Lukasz's chin. "Whiskers. They buff them off the nails and sort the good from the bad." Next, they got a closer view of the wire pullers, their work a combination of skill, art, and machinery. "That's not a job most can do," Nathan said.

They went into the locker room, then the break room, where the employees ate lunches from round metal pails with lids or from trucks that sold sandwiches. Finally, Mr. Griffen showed them where some of the wire was bundled and loaded onto the trucks. "Shipping," Nathan said.

Lukasz watched as two men grabbed a side of a coiled bundle, counted, then heaved it into the back of a truck. He nodded, thinking that this mill would suit him if he was hired.

A siren sounded, startling Lukasz and making him cover his ears. The others just surveyed the space, looking for what had caused the alarm. Some yelling cut through the grinding metal noise. One man at the end of the space raised his fists and crossed them at the wrists. Another man answered with a palm raised while some men scrambled, all of it followed by the distinct sound of gears slowing, the screech of motion halting as loud as the working noise itself. Now the shouts were clearer.

Lukasz looked around and saw two things happening: something on the nail line where the women were and something with the wire pullers. The men signaled with their hands to communicate what to do next. Mr. Griffen waved a blonde girl over from the nail line where the operation had been halted.

She jogged toward him with another following.

"Peggy," Nathan said her name to Lukasz as she began to explain something to Mr. Griffen. "And that's Weira. From church last night."

Lukasz nodded, remembering meeting her.

Out of the corner of his eye, Lukasz saw the argument between two men who'd been loading the wire bundles. One pushed the other into a stack of bundles, knocking it over, the wire scattering and nearly taking their feet out from under them before they could get out of the way. The two men froze, glaring, then started circling each other.

"Oh no," Weira said in Polish.

Nathan translated what Peggy was saying. "Fishtail's drunk again. Can't keep out of that bottle."

One man stumbled. "That drunk one's called Fishtail," Nathan said.

"Like a fish out of water once he goes down." Peggy gestured. "Flip, flop. Promised no more drink, but . . ."

Fishtail threw a punch at the other man. All attention turned toward them. Two managers joined Mr. Griffen.

"What the hell's happening?" Mr. Griffen shouted above the grinding din. "The whole mill's going down."

"Not a good day to hire on," Peggy said. "Everyone's hair is on fire."

Nathan explained that meant that everyone was angry.

Lukasz studied the white-shirted men's faces, unable to understand their words but able to read the anger that hardened one man's face while worry creased the other's. The two managers rolled up their sleeves as they called other men over, berating them. Mr. Griffen took off his coat and handed it to Nathan.

Peggy leaned into Lukasz and shouted into his ear. Her Polish was rough but understandable. "Drunk men who load the wire. He'll fire them without a cent earned this week."

Fishtail saw the white shirts approaching and his shoulders drooped. Before the managers reached him, he ripped off his gloves, threw them to the ground, and stormed away with the other man following suit.

"Lefty must be drunk too," Nathan said. "That's a good way to get killed. Coming to work drunk. At the very least, it gets you fired."

At that moment, Lukasz understood the tension in the mill, the need to keep things running smoothly. He thought again of what Zofia had advised about working hard, and the man at the blast furnace who had jumped into the open job before Lukasz had a chance to be given it. He eyed the bundles. He could make himself useful in every way, the way he had in Myscowa.

More screaming came from behind them. Another two white-shirted managers stalked toward them, bellowing. While the men screamed, pointing in the direction of the nail line and then back at the wire bundles, Lukasz thought this was his chance. The same way he took action to get to America, he would take action to get the chance to make a living in Donora.

His breath was choppy, unsure. Would it ruin his chances for a job if he did this? He pressed his chest. He would not sit on his ass waiting for another drunk to be fired or another man to be injured.

He exhaled deeply and strode toward the wire bundles, only breaking stride to scoop up Fishtail's discarded gloves. He pulled them on, squatted near the closest wire bundle, and wrapped his hands around it. He jiggled it to get a feel for its weight, the way it was distributed compared to hay bales. The shouting continued, and he glanced over at Nathan and the men. They hadn't even noticed he'd walked away. This was it.

He inhaled, stood, and heaved the bundle into the back of the truck. He wiped his hands. Heavy. But not outside of what he could manage. He picked up another and tossed, then another and another, quickly learning to adjust his grip for the best heave, falling into a rhythm that allowed him to move fluidly, machine-like.

Before long, all but one of the bundles was loaded. When he paced toward the final bundle, he noticed a crowd had gathered, watching. Nathan, the white shirts, Peggy, Weira, and another woman stood gaping.

This brought a smile to Lukasz's face. He bent down for the last bundle, and his back bit with pain. He reminded himself to stay focused on the loading, hoping he hadn't just risked getting a job. He gripped the bundle, straightened, and tossed it, landing it perfectly atop the others. He wiped his hands and began to remove the gloves, wishing someone would speak. When they all just stared, Lukasz panicked.

"Nathan, tell them I didn't mean to—"

Mr. Griffen lifted his eyebrows but maintained a scowl, then shouted something at the two drunk men and pointed at Lukasz.

Lukasz's stomach dropped. What had he done? He turned away.

Nathan grabbed and shook him.

Lukasz had ruined his chances.

Nathan's grin didn't make sense. "Listen to me, Lukasz. You're hired!" He jumped up and down as though a foot race had just been won.

Lukasz turned back toward the white shirts and saw they were smiling, clapping, coming toward him. Each man shook

Lukasz's hand and patted his shoulder, talking fast and emphatically.

Peggy and Weira patted Lukasz on the back too. Only the tall, dark-haired woman hung back, her probing gaze swallowing Lukasz. She held a lunch bucket and a newspaper in one hand and adjusted her hat with the other. Like a willow, a single flower against the darkness of the mill.

She cocked her head and gave Lukasz a little smile. He felt like the sun when a sunflower followed it, noticing him, looking past all the others to keep his gaze. He smiled back and waved, still jostled by the happy hands of bosses whose words he couldn't understand. Finally, one of the white shirts went to the tall girl and took the pail and newspaper from her before sending her out of the mill.

With that half smile, he was sure this woman was the one he'd seen after Candlemas.

"Who's that woman?" Lukasz asked Nathan.

"You just did the work of two men, you won the job, and you're asking about some girl?"

Nathan was right. He'd won the job based on nothing but his strength, nothing but him, no favors, and that was what he should focus on.

Nathan waved his hand through the air. "Mary Lancos. She used to sit behind me in cursive until she quit to work for the Dunns."

"Here?" Lukasz asked.

Nathan removed his hat, smoothed his hair back, then replaced the hat. "Their home. She's too young for here."

Lukasz realized that meant Mary Lancos was younger than he'd thought, that her height and her confident posture had fooled him. No matter. He didn't have time for courting. All he wanted was to save up money to buy a home, a Donora home like the one on the postcard. Just like that.

And he was off to a good start. By the time he left the mill that day, he had a job, ushered in by Alexander's connections but sealed by his very own strength.

Back in Poland, he couldn't have imagined what Donora held for him—the fire-breathing machines that swallowed earth and iron and turned out hot rivers of steel, that the steel could be woven into wire as fat as his forearm.

And though Donora's pewter skies and thick smoke turned him around, and the grainy air burned his eyes and throat, he was buoyed by the promise of steady work, and it made him understand how right he'd been to make the trip across the Atlantic. Meant to be. Just as Zofia had said.

Chapter 20

Mary

In the still of the night, the sun in deep sleep, Mary lay in bed, coiled on her side, unhurried. Ann was beside her but curled into her own sleeping bud, their tailbones touching. Victoria was lying across the foot of the bed, her deep breath indicating heavy sleep. For once, it seemed better for Mary to stay in bed than to get up.

Nearly the instant that Mary appreciated her comfort that morning, the drips came, the slow plunking of water drops hitting the space between her and Ann. At first, Mary wasn't positive it was water, but she rolled onto her back and the drips hit her smack in the forehead, convincing her. The roof. Again.

She jumped out of bed and lit her lantern, holding it up. There it was, a line of water trailing across the ceiling before it gave way right above the bed, releasing the drip.

In her nightclothes and bare feet, Mary went to the kitchen and retrieved a bucket. But when she saw how unstable it would be on the mattress, she woke her sisters. They groaned and moaned.

"That roof leak'll get you moving soon enough." Mary shook the bucket at her sisters.

The mention of a leaking roof made Ann and Victoria spring out of bed. The year before a section of the roof over the boarders' bedroom had sprung a leak and brought down plaster, soot, and insulation with it, leaving Mr. Cermak dripping in horsehair, freezing and filthy.

The girls moved the bed, set the bucket on the floor under the leak, and dressed. In the kitchen, Mary pulled on her boots, coat, and wrapped her scarf around her head. She grabbed a bucket to gather the coal and tossed another to Ann. "Get the water."

Within fifteen minutes, Mary had dug the coal and was scooping it into the stove as Ann came back with water, shivering, mumbling about how this was uncivilized living.

Matka appeared with Rose on her hip and settled her into a chair. Mary handed her mother an apron. "Roof's leaking," she said.

Matka looked upward.

"Our bedroom this time," Mary said.

Face drained, Matka tied her apron strings with force, strangling her waist. "Dammit." She started toward the front room, where she slept with Rose and Mary's father when extra boarders took their tiny bedroom. Papa's morning cough signaled he was waking, and Mary's shoulders tightened, bracing for his yelling at the news.

"All that damn church. Thunder candles. Always bringing good luck." Matka slammed the kettle onto the stovetop. "Protection and prosperity, my hind end."

Mary remembered how Ann had sneezed and blown out her candle before they had even left the sanctuary, and she shot her sister a look.

"Don't look at me, Mary," Ann said. "It's just a fairy tale."

"If you believed, it'd be real," Mary said. "This is your fault." Even as Mary said it, she remembered George had broken his candle before it was ever even lit, but he was too young to blame.

Ann stuck out her tongue.

"Girls," Matka snapped. "Yinz git moving. I'll take care of the leak. *Dammit.* We don't have the money." She spun toward Mary. "Ya may be in the mill before yer birthday. Everyone thinks you're a grown woman anyhow."

Mary's breath caught, but she would not argue, not right then. She was glad to be leaving, to have the chance to work all day at the Dunn home with a woman who spoke in gentle waves of words and gave orders by asking questions which everyone scrambled to answer with action. And later, there would be a dance. This time, she wasn't going to miss it.

**

After a hard but lovely day of work at the Dunns', Mary served dinner at home. Ann filled the glasses with water from a pitcher.

Matka smothered a yawn. "Angelo Alfonsi charged me a pretty penny to fix up the roof. Said we have a month to repay it."

Mary nodded as she spooned haluski onto Mr. Cermak's plate. His gaze was heavy on her but she didn't indicate that she noticed, taking as wide a berth as she could when serving and clearing the table. Mary kept an eye on the man as Ann filled his water glass, making sure he kept his creepy paws and eyes off her. But he didn't pay Ann a bit of attention, saving it all for Mary. He smiled at her whenever he caught her watching him.

"Glad it's fixed," Mary said. "I'll get overtime at the Dunns' with how Mrs. Dunn's been taking this pregnancy. Sick as a dog." Mary added extra scoops to her father's plate.

"Damn roof." Papa turned his head away from the table and hacked. "I told you I'd fix it, Susan. No need—" He turned to cough again. "I told you." He gripped his fork so hard, his knuckles turned white.

"Can't afford to wait. You'd cough yourself right off the ladder. Then we'd have medical bills on top of roof bills."

He dug into his food and Mary could feel his shame at not fixing things that he thought he should. She patted his back and he smiled up at her. "Eat, Mary. Go on."

Once she'd cleared the table with Ann and Victoria and had done the dishes, Mary emptied the last bucket from the leaky roof and washed her neck, hands, and under her arms as best as she could, hoping to get to the dance quickly. She changed into her clean dress, which brushed her boots at the ankle instead of the toes, but she ignored it. There was nothing she could do about that until she had time to let the hem down. She couldn't stop herself from growing.

On the way out the door, she stopped in the kitchen and sprinkled lemon juice on her wrists and behind her ears to smell as fresh as possible and to remind Samuel of the type of home she'd keep someday.

With Peggy and Katya, she entered St. Charles's Hall. Most girls had donned their Sunday dresses while others had a special frock for things like this. Either way, each girl knew the most important thing was to be there and dance and be swept away with laughter, to float on that happy dancy feeling, even if just for two hours or so. She was sure that very happiness was the type she'd feel all of her days once she was settled with a husband and a nice home.

Since Peggy was older, her goal was to find a husband right then. Every dance provided another chance. For Mary and Katya, the thrill of just being there was enough. They checked their coats with the girl at the front and giggled as they linked arms and headed toward the music.

The room glowed with candles, lanterns, and gas lamps, making a staid room pretty, warm, and even romantic. Mary noted that many girls did have on fine silk dresses with delicate matching shoes—clothing made for special days and events.

But the thing Mary noted most was how much shorter they all were. Their dainty feet and graceful features made them more desirable than Mary. Since she was eight and charged with cleaning her first house, Mary had been treated like an adult. She was called on endlessly to fulfill obligations to her family and others, but she was invisible when it came to most boys.

Katya was already filling her dance card, a swarm of boys rushing her. Mary strode across the room, searching for something to focus on, to make her appear occupied. Finally, she saw him. Across the way, Samuel's head jutted over the crowd. He was the only boy she was remotely interested in, the only one taller than her.

Several songs came and went, and Mary's card remained empty. Dread choked her. What was she doing there? Rushing through her chores, angering her mother, and for what? Her nerves on fire, she started toward the exit but caught sight of the punch table. One last delaying tactic. She sipped a drink, praying for Samuel to notice her. Some teachers from school, chaperones, chatted with her, reminding her what a good student she had been. Their close proximity made Mary even less attractive to those at the dance. Katya went soaring by, turning out the best polka, her hummingbird feet taking air as she threw her head back, laughing with Mike Hampton, who couldn't take his eyes from her even for a moment.

This made Mary laugh too, sharing the moment of happiness with her friend, and she didn't notice someone beside her. "Mary?"

She startled and pressed her hand to her chest. "Samuel."

"I've been chasing you down all night. I follow you to the punch, and you turn your back to talk to the chaperones. I follow you to the cookies, and you talk with Katya."

Mary hadn't fathomed that she might have made herself too busy to be tracked down.

"So," he said, holding out his hand. "Dance?"

She grinned and made him sign her card. She wanted to look at it later.

She placed her hand in his outstretched palm and adjusted her gloves, wishing they were as pristine as his white shirt. She told herself to enjoy the dance and ignore her wardrobe shortcomings. He glanced at her and then away, looking self-conscious, the same way she felt. They shuffled closer and he drew her into his arms, stepping on her toes. They leapt apart and each forced a laugh. "Just warming up the engine," he said, growing even stiffer as he prepared to lead.

"Always takes a minute," she said. His engine never really got warmed up, from what she'd seen.

He took a deep breath and coaxed her into the circle of dancers, trampling her feet again. She told herself to keep her clodhoppers out of his way or they'd never dance three steps.

"I'm sorry," he said. They looked at each other, and his discomfort made Mary feel bad for him. She squeezed his shoulder to reassure him and nodded with a smile. She decided she would not depend on him to move her expertly around the floor but would focus on trying to lure him into leading so she could at least appear to follow. She thought of her father's graceful footwork and the reassuring way he led, moving like liquid. Samuel's movements were a mechanical shuffle, feet shooting out, his knees knocking hers, his carriage cold and brittle. He was wealthy and smart, but a dancer, he was not. She was glad to have something she could offer, something money apparently couldn't buy.

When the song ended, they found themselves near a darker corner of the hall, a whoosh of relief settling over Mary. The dancing was finished for the moment, but only for a moment. Despite their awkward partnering, she didn't want it to be her only dance. So she looked up to thank him, and as her eyes met his, he leaned down and plastered his lips over hers. He gripped her shoulders, his tongue shooting into her mouth, making it impossible to breathe. He snaked one arm around her waist and pulled her tight. His embrace felt good, and his strength made her skin come alive. But his kiss—the probing, sloppy tongue trampling hers—was clumsy as his stomping feet, and it left her utterly relieved when he pulled away.

"Thank you, Mary." He stepped away, still holding her hand.

She looked around the room. Had anyone seen him kiss her? A chaperone? Her friends? It didn't seem as though anyone even cared they were alive. He went toward the punch table again, taking her with him. She resisted the urge to wipe her mouth until he looked away.

She didn't know what to say, what to feel, what to think. She'd been asked to dance, and the usual fun she had with friends had now been elevated. But she couldn't have guessed in a million years that a dance could be so awkward, that a kiss could be the sheer opposite of the way Peggy and Katya had described it. Where were the chills? Where were the butterflies?

Still, it was done. She'd been held, danced with someone other than a friend, and she'd been kissed. She replayed it all, fully recalling his body against hers. Though he was tall, his midsection was soft against her, as if she were the stronger one. This made her think of the Pole who'd stepped in front of her candle on Candlemas Day, the same one she'd seen tossing hundred-pound wire bundles onto the back of a truck like they were made of silken threads. If only that man and Samuel could be melded into one man like the earth and metal that made the steel down the hill.

Samuel handed her a glass of punch. This time when she looked at him, she wasn't shocked, just gleeful that she'd experienced three major life events in the course of just one song. Finally, she was like all the rest of the petite girls who never had to look for boys to fill their cards.

"You are so light on your feet, Mary."

"It's easy with you leading," Mary said, stunned how easily the lie came out of her mouth.

He glanced toward the dance floor and shrugged. "Again?"

And so she did, again and again, with bruised feet and swollen lips to prove it. Somehow the entire experience felt like an accomplishment, as though it were part of her transformation from girl to marriageable woman. She knew she could not go further than she had with Samuel. Kisses in a darkened corner of a church hall dance were part of growing up. She'd heard enough about it. And now she knew herself.

Chapter 21

Lukasz

Nothing stopped. Well, almost nothing. Lukasz smiled. One day of work complete at the wireworks. This was what he'd come for. Just one shift, twelve hours of backbreaking toil, and the house that Lukasz was going to buy someday became even clearer in his mind. His mood soared. He removed his gloves, put them under his arm, and massaged his cramped fingers. With the next shift of men in place to bundle and load wire, the sounds of the twelve-hour nail mill shift stuffed his ears. Lukasz headed toward the locker room, lengthening his spine, appreciating the soreness that pulsed in the small of his back.

Mr. Griffen came up beside him. He slapped his shoulder with one hand and offered an envelope with the other.

"Good work," Mr. Griffen said. He rambled on, his words spoken too fast for Lukasz to decipher. By the smile on the man's face, Lukasz knew he was pleased. He nodded and accepted Mr. Griffen's handshake before another white shirt, Mr. Dunn, waved Mr. Griffen up to the windowed offices overlooking the mill floor.

Lukasz wiped his brow with his forearm, peering at the dollar bill and coins inside the envelope. He reread his name on the front, and the *$1.98* scrawled under it. He closed the flap and shook the envelope, pride swelling despite being unsure how much money that actually was. Again, the house with the white fence and lush lawn came to mind. How much would that cost? He could put this away, start looking at homes and the land he might buy. He raised the envelope to his nose and inhaled. Even with his nose clogged with soot and metallic dust, he detected the distinct scent of hope, success, and America. "Thank you, thank you," he said to no one.

He washed his face at the spigot on the wall in the locker room, ignoring the frigid air hitting his cheeks, still hot from twelve hours of loading hundred-pound wire bundles. The fellas from Lukasz's shift were excited about payday and something called the Bucket of Blood.

Cyryl Bankowski shook his envelope over his head. "Come with us, Lukasz."

"Where?"

"Bucket of Blood," Cyryl said. "Drinks. Food."

The men poked fun at each other, recounting tales of fist fights gone wrong.

The easy comradery of men who spoke Polish, or at least could understand it as they all struggled to learn English, reminded Lukasz of his friendships in Poland. He never thought he would feel an instant sense of belonging. He thought of Zofia and Nathan, their wonderful hospitality. Lukasz was expected there for dinner.

Cyryl elbowed Lukasz. "Give your sponsor mother a break," he said as if he could read Lukasz's mind. "You think they won't smile if tonight they have one less mouth to feed?"

Lukasz considered that as he scrubbed his face. He thought of how it felt to be welcomed into this group of men, wonderful in the same way as it had been in Myscowa but better because now he had money to set aside to start a life. He should write to Adam. He deserved the chance at a better life too. He thought of the Kowalks, the way they were stuffed into a tiny, crooked house but were happy. And as Nathan had told him, they simply added on to the house as they could afford it. Lukasz couldn't imagine anything grander, even if it didn't look like the postcard at all.

He bundled up in his coat and followed Cyryl and the others to the Bucket of Blood. "Always a fight," Cyryl said. "Keep to the corners and you won't get a punch. Unless we need you for a punch. With your strength added to ours? We're fine. All fine."

Lukasz nodded, not really sure why there was a sure chance of so much fighting.

Waiting in the long line to get into the bar, someone tapped Lukasz on the shoulder. He turned to see Nathan with his hand out. "Mama needs her money for room and board."

Lukasz drew back, unsure as to why Nathan was asking for the money when Lukasz could have easily handed it over himself when he got home.

"Give it up," Nathan said, his usual warmth gone from his voice. "I can take it to her."

Luksaz pushed his hand into his pocket but didn't remove the envelope.

Nathan jerked his head in the direction of the men spilling out of the mill and into the bar's queue snaking around the corner. "If you're going in there, I need the money."

Lukasz squinted and shook his head, unsure of what he meant.

"The bar. Bucket of Blood?" Nathan mimed the action of tossing back a drink and Lukasz understood.

He shrugged, still confused.

"Mama can't have her money disappearing down your hatch. My dad's fine with you commiserating with the men on your shift. Good to get to know them, he said. Keeps you safe at work."

Lukasz cocked his head and watched as the stream of men leaving the mills began to file into establishments lining the street. There didn't seem to be a single one of them heading up the hill to sleep on payday.

"Three dollars twenty-five cents a month, Lukasz. Leaves plenty of money to save as long as you don't drink your paycheck. Mama knows yours is light this week. That's all right, but she needs some money now."

Lukasz was offended. He'd never had a home of his own, but he'd always either traded for room and board or paid for it, and he was always on time.

"I don't want Mama to take in more laundry on account of a boarder not paying his share on time."

Lukasz shook some coins from the envelope into Nathan's palm.

Nathan took the envelope from Lukasz. He pointed to the *$1.98* on the front. "Earned sixteen-point-five cents an hour." He dumped the coins back into the envelope and fished the paper money from inside. "I'll take this dollar. You keep the coins. More than enough for something and then to save."

Nathan steered Lukasz by his elbow to the entrance to the bar. "Have a drink and a sandwich, then sleep. If you stay here all day, you'll be sorry later."

Lukasz grew more offended. Nathan was treating him like a child, but the sound of jovial coworkers inside quickly did away with any anger. He didn't know how to respond to Nathan, so he turned his back on him.

Lukasz entered the bar, Nathan still close at his heels. A man swept red-hued sawdust into a pan as another dragged a bloodied soul out the door, right past Lukasz. A third worker followed the sweeper, dumping fresh sawdust onto the floor. The name of the bar finally made sense.

Lukasz followed Cyryl to the far end of the bar and stood with his back to the corner, the stone wall chilling him through his coat. He put his coat over an empty stool, sat on top of it, and leaned forward, noting the beef sandwiches lined along the bar. Men slapped over their change, grabbing food and drinks. A man with iron-rod forearms bent toward Lukasz, and

Nathan barked out an order. Nathan patted Lukasz on the back. "Want me to hold half your coins? Just for insurance."

Lukasz wasn't sure he heard him right. Why on earth would he let a young boy hold onto his money for him? "No."

Nathan slapped him on the back and stuck his hand into the air in a wave as he left. "All right then. See you later."

Cyryl moved down the bar toward the food, leaving an open stool next to Lukasz. A tall glass of amber beer and a short glass of caramel whiskey showed up in front of him. A gray-haired man with a newspaper ambled up to the bar and took his place next to Lukasz. Older but still in strapping shape, the man jabbed Lukasz with an elbow.

"Overheard your conversation. Buy the special—ham, four eggs, and a beer for twenty-five cents. Or ask for the special—a boilermaker with two hardboiled eggs instead of the ham and eggs. You'll get nutrition on the cheap. Fifteen cents."

Lukasz raised his eyebrows, not understanding what the man was saying specifically about the money. The man let out a sharp whistle and signaled to the bartender. "Time to learn your lessons," he said in Polish.

The bartender split an egg into the beer and then dropped the whiskey, shot glass and all, right into the beer. It foamed and threatened to overflow like tapped slag.

The bartender handed the glass to Lukasz, who tentatively drank until his tavern mentor rotated his hand, encouraging him to chug it. "*Odsysaj to.*"

Lukasz slammed the empty glass down and tapped his chest with his fist, clearing his throat, feeling the concoction loosen the soot and wash it away.

"Feels good, right?" the man asked.

Lukasz finally understood what the men had been talking about in the locker room. He stuck his hand out. "Lukasz Musial. Just off the train."

"Mark Lisowski, blacksmith. From Warsaw. You're country, though, right? I can hear it in your voice." He cracked a hardboiled egg and slid two over for Lukasz.

Lukasz cracked the shell, but he was already signaling for another boilermaker. He'd never had a drink like that, but in having just one, he knew it wouldn't be his last.

They talked as the volume in the bar rose, the patrons growing joyous with laughter. A lightness filled the space. English, Polish, Italian, Czech, and every Slavic dialect slid past Lukasz's ears, as faces with easy smiles and contentment brought on by hard work and cold cash came and went. In that moment, he felt his place in Donora, in America.

But as the day went on, the cheerfulness was punctuated with flaring tempers. Fists flew for stupid reasons—one man bumping another, neighbors bickering over placement of a fence. The bar earned its name over and over, as patrons were reduced mindless, pummeling fists, bloody noses and split lips. The whisking, rhythmic sweep of brooms sent reddened sawdust into dustpans narrating the action.

In just the right corner of the bar, Lukasz wasn't subjected to any jostling or arguments. He and Mark talked for hours about their lives back home—Mark in a city, Lukasz in the countryside, the mermaid tales born of each place.

Lukasz signaled for another boilermaker, his body swelling with good drink and a great high. "A home. That's what I want. And then a wife." He was surprised that his thoughts came out of his mouth, loosened by the drinks like the soot in his chest.

"Ah, a wife." Mark tinked his glass against Lukasz's.

Thinking of the Kowalks made Lukasz lonely for a woman, but he needed something more than wire animals or a handsome handkerchief to offer a wife. He reached into his coat pocket and ran his fingers over the wire that he'd shaped into a bear.

"Look here," Mark said, pointing out the newspaper listings for homes and property for sale. He'd been in Donora since it had been incorporated in 1901 and was accustomed to reading the paper each day.

"If only I could buy a house with this." Lukasz pulled out the wire bear to show Mark.

"Well, look at that." Mark took the bear and studied it as Lukasz ordered another drink. Seeing a fellow craftsman like Mark admire it made him smile.

Lukasz couldn't have pinpointed the exact time he and Mark left the bar and took to the Donora hills, but they wound upward arm in arm, singing "When You Go to the Field," content at having left their homeland and its skeleton of an existence but lamenting its wide blue skies and open land.

**

When Lukasz woke the next day, his mouth was dry like cotton, his tongue thick and his throat scratchy. He opened his eyes and stared at a low wood-planked ceiling, unsure of where he was or how he got there. He felt beside him. A cot, some canvas cradling his aching muscles. The tinking of a hammer on metal. The sound brought familiarity and melancholy, and the scent of fire and metal lured him into consciousness.

The headache brought the memory of the night before—the money envelope, the Bucket of Blood, the drinking. He sat up and rubbed his eyes. He remembered Nathan meeting him and taking a dollar. He reached into his pocket for the rest of his pay. Nothing. He stood and pulled out the pocket linings. A penny flopped onto the dirt floor.

He reached for it and stumbled to his knees. He scraped at the dirt floor for the penny, his fingers barely working. A tug came inside him. It took him a moment to identify the sensation. Failure. He thought of Nathan. Lukasz had been angry that someone younger had treated him as a child, yet here he was on a dirt floor with one penny. One. His entire pay gone but for a penny.

"I can feel your head's thumping like it's my own."

Lukasz startled, looked up. Mark the blacksmith nodded from across the room. Lukasz got up, then collapsed back onto the cot. Drinking. Deep into night?

"How're you so spry?" Lukasz squinted at the window half-covered by a curtain. "It's morning?"

Mark turned with his pliers, the prongs holding red-hot, half-shaped metal. "Oh, it's morning, Musial. And I don't drink booze. Ever."

Lukasz drew back and rubbed his eyes. Hadn't he suggested Lukasz have a boilermaker? "But you were at the bar. Drinking."

The blacksmith went to the corner of the foundry and kicked a wooden box toward Lukasz. "I was visiting. Tired of arguing with my lazy son-in-law. I went out in search of peace and quiet."

Lukasz got up on his elbow, looking at the box. "Your house must be noisy if you found peace at the bloody bar."

"You have no idea," Mark said, pounding away. He shoved a box toward the cot. "It's wire. Make me an animal. Like the bear."

Lukasz shook his head. Had he told him about the animals he made?

Mark scooped something off his workbench and held up a wire shape. Lukasz squinted, realizing it was the bear.

"There's a bunch of enamel too, like you said you used back home."

Lukasz rooted through the box, shoved some wire aside, and picked up a glass jar with enamel powder in it.

"Have no idea what colors they are," Mark said. "Someone traded me enamel for horseshoes. Been sitting there for years."

"I don't remember half the day," Lukasz said.

"You were talkative. Mermaid dreams," Mark said. "How you saw the Wisla Mermaid in your Wisloka River the night you won the contest for the ticket to come here."

Lukasz jerked back, feeling embarrassed, not remembering, not believing he'd disclose such a thing to a stranger. "Oh no."

"And about Waldemar and . . . well, any time you want to set about making your wire animals, if I'm not working and my cheap-ass brother isn't staying here on the cot, you can use the shed."

"Thank you." Lukasz was grateful, but his face flooded with heat, embarrassed by what he'd disclosed.

"Warsaw has its own mermaids, remember," Mark said, banging away on his anvil. "I know exactly what those dreams are like. I may have had a water woman or two spur me on to America, way back when."

Lukasz let out a little laugh, relieved that Mark was easing his sense of foolishness. The blacksmith understood, as crazy as it was. Mark pointed his mallet at Lukasz. "But keep this in mind—Americans are doers. No mermaid tales or firebird stories, just people working their asses off, hoping for a few minutes' warmth in a house they can call their own. A wife and children. All I ever wanted. Kowalks are good people. Treat them well. Stay out of the bars. Work hard."

Mark went to the window and threw the curtain back, light splashing in. "Come see."

Lukasz squinted as he trudged to the window. Mark pointed. "Through those trees. See that roofline? That's my house. Seven rooms. Too many souls inside it, but it's mine, and my family is warm. We eat meat, we live well. You can have that too."

Lukasz rubbed his bicep where it ached from his work, remembering the smiling faces on his superiors. Then it hit him—he'd missed his shift—there was rarely a day off and it would look horrible that he'd been absent after such a glorious start. His breath caught, and he backed away, searching the room for his trousers and shirt. How could he ever explain to his superiors that it was a mistake?

Mark gripped Lukasz's arm.

"They'll fire me."

"I took care of it."

Lukasz winced. "How?"

Mark shook his head. "That's a story for another day."

Failure. Lukasz spent his pay and missed a shift.

"Work's everything," Mark said. "They're expecting you for night shift instead."

Lukasz exhaled deeply, shame coursing through him.

He'd been given so much by the Kowalks and Mark. He would never drink again, not like that. Hard work and strength were all he needed to make a life in America. That was possible, and he would make his people proud.

Chapter 22

Patryk, Owen, and Lucy

2019

Patryk woke after his late-morning snooze and joined Owen and Lucy in the kitchen for lunch. He shook a bag of meat at Lucy. "You tossed aht the good ham?"

"Expired by days, Grandpa," Lucy said, spreading mayonnaise on his bread.

"Still good," he growled. "Keeps for a week past the date."

She shook her head.

Owen opened an Iron City for Patryk. "Smelled funny, Gramps. It really did."

Patryk grumbled but joined Owen at the table, taking his place in front of the book.

The phone rang and Lucy answered it while Patryk sipped his beer and ran his finger down a page in the book. "Kept reading, did yinz guys?"

"We did," Owen said.

As Patryk looked at the book and read the page, the tension in his shoulders dissolved and the tendon in his neck receded. He snickered. "Shrove Tuesday and Lent. Oh boy. It's been a long time since I've had a lucky almond paczki."

"A what?"

"You never had paczki?"

Owen shook his head.

"You've missed aht, son."

Lucy's voice grew louder, drawing Owen's attention to her phone conversation. "No. He's fine for the moment, Shelley," she said, turning toward the window and looping the telephone cord around her fingers.

"I'll handle it tomorrow. It's been crazy . . ." She rubbed the back of her neck and Owen knew his aunt must've been screaming at his mother for not having gotten Grandpa to the nursing home for his appointment.

"I can handle it, and it's fine. I'm the one with the nursing degree. Not you."

There was a pause as Lucy listened to her sister.

"Well, you might have all the money in the world, but you're a big asshole."

Patryk's eyes went wide and he elbowed Owen. "Your mom's got some fire in her. Just glad she's aiming it at someone other than me for once."

Owen scoffed. "No kidding."

Lucy slammed the phone down, then finished the sandwich she was making and opened a bag of Doritos. She carried it all to the table along with an Iron City. She popped the lid off with the edge of the table, shocking Owen and making Patryk belly laugh. "I forgot that you were quite the drinker as a kid, weren't you?"

She tipped her bottle at him. "That's not a story for today."

"I'll give you all my money if you keep your sisters and brothers ahta my business," Patryk said.

Lucy nodded. "Thank you, Grandpa. That's really sweet."

Owen knew Patryk had nothing but the house and social security. Profits from the house would be turned over to the nursing home once it sold, and there'd be nothing to leave anyone.

She pointed at the book. "Paczki. You were saying? Haven't had it in years."

"At least you've had it," Patryk said. "The kid here doesn't even know what it is. Falling down on the job, are you, Mother?"

Lucy chuckled. That was the least of her failures.

"So tell me," Owen said, pointing to the book. "What's this paczki business?"

Patryk took a swig of beer and Lucy got up and retrieved her blood pressure cuff from her bag. Patryk flinched.

"Come on. If I'm going to claim you're all right, I need to be sure I'm not lying."

Patryk stuck his arm out and sighed. "Well, paczki comes with Shrove Tuesday and Lent."

"I know what Lent is," Owen scowled.

"Well, you get an A for the day," Patryk said.

"Thanks," Owen said playfully.

"So," Patryk poked at the book. "Shrove Thursday until Shrove Tuesday was the time all the wives in town took to empty their kitchens of all the delectable ingredients not allowed during Lent. But in Poland and in Donora, really, Shrovetide was much too much like Lent itself—devoid of meat, butter, eggs, and sweets."

Patryk studied the page in front of him, tracing the drawings of baked goods and a large family gathered around a table. "Shrove Thursday had meant crepe pancakes in the Kowalk home, but even Zofia hadn't enough excess fats and meats in the house to eat extravagantly for six days. One big day, Shrove Tuesday, would be enough."

He winked at Owen. "Mouth's watering just thinking of the food."

Owen looked at his mother. "What kind of mothering have you been doing? Feeding me all that rabbit food and protein shakes?"

Lucy wrote down some numbers from taking Patryk's blood pressure and pointed her pen at her son. "You just pipe down, Owen. Maybe I'll make some paczki while we're here. If you behave."

"And the eggs!" Patryk's face lit up.

"Love me some eggs," Owen said.

Patryk waved. "No, no, not that kind. We have to find the ones your great-grandmother made. I forgot all about them." He started to stand, but Lucy put her hand on his shoulder.

"Tell us the story first, then we'll find the eggs when it's a little cooler. It's an oven in here."

Patryk nodded and squeezed Lucy's hand. "Thank you. I mean it. I'm leaving you everything."

Owen smacked his hands together and rubbed them. "Tell me about the paczki, Gramps."

And he did.

Chapter 23

Lukasz

On Tuesday, February 8th, Lukasz finished his night turn, satisfied. Trudging home, he kept his gaze upward, passing by taverns dotting his path back to the Kowalk home, waving to new friends who beckoned for him to join them for breakfast and beer at the Bucket of Blood. Lukasz doffed his hat, reminding himself that his goal to buy a home was more important that a few hours of joviality, and was certainly not worth a blackout and the loss of a day's pay or possibly his job. Great favors had been done for Lukasz, and he held them dear. He was indebted to Alexander Kowalk, who Lukasz would finally meet that morning after they had missed each other over the course of the first six days he'd been in Donora.

And Lukasz was indebted to Mark the blacksmith, who had soothed the angry foremen and managers with a reduction in horseshoe costs and the promise of fixing their wives' broken umbrellas for free. That job was given to Lukasz to attend to when he wasn't working at the mill.

Lukasz was ready to clean up and get some sleep, but when he entered the Kowalk home, the scent of fried dough filled the air. The four Kowalk girls, Judyta, Ewelina, Janina, and Sasha, were there with aprons on, bustling to and from the eating area. Lukasz scratched his head. Judyta pulled him by the hand. She showed him that there'd been extra tables added onto the main one, placed end to end from the kitchen into the family space that led to the window that overlooked the mill.

Lukasz shook his head.

"Shrove Tuesday!" Judyta said, making her sisters squeal with delight as they spread three runners down the middle of the tables, creating a celebratory mood so early in the day. Red, gold, and black-striped linen and wool runners with beige fringes ran down each side. Extra lanterns had been lit, placed on the runners and around the entire space, creating a golden embrace that reflected the love he felt among the Kowalk family.

"*Serwietka.*" Zofia latched her arm through Lukasz's. "My mother made the runners for Alexander and me when we got married. We use them every Shrove Tuesday." The girls swept past them, bubbling and chattering. Lukasz had never seen them so excited.

"The boys are off getting water. With you and Alexander on night shift, we thought we'd begin the day with a fine Shrove meal. We'll have leftovers the rest of the day."

Judyta lifted a plate of paczki under Lukasz's nose. His mouth watered as though he'd never had a meal in his life.

The fat donuts were rolled in sugar. Zofia described what was hidden inside them. "Bacon, marmalade, and almond paste."

Lukasz bit one in half. Thick almond filling spilled into his mouth.

Zofia patted his back. "Ah, the almond paste. More good luck for you this year."

Lukasz could have shoveled the whole plate into his mouth.

Movement off to the side made them all turn. A man filled the doorway, his blond hair wet and slicked back. The younger girls raced to him and leapt into his arms. He nuzzled them and sent them back to work. He held out his hand to Lukasz. "I'm Alexander."

Lukasz wiped his hand on his pants, realizing he still needed to wash up from his shift, and shook Alexander's hand. "Thank you for allowing me to board in your home. Thank you for this priceless opportunity."

Alexander looked Lukasz up and down and nodded. "Vodka, Lukasz. Lent begins tomorrow, and we don't want it tempting us once we start down the road to Easter, do we?"

Lukasz nodded but reminded himself of Friday night when he had lost his pay except for a penny. Alexander filled and lifted a tiny glass to Lukasz. He almost declined it but remembered Mark's words: *Stay out of the bars.* He didn't suggest not drinking at home.

"Not a teetotaler, are you?"

It would be an insult to decline, so Lukasz took the glass.

"We wanted to cook outside over the fire, but the ice is too thick, the hill too steep. We'd all end up tumbling down the hillside onto Thompson Avenue."

Lukasz laughed and remembered he'd made something for Zofia. He downed the shot, then reached into his pocket and pulled out the enameled pig he'd made her as a thank you and to celebrate Shrovetide. He'd worked on it every free moment since Mark had offered him the space in his forge.

He held it out to her. Lukasz's stomach dropped suddenly, remembering the way Petra had reacted to the gift he'd made her. It had been a long time since he made a gift for someone. He was queasy at the thought of how Zofia might react.

She took it and ran her raw, reddened fingertips over the smooth pink enamel. Lukasz studied her face for a sign of what she thought. She turned up the wick on the lantern on the countertop and held the pig into the light.

Lukasz watched a smile come to Zofia. "It symbolizes good luck and also the sacrifice of Lent because it's—"

"A pig," Zofia said, her voice soft and full of wonder. "How on earth did you pay for this?"

"I didn't," Lukasz said. "I made it."

"Made it?"

"At Mark Lisowski's," Lukasz said.

"The blacksmith down the way," Zofia said, still marveling at the object, filling Lukasz with pride.

"He's allowed me to work in his forge when I have the time."

"Thank you, Lukasz." She set it on the windowsill and patted its back. "I really love it."

"Thank you for letting me stay until I am on my own. Soon, I hope to be out of your hair."

"Yes, that. Well, we need to talk about that. You see, there's a woman, Aneta's her name—"

Nathan and his brothers tumbled in the front door, sloshing water. Zofia moved like a cat toward them, giving Bart a smack on the bottom. "Get that water to the stove then fetch the shirt I made for Lukasz."

The boys scrambled off, quieter. Zofia exhaled and rubbed her stomach, bending forward. She drew deep breaths, and Lukasz could see she was attempting to control her anger.

Bart reappeared with a shirt and handed it to Zofia. She took it from him and shooed everyone away. "We need privacy," she said.

Lukasz moved toward the cellar. Alexander stepped in front of him. "Stay."

Lukasz's throat tightened. He was worried but not sure why.

Alexander took the shirt from Zofia and held it up. "My wife made you this. She saw your shirt was singed from the blast furnace. That one will be your work shirt. Your extra one you brought can be for after work, and this will be for Sunday church."

Lukasz felt like a child but appreciated the new clothing. "Thank you, Zofia. It's a fine shirt. I'll pay you on Friday."

"It's a gift, Lukasz. We welcome you as family," she said, looking away as though embarrassed.

Alexander crossed his arms. "But no more of what happened Friday. No bars. Missing shifts."

"Next comes gambling and then . . ." Zofia's voice cracked.

He'd been worrying that they knew about his Friday night festivities.

"It takes fifteen dollars to keep this family each week," Zofia said. "We scrimp to save to add onto the house. We want to keep you, Lukasz, but you can't miss a shift for any reason. It will embarrass us and make it impossible for you to get a job."

Alexander poured another shot and held it out for Lukasz, confusing him. Was it a test? Lukasz shook his head.

"Drink at home, and you'll never drink too much," Alexander said. "Take it."

Lukasz thanked him. They held the glasses up.

Zofia patted Lukasz's arm. "Let's enjoy the last of these delectable paczki, then stuff ourselves to bursting with sausage."

"*Twoje zdrowie*," Alexander said, tossing back his shot.

Lukasz followed suit, the sensation instantly going to his head.

And with that, the Kowalk children pounced on the plate of sweets on the countertop, licking fingers and emptying the plate.

Zofia shook her head and seemed to right herself again as little Witold wiggled around, waiting for another paczki. "Judyta, use the big biscuit cutter for the final batch. Lukasz deserves something worthy of the wonderful gift he brought—blue skies and lucky pigs! Lukasz, go clean up and put on your new shirt."

"It's for Sunday," Lukasz said.

"Today's special too," Zofia said.

Lukasz glanced at the rest of the family, all dressed in their regular clothes, but he was not about to argue with his kind sponsors and did exactly as he was told.

**

Once Lukasz was clean, dressed, and back in the kitchen, Zofia gestured to her boys to sit at particular seats and the girls to load up the smaller platters and set them along the runner between the lanterns. Next, the girls pulled the remaining mismatched chairs up to the table, between the boys. Lukasz was seated to the left of Alexander, who sat at the head of the table.

Zofia sat to Alexander's right, near the large serving platter full of sausage and pierogi.

"You like your work, Lukasz?" Alexander asked. Lukasz listened to his tone to see if he was punishing him with his questions or threatening him, but the question was asked with curiosity only.

"Yes, yes. I could do another shift if they'd let me. I'm doing some work for Mark repairing umbrellas." He didn't add that it was penance for causing Mark to use up a favor in the mill to save Lukasz's job.

Alexander nodded. "Good. Good to make connections early on."

Zofia filled Alexander's plate to overflowing, then Lukasz's, moving to each child according to age, giving the boys bigger portions though they were younger than some of the sisters. The children squawked and shouted, mouths running like crosstown trains, ramming through Lukasz's head with a throb he couldn't remember having at home. Perhaps he did miss those things—his own cot, flimsy as it had been, open sky, and fresh air.

Working night turn meant he could have the bed to himself instead of having to suffer the boys' feet kicking at him, arms flopping over his head, but that day, Lukasz realized, they were taking the day off school.

Alexander shoveled sausage into his mouth, groaning. At first Lukasz thought something was wrong, but between his swallows and moaning, Lukasz realized the way Alexander shut his eyes and smiled meant that he was expressing pleasure. "Oh my, Zof, this is so good. Your cooking is heaven on earth."

The rest of the kids did the same, making Lukasz think he should moan with food ecstasy as well, but he just quietly savored his meal instead. Alexander finished one plateful before Lukasz consumed one sausage.

Alexander pushed his plate aside and leaned on the table, hands clasped. "We have news."

Lukasz loved that they spoke Polish at home and he didn't have to search for the correct translation for every single word as he did at work and even in the bar. With his fork, he spread the onions and melted butter on his pierogi.

Zofia pointed her fork at her husband. "Confessions first."

Alexander's expression looked coy. "We need to explain about Aneta."

Zofia glanced at Lukasz. "Absolve, shrive first."

"What if I promise to see Father Burak tomorrow?" Alexander asked. "After I get my ashes."

"I'd say you'll have the burden of another sin to confess."

He tapped his empty vodka glass on the table. Lukasz held his breath, waiting for Alexander to explode at his wife for sassing him in front of others. But instead of reddening with ire, his eyes glistened, and a mischievous smile warmed his expression.

Lukasz exhaled, and so did everyone else.

"Well, dearest Zofia, you are indeed correct."

"So." Zofia rubbed her fingertips together. "Time to pardon. Time to let go of grudges."

The children started barking at one another, Raymond rising out of his chair and taking Nathan by the shirt collar.

Alexander groaned and poured more vodka into his glass and Lukasz's.

Zofia smacked her hands together. "*Zamknij się.*"

The kids froze, then moved back into their seats, quiet.

Zofia signaled to Nathan. "One at a time."

Nathan looked up, then leveled his gaze on Judyta. "I forgive you for taking the last apple yesterday."

Judyta narrowed her eyes on Nathan. She spoke through bared teeth. "I was going to absolve *you* for that."

He shook his head and shrugged.

They looked around the room, eyes searching, accusing each child at the table.

Slowly, a hand at the end of the table rose, and everyone turned to see Zofia reaching upward.

"Mama? You never take the last of anything," Judyta said.

Zofia shifted in her seat. "Well, it wasn't me. Not for me. Not really."

Mumbles and confused expressions were passed.

"On account of the baby, it wasn't really for me." Everyone looked at Witold, the youngest boy, the baby of the family who still slept in his parents' room. "Not Witold." She leaned back in her seat. "I suppose I didn't really take the last apple." She patted her belly. "She did."

Everyone's eyes scanned downward to where her belly would be if not for it being hidden behind the table.

Alexander growled, his face hardened as it had been when he had given Lukasz his earlier warning about missing work. He took Lukasz's full vodka and threw it back. The tension in the room rose, tightening the air as though there was a limit on who could breathe it. "Holy hell." He pointed the glass at Zofia. "I shrive you for this."

She pursed her lips, and her eyes flamed with anger. "I shrive you, Mr. Kowalk, for saying such a thing. You are quite the—"

She glanced at Lukasz, and he could see she wanted to say something that wasn't meant for anyone's ears but her husband's.

Alexander reached across the table and clamped on Zofia's hand. Lukasz braced for an outburst.

Alexander pushed away from the table and went behind Zofia. "Happy man." He wrapped his arms around Zofia from behind and nuzzled her cheek. "I'm the happiest man I know."

She relaxed, fastening her arms around his, leaning back into his embrace. She closed her eyes. "We're blessed," she said, barely above a whisper.

Lukasz added his congratulations to the children's cheers.

Alexander straightened, keeping one hand on Zofia's shoulder. "This makes our news even more important, doesn't it?"

He grabbed the vodka bottle and topped off Lukasz's glass. "Aneta Wasco's been left at the altar."

Lukasz took a bite of sausage, the rosemary-infused meat melting in his mouth like the paczki had. Lukasz saw everyone staring at him and realized they wanted him to say something, to be part of the conversation.

"That's sad," he said, still not used to anyone expecting him to participate in so much chatter at every single dinner. He dug into the pierogi, savoring it.

"She's *free*," Alexander said. "And she arrived in Donora just the other night."

The emphasis Alexander put on the word "free" made Lukasz look up from his meal, all eyes on him again. He was confused but understood they wanted him to care about this development. Perhaps she was their relative?

"Send her almond-pasted paczki," Lukasz said, lightening his voice, taking a chance with humor. "For good luck!"

Zofia glanced at Alexander. Lukasz sighed, rushing into his next bite, wanting to end the conversation, get some sleep, then head over to Mark's to repair umbrellas and make more wire animals.

"We've sent word to Aneta's parents back in Poland that *you're* free as well," Alexander said.

Lukasz stopped midchew, his eyes settling on Nathan. Did they mean *him*? He was just twelve or thirteen. They couldn't mean him.

A knock came at the door and Zofia rushed away.

Lukasz exhaled, relieved to have the conversation end.

**

Zofia returned, her arm roped around the shoulders of a young woman. She was blonde, her golden braids bundled at the nape of her neck. Her cheeks were rosy and her lips plump, a perfect V at the center of her upper lip. Her doll-like face enchanted Lukasz. Her petite, shapely curves added to her allure.

"Lukasz, meet Aneta Wasco," Zofia said. "She arrived the other day, from just down the Wisloka from our village."

Lukasz set his fork down. This Aneta had been mentioned for him, he realized. He'd seen that look before when a match was made—the matchmakers so full of hope that they'd selected correctly. But the Kowalks hadn't known him. He and Aneta could not be a proper match. Still, he knew his role in this. He stood and approached the woman, hand out.

Her slender hand disappeared in his. She was tiny, barely five feet. Lukasz felt massive in her presence, and the sense of feeling big softened his irritation toward the Kowalks for arranging for him to meet her without warning. He had nothing to offer yet. Maybe once he had a home that needed a woman's touch, he'd consider a match.

Aneta looked at Zofia. "I thought his name was Waldemar, that he was . . ."

At the mention of Waldemar's name, the idea it was *he* who was originally meant to arrive in Donora took hold. Looking at Aneta, her hand inside his, he was struck by the notion that Alexander had said she'd been left at the altar. He couldn't fathom how on earth that was possible, not someone so beautiful. He wondered what she'd been told about Waldemar.

Alexander cleared his throat. "Well, ahem. Lukasz here bested Waldemar after the initial contest. There was a second contest, and . . . well, here he is."

"Yes," Aneta said. "Here he is."

Aneta's eyes watered. Her lips quivered. Little Sasha pushed out of her chair and ran to Aneta, who dropped to her knees. Sasha caressed Aneta's intricate braids. "*Piękny,*" she said.

"Thank you," Aneta said quietly. She swept her hand over Sasha's hair. "Yours is beautiful too."

This made Lukasz smile. Sasha's hair looked as if rats had been nesting in it.

Alexander nudged Janina out of her chair to seat Aneta beside Lukasz. Zofia heaped Aneta's plate with sausage and pierogi. This told Lukasz that they were attempting to impress her.

We've told her parents you're free too.

If Lukasz had conjured up a woman to marry, she would have looked exactly like Aneta, but he couldn't shake the anxiety that knotted his belly. Her arm brushed his as she reached for her glass. Lukasz tried to eat, but he lost his appetite as the Kowalks attempted to connect Lukasz's life to Aneta's in every way imaginable.

A heaviness formed in his chest, as if an anvil had been placed there. He had nothing to offer. Especially to someone as beautiful as Aneta.

Little Raymond bounced in his chair. "Tell her how Lukasz won his job!"

Alexander took a piece of sausage from his wife's plate, ate it, and leaned on the table, plucking at his shirt buttons. "Tossed two dozen hundred-pound bundles right into the back of the truck like they were feather pillows. I recall your father was once a champion ax thrower, Aneta. Strength grows on both sides of the Wisloka River. Look at this man."

Aneta blushed. Lukasz's cheeks burned.

Zofia took her husband's plate and brought it back full of meat. She touched his shoulder, her thumb caressing the seam.

Witold announced he needed a trip to the outhouse. Zofia got his coat and ordered Judyta to take him then she returned to the conversation. "Lukasz's strong as steel, Aneta, but look at what else he can do."

Zofia set the wire pig in Aneta's palm.

She studied it, her long brown eyelashes blinking. "Very sweet."

Lukasz's heart stopped, realizing that Aneta liked what she saw.

Aneta handed the pig back and Zofia held it up, examining it. "Heaven-sent." She set it beside her plate, smiling. "I'd like an entire set of animals from Lukasz. A miniature circus train."

Lukasz smiled, heat rising from under his collar into his cheeks. He sensed Aneta staring at him and he turned to her. Her bright blue eyes—almond shaped, wide set, probing—made his stomach flip with excitement. Any sense of dread dissolved.

He nearly laughed out loud.

Blue almonds. Adam had insisted they didn't exist. Perhaps the old Polish phrase led him to something, someone, as real as Lukasz himself. His mind whirled. His American dream had a name. He didn't just want a warm home to call his own; he wanted a cozy home for Aneta.

"You'll see someday, Aneta. The smallest gestures can get you through the day," Zofia said.

"A sturdy home. That's what matters," Alexander said. "Lukasz here got hired into the mill the first day he tried. He's here. He's free." He held up his glass. "To freedom. To America."

Everyone raised their glasses and even the children cheered, "America! Home of the free. Home of the brave."

Aneta lifted her glass. "To a grand future."

"And love," Zofia said, nodding at Aneta then at Lukasz.

Aneta broke into a large grin and Lukasz saw a bit of life behind her eyes like when she had knelt down to talk to Sasha. He remembered again that Aneta'd been left at the altar. He wondered when it had happened. Aneta radiated a mix of sadness and frailty that made him want to know her.

A flutter came inside Lukasz again. The lantern bathed Aneta in golden light, making her appear angelic. This pretty woman beside him had been offered as a match. Well, at least she'd been offered to Waldemar. She'd been expecting the handsome bear, and that unsettled him, making him forget his own strength. He concentrated on Alexander's praise and vowed again to make his Polish compatriots proud.

Chapter 24

Mary

Each pull on the oars propelled Mary over the dark Monongahela water, giving her the chance to consider Samuel. She'd known for a while he was a terrible dancer. But standing with him lent her a daintiness no other boy provided. But there was his awkward kissing. That kept coming to mind, making her question if the clumsiness was her fault or his. She had plenty of evidence she was a good dancer, but what if she was the lousy kisser not Samuel? Even with the kissing matter, she had to admit something lured her to him, something made her bake extra loaves of bread for him and hide them from her mother.

Earlier that day, with the extra dough, Mary had made two smaller loaves to take to Samuel at the library, where he'd be studying. She had spread generous amounts of butter on them and dusted them with sugar and cinnamon. *That's* what it was—it was the idea of a home with someone like Samuel that attracted her, no matter how he kissed.

She pulled and released the oars, adjusting her angle instinctively as the current attempted to take her off course.

The fiery blast furnace shot up the sky. There was beauty in the harsh work done in the mill.

Though she yearned for a lemon-scented life, for a white-shirted husband who worked in management, she admired the men who worked on the floor. Every time she took a lunch pail to Mr. Dunn, she found herself stopping to watch the men he supervised, the men who fed the steel, pulled the wire, bundled it, and loaded it. Their work was a balance of art and muscle as they coaxed scorching hot steel into the flexible wire, brawny little nails, and massive girders that helped build America.

But she was old enough to understand the layers of society in Donora. In school, the children of every nationality and financial condition blended, but at home, one family spoke Polish, another Italian or English. Even the Catholic churches revealed economic and social striations, marking their members with old-country traditions and language.

She was lucky Samuel wasn't Presbyterian, as many of the mill managers' families were. If he had been, there'd be no use in Mary even fantasizing about a life with him, no matter what her qualifications for being a wife were. He attended St. Charles Catholic Church. Mary had only glimpsed the inside of it a couple of times, and though she couldn't deny her draw to Holy Name of Blessed Virgin Mary for being her namesake, and St. Dom's for being their ethnic parish, she thought she could see her way to finding comfort in St. Charles too. That church came with the lemon-fresh life.

Monongahela waters sloshed against the boat as she dug her oar into the water to turn the boat into the dock. It bumped up against a piling, and Mary tossed the rope around it. She climbed onto the dock and started toward the shore. A man stood at the end, and even with him just being silhouetted in the dark, Mary knew the short, stout fellow wasn't her father. She drew closer and recognized him, his bright green eyes always with a smile in them.

She bit the inside of her mouth to keep from saying something sassy about her father not being there waiting. "Hello, Clyde."

Her father's dearest friend stood with his hands stuffed into his pockets. "You're mad," he said. "Your papa said you'd be."

Mary spread her arms to agree with him without losing her temper.

Clyde removed his hat. "He'll head back with Always Late Larry. But early. Just one drink to celebrate Larry's wedding. Early night, they said."

Mary laughed. "Late Larry'll bring Papa back early?"

"Said so."

She looked away, the wind grabbing her hair from its tie and whipping it across her mouth. She pushed it behind her ear and adjusted her hat. "Early this time, but never early any other, not even for his own birth? I'm supposed to sell that week-old bologna to my mother?"

Clyde clenched his teeth and scratched the back of his neck. "It's Shrove Tuesday."

She jerked her head. "My father's suddenly observant, is he?"

He shrugged. "He's not a big drinker, you know. It'll be all right."

"Why aren't you with 'im?"

"On account of my Ingrid being fast and hard with the rolling pin. I chose to forgo the merriment."

Mary punched her fists onto her hips. "On account of you being intelligent, I'd say."

"Ah, go easy, Mary. Yer pop's blowing off steam. Working bent and black-dusted in the mine for pennies requires it. You know."

She sighed. "Matka works bent and sore and tired too." She started back down the dock, angered at the waste of time, knowing Matka wouldn't accept the excuse.

"Wait," Clyde said.

Mary turned.

Clyde held something out. "He gave me this, though. Said yinz had trouble with the roof."

She went back. Dollar bills.

"Wanted to be sure you got this to his Susan."

Mary held her hand out. Clyde placed the money in her palm, his crooked, coal-black fingers petting the money, then closing her fingers around it.

"There's three. Kept just one out for the party," he said.

The anger Matka was going to feel swept through Mary. Her father should be returning home with the whole four dollars. Matka didn't get breaks or parties with lady friends. Work, work, work for her. Yet Papa seemed to have reasons to take a break in the company of others more than a few times a month.

She considered the one dollar she'd been given for a month's worth of work at the Dunns'. She'd spent a portion of it on extra flour to make the loaves for Samuel. She thought also of the pennies and dimes she'd hidden in the fireplace as part of her dowry.

She'd give that to her mother to help make up for this, but that would only soothe her so much. Her husband was out gallivanting, maybe getting into fights with the rest of those crooked-backed, coal-mining drunks, getting so overdone with liquor that he might miss work or come home fuming, tossing things around like chairs were made of nothing but cobwebs.

She understood Matka's concern. They had to pay someone on credit to fix the roof, and she wanted to pay it back before interest was due. With Papa's bad lungs, he couldn't afford to get lost in a bottle. Every single time he had even a few drinks, it stirred up a cough that rattled him for days, turning him gray. The layers of trouble that came with the bottle were overwhelming.

Mary could borrow from her stash behind the fireplace bricks and soothe her mother with that, but she didn't dare touch it. Once she started spending that money, she wouldn't stop until it was gone, and then she'd never be free. She'd seen that happen to many people, both with drink and money.

Once they got a little drink in them or once a woman's hand was inside her purse, they just consumed and spent like the world was coming to an end.

"Thanks, Clyde." Mary held up the money before shoving it into the deep pocket of her work dress. "Appreciate you meeting me like this."

"Just lookin' out," he said as he started up the hill, his misshapen hand pushed into the air to wave goodbye.

**

From inside the boat, Mary lifted the rope off the piling and started back across the river, furious. Not because her father was spending this evening with his soon-to-be married friend on Shrove Tuesday when everyone was busy emptying their vodka, beer, and whiskey for Lent, but because of the time she had wasted coming to fetch him.

She splashed the oars into the water, pulling back so hard that she thought she might make it back to the Donora side of the Mon in just ten strokes.

Between strokes she shouted, "I. Will. Never. Live. Like. This." Somewhere in the middle, she stopped rowing, exhausted. "I can't live with a man like him. Not ever," she whispered. She wanted the words back. Her throat tightened. Ashamed, she worried her words would waft on the wind, float along the Webster flats and find her papa's ears. It hurt that she thought such things, that her father had given her reason to. She wanted to make a family completely different from the one that lived on Marelda, the one that made her say awful things, then feel disgusted for saying them. She thought of Samuel—the clumsy dancing, the sloppy kissing. She could teach him to be better. She was sure of it.

She stood and spread her arms wide, head back. The clouds shifted to reveal a crescent moon. Pink. It was unusual to see it so clearly, and certainly unusual to see it pink. She could feel the moon rays hit her skin like sunshine. She'd seen pink moons every so often when the mill flames and moonlight mixed just right, but usually in summer. She wished

Papa was there to see it. "God, please watch me, listen to me. Hail Mary, full of grace, listen close. Mother Mary, all of you. Please let there be more in store for me than this. More. Please don't forget me. Please let my name mean something important."

The wash of machinery noise created what she thought of as silence. What was she thinking? God was listening to a girl in a boat under a pink crescent moon? A bout of laughter rose up and out of her at the insanity of her prayer. Certainly there were more important blessings for the Virgin Mother to grant than what Mary requested.

She sat down and rowed again, smoother, calmed by what she felt was Holy Mary's grace raining in the form of pink moon rays.

As she neared shore, she stopped rowing. She wanted to see Samuel's face light up when she gave him the bread, but dreaded the turmoil that would result from telling her mother that Papa wasn't coming home.

When would he be home? *Early.* Mary's mother would scoff and maybe throw something across the kitchen. The boat bobbed, the current splashing against the wood. Cradled in the river's lap, she enjoyed the peaceful moment. She looked at the crystal-pink moon again, clouds and smoke careening toward it.

She stood for the second time that night, removing her hat and hair tie to let the wind blow through her locks. Arms wide, head back, she inhaled deeply, pink moonlight bathing her as the boat bobbed and turned, free of her guiding oars.

More reluctant than ever to return to her mother, Mary lay back in the boat, dangling her fingers over the sides. Frigid water bit her fingertips. She didn't care that she was floating past Gilmore Docks, the current having its way with her.

She sang "Ave Maria" and dreamed of a clean home, just a small one, imagining every surface sparkling. She didn't need a mansion like Mrs. Dunn's, just a little home that she could keep spick-and-span, one that would house a little family with lots of love.

Chapter 25

Lukasz

It all made sense—the whispers and half-started conversations, the new shirt Zofia had made for him and insisted he wear for breakfast even though she intended it for Sunday best. Lukasz pulled his hat down over his ears. He fastened the top button on his coat collar as the chilled air ran over the Monongahela River, up the bank, and through his clothes, sinking into his skin. Still a little drunk from Shrove Tuesday drinking with Alexander, Lukasz had taken a nap, then decided fresh air would sober him up before heading to the night shift. Standing on the bank above the river, he thought of Aneta, her tiny hand soft and fragile in his when they were introduced.

She was a beauty, but the sadness behind her crystal-blue eyes piqued his curiosity. Seeing Aneta with the Kowalk children—her natural way with them, their instant affection for her—made him want her to like him. He was taken aback by the idea he'd been matched to someone unbeknownst to him, and that Aneta had been expecting Waldemar. Her reaction to Lukasz had betrayed disappointment though she had quickly covered it up. He would prove himself to her, to the Kowalks, and to Mark.

Things were making sense for Lukasz. The cacophony of Donora, an opera of every machine noise, was becoming familiar. It saddened him that he didn't recall what true silence sounded like, what it was like to not feel the vibration of nails being molded, levers pulled, and gears turned. But he absorbed it all, trading nature's silence for opportunity.

He looked skyward. The clouds were parting, and what he saw took his breath. The crescent moon shone bright, but it was pink. He blinked and stared. He'd never seen it look that way. He'd certainly noticed that the Donora moon was shy like him, usually hidden away unless the clouds, fog, and smoke parted at exactly the right time, forcing her to show herself. The crescent glinted, a star to its left twinkling. Mesmerized, he walked closer to the crest of the bank, wanting to bathe in the magical light.

Movement out in the river, partially hidden by a low, rolling fog, caught his attention. Drawn to it, he inched down the bank, closer to the shoreline. He thought he heard someone yell something. Was someone in trouble? He strained to hear.

There. The sound came again. Laughter? *Singing?* He was sure it was a woman's voice. He ran down so close to the river that water seeped into his shoes.

He squinted into the night, straining to see. The fog shifted again and a figure appeared. A woman stood atop the water, arms raised, hair blowing, basking in the moonglow. He yelled to see if the person was all right. *She* . . . it was definitely a she.

She stayed like that, the pink moon illuminating her. An angel on earth. Her arms were raised high as she slowly rotated, her profile now obscured in moon shadow. Lukasz moved closer still and yelled again, raising his hand, waving. He shook his head, trying to make sense of what he was seeing. His Wisloka Mermaid came to mind, the night she had seduced him from a frozen river. Had he passed out from drinking?

It was foggy, but not the black, smoky fog that he'd seen in town so many times since arriving. The mermaid on the river slowly lowered, disappearing into the fog that skimmed along the river surface.

He cupped his hands. "Hello!"

No response. He rubbed his eyes. She was *there*. Hadn't she been? The fog thickened, obscuring the space where he saw her go under. He went back up on the bank and got on his toes, craning. He looked behind him. Was anyone there to bear witness with him? No one. He turned back to the water. Nothing.

He shook his head, stretched one direction, then the other. He rubbed his jaw. He wasn't that drunk, not after sleeping it off and taking a walk. But no one was on the water.

He sighed and bent forward, hands on his knees. He'd sworn he'd seen the Wisla Mermaid emerging from the Wisloka waters the night of the contest, but he'd drunk a bottle of potent liquor. Was there such a thing as a mermaid of the Monongahela? He went back down toward the shoreline, hoping to peel away fog layers with nothing more than his gaze.

Nothing.

He adjusted his hat and headed up the bank toward Meldon Avenue, toward the bars. His wet feet would be dry in no time once he started work in the hot mill. He looked over his shoulder again, thinking he was going crazy.

Something about what he'd seen or had conjured was comforting. He exhaled and stopped short, looking back again. Aneta. Maybe this foggy appearance of a woman, a hazy conjuring of a mermaid all over again, was a sign that Aneta was indeed the woman for him. It was too much of a coincidence that she had arrived and then he'd seen a mermaid, the Monongahela Mermaid. His.

Aneta was certainly beautiful enough to be drawn into a storybook and have tales told about her, passed down for generations. He shoved his hands into his pockets as he passed a bar. The owner stood in the doorway with a filthy apron around his waist, grasping the doorjamb.

"Happiness is between the lips and the rim of a glass," the man said in Polish, jerking his head to invite Lukasz in.

He hesitated, looking beyond the owner to see the bar nearly empty, open seats waiting for shifts to change and tired bones to warm them. Lukasz considered heading in for a drink, but he was inspired by the mermaid, by Aneta, and by his own vow to stay out of the bars and keep any money he earned for the home he wanted, a home fit for beautiful Aneta.

"Not today," Lukasz said, and off to work he went.

Chapter 26

Mary

It wouldn't go well. Mary braced, gripping her front door's handle. She reminded herself that Samuel was waiting at the library and she wanted to surprise him with the special bread she'd baked. She would let her mother's anger rush over her, eat dinner, do her chores, and be on her way. One more deep breath before she pushed through the front door.

Two boarders, all of the children, and Matka were standing around the table, ready to sit, as though they knew the exact moment Mary and her father would come through the door.

Matka smiled, but when Mary shut the door, her mother's face hardened into a scowl. Mary swallowed hard and shook out of her coat. Guilt coursed through her. She had failed to bring her father home. Feeling her mother's anger more than usual, her breath stopped. She wasn't Papa's keeper.

Matka clenched her knife and fork as if she was about to defend her table from an intruder. The boarders looked down at their plates and the children shushed one another. Mary's heart beat heavy and fast.

Mary had always loved Shrove Tuesday supper, but now she just wanted to grab the loaves of bread she had made for Samuel and run. She surveyed the table and saw the haluski hadn't been put out. She told her mother she'd get it and strode to the kitchen. Matka came behind her and gripped her arm.

"Where's Papa?"

Mary shook free of her mother and hung her coat on a hook near the back door. She wanted to lie, to say he had taken on an extra shift.

Matka gripped the table edge. "Draining Webster of all its Shrove Tuesday vodka." Her words hit like knives.

Mary untied her hat. "He's celebrating Late Larry's engagement."

"You let him just leave?"

"He wasn't there," she said. "Clyde told me." She took off her hat.

"Put that back on."

Mary shook her head but put it back on and braced.

"We're gonna drag his ass home."

"I don't know which bar he went to," Mary said.

Matka wagged her finger. "Enough with the sass."

Mary didn't mean to sound disrespectful, but twice across the river was enough for one day. "We'll never find him."

"We'll scour every damn watering hole in Webster. We need his pay."

Mary remembered the money, went to her coat and pulled the bills from the pocket. If only she could retrieve another dollar from her hidey-hole in the fireplace . . . but that was impossible with everyone at the table. Mary held the money out to her mother. "From Papa. He barely drinks, Matka. With his lungs and all. He's just being a good pal is all."

Matka stared at the scrunched-up bills. She put one shaking hand to her forehead as though her headache was returning. "It's *not* the drinking. He'll come home sick and tired, then he'll lose shifts and . . ." She lifted her shoulders and let them drop. "We'll take in another boarder. We have to pay Mr. Alfonsi for fixing the roof. The interest he charges is criminal."

Matka snatched the money and went to the pantry, where Mary knew she was stashing the cash in an old detergent tin. "Papa's pay covers most of the mortgage, but we need more than that to keep the house and all of you."

Mary held her breath. She thought of the bread she'd hidden in the pantry for Samuel. Her mother would see it, and Mary would have to explain. She could hear her mother shuffling things around, and she kept waiting to be summoned, questioned about why she would have covered and stashed bread away from the other loaves. She heard nothing but the sound of a tin opening and closing.

Matka exited the pantry and headed toward the boot room. Mary was halfway into the pantry to check on her bread when her mother screamed her name and tossed her coat to her. "Let's go."

Mary's heart dropped. There would be no time to take her bread to Samuel that night. She was relieved her mother hadn't discovered it. She could use the bread to make it up to Samuel for not showing up at the library.

Matka strode out of the kitchen, Mary following. The scent of noodles, cabbage, and sausages made her stomach growl.

Matka shoved hat pins into place. "Ann—make up three plates when you're done. Keep the fire. Victoria—mind the boys and baby."

Ann and Victoria nodded.

Mary took a serving fork from the center of the table and stabbed a piece of sausage. The salty, herb-filled meat melted in her mouth, making her even hungrier.

"Mary." Matka opened the door, a gust of wind making the fire dance and everyone shiver.

Mary put her fork back, and that's when she saw. It couldn't be. She hadn't noticed when she first came in, but it was true.

Ann was pulling a hunk of bread from one of the loaves Mary had made for Samuel and popping it into her mouth. Mr. Cermak, the man Mary detested most in the world, took nearly half the loaf for himself and buttered it, devouring it in one chomp. Mary wanted to rip it from his filthy hands. They'd found the bread. That's why her mother wasn't angry about it. Matka thought Mary had made it for them.

Johnny jammed the special cinnamon bread down his throat, smiling, pleased with something as simple as bread. Mary's heart seized. She grabbed her skating lantern and lit it. Samuel would feel the same when he was finally the recipient of her baking. If that ever happened.

**

Mary and her mother trudged to Thirteenth Street, then took it straight down the hillside past Thompson to the stairs that led the rest of the way to Meldon.

Her mother's foot slipped at the top. "Goddamn darkness! I'm part mountain goat by now," Matka said. "Give the lantern here."

Mary passed it to her mother and followed. The fifty-degree angled stairs carved a path from Thompson to Meldon.

"Goddamn stairs," her mother said as she slipped again. "Hold this." She handed the lantern back to Mary. "Keep it high."

Mary obeyed as they headed north on Meldon to Scott, her mother breaking into a jog as they neared Gilmore Docks. With her mother's anger filling the space between them, the peace of the river was gone. Mary rowed as fast as she could, the stars and moon tucked away behind smoke and clouds.

Matka pointed toward Webster. "Straighter."

Mary didn't need rowing instructions. She fought the current and cut a clean line even with a rougher river than she'd had coming back just a half hour before.

Matka launched into a diatribe about Papa's behavior, spooling out a lifetime of grievances, saying she should have remained in Bohemia with Gustik Beranek.

Once docked in Webster and out of the boat, Matka stalked ahead, coat billowing in the wind and fog. A force. Mary could only describe her mother that way; energy blazed off her like lightning lit a sky. They stopped in three bars before someone pointed across the room.

Matka glared, breathing hard.

Papa's metallic cough came inside his raspy laugh and cut through the din. Mary smiled, but her throat was tight with sadness. She rarely heard that laugh but knew it instantly. Her mother tramped toward the sound, plowing through the men, knocking them aside like bowling pins.

Mary followed, but the horrified looks on the other miners' faces registered, and she stopped. Papa must have noticed the shift in energy in the bar. He turned, his eyes widening, his jaw slackened as his wife clinched his arm. His grin disappeared. He resisted his wife's tug.

The men watched, some whistled. "Baby needs his feeding."

"Baby needs more than that," another man said.

Mary's skin crawled, shame gathering in her belly.

Matka yanked Papa right out of his seat.

Mary stared, her breath gone and her heart seizing.

Papa was so stunned, the cigarette fell out of his mouth. It took a moment before he tore his arm away from Matka, but inside those seconds, embarrassment flooded his face, making him instantly small, weak in the shadow of his wife's fury, unrecognizable to Mary.

Her stomach clenched. The aching in her chest grew to a throb as Papa's friends turned their backs to keep from humiliating him further. Some glanced at Mary but quickly looked away as though everyone in the bar shared the shame.

Everyone but Matka.

Mary's mother squared her shoulders, dragging her woozy husband by the collar. Mary's breath quickened with her distress at seeing this unfold. Nausea came with anger, but this ire was no longer for Papa wasting her time. It was for Matka. The bar's silence choked her and she couldn't stay.

She ran all the way back to the docks and waited, pacing. She wanted to leave them there. Let them fight it out without her witnessing it. She wanted to disappear, wanted God to hide her away in a dark space beyond the clouds, between the stars.

She steadied her breath. Matka was abrupt by nature, and other than when she took a baby into her lap and got lost in a rocking motion, she was not soft.

But this.

Mary forced back rising sobs, her throat burning, her heart breaking for her papa. Matka and Papa yelled plenty at home, but Mary understood their rough words as a means of releasing anger. It was nothing like tonight, not emasculating Papa in public.

Matka's scolding voice came through the fog as they neared the dock.

Mary swallowed Papa's humiliation, hoping she had somehow managed to lift it off him. She shook her head, wanting to erase the vulnerable look on Papa's face from her mind. The recollection of his face physically hurt. Tears stung her eyes.

Papa shouldn't have gone to that celebration. He should have come home with all his pay.

Still.

Even with her own anger at him earlier, she knew then she'd *never* treat her husband or anyone like that. Ever. Mary didn't care what sins he had committed, she couldn't imagine stealing away someone's pride, ripping it from him like she ripped a quilt from her lazy sisters just to get them moving in the morning.

Did Matka love her father at all? Did she *like* him? Did she like anyone? As her parents emerged through the fog, she saw Matka's friendless isolation, her angry existence where all she wanted was the next installment of money to fill her hand and pay the bills. Mary was sure her mother had been cut from stone rather than born of a living, breathing, loving woman. What else could explain Matka's lack of care, her lethal handling of her husband's heart? What else could possibly explain such a thing?

Chapter 27

Lukasz

The Kowalks' kitchen table was set for a simple Lenten supper, no vodka or fat donuts or rosemary sausage bursting from its skin. But there was cabbage soup, Zofia's bread, and a plain, faded-blue cotton cloth on the table. Lukasz wiped his hands on his pants and told himself not to be nervous. Even though he'd learned Aneta was descended from kings, she was still a young Polish girl born on a Wisloka River bend, not far from where he'd lived most of his life. She was more like him than not, no matter how beautiful and poised she was.

When Aneta whisked into the house in a blur of sky-blue coat and matching dress, she brightened the space, filling it with magnificent energy. Zofia pulled Aneta into her arms and kissed each cheek. Aneta nodded hello to Lukasz.

She shed her gloves and lifted her bag. "I have some things for the girls."

"Judyta! Bring the little ones. Aneta's here."

The children, giggling, scrambled to Aneta, who got down on one knee and gathered them into her arms. "You remind me of my sisters," she said.

Lukasz took it all in. He would ask about her family when they had a chance to talk.

Aneta removed a satin sack from her handbag and opened it. The little girls reached inside, each one's face brightening with delight. Dolls. They hugged them to their chests, patting their backs, smiles on their lips. They hugged Aneta before scattering away to make little beds for their new babies.

Lukasz's blood raced at the sight of Aneta's affection for the girls, for her warmth, a fount of maternity.

Aneta stood and handed Judyta folded white fabric. "My family's lacemaker created the pattern. It's enough to edge a large tablecloth for your trousseau. I'm sure you've already got quite a trove, but I thought you might like—"

Judyta threw her arms around Aneta, yanking her close. "Oh my goodness. It's gorgeous. And it's my first . . . well, this will be so special. Mama, look."

Zofia's eyes were brimming as she looked on. She studied the lace, holding her hands away from the fabric. "Hands are filthy. Wrap that in the clean sheet and stow it on the shelf in the closet high up."

Judyta nodded and rushed away.

"Thank you, Aneta. We've done well here, but a hope chest for Judyta hasn't taken precedence. I have a few things to pass on, but . . ." Her voice cracked. "Thank you."

Aneta's smile broadened and she took Zofia into her arms. "You're welcome. Mother said you'd both love it."

Lukasz hadn't thought about hope chests and trousseaus, but he could see from Judyta and Zofia's reactions that having one meant a lot, even in America. Though he'd had no idea he was to be matched with anyone when arriving in Donora, he could not think of someone else he'd consider marrying, and he imagined Aneta must have a trunk overflowing with household wares. It didn't matter that they knew little about each other. Lukasz counted himself extraordinarily lucky right then.

He took Aneta's coat, hung it on the rack, and again invited her to sit.

Zofia called the children to the table. "Alexander's working a double, so I'll keep the soup on for him," she said. Aneta offered to help Zofia, but she insisted Aneta sit beside Lukasz.

Lukasz asked her how she was.

"Good." She smiled and looked away. She rubbed her arms, antsy, as though unaccustomed to being served. Lukasz had been told she lived a comfortable life with servants until her family had lost everything two years before. Perhaps she was just shy like him. This reduced his nervousness, making him even more grateful he'd won that ticket.

The girls and Zofia set a steaming bowl of cabbage soup in front of each person and three baskets of bread in the middle of the table. Finally, Zofia sat and clasped her hands, closing her eyes and starting the Lord's Prayer. The others joined in, Lukasz too, easily reciting the centuries-old words. But he opened his eyes, and Zofia's peaceful prayerfulness struck him. The three girls had similar expressions, but the two younger boys squished their eyes shut, mumbling the prayer, appearing as though the words pained them.

Nathan was reverent, though, a good son. Lukasz hoped someday he had a boy like him.

Lukasz turned to Aneta at the same time she turned toward him. Her gaze startled him. He smiled at her, but she just turned back and closed her eyes, her long lashes wet before releasing a tear.

Lukasz wanted to wipe it away, remembering how his mother had once cried silent tears that no one else but Lukasz had noticed.

"Are you all right?" he whispered.

Zofia cleared her throat and shot a look at him. Lukasz shut his eyes and tried to be as prayerful as the rest of them. Zofia continued thanking God for their meal, the children, Mr. Dunn and especially Mr. Griffen for hiring Lukasz, and a dozen other mill managers and bosses who made mill work possible. On and on she thanked God, her words fading into the back of Lukasz's mind until he heard his name. ". . . Lukasz's match. Thank you, good Lord Almighty, for giving Aneta her earthly king."

His eyes widened, and Aneta pushed away from the table.

"Amen," Zofia said, the children providing a chorus of amens. "What's the matter?" she asked Aneta. "Soup's on."

Aneta shook her head. "Excuse me for a moment. I need to use the . . ." She dashed from the room and out the door.

Without thinking, Lukasz rushed after Aneta. Outside, the cold air struck him. Aneta stood with her arms crossed, her back to him. She was either shivering or crying. He went closer, wanting to warm her, to comfort her, but sensed her wariness. He went back inside and grabbed her coat, putting it around her shoulders.

"Thank you," she said but didn't look at him.

He wanted to tell her he knew it was hard to be here, not knowing the language, not having family and familiar friends to smooth the path.

She wiped her tears with the back of her hand. His tongue was tied with all that he wanted to say, so he simply pressed his hand between her shoulder blades. "Come inside."

She nodded and looked down. "In a moment."

Lukasz wanted to pull her back inside, to soothe her. But her steely mood backed him off.

"Tell them to eat," she said. "The children are hungry."

"Yes," he said. Again, he was taken by her concern for the children and was struck by the urge to protect her, to keep her far away from whatever it was that had put the obvious hurt behind her stunning blue eyes.

But he honored her request and returned to the dinner table. "She'll be right in."

Zofia grabbed Lukasz's hand. "I had the same nerves when I met Alexander. Now look at us. We share a fine marriage and this passel of children."

Lukasz nodded, appreciating Zofia's kindness. Imagining intimacy with Aneta excited him. He wondered if she entertained such thoughts, or at least shared the understanding that they were to be together. He spooned his soup. Did Aneta even see Lukasz as the potential father of her children?

"Don't worry, Lukasz. We promised her father a match. He promised to send her. And so it is."

Lukasz hoped Zofia was right. America was about making choices—choosing a life, a home, a wife—not following the same rules of kings and queens. Not that Aneta would've even been offered to him if they were still in Myscowa. He was a peasant. She was the daughter of a landowner, even if the family had lost everything.

Zofia squeezed Lukasz's hand. "And so it will be. Aneta's heart will fill with all the love needed to make a good home. You'll see."

Lukasz wondered if he would ever see that sentiment reflected in Aneta's eyes. He thought back to the night he'd met her, when she had asked about Waldemar. This niggling memory wouldn't let go. He knew it was weak to ask, but for once he couldn't stop himself. "Did Aneta know Waldemar any more than she knew me? Did she know anything about him?"

Zofia's eyes widened. She looked away and sighed before looking back at Lukasz. "Oh, Lukasz. Do we ever know anyone before we really know them?"

A squeal from one of the little girls made Zofia leap up, leaving the topic of Aneta and what she'd been expecting when she arrived in Donora closed. His doubts about what Aneta thought of him opened the hole inside him that had been bored years before. He'd thought it had been closing, but no, it was barely healed at all.

**

Supper was complete, and Lukasz and Aneta headed to the dance at the Royal Dance Hall, with Zofia escorting them down the hill toward McKean Avenue. Aneta was cheerful now, talkative, sharing memories of family kuligs. These great outdoor festivals for the ruling class were full of dancing, decadent food, laughter in the pristine snow, warmed by fur coats, served by people they considered family under bright, starry skies. The sound of Polish bantering and the lightness in Aneta's voice gave Lukasz hope, and he decided that she simply needed time to adjust to America, to him.

"It's the light I miss so much," Aneta said as they neared the theater.

"Light?" Zofia asked.

"Back home. You remember. Even on the darkest winter night, the snow reflected the moon and stars like jeweled tulle. Here . . ." She looked up at the dark, starless sky. "Surely you haven't forgotten the wide-open spaces, the crisp air . . ."

Lukasz nodded. He called to mind the blue skies and butter sun. He was pleased to have something in common with Aneta. "I remember."

Zofia shook her head. "Empty bellies and sleeping like dogs. That's what I remember. I'll take food on the table and a home with a topping of smoky, black sky any day. Any day I live and breathe." Zofia steered Lukasz and Aneta toward the hall. "Enough of this talk. Go dance."

**

Inside the hall, Lukasz helped Aneta off with her coat and checked it with the girl near the front door. He took Aneta's elbow and led her toward the room, ribbons of music reeling them in. She stuck close to Lukasz, making him feel protective again.

The doors swung open, releasing the full weight of the music, revelry, and perfumed air. The rhythms beat in his chest as though they emanated from him. The large band played loud and fast, musicians playing instruments he'd never seen before. The musical notes were gentler even though louder than what he was used to. Still, he could hear and feel similarities in the rhythms. Couples flew around the dance floor, laughing. Lukasz didn't know what direction to focus on. Off to the left, near the entrance, was a table with lemonade and tea. The music slowed and ended before changing to a familiar polka, the music sending couples whipping around the floor, their energy spinning off toward Lukasz and Aneta.

He tapped his foot and scanned the room. Aneta's gaze stopped on a group of people huddled near the band. Their heads were bent together to talk over the music, their friendship and closeness radiant.

Aneta stiffened, and he remembered how uneasy she must feel; it was her first dance in America, a room full of strangers. He was glad they had each other. This beauty on his arm was his match, and he would provide what she needed to feel comfortable in a strange place.

The song wound down and another polka began. He knew Aneta must have been given dance lessons as a girl, but every Polish girl loved a good folk dance when her parents weren't looking. Dancing would settle her nerves. Lukasz gestured toward the dancers, and Aneta nodded. He clasped one of her hands and gently pressed his other into her back, leading her onto the floor and around it, their feet catching a few times as though she wanted to lead. Eventually, she relaxed into him, and they fell into the music, her steps meeting his, their bodies tilting and rotating as one.

When the song ended, both of them were breathing hard. "You're light on your feet," Lukasz said as they slowed to a stop and caught their breath. Another dance started, and they watched the dancers execute a few simple moves.

"We can do that," she said.

"Yes!" he said, and they headed back into the mass, feet flying, feeling the unfamiliar American tune as if they'd been raised on it. After a few more songs, they left the dance floor. She held her hand to her chest, her cheeks pinked more than they naturally were.

Her beauty turned him mute. He was so glad they had decided to attend the dance even though both had been hesitant. His body tingled at the thought of holding her again, that a slower tune might be coming soon. "A drink?" he asked, and she nodded.

At the drink table, he pointed to the iced tea, forgoing the sweet lemonade since it was Lent. Aneta took it seriously. With drinks in hand, he searched for her, but she wasn't where he'd left her. He sipped his tea, checking out the tables scattered around the perimeter of the dance floor. They could sit at one of them. He would make himself be talkative the way women liked. It was hard for him to imagine that just two months before, he'd had nothing, and now his future seemed as bright and clear as the sky he'd left behind.

His eye finally caught sight of her dress. She was nearly swallowed into a group of people. She was laughing, her head thrown back. It was the same group he'd noticed when they had first walked in. Americans. Lukasz could tell from their easy posture. They filled the space with their confidence and style, and all eyes tracked toward them. But how could Aneta know them? Hadn't she just gotten teary-eyed up at the Kowalk house and had to run outside to hide? How did she radiate the same effortlessness as these Americans? How did she know them when she had only arrived weeks before?

The entire group focused on Aneta. She was animated and warm, and when he walked over to them and offered her the iced tea, she pulled him toward the group. He was finally close enough to hear them speaking English. *She* was speaking English, slipping Polish into her words when needed. This only drew the group into her further, as though they were physically bridging the gaps between her Polish and English, as though there was nothing else in the world to do.

Aneta introduced him to Sally, Bernice, Maggie, Tom, Bugsy, and Harold. Each shook Lukasz's hand, smiling. They spoke so fast, one handing the conversation off to the other, that he could barely make out the simplest English words.

Within seconds of the introductions, an invisible force began to suck him out of the group and away from Aneta's orbit as she was drawn deeper into the Americans' universe. The joy she emanated, the ease she now exuded, echoed how she'd been with the Kowalks' children. Only then did Lukasz realize that Aneta wasn't shy, she wasn't lost. She didn't need him to protect her at all.

"There's a party after the dance." Aneta yanked on his arm. "They've invited us."

He nodded and looked at the group, who didn't seem interested in him attending their party in the least. Though he was certain they'd love Aneta's company, he couldn't imagine spending extended time with people he couldn't understand. Aneta must have seen his hesitancy on his face. She said something to the group, then pointed across the room. "Cookies?"

Lukasz nodded and they went toward the refreshment table. She finished her drink as they walked.

Just being away from that group reduced his anxiety. "You know English?"

"My father spent three years in New York. He taught us a little. The rest I just picked up."

"In two weeks?"

She shrugged. "When you want something bad enough you just. . . You *must* be learning English at work. Right?"

Lukasz's chest burned, chastised. He was learning, yes, but it certainly hadn't been a goal to use English to work his way into parties with strangers. All that he knew about Aneta—being left at the altar, her family losing all their money, her tears at dinner—none of it fit with the Aneta at the dance, the butterfly suddenly sprung from its cocoon.

He swallowed his questions along with the cookies, thinking of how little his father used to talk, even when things were good. They danced a slow waltz. Aneta relaxed in his arms, and that encouraged him to be bold, to convey the same poise the Americans had. He pushed words from his mouth no matter how strange it felt. "I'm sorry about what happened back home, about your family, that they—"

Her face hardened and she put more distance between them as they completed the steps, making it obvious she wasn't interested in talking about it.

He should have known better. "I'm sorry. I just wanted to say that I know what it's like to have nothing. I never had anything like you did before, but I understand how you feel and . . ."

She looked up at him with tears in her eyes. He could see she was forcing back a sob, and he pulled her close. She let him hold her, but Lukasz worried that what he'd said had increased her discomfort instead of lessening it.

The music changed to a faster tune. This was his last chance to tell her what he wanted to. Once they left, he'd never get the words out. He whispered into her ear. "I'll take care of you. I have a job, and I'm saving for—"

She ripped away from him and bolted toward the exit. He was so stunned, he couldn't move, his arms hanging empty. With the music in full polka, couples whizzed past him.

A tall couple spun toward him. The man stepped on the woman's toes and she tripped, bumping into Lukasz. He steadied her. "All right?"

She grimaced and rolled her eyes before going back into the arms of her partner. Lukasz followed their progress around the room, and he could tell the woman was willing herself to continue dancing with the man with the two enormous, clumsy feet. He wondered if Aneta had willed herself to keep dancing with him.

He recognized the tall woman from Candlemas Day when he had stepped in front of the wind to save her candle flame. She'd been there the day he had gotten the job at the mill. He hadn't realized how tall she was. He didn't know her or her dancing partner, but all he could think was what a mismatch they were.

And then he thought of how graceful he and Aneta were on the dance floor. He told himself he pushed her too fast about too much. Maybe if he'd just stuck to dancing, things would be all right. He should have known better. He'd never been a conversationalist.

He would apologize and make it up to her with more dances and less talk. He made a move for the exit where he'd seen her go and stopped cold. Aneta was being pulled onto the dance floor by a young man—Bugsy? Was that Bugsy or Tom? It didn't matter. It was someone other than him.

Chapter 28

Mary

Mary sat at Mrs. Dunn's kitchen table, surrounded by eggs. Some were raw, in preparation for making traditional Kraslice, others were hardboiled, but all of them had to be dyed. The cook, Mrs. Harper, bustled between the stove and sink, mumbling about everything she needed to complete before leaving to nurse her husband's fractured hand. "That mill." She shook her spatula at the sky. "A blessing and a curse."

"I'll take the casserole out of the oven," Mary said. "Go on home."

"Lucky to be alive at all." Mrs. Harper stepped away from the stove and plugged her fists on her plump hips. "Hurry with that, Mary. The missus'll want your full attention on the boys when I leave. You're going to have to run the kitchen and ready the meal I prepared when she asks and—"

Mary turned in her seat and looked at Mrs. Harper. "I will. Go on, and please be sure to tell my mother that Lefty Smith will row across for my father. And that—"

"Mrs. Dunn'll pay for it. Heard ya the first eighty-three times."

Mary sighed, accustomed to brusque women who offered short-tempered scoldings as often as polite hellos. "I can handle this. Go to your husband."

Mrs. Harper looked at the floor. "You're right." She reached behind her back to untie her apron. "I trust you. Not like that ninny who worked here before. I couldn't—"

Mary glanced at the door, hoping to remind Mrs. Harper she should be leaving. The older woman hung her apron and surveyed the kitchen one final time before grabbing her coat and hat to leave.

Peter was asleep upstairs, the older boys played cards in the keeping room off the kitchen, and Mrs. Dunn rested in her room with the new baby, Clara, her first daughter. Mary cherished the few quiet moments alone in the kitchen. She dipped hardboiled and raw eggs into dye she'd made from vegetables and flowers and separated them into sets on newspaper to dry with the others. The sharp vinegar scent filled her nose as she watched the cranberry-red, navy-blue, and cocoa-brown colors absorb into the shells, turning plain eggs into art.

She worked into an easy pattern and thought of her night dancing with Samuel. She'd had to slip out of the house since her mother had barked a "no" to Mary asking to attend yet another dance. She'd had to bribe her sisters to cover for her in return for doing their chores for two days each. She was proud of her successful maneuvers, sneaking out and back into the house, but she wasn't sure she could say her bruised foot, which Samuel had clomped on all night long, had been worth the risk.

She had spent the night flinching from foot pain, trying to lead him to lead her. Mary adored polkas but they turned into her least favorite dances when she had to dance them with Samuel. Every time they turned a bend, he lost his grip on her, tossing her into whomever happened to be standing in their path when they stumbled by like a couple of five a.m. drunks.

But. But, but, but. Samuel was what she and her friends thought of as fully American, with his Scotch-Irish ancestors, his easy confidence, and his limitless future. And he'd picked *her* to dance with. He'd even left another girl by the wayside to do it. Mary didn't like that, but no one could be forced to dance with another. She knew it better than anyone. She'd spent hours, entire dances alone, milling around the cookie table when all the shorter boys looked past her to the petite girls who batted eyelashes and wore delicate shoes on teeny feet.

And once Samuel began tromping over her feet, she figured she was saving the other girl, Melody, a lot of pain and trouble. Mary pacified her guilt with the knowledge that Melody had only milled at the cookie table for about sixty-one seconds before another boy swooped in, luring her into a very expert hesitation waltz.

Mary transferred the dry hardboiled eggs into a bowl and sighed. She touched her lips. Samuel had managed to kiss Mary in between a waltz and a polka, even with few dark corners to do it in. Like the first time he had kissed her, it was bad. No, worse. His lips were lumbering like his feet.

This time, in a rush, he had dug his tongue past her lips, snaking around her teeth and nearly making her gag. She shuddered again, wondering how it was that what she'd experienced didn't fit with what the other girls described.

Still, still, still.

Samuel had picked her. She would focus on that.

While waiting for the newly dyed eggs to dry, she took an uncooked egg and knitted a diamond pattern around it with thin wire, making it into Kraslice. When she'd completed twisting and shaping the metal around the entire egg, she poked a hole in each end and blew out its insides into a bowl. She would use the yolks for cooking later.

"Mary, Mary." Michael Dunn pulled at Mary's sleeve. "It's Mama."

Mary turned toward the back staircase.

Mrs. Dunn peeked around the corner. "Is she gone? Mrs. Harper?"

Mary nodded and leapt up, taking the little one from Mrs. Dunn's arms.

"That awful woman is suffocating what's left of my life right out of me," Mrs. Dunn said. "She sticks to me like a snakeskin. Ordering this and that."

Her face looked unusually pale to Mary. "Did you ring? I didn't hear it."

Mrs. Dunn brushed the baby's cheek with the back of her fingers and shook her head, shuffling toward the stove. "Oh no, no. I had to get out of that room. I opened every window to let the stale air out, and a blustery wind brought all the smoke inside. The python won't let me out. Thank God you're here."

Mary cradled Clara in one arm, her pink, chubby cheeks still splotchy from a rough birth. "Let me get the water on. Sit."

Mrs. Dunn leaned against the sink, her shoulders slumping forward. She'd lost significant blood in giving birth three days before. Mary held the baby in one arm and took Mrs. Dunn around the waist, leading her toward the table. "There's fresh bread for toast. And eggs." Mary jerked her head toward the table. "Plenty of eggs."

With Mrs. Dunn seated, Mary retrieved the Moses basket from upstairs, laid the baby in it, and saw the blanket was missing. She asked Mrs. Dunn where it was.

"In the drawer there," she said.

Mary looked at her, confused.

"The butler's pantry. Bottom drawer in the middle."

Mary opened it and gasped. White lace linens and brightly colored embroidered fabrics filled the drawer, with a couple of the softest wool blankets she'd ever felt. They were separated into three neat piles of the sweetest smelling linen and cotton material, as if someone had described what comfort was like and created the blankets to exemplify it. The stunning embroidered fabrics were like the two Mary's mother owned, except here were several piles, ten deep.

"The small woolen one. Gray-and-pink check," Mrs. Dunn said.

Mary covered the baby with the soft blanket, patting her back.

She poured Mrs. Dunn's favorite English Breakfast tea, pulled a few biscuits from a tin, and set them in front of her. She peeled a hardboiled egg and sliced it thin.

The middle child dashed into the kitchen, wanting to help Mary dye more eggs. With a wet cloth from the sink, she swiped clean his grimy hands and face.

Mrs. Dunn studied the deep-red, navy, and natural-brown dyed eggs. She picked up one of the navy-blue Kraslice eggs and ran her finger over the silver wire. A smile crept across her face.

"Mr. Dunn gave me that wire to use. Said he was going to—"

"Make a frame for his bees with it," Mrs. Dunn said. Finally, she looked directly at Mary. "These eggs are exquisite. I remember back when my family made these for Easter."

Mary swelled with pride at Mrs. Dunn's admiration and gave each of the boys another hardboiled egg to dye. She wondered if Mrs. Dunn missed the old days. The embroidered fabric in the butler's pantry drawers was so similar to the four special linens her mother had brought from overseas. Mary hadn't seen Mrs. Dunn serve traditional meals or celebrate holidays in traditional ways, but perhaps she just hadn't noticed her doing so.

"Would you like me to make you a blessing basket?"

Mrs. Dunn appeared confused.

Mary shouldn't have assumed she would want one. "I'm sorry. I thought with the baby, you wouldn't have time . . ." Mary glanced toward the pantry. "I saw the cloths in the pantry, and we've talked about you being from . . . that you're also Czech."

She nodded, picking up another egg and examining it in the light. "I'd love a basket, Mary."

"Should I select one from the pantry? I can take it to St. Dominic's with me when I take my mother's on Saturday. I know it's not your church, but still. We're both Catholic. We share the same root country. Deep down, you know."

Mrs. Dunn gave a small shake of the head and looked lost in thought, as though tumbling back through memories far from the Irish home she now kept.

"It's no trouble. I'd be happy to put it together and take it."

Mrs. Dunn cocked her head. "Sure. Thank you. Yes, please make one."

They worked with the boys to finish dying the eggs. Mary expertly knitted the wire into various triangular and diamond patterns around the uncooked eggs, attempting to teach Richard how to do it. But after three raw eggs crushed in his paws, Mary and Mrs. Dunn had him stick to dyeing boiled eggs.

At one point Mrs. Dunn attempted to wire an egg, looping and twisting the wire. It was almost done when it shattered in her hand. She held her hands up, yolk dripping through her fingers. "I'm as bad as the boys."

Her eyes welled. "It's been years since I made something like this. I think . . ." Her voice trailed off, and she shuffled to the sink to clean up her hands. When she turned back to Mary and the children, she pressed her temples and squeezed her eyes closed. "I thought I felt better than I do."

Mary nodded and followed her up the back staircase with Clara in the Moses basket.

Mrs. Dunn removed her robe and slipped into bed while Mary transferred the baby from the basket into the bassinet. She slid it close to the bed so Mrs. Dunn could easily reach her daughter when the time came to nurse.

Mary pulled the covers up on Mrs. Dunn and stoked the fire.

"Thank you, Mary. My sister'll be here tomorrow to help. Be sure to use the embroidered cloths for the baskets, the ones in the drawer where you got the baby blanket. Use anything you want from the larder and make a basket for your family. Anything you want. It'll be beautiful. It's been such a long time since I had a basket blessed."

"I'll make yours the most beautiful ever." Mary remembered what her mother had said about asking for money instead of taking gifts. "I sent word that I'd be staying overnight. But . . ."

"What is it?" Mrs. Dunn looked over her shoulder with half-closed eyes.

"I was wondering if you were paying extra for the extra time." Mary's breath stopped.

Mrs. Dunn got up on her elbow and looked at Mary quizzically. "Why, of course. Of course."

Mary's shoulders relaxed and she exhaled. "Thank you so much. Our roof is broken down, the price of—"

"It's all right, sweet Mary. Always more money to be had. Remember that. With the right people . . ." Mrs. Dunn curled onto her side, leaving Mary to consider the right people, the ones who enjoyed rivers of more money.

**

Back downstairs, Mary found the boys tossing the undyed eggs at each other—raw and hardboiled. She grabbed the two youngest by the back of their collars. "What the blue hell?" She chomped down on the last word before she let it fully out, and in that instant, became more like Matka than she'd ever wanted to. The anger snapped to her lips like it had been born there. She forced calm into her voice. "Outside. Be home five minutes after the mill whistle blows. Not a second longer."

She stuffed them into their coats and hats despite them claiming that the forty-five-degree weather was warm enough to go coatless. She remembered how upset Mrs. Dunn had been when she found out they had been running in the streets. "Wait," Mary said, closing the door to block their exit. "Stay near the house. You can have the run of this block and half the next. If you can't see some part of the house or the Johnson's, come back." She dug through a lidless milk crate and pulled out several baseballs and mitts.

Michael shrugged. "No bat."

She reached across the cloakroom and tossed him a broom. "Here's your bat."

She watched them knock each other around as they meandered down the walk, stabbing one another with the broom before stopping at the Mayhews', clambering up their front stairs. They'd be all right. They weren't fine china.

Mary looked through the pantry for all the items she'd need to make two blessing baskets. She would bake mazanec for the family. Her mouth watered as she thought of the Easter bread made properly. Like most of Mary's friends who couldn't afford all the ingredients, they still made it without raisins and almonds and nearly all the sugar needed. She imagined her mother's face when she appeared back home with mazanec and all its traditional ingredients included. Mary would also have to appear with money in hand, but she trusted Mrs. Dunn. She poured raisins into a bowl with some rum to soak in preparation.

From the big bottom drawer, she pulled out the linens. Each had a label pinned to it stating the type of lace or material, along with the relative who had made it, and for what occasion. Mary selected the prettiest navy-blue linen with cream embroidered flowers to line the bottom of the basket for the Dunn family. She selected a delicate lace called Battenberg to top the basket. "Battenberg," she repeated the pretty word, wishing that saying it would conjure more beautiful things right out of thin air.

She imagined Saturday's blessing at St. Dom's, strolling down the aisle, seeing— no, *feeling*—everyone's eyes settle on the regal, overflowing bounty. People were judged on the size and fill of their baskets. It didn't matter that they were in the Lord's home; people still judged. This time, they'd all be green. No one would know it wasn't the Lancos family basket.

Next, she found a deep-blue organza ribbon to tie around the basket handle. Once she nestled the blue cloth into the bottom of the enormous basket, she located a large ivory candle to symbolize Jesus's love and light and set it in the basket.

She rubbed her chin, inventorying the kitchen and cellar for the traditional Czech foods that comprised an Easter basket. She wasn't surprised she couldn't find a lamb-shaped butter mold in the pantry, so to signify the end of Lenten sacrifice, she pressed butter into a shot glass to be added later.

She located sausage that represented Jesus's kindness. She selected the best of the dyed and wired eggs to signify the daily opportunity for fortune and hope. The navy-blue Kraslice eggs appeared like new winter moons, full and draped in silver moondust. She added cheese to remind people of soberness even when celebrating. There wasn't any fresh, so she added aged white cheddar, knowing Mrs. Dunn wouldn't care. Next was horseradish to recall the losses and deprivation, salt for the unexpected bite life can bring, and sweets to recall that even when things are difficult, life can get better, that people can be transformed.

She was missing bacon and ham to remember God's generous grace, so she opened the back door and bellowed for Michael just like all the wives in town did when they needed to summon a child. He returned breathless, and she sent him down to Murray's for half a pound of bacon to ensure the basket was the very best it could be, that it would bring all the best blessings for the year.

After making dinner, taking a tray to Mrs. Dunn, and feeding the boys, Mary made the mazanec. It took several cycles of kneading dough and letting it rise before it was ready to bake. The fact that the oven for baking was inside the house instead of outside as it was at her house was enough to make Mary hum as she worked. In the morning, she would arrange everything, the candle held in place by the bread, a cover on top, and sprigs of green to decorate the Battenberg lace.

Battenberg.

Mary prepared a basket for her family as Mrs. Dunn had directed, finding the most worn fabrics so nothing would be ruined while in her care. The act of making a modest but beautiful basket, even if it was missing a few ingredients, made her feel as though she was disobeying her mother. But Mrs. Dunn said she'd be paid for the extra work. That should make her mother happy. Mary should enjoy this opportunity, not feel guilty over it. It was a time for forgiveness, after all.

**

Once Mary had tucked all the boys into bed, she went to the study as directed. Before entering, Mary noted the blazing fire, Mr. Dunn bent over his ledgers, and Mrs. Dunn holding Clara in one arm and a book in her other hand. The tick of the clock, the crackle of the fire, and the scratch of Mr. Dunn's pen over paper sank into Mary's mind as marks of exotic but truly perfect family life.

A gurgle from Clara made Mrs. Dunn lean down and kiss her baby's forehead. Even with all the luxurious things the Dunns owned, it was this scene—the boys snug in their beds and the Dunns' sweet stillness, tucked into the study—that made Mary fully see the contrast with the constant blare of her household. Matka couldn't read Czech or English, and other than signing his name, she'd never seen Papa write or pick up anything to read, even though he could.

Mr. Dunn glanced up to say good night as Mary and Mrs. Dunn took Clara upstairs to put her down for the night. Mrs. Dunn escorted Mary to the guest room at the far end of the house. Mary had never been in the room before, had never known there was a designated place for visitors. Mrs. Dunn opened the door and the hall light splashed into the space. Even before the bedroom light was on, Mary could feel the hugeness. When she hit the light switch, Mary's mouth fell open.

The large bed was covered in a blue coverlet, and there was delicate blue-and-cream patterned wallpaper, cream and blue everywhere. It had a high ceiling like every other room, paintings of streams and lush green trees, bookshelves, and a gathering of little dolls on a bench that Mary imagined would be Clara's someday.

Mary had cleaned the Dunn house for years, and to her, every decorative household item represented something her family didn't have as much as something the Dunns did. But to decorate a bedroom that no one ever even used? Mary couldn't have imagined it before seeing it herself.

"I hope it's all right," Mrs. Dunn said. "There's always a chill in here when it has been shut like this, but I don't want it covered in ash and soot from the mill. Well, I don't have to tell you."

Mary walked to the fireplace across from the bed and ran her hands over the smooth marble mantel.

Mrs. Dunn pointed. "Matches are in the tin. Kindling is set. Just crumple the newspaper and . . ." Mrs. Dunn waved her hand. "Silly me. You know how to light a fire." She gestured toward a closed door. "Bathroom's through there."

"*Bathroom?*" Mary covered her mouth with both hands, feeling like a little girl instead of the mature woman she'd come to think of herself.

Mrs. Dunn leaned against the doorjamb and crossed her arms across her still-round belly. "You make me smile, Mary. Always in *so* many ways. I hope little Clara's just like you when she grows up."

Mary pulled herself into her full height, basking in the compliment. "Thank you."

"Well, I know you want to head to church tomorrow for the blessing of the baskets, so go ahead and bathe, use the nightgown in the wardrobe, and pull the extra blankets from the top shelf of the closet. It'll be cold tonight. Books over there, a teapot, tea and honey there if you'd like some before sleep. That's what the grate is for in the fireplace—the teapot."

Books. In a bedroom. Tea. In a bedroom? Volumes of books lined the front parlor, the library, and were stacked and shelved in Mr. Dunn's study, but in a bedroom? Tea? Mary couldn't believe her job included such pampering.

"Go on. Take a look at the bathroom."

Mary bolted. It was tiled with white and blue from top to bottom, and the tub was circled by an embroidered curtain that hung from above.

Mary shook her head, disbelieving as she looked at everything. Every porcelain container was filled with swabs, cotton, lotions, and washes.

"Use anything you want," Mrs. Dunn's voice echoed. "Lavender, lemon . . . lemon, vanilla."

Of course there were lemon washes and lotions. Fluffy towels hung by the sink and were stacked in the closet. Hairbrush, ribbons, pins. Everything.

"The only thing I ask is that you strip the bed tomorrow and remake it. Fresh sheets are on the bottom shelf, below the towels. My sister is persnickety as can be, and I don't need her in a snit over the guest room."

"Oh yes, I will," Mary said. "Thank you." She ran to Mrs. Dunn and threw her arms around her neck, holding her tight, holding her until Mrs. Dunn had no choice but to hug Mary back just as tight.

Mrs. Dunn patted Mary's back. "I wish I could trade the python and my sister for a week with you, Mary."

Hearing that, Mary squeezed Mrs. Dunn so tight, she choked. "I do too. You have no idea."

Mrs. Dunn cleared her throat and let go. They backed away from one another. "Sleep tight," Mrs. Dunn said.

"I will. I will," Mary said, already turning the tub faucet on.

After a bath, Mary sat on the chaise longue by the fire in a clean nightgown. With every inhale came the scent of her freshly washed hair and her soft lemon and lavender skin. She didn't care if Mrs. Dunn paid her a cent for the work she had done that day. Once her hair was dry, she put another few logs on the fire and tucked herself into the wide bed. The linens smelled of . . . well, cleanliness. No—spring wildflowers.

First she kept close to the edge of the bed and turned toward the windows as she always did at home. She half expected to feel a kick in the kidneys or to have Ann's hand flop over her face. What was she doing hanging off the edge? She scooted to the center, flung her limbs wide, and inhaled deeply, watching the crackling fire dance. The fragrance of flame mixed with the soapy bathroom scent transported her to her future, to a place she couldn't really visualize clearly until that moment.

But the bed was too big, too empty, and she was too excited to sleep. She didn't want to waste a decadent moment on sleep, so she pulled the top quilt to the chaise longue. She went to the bookcase and ran her finger along the spines—poetry, the art of flowers, the science of vegetables, the story of a prince and his waif wife. Nothing interested her until she saw *The Short-Stop* by Zane Grey. Baseball. A book about baseball? People wrote and read about baseball? Beside that was a story called *Making the Nine* by Albertus Dudley and *With Mask and Mitt* by the same author. Bliss. She laughed aloud and pulled them from the shelf. Another discovery to add to her list for the day. The baseball book didn't fit with the others in the room, and she wondered who'd been reading it. She settled into the chaise near the fire, the books spread on her lap.

She looked at the bed. What was she doing not sleeping in it? But the chaise gave her the perfect amount of space. Its royal velvet arms embraced her while the fire roared, toasting her toes. She'd daydreamed plenty of a lemony home, children, a husband kissing her hello each evening—without the snaking tongue—but until that very moment, she hadn't understood what that kind of life would *feel* like, how different it would be from the life she lived at home.

She thought again of Samuel and his clumsy feet and lips. She sat with the feelings that he invoked in her. What were they? She didn't quite know. She certainly didn't feel the way other girls had described when they fell in love. She laid the book on her lap. Could someone like Samuel make her happy? Did she like him at all? She imagined him and his life when he was away at school. He held the world in his hands, had everything a person could want. Everything except Mary's heart.

She crossed herself, said a Hail Mary, and added a list of names for God to bless. "And thank you for this day. Thank you for showing me the kind of life that's possible. Thank you for Mrs. Dunn and all she thinks of me, God. Thank you for her wanting her daughter to be like me. Thank you for that, for having someone see the good in me."

She looked at the bed again. Its expansive emptiness brought the familiar loneliness she was always trying to tamp down. She wanted a life that came with a room saved for people who visited, but she knew right then the longing that followed her to this beautiful home meant she only wanted such grandeur if she could share it with family. As much as her parents and siblings troubled her in different ways all the time, they were hers. Someday she would bring them all into a luxurious home, even Ann with her ice-block feet. Yes, even her.

And with that, Mary pulled the heavy woolen blanket up and opened the book, reading until her eyes fell shut.

Chapter 29

Mary

Mary arrived at St. Dominic's for the Holy Saturday blessing of the Easter baskets. She took her place behind Katya Svoboda at the end of a line of girls and women snaking out the door and around the corner.

"Why the hound dog face?" Mary said.

Katya held up two weather-beaten baskets. Each held mazanec, but Mary knew from its dishwater-gray color that it had been made without rum-soaked raisins, sugar, or almonds. Each basket also had tiny salt boxes and a few lengths of sausage. No eggs, no cheese, no linens. Mary knew too well the embarrassment that came with arriving at church with such sad baskets. It was supposed to be about love and renewal, but sometimes it was simply a competition that most never won.

Katya bent over Mary's bounty. She fingered the blue organza ribbon on Mrs. Dunn's basket, her eyes wide.

"It's for the Dunns," Mary said. "I'm just helping out."

Katya looked at Mary's smaller baskets, which overflowed as well. Mary took a Kraslice egg from Mrs. Dunn's and one from her own family's and put them into Katya's.

"Thank you, Mary." She set down the baskets and grabbed Mary around the neck. "I'm ready to hand this job of parading our pitiful baskets in public to my sister. It was so exciting before I understood how awful it could be. Everyone staring at everyone's wares. It's like seeing inside our houses, seeing all that we . . ."

"Don't have," Mary finished. "You know my basket normally looks like that."

"I know, but it's just . . ."

Katya shrugged.

"What?"

"You're always so lucky," Katya said.

Mary nodded, knowing it was true in many ways. "Mrs. Dunn's been very generous."

"I should say." Katya shook her head. "You get these great jobs with good people. Christine Allison got beat by Mrs. Mason last week. For not changing the twins fast enough. The twins Mrs. Mason had ignored until Christine arrived."

Mary gasped. "She quit, right?"

"Fired."

Mary couldn't believe it. She studied Katya's face. "Don't you dare go apply for that job."

"We need it. I sure wish I had your luck."

Mary considered the fact that Katya thought she was lucky. To Mary, Katya was the fortunate one. At dances, her diminutive, shapely figure ensured her dance card was so full, she had to waltz out the door with the boys who couldn't get enough of her pretty face and light feet. No one cared that her dress was worn and patched, let out at the seams, its hem taken down. "I'll keep my ears open for a job opening. Mrs. Dunn sometimes tells me when someone's looking."

Mary had planned on giving the next job she heard about to her sister, Ann, but she couldn't let her friend work for Mrs. Mason.

"Thank you, Mary. You're always kind and generous. Always."

Mary stopped herself from revealing the decadent bath and overnight stay she'd had the night before and concentrated on the line moving slowly around the corner and into the church, down the aisle to where their baskets would be blessed.

There was a steady stream of children and families to the church that day, with the oldest child in a family often given the privilege—or, as Katya saw it, the burden—of taking the basket to be blessed. Mary was proud to carry the enormous basket for the Dunns, basking in the double takes and whispers between friends. All of it evoked a mix of pride and humility because the basket wasn't hers.

"Ah, Mary," Father Kroupal said as she came to the altar. "Your cup runneth over."

Her cheeks warmed and she held up the big one. "This is for Mrs. Dunn. She's confined at home with a new little one." She set that down. "This one's for my family."

It was small but was made with fine linens and topped with Battenberg lace from Mrs. Dunn. Thanks to Mrs. Dunn, the Lancos basket overflowed beyond anything Mary had ever imagined taking to church. "A fine basket as well," Father Kroupal said, hands clasped against his belly.

"And this one's a gift." Mary showed him the diminutive basket with plain fawn-hued linen that she would give to Samuel. She hoped Father Kroupal wouldn't push her to confide who it was intended for.

He dipped his straw brush into holy water. "A generous streak. The recipients will be pleased to find someone has thought of them on this very holy day, Mary." He whipped the holy water at the baskets, sprinkling Mary with it as he did. He said his blessing that singled out the items inside and what they meant, praying for the foods to nourish their bodies the way that Jesus and the church nourished their souls.

She broke into a smile as he passed his fingers over the handles, closing his eyes before finishing the prayer. He gave her back the baskets, looping their handles over her arms.

"Of all the baskets, I like the small, simple one best," he said. "It's the one most in keeping with Jesus, don't you think?"

Mary flinched, then smiled. She hadn't considered such a thing, that the modest basket might actually be the most special. "Thank you, Father. Thank you."

He patted her shoulder and sent her on her way.

She was so pleased with what Father Kroupal had said about her basket for Samuel that she swelled with confidence, imagining his face when she gave it to him.

**

At Samuel's house on Prospect Avenue, Mary paused, her foot on the first of several sets of stairs leading to the whitewashed porch. Very few people were willing to spend money on a new paint job every spring, but Samuel's family apparently was.

Mary drew nervous breaths. She'd met Mrs. Blake at the Dunns' house when she'd served them drinks but doubted the woman would remember her. She hoped that one of his sisters would answer the door and that she could have the chance to talk to Samuel without his mother watching.

His enormous home sat high on its property, looming over Thompson Avenue and the mills below. Mary counted the thirty-one stairs that led upward. The angles and woodwork were perfectly kept. Mary was sure there were no holes in this roof. Even the porch had pretty green wicker furniture dressed in pink and green flowered fabrics, surrounded by Easter flower pots. Right then, she knew Samuel's home had a guest room. It must, and she wanted to see it. She laughed, imagining asking him about it.

Halfway up the second set of stairs, she wondered if she should even go to the front door. She always entered Mrs. Dunn's by the kitchen door around back. But this was different. She wasn't coming to work. She squared her shoulders and ascended.

She reached the porch and heard voices. She looked at the open windows. Samuel. His voice rattled deep in his chest. Mary moved toward the sound. The family still had their winter drapes up, but they were parted, billowing in the wind, exposing and covering Samuel's back with each gust.

She was about to say his name when she heard a female laugh. A giggle, coy and playful. Mary moved closer. Samuel's sister or mother? She forced a swallow. Samuel turned to the side, and the giggly girl came into view. Melody. The daughter of his father's boss. She dug her fingers through her hair. Shiny combs held up its sides, and the back of it was loose, swinging in sumptuous curls.

Melody moved closer to Samuel, reaching up around his neck, latching her hands as he bent down and lifted her up, hugging her. He put her down and leaned in, kissing her. The delicateness of his movements—of Melody herself—made Mary look at her own body, her big feet, and her mitts for hands. Her robust guffaws never even began as giggles.

Maybe that's why her kisses with Samuel had been so awkward, why they couldn't dance without him tromping over her feet. The spot on her arch where he'd bruised her began to throb.

It's me, not him.

Anger agitated Mary. Samuel was hers. His height made him hers. Melody could have any old boy. Before Mary knew what she was doing, she flew to the window, her baskets crashing together.

She stomped her foot. "Samuel."

Melody and Samuel spun toward Mary and released each other. Their mouths gaped. Melody smoothed the front of her dress and tossed her curls back over her shoulder.

"Mary? What . . ." Samuel said.

She stared at him She was so confused at being so angry. It wasn't as though she wasn't aware that he had to entertain Melody and her family. Mary hadn't enjoyed their kiss or their dancing one bit. But he was the only one for her. He was the only one who had asked her to dance. He was the only boy who was tall enough, who lived in a lemony house.

Someone called his name, causing Samuel and Melody to turn away from Mary and toward another room. This gave Mary the chance to get away. She stormed down the front steps and ran to the Dunns' house. When she reached it, she turned back to see if Samuel was following her.

Behind Mary, a clump of people going about their business was shrouded in the smoky air, but not one of them was Samuel. She would have known his shape anywhere, the way his head always bobbed over the crowd. She leaned against the short stone wall, breathing heavily, going over what she'd just witnessed. It was obvious he had wandering hands and lips and, well . . . that wasn't the point. The point was that the girl seemed to find it lovely instead of awful.

It dawned on her. Samuel had practiced on her with his probing, awful tongue.

"Mary?"

Mary looked up, startled. Weira Dominska walked toward Mary with a man on either side of her.

Mary's heart continued its pounding, her thoughts confused. She wasn't formally Samuel's girlfriend, but still, seeing him with Melody, kissing her, stung.

Weira hugged Mary tight, the baskets between them. "Your baskets! How beautiful!" Weira held up a modest one similar to the basket Mary had intended for Samuel.

Mary's eyes prickled, tears threatening to drop over her lids. She couldn't shed the feeling she'd been slapped.

"What's wrong?" Weira asked.

Mary shook her head and glanced at the two men.

"My brother, Wilhelm," Weira said, "and Lukasz. The Kowalks are sponsoring him."

Mary didn't know the Kowalks, but she remembered this man from the mill and from church. She forced a smile through her tears. She looked down at her basket, the tiny one. The handle, arched over her forearm, was pinching her skin. She wanted it out of her sight. She offered it to Lukasz.

His eyes lit up, but then he held up his hand to decline.

Mary pushed it closer to him. "No, please. Take it."

He squinted at it and shook his head again.

"Go on."

He finally took it by the bottom and held it up, inhaling the confluence of scents. Mary could see he was pleased.

"Thank you," he said. That glimmer in his eyes that she'd seen on Candlemas was there again and she saw it, the blue that hid inside the gray.

She nodded and stepped back.

Lukasz picked up one of the wired eggs and studied it. "*Piekny*."

Mary shook her head, not knowing the word.

"Beautiful," Weira said.

Mary's throat tightened. She had wanted Samuel to react that way to the basket. "*Dziekuje Ci*," she said.

"I came *za chlebem*," Lukasz said, holding Mary's gaze.

"He came to America for bread, for food," Weira said.

"*Ameryka jest świetna*," Lukasz said.

Weira nodded.

"*Przyniosłeś mi to. Jak magia*," Lukasz said, staring at Mary.

"What?" Mary kept Lukasz's gaze but patted Weira's arm. "What'd he say?"

"America's great."

Mary shot her friend a look. "No, the other. The beautiful words."

"And *you* brought the bread to him. Like magic. Here it is," Weira said.

Mary repeated the phrase as best she could, touched by the sentiment. He came for bread, and she had brought it to him. Simple, like the basket.

Lukasz held up the basket. "Thank you."

She nodded, a flood of tears threatening to drop. She was pleased that Lukasz appreciated the basket but she still smarted from Samuel's affection for Melody. Mary bent down for the remaining baskets and headed toward Thompson Avenue.

"Happy Easter," she said over her shoulder and left the three Poles to get their baskets blessed that day.

**

Mary took the walkway around the back of the Dunns' house, knocked on the kitchen door, then entered. A tall woman in a faded black dress was at the sink. She turned, questioning who Mary was.

"I work for Mrs. Dunn."

The woman's face lit up and she dried her hands on her apron. "Mary. I've heard about you. I'm Miss Dvorak. The sister."

Ah, there it was—the Czech name hidden by Mrs. Dunn's married name.

Mary felt a surge of goodness hearing that Mrs. Dunn had told her sister about her and that the woman seemed excited to meet her. Mary held up the basket. "It's blessed and ready for soup tomorrow."

Miss Dvorak waved Mary toward her. She pulled out a canning jar filled with golden broth. She fitted it into the large basket. "Chicken broth. She wants you to have the basket for all the work you've done the past few days."

Mary's mind spun. First, the idea of owning the linens inside it was dizzying. Second, the food! It would feed them all after Easter Mass. But third . . . oh, that third thing.

Matka.

Mary needed to return with money, not just beautiful presents, presents that Mary would ferret away in her brick hiding spot. She remembered the tiny pieces of paper that had been pinned to each linen cloth. "I can't possibly. These are family linens."

Miss Dvorak bent closer to the basket and shifted some of the items to get a closer look. "This was from her aunt by marriage, Maisy O'Toole, correct? For her first Christmas married?"

Mary nodded, remembering that notation. "That's what the paper pinned to it said."

Miss Dvorak patted the items, shifting them again. "If we were to list our relations in order of likability, Miss Maisy O'Toole would be dead last. Though they are beautiful, my sister would prefer you tuck these away for a time when you start your home. She said you'll certainly have a home worthy of the embroidery in no time. The lace—"

"Battenberg," Mary said.

"That was from Maisy too." Miss Dvorak fingered the edge. "Such beautiful things, such hateful people."

"Hateful?"

Miss Dvorak looked as though she were lost in a memory. She shook her head. "So beautiful. But I agree with my sister. Better to be in your hope chest than her pantry with memories of a woman who couldn't accept an immigrant wife into her family."

"Then why'd she give Mrs. Dunn these beautiful things?"

Miss Dvorak fingered the cloth again. "She was embarrassed that her nephew might have a wife who didn't bring these things to the marriage, to their social world."

"But she's so wonderful, so . . ."

"Doesn't matter. Not to her. My sister's Bohemian, barely off the boat when she met Mr. Dunn. That colored everything else in Maisy O'Toole's eyes."

Mary thought about Samuel and his family, of all the families in Donora, some rich, some poor, and some in between. Except for four homes in the Terrace area, they all lived in the same congested neighborhoods, rich and poor alike, attending the same school, the same dances.

Mary was relieved that things had changed. It was 1910, after all. And yet, she understood what Miss Dvorak was saying. She recognized it more than she wanted to. Mary knew of the law that demanded an American woman who married an unnaturalized immigrant take on the citizenship of her husband's country. The insanity of such a rule, as though immigrant men were spying for foreign governments in between their mill shift, sleep, and quick meals.

Mill owners needed the foreign men fresh from the train to work for them, and their wives needed immigrant women to keep house, but those employees weren't treated the same as those who'd been naturalized or born in America? Mary saw the definition of a proper marriage was tied into those very considerations. Being American one way or another was everything when it came to the rule of law in America and to the social set who made rules. Why on earth the government wouldn't allow a foreign man to become American when he married an American woman was stupid as anything Mary could have dreamed up. Still, it was the law. Luckily, this wasn't going to be a problem for Mary. Her marital prospects, imagined or not, were always, already rooted in solid American citizenship.

She sighed. Having a hope chest with fine things like Mrs. Dunn's linens would help Mary when she was ready for marriage, making her more appealing to men like Samuel. Still, she shook her head. She couldn't accept Mrs. Dunn's gift.

Miss Dvorak took Mary's shoulders. "No argument. My sister's stubborn and very emotional right now. If you refuse her gift, she might cry for days, and I can't stand a crying woman. I just can't stand it." Her lips pulled into a smile that told Mary she was joking.

Mary laughed. "I'm so touched. I just can't even say . . ."

"She knows. She sees big things for you, your life. So not another word."

Mary looked at the stunning basket and thanked her again. She wanted to ask about the extra pay, but it wasn't right. Miss Dvorak would have given Mary the money if she had known anything about it. Mary's stomach clenched, thinking of Matka's reaction. Too old to be spanked, Mary wouldn't have to dodge a smack, but the sound of Matka's yelling? Mary felt it in advance. And so, Mary would have to lie.

As she walked home, she glanced at the basket Mrs. Dunn had given her. She didn't need Samuel, did she? She had Mrs. Dunn, who saw big things for her. A hope chest.

She certainly didn't have a chest, but she had the space behind the bricks. She couldn't hide these fabrics there. They would be ruined. Every time she thought of Samuel or her mother, she forced herself to be hopeful instead, and focused on having a nice home someday, a drawer in the butler's pantry filled with stunning linens. The ones Mrs. Dunn had given her would remain her most precious, she was sure.

Chapter 30

Lukasz

On Holy Saturday, Lukasz presented Zofia with the basket he'd been given by that girl. What was her name? He was bad with names because on nearly every outing, he met someone new. He remembered seeing her at the dance with that boy tripping over her feet, though. She was the girl with the candles.

Zofia had been thrilled at the sight of the basket, but after she learned Aneta hadn't given it to him and another girl, a stranger, had, she spat on the floor, stomped it, and brushed her hands together to finish it off.

"Gifts from another woman? Bad luck!"

"But Aneta and I—"

Zofia smacked her hands together. "*Dosc.*"

Stop? Zofia's passionate response startled and confused Lukasz. "I'll get rid of it." He took it from the counter, but Zofia snatched it from his hands.

"That's worse. Toss out good, blessed food? I don't think so. But no more gifts from other women."

Lukasz sighed. "It wasn't a gift like you're thinking. I just happened to be there when . . . As I told you, I don't even *know* her."

Zofia squeezed her eyes closed. "*Even worse.* Stop it with whatever you're doing that's letting women think you're available."

He searched his mind for what he might be doing to that end.

Zofia rubbed her growing belly, then pulled a chair out for Lukasz. She sat beside him and took both of his hands. "Please, Lukasz. We promised Aneta's parents a good match."

He looked away.

"Why're you making that face?"

"What face?"

"Sour. Like you're having a bellyache."

He shrugged.

"You and Aneta are a wonderful match. The stars aligned. Think of it. You won the handstand contest after losing the hay contest. You're meant to be together."

"How do you know?"

She rubbed her belly. "Like I know this baby'll be a girl, I know you're the man for Aneta. We have housed you and helped you get a job, right?"

"Yes."

"So you need to trust us. She's a beauty. Descended from kings. What's wrong with you? All this wondering."

It stunned Lukasz that Zofia couldn't see Aneta's disinterest in him. She slipped into English half the time she came to dinner, always surprising Zofia. Didn't she wonder what that meant?

Zofia squeezed Lukasz's hands again. "Love can grow between two wandering souls. God links them in marriage, then time allows love to take hold, shared like tree roots weaving in and out of each other, clutching at the earth, fixing each other as one. I *know*."

"Why's this so important to you?"

She leaned back in her seat. She looked off, her jaw clenched. "Aneta's father got us to America all together, all at once. Gave us money to set up here. Got Alexander into the mills."

Lukasz knew how difficult it was to pay for an entire family's passage to America. "Why would he do that?"

Zofia looked pained. She glanced over one shoulder, then the other. "I'll tell you, but you keep this secret for eternity." She mimed putting a key to her lips and locking them.

Lukasz nodded, not sure he wanted to know.

"Alexander found a man on Aneta." Zofia closed her eyes and spit out the words. "She was fourteen. Alexander ripped him off and pummeled him." Zofia gestured, and her face bore an expression as though she had been there when it had happened. "His legs are only half good now. It was the son of Lipinsky."

"Royalty."

Zofia nodded. "Alexander crippled the bastard. He was going to be thrown in jail, so Aneta's father got us all out. All at once, he was so grateful. But then the baby . . ."

"Baby?" Lukasz asked.

Zofia covered her mouth. "What baby?"

"You said 'baby'."

She wouldn't look at him. Lukasz ran the story through his mind again, putting the pieces together. "Aneta had a baby?"

Zofia rubbed her sternum. "Acid," she said, uncomfortable. "I shouldn't have told you."

Dark sadness for Aneta filled Lukasz, reminding him of his own loss—his mother especially. "What happened to the baby?"

Zofia shrugged and finally looked at Lukasz square again. "What always happens. They passed the baby off as Aneta's sister."

"What about the man who left her at the altar? Why?"

She sighed. "The attacker somehow managed to get the word out that he'd fathered the baby, that Aneta . . . well, he taunted her intended and embarrassed him. The in-laws got a look at the baby, who was now a little girl, and her black curls and coal eyes said it all."

Lukasz couldn't talk.

"It wasn't Aneta's fault."

Lukasz nodded. "'Course not."

"You can't mention this. I'm trusting you to take this to your grave."

"'Course."

"Aneta needs you, Lukasz. She's a little standoffish, but it's understandable. You're exactly what she needs to make her whole again."

Lukasz inhaled deeply. He thought of the exchanges that had occurred in Alexander's name when he had been granted a chance at the job in the blast furnace and then in the wireworks. Every deed in the Kowalks' lives was recorded as a give or take.

"I promise Aneta will make a fine wife," Zofia said. "And with my baby coming, the sooner the better. You're saving money. It's March. Let's plan a wedding date for June. It'll be lovely."

Lukasz flinched. June? "Next year?"

"Three months' time, Lukasz. Ready your mind to take your match in holy matrimony."

Lukasz wasn't sure he was breathing anymore.

"What's wrong?" Zofia asked.

He rubbed his eyes, trying to ground himself.

"You get it together, Lukasz Musial. Romance her, lure her, show her why you're the man for her. For us. For what we did for you."

Lukasz forced his air out. He thought of other options. He could leave Donora. But go where? He wasn't fluent in English yet, and he didn't want to leave Donora.

No. He had come to America to start a life, and if Aneta was to be part of it, well, so be it. As Zofia often said, *so it will be.*

**

The conversation with Zofia left Lukasz exhausted. He was also far more open to Aneta, becoming more protective of her. He would do a better job of showing her he was not only interested, but that he would make a good husband. He would never mention what Zofia had told him, but he wanted to convey his strength. He was strong enough to keep her safe and give her the family she deserved after she had been through so much.

How alone she must have felt since the day she was attacked, forced to carry her secret, shunted away, matched with someone in a far-off land. He knew the emptiness that loss brought, but nothing like she had experienced. He would be her strength, the man to make her past fade like the moon behind smoke and fog.

Between talking to Zofia and heading to his shift on Holy Saturday, he took refuge at Mark's forge, working on enamel Easter gifts for Zofia and Aneta. He made Easter eggs, his most intricate pieces yet. He heated and hammered the metal pieces so thin, he thought they might break. Then with delicate, rhythmic movements, he worked the wire into place, lacing loops, flower petals, and squiggles around the steel orbs, creating a sense of movement on the surface. He made an extra one for Mark as a thank-you for lending him the space.

Lukasz put away the thin wire and thought of the Kraslice eggs that the girl had put into the basket. Her eyes had filled with tears. Now he remembered that Nathan had said she was fourteen or so, but looking at her, she was as mature as any woman he knew. The way she smiled when he held up the wired egg she'd made. The pride. He knew the power in being able to make something beautiful, to leave little bits of himself behind. He imagined she experienced that same sensation right then, and he knew he was in the right place.

To be in America, to marry beautiful Aneta, to make a home together—there was nothing else to want. "So it will be." He repeated Zofia's words aloud like a prayer, every repetition making his future as real as the mermaid who'd sent him on his path just months before.

Finished with the eggs, Lukasz played with steel plating and wire, attempting to make a ring. He would use cast-off steel to create one that would shine like jewels worthy of a woman like Aneta, a woman who deserved to know she was safe, that she would soon have a loving home.

He exhaled. It was time to repair the broken umbrellas standing near the entrance to the forge. The cold March weather brought cycles of frozen rain, buckets of it, interspersed with blizzard winds and heavy snowfalls. Lukasz retrieved an armful of umbrellas. Good. The repairs he did to repay Mark for his kindness kept Lukasz straight. And with a wedding just three months away, he'd never been so glad that was the case.

**

Easter came, and Lukasz got off the night shift and arrived home to find the Kowalk children rushing into the brisk March morning, searching for treats hidden around the frosted but mud-covered yard.

He entered the house, inhaling the scent of the soup made from the blessed basket's ingredients. Zofia was at the stove frying paczki, simmering sausage, and scrambling eggs. Alexander patted his wife's bottom to get her to move aside so he could pull out the bottles of vodka that had been stowed away for Lent.

"Lukasz!" Alexander held a bottle and two shot glasses over his head. "Quench thy thirst."

Zofia shook her spatula at her husband and scooped paczki onto a cloth-covered plate. Lukasz tossed back a few shots. As the warmth of the vodka filled him, he agreed to go to Mass, even though he hadn't slept.

The streets teemed with people walking to the various churches to celebrate Jesus's resurrection. In the foggy morning, glimpses of blue, pink, and green Easter coats, hats, and purses peeked through the dark morning.

When Lukasz and the Kowalks arrived at St. Mary's, Aneta and her sponsor family, the Bielawas, were entering church. She wore a hat Lukasz hadn't seen with a small veil over her eyes, making him think of a bride.

The Kowalks sat one row behind Aneta. The Bielawa children piled on either side of her with the youngest, a toddler, snuggled onto her lap, her head on Aneta's shoulder, staring at Lukasz. Aneta rocked the child and rubbed her back. Lukasz thought of her baby who had been left behind.

The priest began Mass, the monotonous Latin lulling Lukasz's thoughts toward the money he'd stashed at the blacksmith's forge. He kept it in a small box he'd made just for that purpose. Even though it was far from enough to purchase property and build a house, he felt strong and confident in his work at the mill and his determination to stay away from the Bucket of Blood.

He earned extra money from the enamel animals that Mark sold for him, and once in a while Mark gave him a few coins for umbrella repairs.

Father Burak launched into his homily. Lukasz's gaze settled on Aneta's intricate braids peeking out from under her hat. Her long, elegant neck. He looked away, crossing himself, absently saying his prayers. At some point, his thoughts moved away from his attempt at pious prayerfulness back to Aneta's creamy neck, imagining his lips exploring her skin.

The child to Aneta's right spun in the pew and waved to him. Aneta looked over her shoulder and smiled, making his heart leap. Adam had been right. It *was* his turn to live under the lucky star that Waldemar had crowded him out of back in Myscowa.

After church, Aneta came to the Kowalks' to eat. She smiled at Lukasz and even touched his arm at the table when she asked him to pass the Easter bread. Aneta's gentleness and warmheartedness signaled that something was growing between them, that she felt it as much as he did.

When the meal was finished and the children had enjoyed fresh paczki, Zofia nestled three fat marmalade-filled ones into the small basket that Lukasz had gotten from Mary and handed it to Aneta. She thanked Zofia, kissing her on the cheek.

Lukasz nodded, pleased. Aneta was adjusting to America, to him. A tap on the small of his back made him leap. "Walk her home," Zofia said.

He was excited at the thought of being alone with Aneta. "Of course."

He handed Aneta her coat and hat and pulled his own on as they stepped into the cold. Night was just beginning to darken daylight's edges, and it gave each of them the chance to mask their expressions, to silence the pressure for words. The day had been warm but grew icy with the setting sun.

Aneta shivered. Lukasz slipped his arm around her and pulled her close. She leaned into him, the increasing darkness lending them cover. He didn't know what to say. He tried to talk but his words tripped like a drunk headed home from the bar. When had he had the chance for extended talks with girls? He'd certainly had dates back home, plenty of romps in barns and behind the bushes at the bend in the Wisloka. There was never much conversation then, just fumbling, groping for affection, attention, warmth.

"A beautiful day," he said.

"Mm-hmm."

He wanted to talk to her about their future, his plans for a home, and about Zofia and the Bielawas deciding that they should get married in three months. "Zofia told me that three months is—"

"Such a beautiful day today," Aneta said.

"And there'll be many more when we—"

"The children were so funny. That Witold always—"

"Aneta." Lukasz interrupted then stopped from pushing her to discuss the wedding.

She smiled at him. Perhaps it wasn't that she wasn't interested in discussing it, but preferred to enjoy the wonderful day. Perhaps he should just enjoy their quiet walk, feeling their synchronized pace, gait, breaths. He told himself that this unspoken harmony was more valuable than any of the things he couldn't say.

Aneta's toe caught on her skirt's seam. She stumbled and he caught her, steadying her, then straightening her hat. Standing close, he inhaled her rose fragrance.

They smiled, her penetrating blue almond eyes stirred him. Before he formed a conscious thought, he brushed her cheek with the back of his fingers and pulled her in, kissing her, his heart pounding against her. She nuzzled into him and wrapped her arms tight around his back. He breathed into the kiss relieved at her response, reassured that she did want him.

The sound of laughter and footfalls made them pull apart, but they held each other's gaze. His heart sped. Her breath was shallow, quick. Lukasz took Aneta's hand and escorted her to the front door. They said goodbye twice, neither moving to end the evening, kissing again when no one was passing by. Finally, she disappeared behind the door, and Lukasz took off to change into work clothes. Zofia had been right about Aneta, and Lukasz couldn't believe it was so.

**

Lukasz bolted awake, his vision blurred with fatigue. He patted beside him. Three—no, *four*—boys were stuffed into the bed. Jan, the boy from the house down the way, was there too. Their arms and legs were splayed like snow angels, jutting in every direction. Lukasz shoved mismatched limbs off him and shifted to the edge of the bed, rubbing his pounding head. The mermaid had come to him again.

Since meeting Aneta, he'd always thought his dreams and river sightings of the mermaid hinted of Aneta and their future, but now he wasn't sure. The dream left a residue, a sense of another woman that he couldn't shed. The mermaid had long dark hair that swirled and twisted in the water, covering her shoulders. Her earthy eyes beckoned, seduced. And then she touched him like she had that night at the Wisloka, her velvet fingertips trailing up his arm and electrifying his skin.

So real, but impossible. And not Aneta. He dug his fingers into the back of his neck, relieving the ache that came with sleeping in curled, crooked positions, draped by arms and legs. He wouldn't complain. With Zofia's baby and his pending wedding, he'd have to move soon anyway. Zofia would make room for them if necessary, but it was time to prove himself. He was proud that he'd resisted the urge to go with friends to the Bucket of Blood using a shot and a beer to rinse away the mill soot that collected in his throat.

After a trip to the outhouse and washing up, he sat at the kitchen table and Zofia poured coffee. He added the sweet evaporated milk he'd come to love, the fatty flavor enough to fill him. Zofia set leftover Easter sausage in front of him and sat beside him. She separated a bundle of pussy willow and ribbon into sets, tying each. "Smigus-Dyngus today," she said.

He stared at the items. He'd forgotten. Wet Monday, the day after Easter.

She stopped tying and cocked her head. "Time to celebrate the coming spring, fertility, hope, new life, marriage."

"Silly," he said.

She sighed. "Alexander doesn't douse me with water anymore, but Aneta's young, you're young. Things are going well between you two. Today's the perfect time to show her you're thrilled to be matched."

He thought of how Aneta had been attacked and her baby taken away from her, then she was left at the altar before being sent to a new country. Aneta probably did need extra attention and reassurance, but not this. She didn't seem the type to enjoy being drenched with water.

"Mrs. Bielawa's expecting you to do it." Zofia pushed a bunch of fluffy pussy willow toward him. "That's my best ribbon. She can use it afterward. Or perhaps she'll just keep it under her pillow to think of you."

"I don't know." It certainly was tradition to douse single ladies with water and brush their legs with willows, but still, it didn't quite seem to fit their situation.

"You're expected."

"I don't know."

"Tradition."

"After all she's been through? I don't—"

Zofia shook a bundle of pussy willow in his face. "Shush. Pretend you never heard that."

"But—"

"Shush. She's young. She'll want this."

Lukasz had a bad feeling. "I'll do it if she comes outside. I'm not going inside to surprise her."

"You could sit there all day waiting. Mrs. Bielawa's expecting you to burst in and douse her as custom dictates. I told her you would not drag her back here, as is tradition. But you go in and wet her."

He rubbed his tired eyes.

"Hit her with the water good. It'll be bad luck if you just sprinkle her. Then come back and sleep some more before your shift."

Lukasz exhaled. He picked up the pussy willow bundle and a jar for the water.

Zofia pointed. "The bucket."

He sighed.

"Every Polish girl appreciates Wet Monday. Even in America."

Lukasz doubted that was the case for Aneta, but what did he know? He'd been wrong before. He would have to trust Zofia and Mrs. Bielawa on this.

**

As he neared the Bielawa house, the door opened and out came Aneta, snatches of her blue coat and blonde hair flickering through the smoky fog. The regal way she carried herself as she dashed down the stairs made Lukasz look at his bucket and pussy willow bundle. It was stupid. But again, Zofia had been right so far.

He called out to Aneta and a mill whistle blew two short and one long time, letting them know something had stopped the rolling mill. His voice, obscured, gave him the perfect cover to approach her. At the bottom of the stairs, she dug through her purse. Now was the right time if he was going to do it.

Just toss it.

No.

Lukasz ignored his doubts. He thrust the bucket through the air and drenched her, her hat flying right off her head. It was as if she'd been caught in a wild rainstorm.

She dropped her purse and gasped, spreading her hands before furiously wiping at her eyes. Lukasz gently swiped at the backs of her legs with the pussy willow bundle as was tradition.

Finally, she focused on him, and he expected that now the shock had worn off, she'd smile, laugh, and throw her arms around him for bringing a little bit of home to Donora for her.

She grabbed the pussy willow and swatted him on the shoulder.

Still no laugh. Her eyes narrowed, and she looked indignant.

He laughed at her reaction, the anger, as though she had no idea what Dyngus traditions were.

She swatted his other shoulder. "*Dupek,*" she said.

"Asshole?" All the warmth between them the night before—the kiss, their bodies pressing together—gone, quick as a rabbit down its hole. Zofia may have been right about a lot of things, but not this. "Oh, come on, Aneta. Zofia said you were expecting it. It's just fun."

She straightened. Her jaw clenched. "When you're standing in the cold, drenched, you tell me if it's fun."

"Aneta."

She picked up her purse and swatted his belly, barely making contact. He laughed.

She pressed her chin into the air, her hair dripping. "We're not in Poland anymore, Lukasz." Contempt filled her eyes.

He was utterly confused. "But *you're* still Polish."

"Not for long." She hit him again with the willow bundle, then threw it at his feet. "There's no reason for Smigus-

Dyngus in Donora. That stupid tradition's not going to make those choking mills turn out more steel. There's nothing growing here." She dug her foot into the muddy yard. "Grass doesn't even grow here. It's all dirt and smoke and . . ." She swept her hand over her head. "Do you even see any of it?"

He was so stunned that he couldn't speak. Of course he'd noticed. By this time, he even realized why they had all been so excited when the sun had shone on the day he had arrived, why they credited him for bringing the blue sky.

"There's rumor of blue sky tomorrow," he said, his voice as light as he could make it.

She stomped up the stairs.

"I brought the blue sky the day I came," Lukasz joked. "Didn't they tell you?"

She turned back, chin pushed high. "Well, it's gone now." She stomped into the house and slammed the door, the sound hanging on the hushed Easter Monday air—Wet Monday.

Lukasz scratched the back of his neck and shook his head. If tradition held true, then the prettiest girl in town, Aneta, would find herself sopping wet all day long.

He started back toward the Kowalk's and heard the pounding of feet behind him. He turned to step out of the way and before he could see who it was, water splashed over his face. The person, a girl, kept running, but she slowed down to douse another boy who was farther up the street.

"Mary Lancos!" the boy bellowed. He held a bundle of willows in the air and took off sprinting after her. Mary Lancos's laughter trailed behind her, roped into the gentle wind, reaching Lukasz's ears long after the fog had hidden her away from sight.

He shook off the water, chuckling, and headed home to dry off. He replayed Mary's big laugh, the joyous look on her face when she had doused him, wishing that Aneta would laugh just like that.

Chapter 31

Mary

Przyniosłeś mi to. Jak magia. Mary played with the words again. There was something in the way Weira's friend had said them that made her feel his tenderheartedness. He didn't even know her, and he had been sweet and kind to her. Samuel paled in comparison.

Easter Sunday had been full of work, and though she enjoyed every minute of Mass and preparing and eating the blessed food, there was an emptiness widening inside her. Like the fireplace hearth where she hid away the things that she'd take into her marriage someday, there were hidden dreams and empty spaces inside her, wanting to be filled. The rejection burned. She told herself to ignore it, but the sensation persisted.

Mary was more cheerful on Easter Monday. She, Katya, and Weira turned the Smigus-Dyngus game on all the boys and threw water on every single soul they saw in town. They moved so quickly from person to person and house to house that Mary accidentally doused Dr. Friday as he was leaving the Westchester's on Thompson. Mary and the girls got their share of dousing as well, but that was good; it meant they were desirable. That eased her heavy heart, at least for a time.

"*Przyniosłeś mi to. Jak magia,"* she said aloud.

"Why do ya keep repeating that Polish?" Matka came behind Mary as she was cleaning the supper dishes.

Mary shrugged. *It's elegant*, she wanted to say. But that wasn't an answer her mother wanted to hear.

Matka took Mary's chin and turned her face one way, then the other, studying her. When she saw whatever it was she was looking for, she stepped back and crossed her arms. "English, Mary. Or Czech." She threw a spoon into the dishwater, her frustration obvious. "Was gonna wait on Papa to talk to ya about this, but he's pullin' doubles and you're getting dreamier and dreamier."

Mary narrowed her eyes on Matka as she imagined Papa crumpled over in the mine, every inch of him catching the coal dust that choked him as he worked.

"What?" Mary asked.

Matka took her apron off the hook and tied it around her waist. "A match."

Now Mary was frustrated. "Match?"

Matka removed cans and celery from the bags. "Ya know what I mean."

Mary shook her head, feeling sick, her thoughts tangling.

"Ralph Zacpal. Perfect for ya."

Mary visualized the boy. She knew him from church and school, but his family was never considered friends of the Lancoses.

Matka stalked across the kitchen, her arms full of cans for the pantry. "They bought a store on McKean. Hardware. That's what ya should be repeating every five minutes, not that Polish nonsense."

Mary groaned.

"He's the one."

"Why?"

"Tall. And, like I said, his family's got a hardware store. He'll give ya the easy life with a girl to help clean."

"He's shorter than me."

"Not anymore. Leaving church on Palm Sunday, he was right behind ya. Good three inches taller."

Mary shook her head, remembering how Ralph used to pick at scabs in elementary school.

"Size is important," Matka said. "Don't want ya hunching like an old fortune-teller the rest of your life, like you do when ya stand around your friends."

Since when did Matka care about such things? How did she know that her height had been such an enormous deal to Mary? It was as if she could see right into Mary's mind, feel the worry in her heart that no one would ever really want her because of her height. "I don't slouch."

"You droop like wilted daisies with yer pals. Other times ya strut like Queen Victoria. Do *that* every time. No hunching."

Mary exhaled dramatically.

"Ralph's father sells screens, wrenches, every single thing a person needs for a home." Matka pointed at the ceiling. "Hell, maybe we can fix the roof for good if—He's got *tools*, Mary."

"Tools?"

"Implements of progress."

Mary wondered where Matka picked up that word. "Papa mines the coal that makes the coke that heats the iron that makes the steel that makes the bridges and buildings and those implements of progress that Ralph's father simply sells. Real hard."

"Mary Lancos."

Mary was confused. Matka was normally bitter toward successful men. Was the only difference that Ralph's family shared the Lancos heritage? That was it? "Why don't you talk about Papa like that, with all that awe in your voice? It's like you don't even realize how hard he works. There wouldn't *be* tools for a store if not for his share of the process."

"Mary." Matka spoke through clenched teeth. "Watch that tongue. Yer arguing against yer own case."

Mary crossed her arms. "I'm sorry, Matka. But I don't want to marry Ralph. Please don't talk to his parents. It's un-American to force people to marry like they're animals."

"How do ya know ya don't want to marry 'im?"

"This is stupid. He has his eye on other girls. I've an arm's-length list of them if you want it." Mary thought of all the girls he always chose at dances.

"He'll see yer worth. It's not happening tomorrow. Ralph's finishing high school before he takes his father's store. And we need yer income for now. Papa's not ready to send ya off yet. Too young, he says. Nearly old enough I say."

Mary's throat tightened.

Matka grabbed Mary's arm. "*We* know what's right. Yinz two would make a fine pair. Everything'll be easier, and ya can stop worrying about . . . whatever it is that has ya reciting Polish while ya do the dishes."

Mary shook her head. Nothing about Matka, even her suggestions, seemed to make anything easier.

Chapter 32

Mary

May 6, 1910

On Mary's fourteenth birthday, she entered the Dunns' kitchen to find Mrs. Harper washing breakfast dishes.

"Mister and the missus want ya in the study."

Mary hung her sweater and placed her hat above it in the cloakroom, confused. "Mrs. Dunn?"

"Both."

Her hands shook. She glanced at the clock. Was something wrong? Mr. Dunn should have been at work, and Mrs. Dunn was normally getting ready to leave for the Women's Club. *Both of them.* Had she broken something while cleaning? Let the boys out too far again? Her blood rushed in her ears. "Why?"

Mrs. Harper pushed her fat hands into the sink and scrubbed at something. "How in the hell do I know?"

Mary swallowed hard, smoothing her dress. "Did I do something wrong?"

"Do I look like a corresponding secretary?" Mrs. Harper asked. "Scoot."

Mary headed through the butler's pantry and into the foyer, where she checked her hair in the mirror. Hesitant, she moved toward the back of the house to the study.

As she drew nearer, she saw the door was open. She knocked on the doorjamb and Mrs. Dunn turned in her chair. Mr. Dunn rose from behind his desk.

"Come in, Mary," Mr. Dunn said.

At the edge of the rug, Mary's toe caught and she lurched. Mrs. Dunn hopped up to steady her. "Happy birthday, dear Mary."

Mary smiled, pleased that Mrs. Dunn would remember such a thing. "Thank you."

Mr. Dunn came around the desk and held out his hand. Mary shook it.

"Well." He leaned back on his desk and crossed one foot over the other. "You're all set for the mill. Monday. Daylight shift, nail girl."

The air left Mary's lungs. She glanced at Mrs. Dunn. Mary knew Mr. Dunn had planned to hire her once she turned fourteen, but she hadn't expected it to be that very day.

"I'm glad you're pleased," Mr. Dunn said. "I know your parents are."

Mary nodded, not sure how he could think she appeared delighted. She was nauseated. Though she was sure she could do the work, she wasn't ready to leave Mrs. Dunn.

"You'll work for me on Wednesdays," Mrs. Dunn said. "And anytime we arrange it on the weekends."

Mary nodded, feeling herself lift out of her shoes.

"Peggy Matthews will train you on the nail line," Mr. Dunn said. "But in addition to sanding the burrs off and sorting nails, I'd like you to keep an eye out for me."

Mary didn't know what he meant. "Keep an eye out?"

He crossed his arms. "People have been leaving shifts with pockets full of nails, wire, and such."

Mary still wasn't sure what he was getting at.

"If you see anyone take my steel, you tell me. And if you overhear someone being paid to look the other way, you tell me. And if you hear one bit of chatter about organizing the union again, you tell me. They talk in Polish or Czech or Italian when we"—he touched his shirt collar—"walk by, but you'll hear what we don't."

Mary's breath caught. "You want me to spy?"

"That sounds rather official, Mary. I simply want you to notice and report."

She hated the idea. "If I'm working, how would I notice such things?"

"If there's something to notice, I'm sure you will. My wife has assured me of that." He nodded at Mrs. Dunn. "See you Monday." He waltzed off, his footfalls growing quieter as he trailed through the house.

Mary's blood drained to her feet. She was devastated that everything had changed so quickly.

Mrs. Dunn guided her into a chair. "Not to worry. You'll be here on Wednesdays. Your family needs the pay and . . ."

Mary nodded, looking into her lap, clasping her hands so tight, her knuckles whitened. She wished her family wasn't so desperate for money.

Mrs. Dunn pulled a slim box off the table and handed it to Mary. "Happy birthday."

The white box was belted in ribbon a shade of blue Mary'd never seen before. She ran her finger down one piece of it, then wiped her hand on her dress, afraid to get it dirty.

"Peacock blue. Isn't it gorgeous?" Mrs. Dunn asked.

"Oh yes, but you shouldn't have, Mrs. Dunn." She couldn't take her eyes off the present.

Mrs. Dunn leaned back against her husband's desk. "I would give you gifts every single day just to see your face, Mary. You truly love and appreciate each and every thing."

"I can't tell you how much I do." She yearned for a time she could give special things to people and evoke delight in them.

"And I know what you're thinking," Mrs. Dunn said. "But you give me something every time you show up. You care for my children like you're their second mother. That debt can't be repaid."

Mary swelled at the thought. "I don't want to work at the mill. I can work even longer hours for you to make extra money."

Mrs. Dunn shrugged. "Mr. Dunn needs you at the mill. And your family does too. I have a household budget and can't give you more. Cash, I mean. I wish I could, believe me."

Mary had never considered that Mrs. Dunn might be constrained by finances in any way.

"You'll see someday. Your husband'll buy you a beautiful home to keep, and you'll find there are limits on just about everything. But you'll be magnificent at it, Mary. That I know."

Mrs. Dunn's eyes were filling and her voice cracked. She pushed her chin into the air. "Enough of this. You're not leaving town. I'm not leaving town. You'll come on Wednesdays and more when possible."

Mary nodded, swallowing the lump in her throat. She had to be practical. Mrs. Dunn put aside her sadness, and Mary would do the same. She would listen and learn and keep making Mrs. Dunn want her around. Who knew what might happen?

Mrs. Dunn got down on her knees and put her hand over Mary's. "Now open the gift. I can hardly wait."

Mary pulled the ribbon and removed the lid. She spread apart the paper inside, and it revealed an ornate spoon. It was heavy like the dinnerware Mary had set for the Dunns' fancy parties. The thick handle was engraved with flowers of every sort.

Mrs. Dunn smiled. "It was Mr. Dunn's mother's. Her father was given a trunk load when they lived in Baltimore. A reward for some act of valor or another. Mr. Dunn's mother turns the fact that her family lives and breathes into acts of valor. Like I said, there's a trunk load of things we've never even used. And she doesn't like me much, so . . ."

Mary pushed the spoon toward Mrs. Dunn. "I can't take this."

Mrs. Dunn pushed it back. "You told me about the sterling spoon your parents were given when you were born."

Mary's throat constricted. Her parents had sold it for a down payment on their house. She was flooded with shame.

"I understand why they sold it," Mrs. Dunn said. "You've a home now, and, well, I had to trade something beloved once. I know the desperation that forces the sacrifice. But every young woman—"

"Needs a hope chest," Mary finished the sentiment that Mrs. Dunn often repeated.

"Especially you. You'll be great, Mary. Different from all the rest."

Mary couldn't look up for fear the tears gathering would tumble down her cheeks.

Mrs. Dunn stood and brushed her skirt. "Now pop that into your coat pocket and get to work. There're no ladies of leisure in this household."

Mary sniffled, pulled her handkerchief from her sleeve, and dabbed her nose. When she realized how dingy it looked, she jammed it back into her sleeve. She replaced the spoon and covered it with the delicate paper, tucking it in like a baby.

Chapter 33

Mary

Six weeks into her work as a nail girl, Mary was at ease inside the belly of the wireworks, among the power and grind. Since Mary had moved with her family to Donora at the dawn of the mills' founding, she couldn't remember not hearing the racket, feeling the shudder of machinery as it hummed, ground to a halt, and then roared to life again. She'd been in the mills to deliver things to Mr. Dunn plenty of times, but until she worked there, she didn't fully absorb the power. The grating, spitting, cutting sounds worked right through her skin, making her feel as though she was one with the mill instead of a distinct being.

Mary straightened, her hands on the small of her back, and squeezed her shoulder blades together, hoping to work some of the fatigue out of her body. She stretched her head to one side then the other as she reached down the line to grab any nails that might have gotten past her when she had looked away. Most days, there was nary a defective nail in the bunch. American Steel and Wire prided itself on the quality of the coke, steel, and wire of every type it produced in record time, but that afternoon, Mary removed bent nail after headless nail.

She furrowed her brow. "See those?"

"What?" Kasandra, the girl beside her, answered her in Polish. It was her response to nearly everything. Mary knew what it meant. She sighed again. The gang leader, Peggy, was nowhere to be seen. Mary nudged the Polish girl with her elbow. "Keep going. I'm going to find Peggy." Mary mimed the act of working to the girl. "*Szybciej.*"

The girl smiled and nodded, understanding. "Faster," she said in English, the word muddled by her thick accent.

"Yes, yes, faster," Mary said. She backed away from the line, making sure Kasandra understood before she went to look for Peggy.

Mary knew where she'd be. Peggy was sweet on the wire-pulling boss who always took a coffee break smack in the middle of a shift.

Mary pushed into the room to find Peggy leaning against a table and smoking, the hem of her dress revealing her legs midcalf. Jim Byrne sat in front of her, coffee mug to his lips, his eyes tight on Peggy as if she'd cast a spell.

Mary cleared her throat. Peggy pushed away from the table and smoothed her dress, the hem falling to her ankles where it belonged. Jim stood and shuffled toward the coffee. "Mary," he said when he passed her.

"Jim," she said, watching him as he stirred sugar into his coffee. She tapped Peggy. "Something's wrong with the line."

Peggy sighed. She sashayed toward Jim, who was sipping his coffee. "Well, that means nails for my father's house. Good. He's looking to add on this summer."

The comment confused Mary but made her remember what Mr. Dunn had mentioned—nails were walking out of the mill as though they had feet. She had imagined that if someone was taking nails, it would be that a man was dragging three kegs out, not that Peggy might be taking some damaged ones.

"Hey, you take nails?" Mary asked.

Peggy's brow furrowed. "Who doesn't?"

"Who does?"

Peggy sighed and rolled her eyes. She took Mary by the shoulder to walk her back to the line. "Anything damaged isn't used—"

"Scrap for the heat in the open hearth," Mary said.

Peggy stopped and looked Mary in the eyes. "Who made you officer know-it-all?"

Mary was ten years younger than Peggy. She liked Peggy and knew better than to make her feel threatened. Still, she didn't want her to get into trouble. Mary didn't want to have to tattle on anyone, least of all a friend. She thought of the Dunns. She didn't want to disappoint them either.

Peggy was aging and needed a husband. Mary understood why her eye was more attuned to Jim than the nails missing half their heads. Still, if Peggy couldn't lure Jim into marriage, she was going to need her job even more.

"Don't take things, Peggy. It's not worth it."

"The only one who doesn't take scrap is Mr. Dunn. He actually pays for it. Jim told me that."

Mary thought of the wire she'd used at the Dunns' to make the Kraslice eggs.

Peggy put her arm around Mary. "Just sort your nails, and everything will be fine. There aren't more than ten houses in Donora that aren't at least half built with pilfered nails. They owe us for stiffing us, paying too little half the time. Jeez. They don't even stop the line when a fella crushes his hand in the roller. So yeah, we take a nail or two. Who cares?"

Mary's father worked for the mine, so it wasn't something she would know personally, but she was surprised she hadn't heard that before.

They walked back toward the line and passed the shipping department in time to see Lukasz Musial tossing his wire bundles as though they were made of spiderwebs instead of braided steel. She and Peggy stopped to watch. When Lukasz and his partner finished the load, they bent over to catch their breath. Lukasz had tossed double the number as the other man in just the time Mary had been watching. Lukasz straightened, rubbed his shoulder, and turned. Peggy waved, and he returned it with that shy smile Mary had come to see anytime they ran into one another. Before Mary could wave back, he looked away.

Peggy pulled Mary's arm and jerked her head upward toward the offices. "Go hit the button. I'll start explaining what's wrong to the white shirts. The only thing they'll stop for is quality. You can bet that takes precedence."

Mary nodded and crossed herself, hoping she hadn't done anything that might get her into trouble. It's not like she had seen anyone take nails. Merely discussing it didn't rise to the level of a report, she told herself.

But it did. Of course it did.

**

Mary's shift ended, and with it being June, sunset wasn't until well after nine at night. There were no dances planned at Eldora Park or the grove, but at only seven p.m. it was early enough to do something fun. "Peggy, Kasandra," she said as they washed their faces at the spigot at the end of the shift. "Let's go swimming."

Peggy jerked back from the sink, water droplets spilling off her chin.

"Swim?" Kasandra shook her head. Mary mimed the action, and Kasandra smiled. "Yes. I'm so hot."

Peggy wiped her face with a hand towel that had been left for them to clean up. "First really hot week in summer is always the worst. After that, you'll be used to it."

"So, yes?" Mary asked.

"Why not? Tomorrow's payday. Things are looking up," Peggy said.

They walked down Meldon to Gilmore docks. Mary's family's boat was there on the days Papa took the ferry to work. Sometimes a friend would borrow the boat for the day and shuttle Papa back and forth but this particular night, it was there, waiting for the girls. They spilled into it, and Mary had them out in the middle of the river in no time. She lowered the rope with three horseshoes to anchor them, and they peeled off their dresses and dove into the water one after the other, bursting back up, bobbing and giggling.

Kasandra spit out the water, making a gagging sound.

"Keep your mouth shut, silly," Mary said, floating on her back. "I could stay out here all night."

"Watch for the barge or this will be our final resting ground," Peggy said.

Mary laughed, turned onto her belly, and dove down as deep as possible before letting her body rise slowly, the water cooling and cushioning, releasing all the tension that hid in her neck, gripped her shoulders, and strained her lower back.

When she broke the surface and began to tread water, she was startled by Peggy and Kasandra's panicked breathing.

"What the hell, Mary? Yer part fish," Peggy said.

"We thought you got caught up in a current or something," Kasandra said.

Mary narrowed her gaze on her two friends and shrugged.

"You were under there forever. You know there're giant catfish down there. I thought . . ." Peggy said before she began to laugh. She splashed Mary, who splashed her back before rolling onto her back, arms out, chemise floating.

"It's the best. Just lay back and let the cool water take you," Mary said.

Peggy floated easily. She tapped Mary's arm. "You must have been born underwater or something."

Mary splashed at Peggy without even looking, feeling light and unburdened. "I may have, Peggy. I may have."

Kasandra hung onto the side of the boat, gasping. "Well, I wasn't born anywhere near water. I'm gonna drown."

Peggy and Mary hoisted Kasandra into the boat, where she lay between the seats, gasping.

After a few moments, Kasandra sat up and pointed. "Look. Who's that?"

"Dunno," Peggy said. "Great. We're in our underwear."

"Everyone swims in a chemise," Mary told her.

Peggy grasped the side of the boat with one hand and shaded her eyes from the setting sun reflecting off the water. "I once had a fine swim set to wear."

Kasandra faced the shore directly. "I can't see who it is."

Mary pulled up the rope with the horseshoes and tossed them into the boat, staying in the water.

"Oh, that's the gang from up Short Street," Peggy said.

Mary squinted.

"That's Lukasz," Peggy said. "See how stocky? Blond hair." They dragged the boat closer to shore. "See. Told you."

Mary stared.

Peggy splashed Mary. "Enjoying yourself?"

"What?"

"I see you gawking at him every time you pass him at work."

Mary smiled as she envisioned him tossing wire bundles. "It's like the bundles're made of air. It's just that. Interesting, is all."

"Oh yeah, that isn't *exactly* what I just said," Peggy said.

Mary kicked harder, panting. "Too short."

"Too engaged," Kasandra said, peeking over the edge of the boat at Mary and Peggy.

"Engaged?" Peggy always had a bitter edge to her voice when she heard of yet another woman finding her mate.

"Aneta Wasco."

"A Pole?" Peggy let go of the boat and backed away from it, treading water.

"*Oczywiście*," Kasandra said.

"Don't you people want to mix things up a bit?" Peggy asked. "I mean, you did come to a completely new country an'at. Why not marry someone like me? A mutt." She splashed at Mary. "Or at least someone like Mary here. She's American but still Czech in a way."

Mary and Kasandra laughed.

"You're right," Kasandra said. "We came to find better, new. For bread. And when we get here, we huddle in the same church, same clubs. Why *not* mix it up? I'm going to find myself an American. Maybe . . ." She wiggled her eyebrows at Peggy. "Jim. I'll take him."

Peggy glared then laughed.

The girls laughed harder, attracting the attention of the men on shore. They all waved but didn't come closer.

Peggy went onto her back and kicked water at Kasandra. "Keep your gloves off of Jim. He's all mine."

Kasandra flicked water back at her. "I know."

"So Lukasz is engaged," Peggy said.

"Arranged," Kasandra said. "Aneta's descended from kings. They're a very good match, even though Lukasz comes from peasants."

"Ugh, arranged. That's awful." Mary stretched her arms over her head and dropped under the water, knifing downward.

When she came back up, Peggy was still talking. "Arranged is looking pretty good to me right now." She pointed at Mary. "If your parents arrange a match, take it. You're young, but the difference between fourteen and twenty-four is about ten seconds."

Mary couldn't imagine such a thing.

Kasandra pointed to the men on the shore and the women who were joining them. "What're they doing?"

Mary squinted. "Setting up for a picnic dinner?" She counted. "Eight of them. Yep. Looks like a dinner date to me."

"You need to watch it, Mary," Peggy said. "You're like me. All full of ideas and standards and hopes and dreams and a mouth, always speaking your mind."

"Watch what?" Mary asked.

"Watch that you don't talk yourself out of the marriage pool. Men like a quiet woman who knows her place. I almost think I'm too capable. Sometimes I don't even want a man."

Mary and Kasandra laughed at that. As they neared the shore, Lukasz put two large baskets on his shoulders and walked along as though they weighed nothing.

"His strength makes him look taller than he is," Peggy said. She knocked on the side of the boat. "You sure he's taken, Kasandra?"

Kasandra narrowed her eyes at the group on the shore. "Oh yes. The Kowalks shoo away every girl who looks his way. Except for Aneta."

Mary had seen him at the dance way back before Easter with a blonde girl—very pretty. The two of them must have been a good match. But a match made more sense for them—they were new to America, not born here like Mary.

"I hear Aneta has eyes for other men. Irishmen, Scotchmen, the leading citizens of Donora," Kasandra said.

"Really?" Mary and Peggy asked in unison.

"*That's* interesting," Peggy said.

"The Kowalks are having none of it," Kasandra said. "And I'm not sure Lukasz sees it."

"Blinded by her beauty," Kasandra said.

"Or resigned to his prison," Mary said.

"Descended from kings, Mary," Kasandra said. "She's everything a Pole would want in a wife. Quiet. Beautiful."

Mary yawned, beginning to feel the exhaustion of the day. "I don't know. I may have a mouth, but I'll make a darn good wife. That much I know."

"Watch it, though."

"Watch *what*?"

"I see you dancing an awful lot with that Samuel fella. He's busy, that one. Take whomever your parents find if he's good enough. Just enough. That's all you need."

"What do you mean Samuel's busy?" Mary knew what Peggy was getting at—Melody.

"I know he's just sixteen, but Mr. Smarty-pants is charming you one minute, taking another for a soda the next, another to the show, another to sorority dances down at the University of Pittsburgh. I hear it all, Mary." She pointed at her head. "Every bit of Donora's dating information funnels through these two ears."

Mary certainly knew Samuel was busy with Melody, but all of those other girls? "He's too busy studying for any of that. Always at the library."

"Oh, Mary," Peggy and Kasandra said at the same time.

"What?" Mary splashed at them.

The two women studied her then rolled their eyes.

Peggy sighed. "Barge's coming. Kick! Row!"

"Kasandra, row," Mary said.

They got the boat to the dock, getting dressed under the falling darkness as the dinner group was too busy with each other to notice the three girls at all.

Chapter 34

Mary

June 23, 1910
St. John's Eve

Ever since Mary had learned to swim like she'd sprouted fins, she had found the festivities that surrounded St. John's Eve to be some of her favorites. Now she was at the age where she needed to act ladylike and remain dry in her white summer dress, she missed the chance to splash around, not caring about whether some boy plucked her crown from the candlelit water.

Down on the banks of the Mon, tables were set with white crochet and flowered linens that wafted in the sticky, hot wind. St. John's Eve, the day before John the Baptist's feast day, was also called Midsummer's Eve for those who weren't so religious. The Irish brought goody—bread soaked in hot milk—the English brought beer, and the Slavs brought the music and set the bonfires for cooking and jumping over. The Poles brought the flowers for the crowns used for rzucanie wiankow—the tossing of the wreaths—and the herbs to sprinkle into the fire.

At tables under a canvas tent were vines, leaves, flowers, candles, and floral wire. Girls and single ladies twined their vines into crowns, measuring each other's heads before decorating the wreaths. Flowers and ribbon were added, with spaces to hold small candles. Later, the girls would release their wreaths into the river, hoping they'd float toward the men of their dreams.

Matka didn't care for the event. "Stupid waste of time. As though all them ladies' houses will redd-up themselves." Still Mary asked her to attend.

"Nope. Someday you'll see, Mary. Sad day that'll be."

Mary squinted at her, praying she was wrong then left for the river.

The committee of women who'd arranged the celebration had brought fennel, rue, rosemary, lemon verbena, mallos laburnum, foxglove, roses, and elderflower along with lavender and St. John's wort. Some of those supplies were used for the crowns, and the rest were divided among the women so they could be kept outside overnight in a shallow water bowl, collecting dew. The next day, they would use the flower water to wash their faces, a ritual to protect them from evil and increase their fertility and beauty. As she saw it, Mary was never in danger of having too much beauty and couldn't wait to wash her face in the special water the next day.

Many of the families who lived in Donora hosted relatives for the summer to visit and enjoy the river. Mary eyed the crowd, wanting to avoid Ralph, her mother's idea of a match for her.

She still thought an awful lot about Samuel, who had been her most ardent dance partner, even if he'd been horrid, even if he'd turned his eye toward Melody. But she was looking forward to the chance to see boys visiting from other places as well. Though Mary hadn't seen Samuel with Melody lately, she couldn't get out of her mind what Peggy and Kasandra had told her about his packed social calendar.

Tents had been erected for the men and women coming from work to change clothes. The music and laughter filled Mary as she and her friends washed up and changed after their shift. The chatter in the women's tent was exciting. Maybe Kasandra's future husband would be someone visiting for the summer. Maybe tonight would be when everything in Mary's life changed and the perfect unknown man retrieved her crown from the river. Or maybe Samuel would claim hers.

Mary and her friends worked on their crowns, but she helped fit her sisters' vines onto their heads and searched out unique flowers to make their crowns noteworthy enough to interest boys. Unmarried men and mischievous boys snuck peeks under the tents to be sure they retrieved their favored girl's crown when the time came.

Downstream from the females, the boys and men gathered around bonfires big and small to drink beer, roast meats, and leap over fires to entice the sun to stay longer. The flames were to cleanse the earth and air and lure the luck needed for a fruitful harvest. In Donora, the lore was modified to influence the output of steel and bring ever more jobs.

The blast furnaces worked hard, shooting their flames in the distance. The bonfires were like miniature echoes, reminders of the immigrants' farming pasts and a reflection of their present industrial lives.

"I'm too old for this," Peggy said as nine p.m. approached, bringing the first whispers of night.

"But maybe this'll be the year," Kasandra said.

Mary noticed a single sunflower that had fallen off the table. She fastened it into Peggy's crown and was satisfied that it could be easily identified later. "No one else has a sunflower. Jim will find yours for sure."

Mary patted her crown, satisfied that the pattern of foxglove, rose, and gladiolas was unique. She put it on her head and glanced around to see if Samuel was watching from afar, attempting to see which crown was Mary's.

No sign of him.

She readjusted her wreath on her head, took a lemonade, and crept toward the bonfires to see which boys had arrived.

"Ladies, ladies!" Mrs. Sarto's voice rang out behind Mary. "Sun is setting. It's time."

Mary backed away from the bonfires and joined the young women waiting to release their crowns on one of the docks. She removed her crown. When it was her turn, Mrs. Sarto put two candles into the woven flowers and lit them. Mary gently laid it onto the water's surface. "Please let someone wonderful get mine." She gave it a brush of her fingertips and sent it scooting far into the water, watching the current catch it and take it along.

One by one, the candlelit crowns went into the water, the darkness swallowing everything not illumined by the wicks' flame. Mary didn't think she had ever seen a more beautiful sight—her river, the river of work and play, decorated with crowns of light and hope.

Peggy tapped Mary's shoulder. "Let's go to the fires."

They drew closer to the bonfires, and the sound of hooting and hollering men was followed by splash after splash as they leapt into the river to retrieve wreaths. The elder women followed the running girls, clapping and encouraging the boys to bring them in. Mary took a bowl of the herbs and tossed handfuls into the fire as she did each year.

"Hi, Mary."

Mary jumped at the sound of her name. "Samuel. Hi."

He held a crown out to her. "This is yours, right?"

She stopped tossing the herbs and looked at what he held in his hands. His wet fingers glistened in the light of the fire. His dripping hair had flopped over one eye. Mary exhaled and pushed the lock off his brow.

"Nope. Not mine." It was full of daisies, not even close to the flowers she'd chosen.

"Oh. I always saw you as a daisy girl."

Mary flinched, not sure what that meant. She certainly wasn't dainty.

"Oh well," Samuel said. "It's a silly thing anyway, isn't it? Why don't we—"

A girl squealed from somewhere near the riverbank. They turned to see Hanna Applegate and Maxwell Thurston running toward the fire, smiling and laughing. They stopped, letting the golden glow color them like royalty as Maxwell fitted the crown onto Hanna's head. Maxwell got onto his knee and asked her to marry him. There was more squealing and arms looped around necks and waists.

Samuel and Mary looked at each other. "Not so silly," she said.

"I guess not. Listen, Mary. I wanted to—"

"Samuel."

They turned toward the calling voice.

"That's my crown," Veronica Murray said. "Oh, I can't believe it." She came nearer, covering her mouth with her hands. She spread her arms. "You know what this means."

Samuel exhaled. "You're a daisy girl?"

"She's definitely a daisy girl," Mary said, backing away. Heaviness filled her chest, thick as the humid air.

"First dance is with me." Veronica stepped closer to Samuel, her eyes closed, her head bowed forward, signaling for Samuel to place the wreath on her. He did, and she grabbed his hand, dragging him toward the music near the food table. They disappeared into the darkening night, Samuel not even glancing back.

Mary turned back to the river, looking for a sign of the crown she'd made. The river was still littered with them. Boys who weren't interested in finding a girl or retrieving a crown splashed and dunked one another. Mary crossed her arms, dying to just dive into the water and swim among what looked like earthbound stars. The crowns should just stay in the water, bobbing, lighting the night, each hopelessly isolated on an unrealized path, similar to her own.

A boat came into view, cutting through the trail of crowns. Mary didn't pay much attention to it until she heard the laugh, followed by a near-crippling coughing fit.

Papa.

The craft drew closer, and she saw the fella rowing—String Bean, the man her father had been sharing rides with since Mary had started as nail girl. Papa sat upright, singing, coughing, yelling, coughing. He should have been home hours ago.

Mary glanced around to see if anyone else had noticed the ruckus, but neither her friends nor Samuel were in sight. Relieved, she walked toward the shoreline. Papa stood when he saw her, waving his arms, his shirt untucked, his coal-smeared face lit by sunset and candlelight.

Mary lifted her hand and signaled to her father. "Down a little further. Go to the docks," she said as the boat knocked into the crowns, extinguishing candle flames. She glanced around again, hoping no one had noticed. None of her friends were watching, but lots of other hopeful girls were.

Papa stopped coughing and leaned out of the boat, stretching wiggling fingers.

"Papa, no!" Mary said.

He bit his lip and stretched farther, snatching a crown out of the water. He wrestled it onto his head. "Where's my maiden?" he asked, laughing again, drawing the attention of anyone in earshot.

"That's mine!" a voice yelled. "Put that back!"

He took it off and tossed it with all his might, the candles falling out and dropping into the river. The flames went out like firefly light extinguished at dawn. Papa's arms spun, but he lost his balance and toppled into the river. The owner of the crown, Melissa Franklin, burst into tears, dropping her face into her hands. Her mother comforted her, glaring at Mary.

"I'm sorry, I . . ." was all Mary could say. No one spent more spare time drunk than Melissa Franklin's father, but he wasn't the one here making a fool of himself, ruining a young maiden's dreams.

Papa surfaced, choking, grabbing the boat. He pulled himself halfway up but flipped the boat, sending his pal, String

Bean, into the water as well. Mary edged closer, removing her shoes.

Papa surfaced, choking harder. She lifted her dress hem, wading into the water. He reached for her, and she latched onto his hand, dragging him onto the bank. On wobbly legs, he staggered then crashed straight onto his back, knocking the wind out of himself.

He heaved for breath, his face apple red. String Bean crawled onto shore, popped up, and waltzed away. "Beer!" he yelled. "Get this sailor beer, you landlubbers!"

Mary pulled her father to sitting and slapped his back until his breath came back to a normal rhythm with little coughing. She helped him to his feet. "Easy now. Let's get you home." She moved him slowly, glancing around to see most people looking away, giving them space.

Mr. Lubinsky came to them. "I can get him back home, Mary. I'm already married. I don't need a crown."

Mary forced a laugh. "Thank you. I'll get my sisters and be right behind you. Tell my mother we're coming."

She bent over and brushed the debris from her skirt, but that made it seep further into the material. When she straightened, she saw that someone was pulling her boat to shore.

"Thank you," she said, going nearer. "Oh. Lukasz, right?" She pulled the top layer of her white dress away from the chemise that clung to her skin underneath.

He nodded. "You're welcome."

She moved toward the water. "I'll take the boat."

He motioned that he would drag the boat down to the dock.

She smiled, and they stared at each other. "That's all right."

"All right?" He looked at her drenched and dirtied dress. She was suddenly embarrassed and wanted to run. Her feet slid in the sludge and he grabbed her hand. He pointed downriver. "No problem. I'll take it." He struggled with the words, but she appreciated him trying.

His hand was warm. Though he was considerably shorter than she, his hand dwarfed hers. His grip was firm, reassuring.

"Yes. Thank you."

"Moja przyjemność."

"Lukasz." A voice came from higher up on the bank. It was Aneta, Lukasz's fiancée. Her lacy white dress billowed, her loose, golden hair dangled down her back, lapping in the wind. She looked like an angel.

Lukasz said something Mary didn't understand. Aneta answered him in sharp Polish, her face twisted in anger.

Mary grabbed the boat. "Go on." She gestured toward Aneta.

"I'll help," he said, pulling the boat back.

"Lukasz. Now," Aneta said in English.

He straightened and stared at her. "I'll be right there."

She shook her head. "Get the crown. That's what I want," Aneta said in nearly perfect English.

"I'm sorry, I—" Mary said. Aneta glared, silencing Mary.

Lukasz eased the boat off the shore farther into the water, wading into lapping wake.

"Your shoes!" She pointed and he shrugged, smiling.

"Really," Mary said. "I can do it. I used to row my father to work all the time."

Lukasz looked confused but continued pushing the boat further in. Mary looked over her shoulder at Aneta, who was coming down the bank, slipping then recovering her balance then slipping and recovering again. Lukasz stopped and held a wreath over his head. It was outlined in blaze orange, caught by the setting sunrays. He held it up to Aneta. "*Czy to twoje?*"

Mary could tell Lukasz was asking Aneta if the crown was hers.

Papa trundled back toward the river, heading in the direction of Aneta. Mary lifted her hem and started for her father.

"*That crown?*" Aneta said in English, snapping her words off short.

Papa's voice came again. Mary had to get him home. She turned back to Lukasz grateful he offered to take the boat to the dock. "Are you sure, Lukasz?" she asked.

He nodded.

"Thank you." She shielded her eyes and saw the crown clearly for the first time. It was hers. She laughed. Samuel was right—it was silly. An engaged man plucked Mary's wreath from the water.

"I'm going to eat," Aneta said, stomping away just as Papa barreled past and tripped into Mary's arms.

She jerked her head toward the water. "Toss that back, Lukasz. Belongs in the water." *Like me.* She steadied herself and turned Papa toward home.

Mr. Lubinsky was already coming to help her along. They each took an arm and escorted Papa back past the fires toward home. Mary looked over her shoulder to see Lukasz walking the oarless boat downriver. Her sisters were occupied with friends, making Mary glad they weren't watching this unfold.

Papa coughed again, unable to catch his breath. They'd barely walked thirty yards when he threw up. He told Mary he'd lose work the next day and that Matka would give him hell. Mary patted Papa's back. "No, no, Papa. She knows your lungs are bad."

Papa chuckled. "Thank you, sweet Mary. You're a good daughter. So good."

"Thank you, Papa." Mary helped him upright, warmed by the special relationship they shared.

When they resumed walking, she noticed Samuel watching. He lifted his hand in a half wave, and Mary pretended she didn't see. He'd never speak to her again. All her work in presenting herself in a particular way had dissolved into the night like herbs in a bonfire.

Chapter 35

Lukasz

It was the end of August 1910. The wedding hadn't happened, but not because Aneta and Lukasz hadn't wanted it to. Aneta had declared she simply could not walk down the aisle until her parents had arrived to witness the nuptials. That was still being arranged.

With summer temperatures pushing one hundred degrees, the heat and haze suffocated Lukasz. The mill was hotter than any hell he could imagine, but he was comfortable in his role in the shipping department, tossing wire bundles into the trucks, the monotonous rhythms limbering his muscles, giving his mind a chance to unfurl his dreams and plans. The boss rigged some tubing to bring water into the mill so they could stand under a steady drip of river water whenever there was a break.

After his shifts, his muscles screamed. But it was good. The aching reminded him of his important work. His strength directly impacted America's growth. His contribution mattered in a way he never could have fathomed back home. Most of the men shared that pride in their work. Many were interested in unionizing. Lukasz had caught bits and pieces of such talk, but he'd seen Jas Schmidt tossed from the line for merely suggesting to another that they think about demanding shorter shifts, even safety goggles. Lukasz put his head down and did his job.

Working meant a chance to amass cash for land and materials to build a home. He was surer than ever that he and Aneta would achieve what every human wanted: a warm home and hot food every night.

Like many employees in the nail mill, Lukasz helped the foreman add a room to his home in exchange for looking the other way when he walked away with a bucket of nails for his dream house. Before he could build, he needed to save enough to buy a tiny plot to build upon. He hadn't fooled himself into thinking he would have expansive property or even the charming little white fence depicted on that postcard the Kowalks had sent to Poland. He would be satisfied with a sliver of land to call his own.

Lukasz and Aneta had settled into a quiet togetherness that included dances, meals at the Kowalks and Bielawas', and baseball games. One particular Saturday, they attended the baseball game between Donora and Monessen at Gilmore Park.

They sat in the stands, shoulder to shoulder. It was so crowded that people were even scattered around the outskirts of the field. Children sat with their mothers on blankets, sharing sandwiches and snacks, tossing balls, and mimicking what they saw on the field.

Lukasz blotted his brow with his hanky and salivated at the thought of the lemonade he would buy after the game. The score was 11-6 with Donora in the lead in the bottom of the seventh inning.

Aneta and her friend to her left chattered incessantly in English, not paying attention to Lukasz or the game. He didn't mind. He enjoyed being with Aneta in the company of others, seeing people taken with her grace and stunning looks. They didn't pay much attention to him, but they were a couple, and he was proud of her.

He understood how important it was to become fluent in English and he was getting better, but Aneta seemed to want to speak it over Polish even at home. She badgered him to learn more and more so he could move up in the mills, make more money, and enjoy the events that she got them invited to.

He reminded her that he'd won his job the very first day he'd had the chance, and he was happy to have any job at all, especially one that made good use of his strengths. He wasn't aiming for any job that required him to talk more than toss wire bundles. A good Polish man was satisfied to keep his family by way of his hands, his back, and his will.

Still, he understood her social inclinations, and he was happy to let her shine over him when they were with others. When the day came and he finally presented her with land and a perfect little home, she would let him shine, and that would seal their perfect match.

He watched the game, marveling at the fun the players had, their skill in turning a silly child's game into something that felt so much more important. The players worked long shifts in the mill and still found the energy for baseball. The entire town turned out to watch, wanting a chance to witness the games that led to bragging rights against other towns and their mill teams.

The batter for Donora swung and whiffed, nearly twisting around a full rotation. The fans gasped.

"Thanks for the cool breeze, Marsic," a woman's voice came from the other end of the bleachers.

The batter scowled into the stands, squinting.

A woman's laugh curled into the air, and Lukasz found himself smiling at the sound of it. He'd heard it before. He leaned forward to see around Aneta and her friend.

At the end of the bleachers, in the first row, a lanky brunette stood with her hands on her hips—the heckler.

Mary Lancos.

She bent over, gripping her knees, fully engaged in the game as though she might be called in to play. She pointed to the third baseman and said something to her girlfriends that Lukasz couldn't hear.

He smiled, watching her, absorbed in her lack of self-consciousness. She was comfortable in her place in the world, unconcerned that some might consider it strange that a woman was so caught up in a boy's game.

Another pitch and another whiff sent Marsic twisting so far around that he lost his hat completely. He steadied himself on his bat and put his hat back on.

Mary cupped her hands at her mouth. "Woohoo! Cooling me off, Marsic. I can use it. It's hot out here!"

The batter spun around. "Stop jeering, Mary. I'm on your team, for the love of Pete."

Lukasz held his breath, waiting for Mary to shrink into her seat, dodging the response of the beloved batter.

"Hit the ball, I'll quit heckling."

"Put a sock in it, Mar," he said.

The umpire tugged on the batter's sleeve to draw his attention back to the pitcher.

Mary laughed again, covering her mouth. Joyful. Lukasz had never heard a laugh quite like Mary's, a laugh that started in her eyes and spread to her lips. He realized right there that he loved it. Mary was bold, without the slightest attempt at being coy or delicate. Lukasz stared. He'd never seen someone so utterly pleased by watching this child's game.

American. The word came to him as he watched Mary, unencumbered by royal dictates or station. He imagined she lived every breath of her life this way—open, loud, joyous. He couldn't imagine feeling all those things at once, and it excited him to think that his children with Aneta would embody all those things.

Aneta slid closer to her friend, their heads bent into each other, further hiding their English words from Lukasz. He nudged her. "Aneta, watch. Big hit coming here." It hadn't taken long for him to learn the rules to the game and enjoy it along with the rest of Donora.

Aneta glanced at him, shooting him an irritated expression and a shrug before turning back to her friend. Marsic stepped back into the box, spread his feet, and bounced a couple of times as he settled into his stance, waiting for the pitch.

The pitcher wound up and sent the ball screaming toward Marsic. He stepped toward the pitch and swatted. The ball caught the top of his bat and fired backward, toward the stands. With a whoosh, everyone ducked in unison, the ball whizzing toward two screeching girls covering their heads.

Mary Lancos leaned forward, one leg off the ground like a dancer in flight. The smack of the baseball against her hands as she caught it, echoed.

"Ooh," the collective audience gasped, hands over mouths, eyes squeezed shut, everyone frozen, waiting for Mary to cry out in pain or join her friends in their squealing.

Instead, she hoisted the ball over her head in triumph. Hopping from one foot to the other. On cue, the stands erupted, cheering as though she was on the team. Lukasz clapped along, mesmerized.

Eventually, the fans sat and the young man Lukasz had seen Mary with at several dances was revealed off to the side, scowling. Mary whipped the ball back to the pitcher, smacking it hard into his mitt. She wiped her palms and cupped her hands at her mouth again. "Straighten it out, Marsic. Today's my day off. Don't make me work so hard. I'm not a charity, you know."

Aneta tugged on Lukasz's shirt sleeve. "Sit down."

Lukasz looked around, realizing he was the only one still standing. Mary heckled Marsic again, making Aneta flinch. "Awful," she said.

Lukasz chuckled to himself, knowing that Mary's behavior wasn't the kind other girls would aspire to when attempting to garner attention from the opposite sex.

Aneta stood. "I've had enough."

Lukasz watched her weave down the bleachers toward the ground. What had turned her so sour? As Aneta made her way, another foul ball shot into the stands. Her head snapped toward the field and she dropped to the ground, arms over her head. This time, a boy in the top row caught the ball.

Everyone laughed at Aneta's reaction and joined Mary in heckling Marsic. Aneta turned blaze red, her confidence dissolving as she tripped away from the crowd. Lukasz bounded down from the stands and followed her, wanting to comfort her. He stole a last glance at Mary, his chest tightening as he watched her gaze slide from batter to pitcher to batter as though she could somehow affect the action with her eyes.

Finally, Lukasz realized Aneta was practically running away, so he took off after her.

Mary's voice rang out again, "Cool breeze, Marsic. Thank you . . ." and something else Lukasz didn't understand. He had to look back. She was pointing, shouting, gesturing.

The batter swung, this time connecting with the ball in a way that sent a crack echoing in Lukasz's chest and he knew it was a home run. The ball flew so far and high, he lost sight of it in the hazy summer sky. What a beautiful game, Lukasz thought. What a glorious day for a girl like Mary to be watching it.

**

Lukasz followed Aneta, the cheers of the crowd accompanying them as they neared the refreshments. Huffing, he caught up to her and took her hand.

"Lemonade?"

She pulled her hand away and kept walking. "Nothing. I don't want a thing."

A cheer went up at the field and Lukasz took one last look to see everyone on their feet, hands pushed into the air as Marsic rounded third base, headed for home. He wished he'd still been in the stands. The roaring crowd made him understand he was missing something that would have made him more a part of Donora, more American.

He grabbed Aneta's hand again, pulling her to go back.

She sighed and stopped near a stand of trees. "What? What?"

He studied her—her beautiful eyes, slender nose, and golden hair tucked under her hat, the ropes of braids beneath the brim.

"What's wrong?" Lukasz asked.

She took a few steps.

Lukasz pulled her back. "What?"

"I see you watching that girl. She's a nail girl, you know."

"I know," Lukasz said.

Her lip curled in disgust. "I knew you knew."

He raised his hands, unsure of what Aneta was getting at. "I see her at work sometimes."

"And you don't notice or care that her dress is filthy? You just stare at her like she's some sort of . . . goddess, or I find you pulling her boat from the water, or . . ."

Lukasz had been staring at Mary, but so was everyone at the game. He'd never seen Aneta insecure. So many times, he was reminded of her royal ancestry. She had to know he understood he was lucky to be matched with her.

"*You're* a goddess. A princess. I know that, Aneta." Why were the words so hard to say? "You know that. Everyone can see."

"You don't even care."

It was true that her ancestors didn't matter in America, but he wished he had the money to treat her like a queen.

Aneta balled her fists and breathed hard. She finally met his gaze, startling him with her intensity. "We're not a match."

"What?"

"We're not good together."

He rubbed his chest. Her words were like a wasp's stinger. She'd been through so much and he wanted to protect her. He had come to really like her. He wanted to be her husband. For her to put words to all of her vague disinclinations, to add language to the unsaid between them, tore at him. "But we are matched."

"This isn't Poland," she said. She was always saying that, always angling away from Lukasz. So many Poles said, "This isn't Poland," longing to get back there, to earn enough to return with treasure for their villages. But it was clear now more than ever that Aneta meant that she didn't want to go back to her wide blue skies, though she missed them. She wanted to separate from her motherland completely.

He was draped in loneliness that hadn't fallen on him in a long time. "You're right." Everything with them had been forced in some way from the time she had found out he wasn't Waldemar.

Aneta played with the ruffles on her collar. "My parents can't come until . . . I don't know when, and I can't get married when they're not here. It'll be even longer. Another year at least."

He nodded. Was she agreeing to continue with their match? "Tell Zofia. She's planning and plotting. She won't believe me if I say it."

Aneta stared at him, longer than she had since they'd met.

He cleared his throat. This would give him time to get closer to having the money for a plot of land. "We'll delay."

"Maybe forever," Aneta said.

Forever? His insides tangled around the thought. "But a deal was made."

"I didn't know it was," said Aneta.

Now Lukasz was offended. He may not have been effusive toward her, but he'd treated her well in planning their future. "I didn't know either." He needed to speak up, to push the words out even if he was clumsy with them. "But now I know you better, and I'm looking forward to being with you, Aneta. I can take care of you."

"I don't want to disappoint my parents." Her voice shook with tears.

"I don't want to upset the Kowalks."

She looked off into the distance and wiped her tears. He pulled out his hanky, the one Adam's mother had made him to give to his true love. He was relieved it was fresh. She pushed it away and he put it back into his pocket.

She squared her shoulders and nodded. "I know my duty."

Was that really what Lukasz was to her? He didn't want to know the answer. He remembered Zofia telling him she'd had a rough start with Alexander. Someday Lukasz would tell his story to a young person wanting to find his way in the world.

"Come on," he said. "I'll show you plots of land I like. I've sketched some houses and—"

She looked away with a shake of her head.

He choked back frustration. What did she want from him? He told himself to be patient. But wasn't it time to push their relationship further? He'd promised Zofia not to mention what happened to Aneta, but it was time to show she could trust him, that he wanted her no matter what. "I know what happened in Poland. You don't have to hide yourself, your past, from me. I understand how much pain you must feel."

Her mouth dropped open and her eyes filled. He readied himself to chase her if she ran off again.

"I'll make you a life here, Aneta. We'll both start again. Together."

He offered his hanky again. This time, she took it and dabbed her nose as she sniffled. She covered her face with it, sobbing into the hanky.

"I'm sorry for how I . . ." She swallowed hard and took his hand, squeezing it.

"It's all right. I know, I know."

Her expression softened through her tears. Lukasz drew her tight against him. She was stiff but finally melted into him. "I'll build you a home. I promise to make it everything you imagine."

She nodded against his chest. Her warmth flooded him with a mix of happiness and sadness; like a shot glass dropped into a beer, his emotions foamed and overflowed. Aneta wrapped her arms around him, accepting him.

His sadness reached for hers, and this moment of mutual sorrow—as important as any joy they might share—gave him the sense that maybe it could work. Zofia had said this was about adjustment. They would fall into love, or at least grow in affection.

He took his hanky back from her and blotted dry her tears. “And so it will be.”

Chapter 36

Lukasz

"Noc Andrzeja Świętego przywiedzie narzeczonego"
St. Andrew's night brings you a fiancé.

November 29, 1910

With his shift in the mill finished, Lukasz exited onto Meldon, his mouth dry and his stomach aching, acid bubbling as though eating the lining away. He hadn't been eating well since Zofia's baby had been born. She was back to her normal chores, only taking two days' rest after the baby came. But at that point, Lukasz was intrusive and intruded upon. The baby screamed nonstop. The rest of the children stomped around the house with hands clapped over their ears. Tensions snapped. Even Lukasz had hollered at Nathan when he kicked him so hard in the kidneys that Lukasz flipped out of bed.

Zofia worked and tended the baby, the screaming seeming to fall past her ears like the mill noise he no longer noticed. Zofia *was* a mill—a never-ending process of consumption and production, no rest unless something completely took over, like deficient material for the mill or childbirth for Zofia. Nothing else stopped either one.

Lukasz was enamored with all of it. Zofia's strength, born of her Polish parents, the mills' fiery power, the product of educated Scots, Irish, and Englishmen. But it only worked because it was fueled by Polish and Slavic muscle. This immigrant vigor, Lukasz's own might, was so important to the steel industry that he trusted it more than anything in the equation.

Even with an achy stomach and a tight cough when his shift was over, he delivered the work, earned the money, and saved it. Education, language, ideas—all of it was invisible, comparatively unreliable except for a few lucky souls who captured their thoughts in the form of money. So few were granted that path. Lukasz had decided, happily so, that two hands and a strong back could provide more than a mind ever could.

Though he'd been doing a fine job of saving his money, earning extra when Mark sold one of his animals, the birth of the Kowalk baby had made him more inclined to stop into the Bucket of Blood. There were days he just couldn't resist, couldn't go home and face the monster infant and the resulting friction that came with it. He was careful not to repeat his first stop at the bar, stuffing his cash deep into his pocket and limiting himself to two boilermakers and a sandwich or two eggs.

He had even entered boxing matches when circuses rolled through town, the strongmen strutting down McKean, always willing to take on a short man like Lukasz. But once the fights started, he beat them in minutes with a few punches and a vice-grip headlock. While he drank one boilermaker with a single chug and the next with a few big swallows, fights would break out all around him, sometimes devolving into wrestling matches, drunks slapping and rolling until one passed out on top of the other, reminding him of home.

Unable to resist The Bucket of Blood that night, Lukasz ordered his usual. He inhaled deeply, dropped his shot glass into his beer, and guzzled it down. He thought of writing to Adam. What would he say? He would tell him about Aneta, his true love . . . but that would be a lie.

He missed his wide blue Myscowa sky, but he knew the mill was the perfect fit for his skills and strengths. He loved that he worked at Mark's forge, making wire animals, decorating them with powdered enamels that melted into colorful pools separated by the precious bits of scrap wire he took from the mill.

With his meal finished, he ascended the hill to the forge, where he would work on his animals. He passed the plot of land he wanted to buy on Heslep Avenue.

Two homes were on either side of the empty lot. Each was wedged into the hillside, positioned at slightly different angles, and Lukasz believed his home would do fine in between. Just a matter of time before he could buy and build. Even with Mr. Dunn and the other white shirts on the lookout for pilfering, he'd managed to get nails and wire out of the mill unnoticed, storing them at Mark's forge.

Lukasz's coworkers had taught him to trade the guards and foremen labor to help build their houses in exchange for them looking the other way. He stood in front of the property, the homes built so high above Heslep that they needed a raised sidewalk to hover over the narrow street. The homes on the other side of the street were built at street level or below, the tops of each roof making him feel as if he were a giant.

He envisioned his dream home—the front porch, fireplaces on each end of the house, and Aneta inside, preparing meals and watching over their children. He'd spoken to the property owner, and he was willing to sell when Lukasz was ready as long as no one else made an offer sooner. Lukasz would have pitched a tent and lived there just to say he had his own property, but he knew that wouldn't impress Aneta, a descendent of kings, with her delicate beauty and gentle ways.

Every time Lukasz took the winding path leading to the forge that was tucked away in the stand of trees behind Mark's home, he entered another world. He lit the lamp and readied his materials. He was working on several projects at once—the umbrella repairs, a set of wire dogs, and several mermaids depicting the ones he'd seen in his dreams. But most important were the rings he was making for Aneta.

He didn't have money to buy a diamond or even a plain gold band, but he trusted his metal work—jewelry made from the very steel that built Donora and brought him and Aneta together. Rings he made would be more meaningful than gold and diamonds dug by some stranger.

He looped the thin wire for the band as best he could to match Mrs. Bielawa's measurement of Aneta's gloves. Lukasz wasn't sure it would be exact, but he hoped it would be too beautiful to matter. In the past weeks of creating the rings for Aneta, his contentment about marriage had grown somehow.

He moved two lanterns closer to his work. His large fingers coaxed the slimmest wires into delicate channels. At the center of the engagement ring, he created a circle, accidentally irregular but prettier for not being perfect. He tapped the enamel powder into the circle and added heat. The powder turned to liquid, revealing an opalescent shade of pink and pearl shimmering in tiny paint waves.

He set it aside to cool and formed slim rectangular channels with wire that would lace around the band as though set with jewels. Each channel required its own heating and cooling, the same shade of pink and white as the round center.

The second band would stack against the first and was enameled in the same rectangular channels. The rings contained no diamond, ruby, or emerald, but Lukasz thought they were better. He'd poured his affection into each tiny pool of hot paint, setting each section with his intention to provide a good and safe home. Though Aneta was nothing like Zofia, Lukasz told himself that Aneta's Polishness—her strength—would take hold and marriage would offer the space for her to fall in love with him. The rings would help her see he was special and deserving of her affection.

He polished the circle at the center of the engagement ring and held it into the lamplight. He was pleased that though the shiny glistening color was merely paint, the overall effect looked as if it was set with precious stones.

He tucked it into a small tin nail box from the mill and covered it with a white piece of linen. He set that aside and polished the second ring.

The door handle jiggled. He shoved the wedding band into the box with the engagement ring and went to the door. Mark's arms must have been too full to turn the knob. "Coming," he said. He opened the door and nearly fell over.

Aneta. Red-faced, pinched lips.

She smacked her gloves into the palm of her hand. "Where were you?"

He stepped back to her let her in, confused.

She didn't budge.

He pushed his hand through his hair. "Come in."

"How could you?"

Lukasz scratched the back of his neck. He shook his head.

"Andrzejki? Remember?"

He closed his eyes and turned away. "Oh yeah. Let's go. I can move the tables now." He started toward her.

She put her hand against his chest. "It's all set up, Lukasz." She sniffed.

He held his breath, not wanting her to see him as a common drunk or see him as weak.

She grimaced. "Were you at the Bucket of Blood?"

He shrugged, wanting to lie, but knowing that wasn't right. "Not all day. I got hired onto another shift and then just went in for one drink. Just one."

Aneta clenched her jaw.

He took her by the shoulders. "I'm so sorry. I'm trying to work extra to save money for . . . I found the property. Our property."

She pushed his hands away and walked across the room to the cot against the wall. She sat down and hopped back up, wiping at her coat as if she'd been sitting in manure. "Buying a house without showing me? This is how things will work?"

She spoke English so fast he only caught every few words.

"Polish, Aneta. I don't—"

She snapped toward him. "Try harder, then."

Lukasz flinched.

"Just a little bit?"

Lukasz's extra time went toward ways to make money to save for a home or for the materials to build it. He didn't have time to learn English.

When she said things like this, his insides clenched and the acid doubled and burned like fire. He knew his value, his strengths. And he'd thought Aneta knew how hard he was working to give her a home. "Sure, sure."

"Well, can you still walk me to the church?"

He knew she was to help coordinate the evening for all the single women in town to find their fiancés in spirit, if not in reality. He looked over his shoulder at the workbench. "I'll clean up fast."

She sighed and joined him at the workbench. He knew she'd never pay attention to the nail box that held the wedding rings and ruin the surprise. For a moment, he thought he should give her the ring right then, right there, but when he saw her hard, angry expression, he decided not to.

She picked up one of the mermaids. "From your dreams?"

He nodded, self-conscious. She had never paid much attention to him when he tried to explain about the mermaid dreams he'd been having. He even once tried to tell her that the Wisloka Mermaid was half the reason he ended up in Donora, her scoffing and eye rolling told him she wanted to be as far from Polish lore as possible.

"Yes."

She held the mermaid into the light and ran her finger down the scales he'd created from hammering heated metal into diamond-shaped, razor-thin plates. They had been so thin, he could practically see through them before he added the enamel. He had wired the pieces together so that each scale moved, appearing to breathe in even the faintest of light.

She glanced at him and shook her head but didn't say anything before setting it down. He was less confident about the ring after that.

"Mama sent word."

Lukasz froze, unsure how to take her tone. Zofia had given him the news.

"They're coming," Aneta said, her voice sharp and hard.

He nodded.

She shook her head slowly, her silence making Lukasz turn toward her.

"February." Lukasz glanced at the tin with the rings inside. His stomach churning intensified, cramping. What was he waiting for?

"I know," Aneta said. "It's November twenty-ninth." Her voice quaked. She didn't view this as good news.

His breath came short and shallow. He had to do it. He reached for the box with the rings. "Listen, I need to—"

She turned and flapped her gloves back over her shoulder. "Let's just go, Lukasz. It's St. Andrew's Night, and I promised the girls I'd be there early. They're depending on me."

Lukasz lifted the lid of the box with a gentle pop. The rings sat on their linen bed, so pretty. Aneta had her hand on the door, turning the knob. "Step it up," she said, the English words blunt in his ear.

He closed the lid and put the box into his pocket. He would do it just before they got to St. Dominic's. The single girls there were all hoping to read their fortunes in wax and come out of the evening knowing who their husbands would be or what job they might do, but he thought Aneta would be pleased to wear the evidence that her future had been determined.

**

Outside, he offered Aneta his arm. She dug her fist through the crook and looped it with his, practically pulling him down the street. They turned onto Thompson, heading toward St. Dominic's.

"What's wrong, Aneta? You must be pleased to finally see your parents."

She shrugged. "Of course."

He didn't want to ask the next obvious question.

Aneta fixed her eyes ahead.

"What's wrong?" Lukasz asked again.

She stopped and whimpered, her face reddening as the tears began. "Today has been the worst day ever."

His heart softened at the sight. He took her hand. "I'm sorry I forgot to help Mrs. Beilawa set up, that I didn't send word after I got the extra shift. I just forgot. But it's not so bad. You've got me now." He did a little jig, hoping to make her laugh.

"Not today, Lukasz. Not today."

"Come on, Aneta. Laugh. Just one tiny giggle."

She shook her head.

He withdrew a fresh handkerchief from his pocket. It was one that Adam's mother had made him. It was fate. It might not be the right time to give her the ring, but the handkerchief? He ran his thumb over the small curlicue of blue embroidery decorating one corner. Was she his true love? Maybe not, but she was to be his wife. And he was sure he would love her fiercely once they were married. "It's clean. Take it."

She wiped her tears, shoved it up her sleeve without a word of thanks and started toward the church. Was she really just going to stalk away without saying goodbye?

He yelled for her to come back. "I have to tell you about the handkerchief."

She turned back. "Later, Lukasz. I want to hear, but later." She smiled at him then, soothing his nervous stomach the way a warm gesture or kind glance from her always did.

Then she strutted away, poised, her royal breeding shining through the dark fog.

Future husband. He had finally accepted his lot in life and patted his pocket and heard the faint ting of the metal against the tin box lid. It was time to act. He would talk to the landowner and convince him to take payments.

He started back down the street, wanting to walk, wanting to make his plan. But before he knew it, he found himself at the river's edge, his eyes searching for movement out in the fog, hoping to get a glimpse of his mermaid just once more.

Chapter 37

Mary

Mary was excited to attend Andrzejki, even though she had to rush after her day at the mill. She finished the dishes and headed into her bedroom to wash up, brush her hair, and change her shirtwaist. Her mother was in the room, smoothing the quilt near the foot of the bed. Mary couldn't remember the last time her mother had straightened her room.

"Matka?" Mary asked.

Matka smoothed the quilt again. "Just redding up your room. It's a mess today." She yanked the bottom of the quilt, but a lump remained. Mary's heartbeat sped up. Matka had no patience for the girls not hanging up their chemises and other things. Had hers gotten stuffed under the quilt when she had rushed off that morning?

Matka sat right on the lump.

Mary's eyes widened, waiting to be screamed at. "I'll get that." She brushed at her mother's hip.

Matka pushed Mary's hand away. "It's nothin'. Ann and Victoria are at the Jones's for children's Andrzejki, and . . ." She cleared her throat. "Have fun tonight."

Mary scrutinized her mother. "Okay."

Matka finally stood, patted Mary's shoulder, and left the room.

Mary crossed her arms, unsure of what caused Matka's odd behavior, but she needed to change quickly to arrive on time for the fun and games. She scrubbed her face and under her arms, smoothed her hair, and changed her shirtwaist. She lifted the lantern to take with her into the dark night, and her gaze went to the lump at the end of the bed. She smoothed it as her mother had, but as soon as she lifted her hand, it reappeared. She threw back the edge of the quilt and reached under, pulling out a long-sleeved undershirt. A man's dingy undershirt. She dropped it on the bed, disgusted. What was it doing there? She thought of Mr. Cermak for some reason, the way he watched her. Could it be his? But why?

Why wouldn't her mother have figured out that there was something actually making the lump, not just a rumpled quilt? She pinched the shirt between two fingers and took it into the kitchen, where her mother was darning socks.

"This was in my bed."

Matka's eyes flicked wide, then her shoulders slumped as though great disappointment had visited her.

"What?"

Matka set her darning in her lap. "Andrzejki."

Mary flinched, then studied the shirt. Her mind started to sort through what her mother was saying. The shirt, Andrzejki, Matka's odd behavior. Mary tossed the shirt onto the table, anger swelling. "Whose *is* that?" She pointed at it as though it were dangerous.

"Oh, Mary."

"'Oh, Mary,' what? Whose is that?"

Matka slumped, mumbling to herself.

"Matka?"

Matka sighed. "Ralph's. Ralph Zapszac."

Mary's mouth fell open. "You took a shirt from Ralph?" She was mortified.

"If you sleep with a piece of clothing from a man, he'll become your fiancé. At least you'll dream of him."

Mary knew the Andrzejki tradition well, but she was so angry, she didn't know what to say first. "You stole a shirt from some boy I don't even want to marry in the hopes that my sleeping with it will result in a marriage proposal?"

Matka gave a slow shrug as though debating whether to admit it. Mary had never seen her so cowed.

"Oh my God. You snuck into Ralph's house and stole a shirt?"

"Don't take the Lord's name in vain. And don't be silly. His mother gave it right to me. We thought it'd be fun. We know you're too young to marry. Not just yet, anyhow."

Mary's mouth gaped. She stared at the shirt and then back at her mother.

"Since when do you believe any of this? You don't even go to St. John's Eve to have a picnic. And since when are you worried about the Lord's name?"

"Where's your humor?"

Mary shook her head. "Humor? My own mother is selling me off."

Matka giggled. *Giggled.* The woman never giggled.

"Never mind. I'm late." Mary stalked out of the kitchen, Matka following.

"Be sure to think of Ralph when the housewives pour yer wax."

Mary left the house with a slam of the door, unsure she even wanted to go anymore. With all this talk of Ralph on St. Andrew's Eve, it might seal her fate with him. She groaned as she broke into a jog. She would need to do everything to try to vanquish him from her thoughts.

**

She reached the church and descended the stairs to the basement to friends and other young ladies busy sewing sleeves onto shirts for boys and men who needed them but couldn't afford to buy them.

Vats of soup simmered on the stove. They would divide it later and take it to people struggling to make ends meet. Anticipation filled the room, the girls' chatter especially light and fun. This was the night a single girl could find out who her future husband might be.

On the stove, next to the hot soup, was a drum of melted wax to be poured through a skeleton key into cold water. Once the wax hit the water, it cooled into shapes that would be removed and studied for clues to each girl's future love. Sometimes the wax cooled into the profile of a man, as it had happened with Lucy Hartman. Two weeks after the wax had taken the shape of Tony Montasano's angular profile, he was on bended knee, proposing. Harriet Hopkins's experience was legendary. Her wax had formed into block letters spelling out "Max," clear as new glass. There was no guesswork for Harriet, and one year later she was married to Maxwell Turner. The girls could only hope for such an obvious miracle. At the very least, the shape of the wax would indicate what job a girl's future husband might have.

By the time Mary finished the shirtsleeves assigned to her and lined up to have her future foretold, the wax was gone. For a moment she panicked, thinking this only locked Ralph tighter into her future. But then she thought better of it. She'd just pray not for a specific fiancé, but that hers would never be decided for her, would never be Ralph.

Mrs. Perry touched Mary's arm, her face full of sorrow at not having been able to let Mary's fortune be told.

"It's all right," Mary said. "My prayers are enough for me."

"No, no, no," Mrs. Perry said. "That's not good enough. You must participate in the lineup."

The lineup. Mary looked down and lifted the hem of her skirt. She'd forgotten to change her shoes and stockings. She blew out her breath. "No, thank you."

Mrs. Perry ignored her and pulled Mary toward the girls. "Nonsense. The lineup's more important than the wax fortunes."

One girl's chance at happiness was just as great as the others', but Mary had to add her shoe to the lineup for the race to the door.

"First shoe to cross the threshold will dream of her fiancé!" Mrs. Perry said.

Mary knew the tradition and didn't want to argue, but she worried that she was thinking too much of Ralph, what with his shirt having just been removed from her bed. She didn't want to take a chance and dream of him.

"We have so many girls tonight that we put each left shoe into three lanes—heel, toe, heel, toe."

"Really, it's all right. I don't need—"

"Nonsense," Mrs. Perry said, dropping to her knees. She yanked Mary's boot laces. Mary stepped back, and Mrs. Perry scooted after her, her fingers working the strings wildly.

She tried to pull Mrs. Perry up by the arm, but the plump woman batted Mary's hand away. She pinched the back of Mary's calf, and when Mary lifted her foot to move away again, Mrs. Perry pulled the boot right off.

She hopped up and hoisted the boot. "One more shoe!"

All eyes turned toward Mrs. Perry. Mary's face grew hot as she stared at the black, scuffed, decades-old boot. With the laces loose, the tongue dropped forward from the maw. The hole in the sole caught the light like a miniature sun, embarrassing Mary. She looked away.

Mrs. Perry put the shoe in the front of the line.

"You can't put it in front. That's not fair," someone said from the back of the room.

"Oh well, all right." Mrs. Perry moved another shoe to the front and slid Mary's in the middle, but that was met with calls of unfairness as well. Mary surveyed the line of shoes, some the same shape as hers, some very clean and new, but all—every single one—tiny.

Mrs. Perry held the shoe in the air again. It was coal-barge big, and Mary was silenced by the sight of it. Finally, it was decided they'd create a fourth lane of shoes, thereby mixing up all the shoes and starting the order all over again. When all was rearranged, Mary's tree-trunk shoe was smack in the middle of the second row, set between a delicate lavender boot with a kitten heel and what looked like a brand-new brown leather shoe with three leather straps across the top, joined with leather diamonds.

Though Mary was embarrassed by her holey stockings, she knew most girls in town wore black boots to work. But they had had time to change before coming to the church.

"That boot's the size of two shoes. She'll have a better chance," a voice said from behind Mary.

She turned to see who had spoken. The Polish princess. Aneta. Mary forced a smile, showing she had a sense of humor, and Aneta glared. Mary turned away. Why was Aneta playing? She was already engaged to Lukasz Musial.

Mrs. Perry clapped her hands and the room grew still. She called out for the girl whose shoe was at the end of each line to move it to the front.

One by one, the girls moved their shoes, each lane working across the space toward the doorway. When the time came for the shoe behind Mary's to be claimed and moved, it was Aneta who sauntered up to it.

Aneta placed her shoe in front of the line and then went back to her friends as Mary went for her shoe. She picked it up and took it to the front. She bent down and set it so that her heel was on top of the toe of Aneta's shoe, then walked to the end of the line. As she passed Aneta and her friends, they giggled and Mary heard the word *giant* as she passed. She pushed away the feeling that came with being called that by someone so . . . dainty. What had Mary done to Aneta?

And so the game went until the four lanes of shoes had nearly reached the threshold of the doorway. The girls moved in closer and closer to see whose shoes would be the first to cross over and who would dream of their great love later that night.

Mary couldn't believe her eyes. The shoes were almost to the doorway, and her turn was coming. Aneta took her shoe and placed it in front, the toe just a smidge from the threshold.

Aneta's face brightened as her friends pleaded her case, saying that toeing the line was the same as crossing it. But Mrs. Perry and the other married women held court, standing over the line and whispering behind cupped hands. Finally, they pointed to the barge of a boot in the back. "Brushing the line with the toe isn't equal to crossing it."

Groans and moans were mixed with cheers as the girls with shoes in the other three lanes converged on Mary's lane to watch. Mary picked up her shoe, holding her breath. Aneta and her friends stood with arms crossed, scowling in their pretty dresses, each wearing one glamorous shoe. She wouldn't let them shame her for something she couldn't control.

Mary raised her shoe in the air like Mrs. Perry had done earlier. She walked to the front of the line as though the shoe itself was a prize and set the boot against the toe of Aneta's pretty, silken shoe. The room erupted with cheers. Aneta stood frozen. Her friends descended on the line and scooped up their shoes, decrying the unfairness of Mary's big feet.

Now the other ladies whose shoes were in the other three lines went to lane three to watch them finish. Mrs. Perry waved them over with her chubby hands in the air. Trying to keep her eye on the action at lane three, Mary bent down to pick up her boot.

As she did, the room went black. Pain spread over her face, and blood poured from her nose.

"You oaf," someone said. Mary forced her eyes open to see Aneta holding the top of her head, rubbing it. "You smacked my head with your face." Mary processed the thickly accented words.

With her attention on lane three, Mary hadn't noticed Aneta standing up with her shoe at the same time Mary was bending down.

Someone grabbed Mary's arms as pain radiated across her cheeks and into her jaw. The girls around Mary scattered, hoping to dodge the blood. Aneta wagged her hands like a little baby. She yanked a hanky out of her sleeve and tossed it toward Mary. Mrs. Perry held it against Mary's nose as she guided her to a chair. Mary's eyes watered and tears fell.

When Mary's nose finally stopped bleeding, Peggy and Kasandra walked her home. The two friends helped Mary up the stairs onto her porch just as her nose began to bleed again. Mary reached for the hanky.

"That's revenge," Kasandra said, helping to hold the hanky against Mary's face. "Bleeding all over Aneta's pretty handkerchief after she was brutally rude to you."

Mary nodded. "And it was her head that smacked me."

Peggy opened the front door. "Well, now you have the Polish Princess's hanky."

Kasandra guided Mary into the front room and to the settee near the fireplace, leaning her back. "Maybe Aneta was just trying to have some fun. It's not like she was out on a date with someone else. Stupid game," Peggy said.

Mary agreed. The game was ridiculous. "I just want to go to bed."

Ann came into the room, her face scrunched up at the sight of her bloodied sister. She thanked Peggy and Kasandra for bringing Mary home, then helped her to bed. Her nose began to bleed again, and Ann stuffed the half-soiled hanky against Mary's nose.

"Keep your blood away from me," Ann said.

"Gee, thanks." Mary turned on her side.

And finally, she was glad to put an end to the day, falling asleep with the Polish Princess's hanky, wondering if it was precious to her and deciding right then she wasn't giving it back.

**

The next morning, Mary's head throbbed and she woke long before her normal time. She got to her knees to say her prayers, to beg for the pain to end. When finished, Mary patted her nose, testing its tenderness, and searched her mind for dreams of the man who might someday hold her heart in his hands. Her inflamed nose ruined any recollection of a dream of her fiancé that she might have had. She pressed it gently, remembering how hard it had been to stop it from gushing. All the blood.

She lit the lamp and held it over the bed. Her mother would kill her if the sheets were ruined with her bleeding nose. She moved the pillow, and a red-splattered hanky fell away. No signs of blood on the pillow or sheets, just on the hanky.

Aneta's hanky. Her angry, moody personality was unbecoming someone so absolutely gorgeous. Mary ran her finger over the fine blue embroidery. It was only fair that Aneta lose a hanky since she'd been mean, since she was the reason Mary was bleeding, accident or not.

Matka would be disappointed to find out that Mary had fallen asleep with a woman's clothing in her bed that night, someone she could never hope to marry.

Chapter 38

Lukasz

December 24, 1910
Christmas Eve

Fatigue lay deep as the marrow of Lukasz's bones. It was Christmas Eve morning, and although tired, he was excited, anticipating the day. He yawned before scrubbing his face at the bucket of water Zofia had left him. She'd piled a stack of clean hankies beside the bowl after having scolded him for misplacing yet another one. He sighed, always unable to remember where he had lost them. Zofia had been pleased that he'd given Aneta one of the special handkerchiefs with the blue embroidery, but she was irritated that he hadn't disclosed the meaning behind it. Lukasz didn't worry. Soon he and his bride would live together, and he would tell her the hanky's meaning then.

Zofia greeted Lukasz in the kitchen, grabbing his cheeks and pulling him closer. She kissed his forehead. "Tonight's a great night to finish a wonderful year. Your future's charmed. You'll write Adam and tell him his mother's paisley hankies have worked their magic and one is in the hands of your true love."

Lukasz smiled, warmed by Zofia's mothering.

She released him and patted his arm. "Show me."

From his pocket, he pulled the nail tin that held the rings he'd made for Aneta. Zofia opened the lid and gasped. She fished the rings out and slid them onto the first knuckle of her ring finger. She moved nearer the lamp and examined them, turning her hand this way and that.

"They are so dainty, yet . . ." Her voice cracked. "Love. They are love."

He nodded.

"With your own two hands?"

"And some wire and enamel." In the back of his mind, he knew Zofia reacted like this to every blessed wire object he made, but still, he let her excitement buoy him. It had been some time since he had finished the rings, and every time he'd considered giving the engagement ring to Aneta, something had gotten in the way—her mood, his mood, someone bursting between them to pull Aneta away to talk at a dance.

Zofia gave him the rings back and he snapped the tin shut and put it into his pocket.

"Tonight, you give one of those to Aneta, and in less than two months, Aneta's parents will be here and you'll be slipping the other onto her finger too. Your own family splintered years ago. Now you're building your own. You've found land you want to buy. So much accomplished." She wiped her hands together like she always did when she deemed a subject settled.

Lukasz started toward the bedroom. Zofia pointed out the carpet under the table. It was made in muted golds and reds.

"Alexander brought it to me last night." She pushed her hand against her chest, staring at it in much the same way he'd seen her look at the children and her holiday linens from time to time. "He's a good man, Lukasz. Look at what he gives me."

"It's beautiful, Zofia."

The baby cried and Zofia picked her up, cradling her and shushing her. Lukasz tried to imagine what it might feel like to hold a child that had been formed from part of him, to stare at her screaming face and only feel love despite the racket. He couldn't call up a sensation that matched what he saw in Zofia's eyes when she held the baby or Alexander's pride when he watched his wife, but he imagined it would happen when the time came.

The girls came in and Zofia told him, "There's stew for breakfast, Lukasz. Judyta'll get it for you. Alexander'll be home to get the tree with you this afternoon." She walked toward the new addition to the house built for their growing family. "Get some sleep. We've a big night ahead of us."

Ewelina, the Kowalks' second-eldest daughter, brought Lukasz a glass of water and bread and Judyta served the stew. He downed the water and requested a beer. He'd skipped the Bucket of Blood that morning to add to the wad of cash he'd show Aneta after he gave her the ring.

"Ewelina, Janina," Zofia yelled from the other room. "Roll out the gingerbread. It's time!"

"Yes, Mama," Janina said and went outside to retrieve a crock full of gingerbread dough. They had made it the week before and kept it outside in the cold for the perfect blend of its ingredients.

As Lukasz's belly filled, he looked around the room to the enormous amount of food that was in various stages of preparedness for Wigilia and felt warm, loved, part of a family.

The girls placed straw on the table and covered it with a cloth white as first snow to symbolize Jesus's birth in a barn. The scent of sauerkraut mingled with dough and cheeses and fish. It was overwhelming, but it reminded Lukasz of times back in Poland when troubles had been set aside to share a rare extravagant meal.

He headed to his shared room, plopped onto the bed's edge, and removed his shoes, both soles worn through in two different spots. The boys were out doing chores for Zofia, and Lukasz had the bed to himself. He changed his clothes, slid to the center, and stretched out. Feeling exposed, unable to get comfortable with so much space, he tossed back and forth. Before long, he'd inched back to the edge and curled onto his side, pulling the blanket up under his chin and falling into deep, welcome sleep.

**

Angry voices pulled Lukasz from sleep. He slipped into a clean shirt, shoved his feet into his boots, and entered the kitchen. Zofia covered her mouth, her face reddened, and Alexander clenched his jaw.

Zofia exhaled and patted her husband's shoulder. "We can't fight today. It'll color the upcoming year with black bad luck. Every year I have to remind you?"

"That only starts once the first star is sighted. Not until," Alexander said, tying his boots.

"Not true," Zofia said. "The clock on the day begins at midnight, and we will be cheerful and happy to ensure the New Year follows the same way."

"It would be bad luck if we *didn't* argue, Zof. We make our own luck."

Lukasz waved as he passed them on the way to the outhouse. When he returned he found them standing at the table, looking down on it as though it were a puzzle.

Alexander rubbed his chin, his stubble whisking under his fingers. Zofia scowled, lost in thought like her husband.

Alexander pointed to each place setting, naming the people who'd be present for dinner. He snapped his fingers. "Twelve courses, twelve people eating on your mother's beloved china. Very good. Very, very good."

Zofia grimaced. "One extra place setting makes thirteen. Not good."

"It's fine, Zofia. Very lucky."

She smacked him between the shoulder blades. "Thirteen, lucky?"

He groaned. "Nonsense."

"We won't set the extra seat; number thirteen seat is gone." She waved her hand.

Alexander shifted his feet and crossed his arms. He appeared reluctant to let his thoughts be known. "But Harry might show, and if there's no extra seat, then what? We'll look like misers and he'll flap his gums all over town about it."

Zofia set a knife beside a spoon and patted it before glaring at her husband. "I don't like him. People follow you home like you're the Pied Piper."

"It's TB Harry," Alexander said.

"Not Hairy Harry?"

"Not this time."

"He's faking sick," Zofia said.

"Who?"

She smacked his arm. "TB Harry. Who else? You know it too."

"Nah," Alexander said. "It's that black lung of his."

"So he doesn't have TB?" Zofia asked.

"Hell no."

"Because if he's got TB, he needs to stay home. He'll bring sickness to the baby. If it's black lung then fine."

Alexander stepped away from the table and dug a cigarette out of his front pocket. Zofia snatched it and stuffed it back into his pocket. "There's enough smoke around here without that."

Alexander sighed. Zofia nodded and shifted around the table, setting the silverware as if she were preparing a baby for christening.

"It's settled."

"Settled?" Alexander asked.

"We'll set the thirteenth place." She lifted her hands and dropped them. "If there's any chance that TB Harry's coming." Her voice vibrated tight.

"He might *not* come."

She stopped. "Don't mess with Wigilia. Everything must be perfect tonight."

Alexander laughed.

"This is serious. A very special night for dear people."

They looked at Lukasz as though they had just realized he was there.

"I know." Alexander stroked Zofia's back. She flinched, knocking his hand away. He put it back, caressing. "All will be well. I promise."

Zofia stretched across the table, adjusting the water glass, ignoring him.

He sighed. "Me and Luk'll get the tree."

She nodded but didn't look away from the table until Alexander had started toward the boot room.

As though she had just remembered something important, she strode to the coatrack near the front door. "Your coat." She held it out to Alexander but still didn't look at him. "Bitter today."

Alexander took it and slipped into it.

She handed Lukasz the coat he'd been borrowing. "You too."

"Thank you," Lukasz said.

"A woman never forgets the day she gets her ring."

Alexander stepped outside but poked his head back in. He extended his hand to Zofia. She took it. He rubbed her bare ring finger with his thumb. "Or the day she gets an oriental rug."

She nodded, blushing.

"Never had the money to get her a ring, Lukasz. You're ahead of the game."

Lukasz had heard the coarse tone between the two earlier, but now the softness buried inside the irritation was evident. It made him think of Aneta and the way they shared a sharpness between gentler moments. He hesitated in the doorway, Alexander waiting in front of him and Zofia behind. The chill coming from outside hit his cheeks and he shivered. He patted his pocket where the ring sat. His stomach ached. Nerves? Or maybe it was the way love felt when it finally began to grow.

He stuffed his hat on tight and turned to close the door, and he saw Zofia at the head of the table, gripping the chair's back. The irritation he'd seen moments before was gone, replaced by pride. Her table, her dishes, her family. Contentment. She filled the room with it.

That was it—if he wanted Aneta to fall in love with him the way Zofia was with Alexander, he needed to give her a home, a place to build a life, a place to let softness unfurl between them. And he was closer than ever to doing it. Tonight was for the ring. After Christmas, they'd put money down on land together, their first act as an official couple.

**

Lukasz carried wood into the kitchen. Across the room, near the windows that overlooked the mills below, the Kowalk children decorated the Christmas tree. The girls had spent the last few weeks making paper flowers, gingerbread ornaments that hung with thin red ribbons, and angels made from golden yarn that Zofia had collected over the year. Underneath were presents wrapped in white butcher paper and tied with red ribbon.

When the time was right, Lukasz handed a present to Zofia. Her face brightened as she slid the twine off. "I hope this is one of your . . ." Her voice cracked as she released the gift from its tissue wrapping. Her eyes glistened. "Oh, Lukasz." She pulled Lukasz into a one-armed hug. "A golden angel. I couldn't have imagined anything more beautiful than this."

She handed it to Alexander, who stood on a box to add the angel to the top of the tree. Proud again, Lukasz was glad he'd taken extra time for Zofia's gift. It was his way of saying thanks for what she'd done.

A neighbor, Mr. Yvenski, arrived for dinner. Alexander welcomed him while Lukasz poured a shot and water for the men.

Zofia was lost in thought, staring at the table again. She shook her head. "We've never had a guest show up uninvited. There's just . . ." She shuddered as though shaking off a chill. "Something's off."

"What?" Lukasz asked.

She looked around the room at everyone settling in and crossed herself. With a shrug, she walked away. "I'm being silly. Thirteen it is."

Another knock came, and Alexander entered the kitchen with Aneta on his arm. The candlelight, firelight, and decorations created a glowing backdrop that lit her like the angel at the top of the tree. She slipped out of her coat and revealed a dress Lukasz hadn't seen on her before. It was purple like a Donora sunset, the kind that was unexplainable, unusual, and made everyone stop and stare.

"Hello," Lukasz said. His stomach fluttered at the thought of giving her his ring, her eyes shining with tears that he'd taken the time to make her something symbolizing their new life together.

"Hi." She smiled before she looked away, making him wonder if shyness was coming over her, if maybe she knew what he had planned for later. Finally, she met his gaze. "You look very nice tonight, Lukasz."

"You too."

She touched his hand. "Later on, could I talk to you—"

Witold flew past Aneta and Lukasz with a gift held over his head.

"Back under the tree," Zofia yelled, interrupting Aneta.

Lukasz nodded at Aneta. "Later. Yes."

The Bielawas had traveled to Pittsburgh for the holiday, and Lukasz thought that when he walked Aneta home after church, he could give her the ring—after a kiss, before the next, before she invited him in to sit by the fire, alone in a house for the first time since they'd met. His breath tripped at the thought of holding her close, the two of them lying together someday soon, exploring each other without an audience.

Zofia clapped her hands. "Children. We can't start dinner until the first star is spotted."

A cheer went up and the kids stampeded out the door, their voices screeching and laughing.

After five minutes, they flooded back inside with little Witold saying that he had spotted the first star of the night. The rest complained teasingly that it was actually Judyta who had seen it. The cloudy night with an especially thick fog meant it was unlikely that any stars could be seen, but they eventually granted little Witold the honor of having claimed it correctly and everyone sat for dinner, with one open seat just in case. The adults, Nathan, Ewelina, and Janina were seated at the big table, with Aneta across from Lukasz like Zofia had planned. "The better for you to gaze at one another," she'd said when she'd told Lukasz where they would sit.

The rest of the children were sardined at the tiny table, sharing chairs. In Witold and Sara's case, they even shared a fork and spoon.

Zofia brought a plate covered in white linen to the table, the *oplatek*. She passed the plate with the large rectangle wafer on it. Each person broke off a piece and ate it, offering their own good wishes for a fruitful new year. As the last of the wafer was eaten by Witold, Zofia got up for the first course of the meal—red borscht. Alexander poured beer, and just as Zofia returned with the tureen of soup, there was a knock at the door.

Her face paled, and she jostled the soup. Lukasz leapt up, steadying the tureen then setting it down, the ladle clinking against the bowl. Silence enveloped the room.

"A guest," Zofia whispered as though she were afraid she hadn't enough food. She looked over her shoulder toward the boot room.

Lukasz thought of their earlier discussion about possible guests and was looking forward to getting a look at TB Harry.

"A guest!" Alexander raised his beer glass and went to admit the visitor. "Good news! A lucky year indeed."

Zofia mouthed the word "thirteen" and stared at the doorway.

Alexander returned with a tall, slender blond-haired man with his arms laden with presents and flowers.

Zofia wobbled, looking confused. Though this man looked like any number of Poles Lukasz knew, there was something different about the way he carried himself, about the way his clothing fit and the glint in his eye. It only took a moment for Lukasz to realize he was American.

"Tytus Hawthorne," Alexander said. "You've met my wife once." Alexander looked around the table. "And yes, Aneta. You've met Aneta."

Zofia glared at her husband and Alexander returned the look with a shrug. "Tytus and his family own the men's clothing store on McKean, the new one by the shoe store. His brother-in-law was the man who . . ." He cleared his throat. "He had the accident in the blast furnace two days ago."

Zofia looked the man up and down. "Yes, yes. Awful. I hope your family got the basket we sent."

Lukasz had heard a man had had his arm crushed in the rolling mill and that it had to be amputated below the elbow.

Tytus nodded and handed Alexander a note. "From my sister for the basket."

Alexander set it beside his plate, patting it.

"And thank you for the invitation, Mr. Kowalk. I wasn't sure I should come, but when you brought Aneta in for her shopping and suggested I come . . . well, you were so kind with your invitation, and I wanted to thank you properly for all you've done for my family since this happened." Tytus looked at Aneta. "Thank you again for inviting me."

Lukasz's throat tightened. He didn't understand everything the man said in English, but he heard Aneta's name and saw how Tytus looked at her. Aneta's pink cheeks deepened to red making Lukasz dizzy, nausea curling inside his belly.

Tytus held up two bags. "*Przyniosłem prezenty.*" Tytus's Polish was clumsy like a novice speaker, broken like Lukasz's English. Tytus strode to the tree and put them underneath. "The *prezenty* you and Aneta bought are in there, Alexander." Tytus gestured toward the bags.

Alexander nodded and Aneta flashed a smile at Lukasz. This relieved him. Of course. She'd been buying a present for him. He smiled back and put his napkin in his lap.

Tytus strolled back to the table, hands in his pockets, relaxed and filling the room in a way Lukasz hadn't seen since he'd left Waldemar in Poland.

"Aneta mentioned younger brothers and sisters, and I brought something for Mr. and Mrs. Kowalk, but I didn't know there was an older . . . brother?" Tytus reached across the table to Lukasz.

Lukasz stood, confused at what was just said, but he shook Tytus's hand.

Alexander translated, staring at the table.

Brother? It was a kick in the stomach to Lukasz.

Zofia rubbed her temples, her face snow white. "Well, thank you for the gifts and for stopping by, but—"

Tytus looked confused now.

"Serve the soup, honey, my apple dumpling," Alexander said. "Don't leave our guest starving."

She hesitated, gaping at her husband. "Thirteen." Zofia's voice wavered. She cleared her throat. "How rude of me. Please. Sit." She gestured to the empty seat and reached for Tytus's bowl. She filled it high with the beet mixture, garnished it with miniscule dumplings stuffed with dried mushrooms and crisped onions, then served everyone else.

Tytus took a spoonful and smiled. "Delicious. Aneta didn't exaggerate your cooking, Mrs. Kowalk."

Zofia set the ladle down and turned from the table, coughing into the crook of her arm.

Aneta smiled at Tytus and looked at Lukasz. "Good?"

He nodded, feeling like he was the guest. Aneta smiled as though she approved of Lukasz liking the soup. She was so quiet at dinners, mostly only animated when talking to the children. Now it was as if he were a child.

"Lukasz," Tytus said, turning to Aneta. "Will you translate?"

She nodded.

Tytus talked at a loud volume, overly concise. "Tell Lukasz to stop by the shop anytime. We've dapper hats just in from New York. I can fit him lickety-split."

Lukasz scowled and Tytus seemed surprised by his reaction.

"Isn't that nice?" Aneta asked Lukasz.

Lukasz narrowed his eyes on Aneta and finally turned back to Tytus. "Thank you."

Zofia cleared her throat again and Lukasz noticed her hands shaking as she gestured for everyone to eat. Lukasz was sure she sensed the odd current Tytus brought with him, too.

"I have to say thank you again, Mr. Kowalk, for saving my sister's husband's life in the mill . . ." Tytus droned on, Alexander pleased with the praise and Aneta listening intently.

Zofia and the girls cleared the soup and brought the carp next. Once everyone was served, Zofia found her voice again.

"Your name, Tytus, is Polish," she said. "You speak some Polish, but you have an Anglo surname?"

"My mother's Polish, but my father's English and—"

Zofia let out a guttural sound and all eyes turned to her.

Alexander coughed into his hand. "Zofia." There was pleading in his voice.

"Just getting to know our generous guest, dear," she said.

"You'll give him heartburn."

Tytus set his fork and knife down. "I'm proud of my mother and all that my family achieved in coming to America."

"Isn't that nice," Zofia said.

Alexander shifted in his seat. "Can we serve the pierogi, please?"

Zofia narrowed her gaze at her husband.

"I'll get them." Alexander stood and jerked his head, signaling Lukasz to follow.

In the kitchen, Alexander popped open a lower cupboard and pulled out a jar. "We're going to need this," he told Lukasz. "Not too much, but enough to get us through." He unscrewed the lid, took a swig, and passed it to Lukasz. "My special blend for emergencies."

Lukasz took a swig and nearly spit it up, it was so strong. It reminded him of Otto's blend.

Alexander grabbed his shoulder. "That's it. One more for good measure."

Lukasz followed his instructions before Zofia joined them and retrieved the platter of pierogi herself.

"How lucky I am tonight," Tytus said. "I can't believe you had an open seat for me at your table. My mother told me stories about these Christmas Eve dinners many times. She warned me that not everyone would set an extra place and I might just have to turn back around for home."

Zofia was overcome with a coughing fit, her husband smacking her between her shoulder blades. The only other sound was Sara and Witold bickering over their shared knife. Eventually, even they went quiet.

Zofia pressed her hand to her chest. "You don't have Wigilia?"

Tytus shook his head, squinting at Zofia. "Well, no. Not since she married my father. But I see what we've been missing."

Zofia drummed her fingers on the table, and Lukasz imagined the rhythm was matching her heartbeat.

"My mother does some of this," Tytus said. "More for lunch. But not the hay under the tablecloth and the . . . well, she'll be envious when I tell her I got to enjoy something like this. And every summer after the Fourth of July baseball game, we picnic with some of these foods."

"Oh yes, *that* baseball game," Aneta said. "It was a close one, wasn't it?"

Tytus smiled.

"I love baseball," Aneta said.

Lukasz glared at her. Hearing the word "baseball" come out of her mouth sugarcoated and sweet made him laugh. She shot him a look.

"You like baseball now?" he said slowly in Polish.

"Of course, Lukasz. You know. Picnics." Her voice caught and she stole a glance at Tytus before plastering on a smile. "Picnics at baseball games. You know I went to nearly every game this summer." She put her gaze back on Tytus, trying to wrap truth around her lie.

"Baseball's wonderful, isn't it?" Tytus smiled, and Aneta nodded along. He pointed to the bowl next to Aneta. "More of that, please?" Tytus stared at Aneta then watched her hands as she served him.

"Braised sauerkraut," she said. "You like this one?"

Tytus nodded. "Oh yes. It's all so wonderful."

"I know. Zofia is a wonderful cook. I hope someday I'll be just like her."

Lukasz could only hope. For what exactly he wasn't sure anymore.

Golabki, *Kutia*, *piernik*, fruit compote, and poppy seed cake were served later. The American devoured every morsel, leaving his plate clean. As Aneta passed the final dish, the poppy seed cake, Tytus's hand brushed hers. They both pulled away, the serving knife slipping off and crashing onto one of the platters, breaking it.

Everyone gasped. The children at the small table put their hands up as if to swear that they were innocent.

Aneta and Tytus stared at each other, then Zofia. "I'm so sorry, Mrs. Kowalk," Tytus said. "That was my fault. I'll replace that as soon as the stores open up after Christmas. I think my mother even has the same pattern at home. I am so very sorry. I just couldn't get to the cake fast enough, everything's so very scrumptious."

Zofia covered her face with her hands. "I can't replace that. My mother's."

Alexander rose and went to his wife, patting her back. He whispered something to her and she straightened, sniffling. "It's fine, Tytus. Please. Don't give it another thought."

As they finished their meal, talk turned to the gifts and Mass. They decided to only open the presents that Tytus had brought and save the others for after Mass.

Each gift from Tytus was a brand-new item from Hawthorne's—wool mittens in pink for Judyta, a cranberry-colored hat for Ewelina, smooth black leather gloves for Alexander and Nathan, a scarf for Zofia, and a matching set of mittens, scarf, and hat in watery blue for Aneta. And so it went. Unusual, expensive presents from an unusual, wealthy man. American.

Lukasz felt as though a great force had drawn him out of the scene, as though he were outside the house, peeking through the window, observing. The pain in his chest reminded him he was very much a part of things. Again, Tytus apologized to Lukasz for not having a present for him and he invited him to select something from the store after Christmas. Lukasz tried to hide his irritation. After Christmas, he and Aneta would be putting payment down on a house, showing off her engagement ring.

Lukasz nodded again, unable to force words of thanks through his lips. He would never go to Hawthorne's to retrieve a gift, not ever. He couldn't wait to get Aneta alone, to put an end to this awful meal. He moved closer to her, reaching for her hand. But when his fingers brushed hers, she leaned over the table, scooping up as many dishes as she could hold. Lukasz stared. Her rebuff sank deep into his bones. He wasn't imagining it.

After the presents were opened, Zofia neatly folded the paper and ribbon and handed it to Tytus for next year. He refused to take it. "My mother has rolls. She'd kill me if I come back with it."

Zofia's face reddened and she looked away. "I'm sure your family needs you back, Mr. Hawthorne. Midnight Mass?"

He stood and checked his watch. Aneta stopped clearing the table, looking up. Tytus nodded, then shook his head. "Mass? No, no. Candlelight service at First Presbyterian. You remember, Mr. Kowalk. I told you that when we prayed for my brother-in-law at the hospital . . ." His voice trailed off and Zofia's eyes grew wide as if she'd just discovered she'd been sharing an evening—the most precious evening of the year—with a snake.

"Get his coat, Alexander," Zofia said.

"No need." Tytus waltzed over to get his coat from the rack, his elegance and ease with strangers infuriating Lukasz. No posturing, no sizing people up, no awkwardness.

He donned his coat and went to Zofia, enveloping her with his arms. It was as if she were his mother. Lukasz tried to remember if he'd ever hugged Zofia like that. She touched him plenty, holding his cheeks, kissing his forehead, or giving him a quick embrace when she saw him after a long shift. But had he ever done what Tytus just had?

Tytus let go of Zofia and moved around the room, joking with each person, remembering something about each of them, shaking hands, and repeating his thanks for the hospitality. Aneta's gaze followed him everywhere he went. When he reached Lukasz, he gripped his hand tight. Lukasz searched the man's face for derision, some snide expression, or anything indicating that he knew Lukasz and Aneta had been promised to each other. He wanted so badly to see something dastardly, something to make Lukasz dislike him for all his wonderful . . . wonderfulness.

But Tytus's face was open and kind, unaware he had knocked a whole house to hell. Lukasz wanted to despise the man but could not. There was nothing about him to even dislike, never mind hate.

Tytus passed by Zofia again, and she picked a piece of lint from his coat's shoulder before stroking it. Although she was put off by his Presbyterianism, she was mesmerized by the softness of his coat.

Tytus lifted his shoulders and dropped them. "Well," he said, searching the group until his eyes fell on Aneta again. Their gazes locked.

Lukasz reached for the box in his pocket. His ring for Aneta. He shifted his feet.

"Santa's coming!" one of the children screamed, breaking the silence. The roomful of people dispersed, everyone grabbing coats and hats. Tytus backed out of the house before disappearing into the night. Alexander led Aneta outside while

Zofia helped Lukasz into his coat. She put his hat on his head, tears welling in her eyes.

He shook his head. He wanted to say what they all witnessed wasn't true. He wanted to reassure Zofia that she and Alexander could repay their debt by seeing Aneta married to half a Pole, a Polish-American.

"She'll come around, Lukasz. Don't you worry one bit."

He shook his head.

"Give her the ring on New Year's Eve. Much luckier then."

A crazy laugh threatened to erupt from him, but he swallowed it. He couldn't let Zofia know his worries. His humiliation was too much to bear on its own, let alone in front of others.

Zofia picked up the baby from the bassinet, put her hat on, and snuggled her to her chest. She patted Lukasz's arm and stepped outside. The children swarmed her, their faces looking up at her, beaming and expectant.

Lukasz pulled the door shut behind him. Zofia pressed her finger to her lips. When the children settled, she finally spoke. "We must pray hard at church tonight. Unlucky thirteen. Bad feelings. An unexpected guest in the truest sense. We must do our best to pray away the bad luck that settled upon the house. Every last little heart must pray. Then you may think of Santa."

She glanced at Lukasz over her shoulder as though she'd said all of that for him as much as for the children. They went into the cold night, the mills ringing out, sending whooshes of flames to the heavens, the red-and-golden glow never ceasing, not even for Wigilia or prayers for presents.

Lukasz stopped, realizing there was probably much he'd missed at dinner. They had spoken a lot of English, and he had difficulty understanding them. Did Tytus really not know Lukasz and Aneta were matched? Maybe he'd missed when that was explained to Tytus. For the first time, Lukasz was angry at himself for not learning English faster. But he didn't need to be a native English speaker to understand that in the moments that spanned one dinner, he'd been removed from the Kowalks, from the promises and the matched, ordained relationship with Aneta. No, not removed. The togetherness shattered. He couldn't breathe. Even if the brokenness hadn't been labeled overtly, the loss was obvious as a splintered leg.

Zofia touched Lukasz's shoulder.

"I'll meet you later," Lukasz said. "I forgot something."

She squinted at him, then nodded as Alexander coaxed her forward. Aneta was already cresting the hill toward St. Mary's, the silhouette of her holding hands with the Kowalk girls breaking Lukasz's heart.

He didn't want to see Aneta in church, to think about what had just transpired. His chest was tight and his lungs burned. He coughed into his hand, heading down the hill away from Saint Mary's. He passed the Slavic church lit from the inside, windows illuminated by golden light. Hope and love emanated from the building, from the voices singing inside it, but he kept going to McKean then to Meldon, stalking right past the Bucket of Blood.

Streetlamps were strung with garlands and red flowers. Every single person Lukasz passed seemed to be radiant like the church, glowing with all the optimism that now eluded him. He stopped, feeling for the first time since coming to Donora the seed of desperation that had sprouted and grown in Poland. There was only one way to stop that feeling from spreading. He broke into a jog, circling back, unable to get into the door of the Bucket of Blood fast enough.

A few boilermakers loosened his lips, and he found himself spouting off phrases he'd heard a million times growing up. Alone, empty except for the booze that he couldn't stop pouring down his throat.

Alone. Queasy.

He stumbled into the night, rubbing his forehead, unsure how much money he'd just spent, how much it set him back in buying a house. He marveled at how quickly his dream dissolved from sight.

Lost again.

Aneta—gone from Lukasz's future with the appearance of one suave, friendly American. The home Lukasz imagined no longer featured her in it, no more children gathered around as she brushed back little girls' hair, telling them it was beautiful no matter how ratty. That much he knew like his name.

Chapter 39

Mary

December 24, 1910
Christmas Eve

"Taxes are due." Matka slammed a spatula into the pan. "It's Christmas, for ever-loving Pete's sake."

Mary nodded, knowing her duty.

"String Bean's docking Papa at Gilmore. I don't give a shit if ya have to wrestle yer father to the ground—"

"Matka," Mary said. She never wanted to see the broken look on Papa's face like when Matka had fished him out of the Hole-in-the-Wall in Webster. "He'll be there. I know it."

"Don't '*Matka*' me. Someday you'll understand. It's a man's world. Oh, to be a man . . ."

"It's Christmas Eve. Let's—"

"Yes, and yer father and I give each other the gift of payin' on the mortgage and taxes for Christmas. I'm aware it's Christmas."

Mary crossed herself and prayed her mother didn't launch into her speech about how there'd be very few gifts this year for the children, most of them for the little ones. That was how it would be, but she didn't want to talk about it and ruin the magic of thinking she would receive something special this Christmas.

Johnny and George flew into the kitchen and circled the table, their faces joyous with thoughts of presents and sweet maple pancakes for breakfast. Little Rose toddled behind them, screeching.

"I'll get the money and Papa." Mary tied her hat around her chin. "It'll be all right."

Matka stopped Mary at the door, holding a lit skating lantern. "Just filled it. No moon tonight."

Mary took the small lantern.

"I know it's earlier than he's expected, but we can't take the chance he beats ya there then . . ."

Mary nodded and started down the hill toward the river, passing a family singing "Joy to the World." She picked up the tune, humming as she went, refusing to let Matka's mood infiltrate her.

Mary was nearly to the end of the dock when the outline of a man sitting at the wharf's edge formed in her lantern light. She hung back, apprehensive, and held the lantern higher. The man glanced over his shoulder.

Mary exhaled. "Oh. Lukasz," she said, relieved it wasn't a stranger. Shy Lukasz was how she thought of him. Bashful either because that's just how he was or because he was new to America and just learning English.

He waved hello before turning his gaze back toward Webster across the Monongahela. Perhaps he'd been sent by the Kowalks or Aneta's family to retrieve a miner as well. She walked to the end of the dock and plopped down beside him, putting the lantern behind them.

"Whatcha doing?"

He looked at her and dug something out of his pocket. He held it up and shook it. A flask.

"Didn't mean to interrupt," Mary said. He wasn't there because he'd just had the best day of his life. They sat in silence but then Mary decided to fill the hush with small talk, just in case he wanted to work on his English. "I'm picking up my father, then it's off to Mass and its 'joy to the world, the Lord has come.'" Mary stared into the starless sky. "I just love that song."

He sipped from the flask and offered her some. She took it and sniffed, grimacing. She'd had a few drinks in her time, but this smelled like liquid wood.

"Joy," he said.

Joy it is, she thought, taking a sip, the liquid burning her insides. She shoved the flask back at him. "That's awful." She wiped her chin, laughing. Things must have been really bad to be drinking whatever was in there.

He looked away, shaking his head.

She wanted to ask him what was wrong but stopped herself from intruding. He may not have understood she was trying to be nice, not rude. She hummed "Joy to the World" and swung her feet over the lapping water. She hit Lukasz's left foot with her right foot, startling him.

"I'm so sorry." She touched his coat sleeve. "I didn't mean to kick you." Her words rushed together so she repeated them slowly.

He waved her away. "I'm fine. Fine."

She held the lantern to see his face clearly. "Sometimes I just don't pay enough attention."

He smiled, his gray eyes sad. She tried to see the blue in them before he looked away.

"Don't need that foot. The other does the work of two."

Mary giggled, surprised by his humor and that he'd got it out in hobbled English. She set the lantern down. "That was funny, Lukasz."

He smiled. "Funny."

They stared into the shadowy river, the train whistling and tugboats moaning in the dark. She loved nighttime, its inherent hopefulness that tomorrow would bring something even better.

"I'm picking up my papa."

Lukasz nodded. "Yes." He pulled a pack of cigarettes from his shirt pocket, selected one, and offered her one. She declined, and he tucked the pack into his pocket.

"In case you wanted to know specifically who I was fetching up. I said that already. Did I say that twice?" She shrugged.

He turned toward her. "Why?"

"Just to talk. Conversation. You know—"

"No. Your papa needs you to pick him up? He's *chory*?" Lukasz grabbed his belly, miming being sick.

Mary shook her head. "No, no. He worked a double. Taxes are due. Matka sent me to . . . well, he should be here any second." Mary straightened, squinting into the night. She couldn't tell the truth—that Papa might lose his money and health in a bar if she didn't intercept him and bring him home. She wouldn't shame him like Matka had.

She realized she was probably talking too fast for Lukasz to understand her. But he seemed to want the comfort of small talk, understandable or not.

He lit his cigarette. "What's his work?"

"Miner. Ella Mine."

He shook ash off his cigarette. "Hard work."

"Very."

"Hard working man needs his daughter to fetch him?"

She flinched at the criticism in his voice. Was it that, or simply the gap caused by their native languages? She had to admit, what he said was exactly right. "No, no. I . . . well, we just . . . I used to row him to and from work every single day to save money until I started in the nail mill. I'm a nail girl . . ."

"I've seen you."

She smiled at having been seen, noticed. Still, she'd never felt so ungainly in a conversation in her life.

"So you come fetch?"

This time she was sure of his criticism. "You say that as if I'm doing something wrong. Papa is used to me getting him. It saved us money at first, and we enjoy each other's company.

Why do you make it sound like everyone in town doesn't fetch her father or husband or—"

Lukasz took her by the shoulder. "Slow. Way slow."

His words had bothered her, but his gaze was warm. A small smile pulled at one side of his mouth. Perhaps it *was* just the gap between his English and her Polish that made him sound gruff.

"You love your papa," he said.

Mary nodded, pleased that Lukasz finally seemed to understand. "And so I come and get him so he can begin to rest. No more worries about getting the money home to my mother or . . . well, he works hard, and his cough . . ." Images of Matka embarrassing Papa at the bar flooded back. "If Papa gets here soon, we can get to Mass and we can put the star on top of the tree and . . . I *love* Christmas Eve. Don't you?"

Mary sighed, realizing she was talking too fast again. "I'm sorry. I'll slow down."

Lukasz flicked the cigarette into the river. "You helped him on St. John's Eve. You hook him out of the water." Lukasz mimed coughing, diving into the river.

Mary gasped, embarrassed, remembering. She'd forgotten Lukasz had witnessed the event. "And you pulled the boat back here to the docks for me."

He nodded.

"I don't think I ever thanked you for that."

"I never thanked you for the bread and basket on Holy Saturday."

She held out her hand to shake his. "So we're even."

He shook her hand with a hard grip.

Mary stared up at the gray sky, a layer of clouds shifting.

"A daughter to meet me at the riverside?" Lukasz lay back and put his hands behind his head. "A good thing."

He dug his hand into his pocket, a metal tinkling sound ringing in the quiet.

He patted his coat pocket and sat back up, pulling things out of it. He found his cigarette pack, shook one out, and lit it.

He set the pack down and Mary noticed a shiny object beside the cigarettes, something he'd pulled from his pocket. It glistened with silver, red, and green. Mary shifted and pulled the lantern closer. An angel. She looked at him. "Can I hold it?"

He nodded.

It was smooth, the colors looking liquid in the lantern light. The wings swooped behind a faceless angel, her eyes cast downward like the ones Mary had prayed to a million times.

He blew out smoke, squinting. "Eyes and lips wouldn't work."

Mary was confused. She shook her head.

He took it from her and ran his finger over it. "Too small. Eyes and nose and mouth . . . I couldn't make it work. So she looks down instead of up."

"What?" Mary processed what he said. "You made this?"

He nodded. She looked closer, tracing the surface, pockets of color chambered off by thin pieces of wire. The smoothness reminded her of Mrs. Dunn's Staffordshire dogs.

"I work for Mrs. Dunn, cleaning house and watching her kids, and she has the most beautiful porcelain dogs. A whole family of them, big and small. This is just as beautiful. You *made* this?"

He nodded.

"It's . . . so real. Like she might answer my prayers right here. How?"

He gestured. "Heat the steel to make the flat parts." He brushed one palm over his other to indicate a smooth surface. "I hammer, cut, make tiny pieces. Then I use the wire to . . ." He mimicked the movement of sewing.

"You thread the pieces?"

"Yes, thread."

"I can see."

"And I heat the wire and make patterns, channels, and add the color."

He mimed all the actions, and Mary noticed the size of his hands, how large they were compared to his height. His thick fingers must have been gentle to create and join together such intricate metal patterns.

"Well, it certainly is beautiful and—"

The sound of splashing drew her attention to the river. Still unable to see the boat, she could hear her father's deep voice and raspy cough.

"My papa." She stood and accidentally kicked the angel to its side.

Lukasz stood and held the angel out. "For you."

"I can't take that," she said.

He pushed it toward her. "Yes. I made for someone to put on treetop each year. But . . . now it's for you."

"Really?" She stared at him, wondering if he wasn't giving it to Aneta or if he had an extra. Clearly, Mary was misunderstanding something about what he said, but didn't feel she should ask. "It's beautiful."

He nodded. "It's nothing."

"*Not* nothing." She found herself whispering, mesmerized by Lukasz's work. She couldn't wait to get it home to put it on the tree. No! She would hide it away with her special things for when it could be all hers. She dug her fingers under her coat sleeve, into her shirtwaist, and pulled her handkerchief out to wrap the angel. The rowboat neared the dock.

"A little light here," Mary's father said from down below.

Lukasz picked up the lantern and illuminated Mary as she wrapped the handkerchief around the angel. Mortified that he'd think she carried dirty laundry, she turned away from the light to hide the bloodstained hanky from Andrzejki.

"A little help," Papa shouted through his cough. Mary stuffed the wrapped angel into her pocket as gently as she could before Lukasz could see it.

String Bean, Papa's friend, hopped out of the boat. "Merry Christmas, Mary. Gotta run. Late for Mass." He tore away, his feet pounding on the wood dock.

She held her hand out to her father, heaving him onto the dock.

He breathed heavy, staring at Lukasz.

"Papa, this is Lukasz Musial. He works in the mill with me. Soon to marry Aneta . . . what's her last name again?"

"Wasco," Lukasz said, grimacing.

She took Papa's arm. He grumbled and coughed, staring at Lukasz, then back at Mary. "You okay? He didn't . . ." His cough wracked him again, and Mary patted his back, starting to guide him down the dock.

"No, Papa. He's a very nice young man."

Papa looked over his shoulder at Lukasz, but his cough turned him back.

"Thank you again, Lukasz," Mary said, moving away. "Merry Christmas."

"Merry Christmas," he said and sat back down on the dock, making Mary refocus on Papa. They inched toward town and Mary hummed "Joy to the World" again, thinking they'd get to Mass just in time if they moved a little faster, loving the feel of the precious angel hidden deep in her coat pocket.

Chapter 40

Lukasz

Two days after Christmas, his shift done, Lukasz trudged up the stairs that hugged Fifth Street. A few boilermakers had eased the edge off his mood but wobbled his legs. He stuffed his hands into his pockets, overcome with a coughing fit. He stopped and bent over, spitting sooty mucus, then stood to see a woman in a sky-blue coat coming through the fog. He knew right away it was Aneta. When she saw him, she started to turn in the other direction, then paused, sighing, her shoulders slumped.

His breath caught. Aneta's blueness, her blondeness, her beauty glowed through the mill smoke and soot that rose and fell from every furnace in town burning to full winter capacity.

She glanced at Lukasz and straightened her shoulders. She looked smaller to him, fragile. Lukasz took her shoulder and moved her to the side of the stairs as three people passed. She wiped her cheeks with her gloves, tears dropping on her soot-smudged skin.

He gently wiped away the soot with his hanky.

She finally met his gaze. "I'm sorry, Lukasz. I don't know what to say except that . . ." She spoke in Polish, something she only did with the Kowalks.

He shook his head, not wanting her to see that he was embarrassed by his appearance, dirty from his shift. He'd known since they'd met that she was different from him, that she had come from an important family, even if she had left in disgrace. But the worthlessness the rejection brought . . . the pity in her eyes? It disgusted him.

"So, this won't be," he said. "You and I. As much as Zofia wants it to be."

She gripped her purse to her stomach. "Every time I'm with you at Zofia and Alexander's, I think to myself, 'yes, I can marry Lukasz. I can help the Kowalks repay my parents. I can do my penance.'"

"Penance?" Another smack of humiliation. He wanted her to shut up, but he also wanted to hear the truth.

"But every other second of my life that I am away from the Kowalks and you, all I can think about is Tytus."

"So you did invite him to Wigilia? Were they all in on the lie? Was Alexander lying about helping Tytus's brother-in-law and his arm?"

"There weren't any lies, Lukasz. All of that was true. I was with Alexander when he met up with Tytus the second time. And then at the store where I bought your present. He was so nice, and I just opened my mouth before thinking, inviting him because he'd never been to Wigilia. I didn't mean to . . ."

He thought of the mountain of gifts Tytus had brought to the Kowalks. "An invitation to dinner at someone else's house."

"It sounds so much worse than it was," she said.

Lukasz bit the inside of his mouth, keeping his angry words at bay. She'd been attacked, left at the altar, and had her child taken; the sorrow he imagined born of those events seeped into him. He wanted to say she was broken and soiled by her past, that she was lucky to have him, and that being left at the altar should have shown her not every man would take her after all that had happened. But he wouldn't—he couldn't—hurt her with those words. "You want Tytus's life, not him."

She shut her eyes for a moment, and when she opened them, she met Lukasz's gaze. "It's the same thing."

He looked over his shoulder at the blast furnaces below, belching fire into the sky. He was making something of himself. It wasn't like back in Poland. He took the money from his pocket to show her. "I'll build us a home. We'll have everything you could want, Aneta. A kitchen inside, children."

She shook her head and looked away. She pressed her hand to her chest. "I wish it could be more than this."

Now he couldn't keep eye contact. His eyes began to burn and his chest felt cold. "No." He looked directly at her. "You wish *I* was more than this."

She put her hand on Lukasz's arm. "You're a good man. There's someone wonderful for you."

"Stop it," he said.

"I just—"

"Stop it!" His bellow surprised them both. He glared, breathing hard, embarrassment coursing through him all over again. He wasn't enough.

She opened her mouth to say something more but must have changed her mind. She raced down the stairs, her blue coat swallowed by fog and smoke.

He stared after her. Soon it would be the first anniversary of his arrival in America, and he was feeling as though he was as poor as he'd been back home. The American dream was supposed to have been his. And now, a girl from his very country—a girl whose family lost their fortune was turning Lukasz away because none of what he offered was enough. *He* was not enough.

Chapter 41

Patryk

2019

Patryk stirred, confused as always when waking. A steady electronic beep nagged and he rolled to his side, trying to slap his alarm clock button off. When the beeping continued, he forced his eyes open. Mottled colors sharpened and blurred then took clear form. Where was he? Antiseptic filled his nose and he knew. A hospital. He'd never been a patient himself, but he'd surely visited plenty in his nine decades of life.

Owen sat across the room, hunched over an electronic screen, his back to his grandfather.

"Owen." Patryk's voice came like a whisper of sandpaper. Owen didn't even flinch.

Patryk called him again.

Still no response. And so he lay there watching his grandson on his toy, amazed at the images flashing across the screen, marveling that although he couldn't read a thing up close without his glasses, his distance vision was as sharp as when he was eighteen.

"Owen!"

Nothing.

It was too much. Patryk was too tired. He allowed his eyes to close, deciding that falling asleep to what he'd just seen on Owen's screen was better than anything he could currently experience while awake.

**

Poke, pull, prod. Patryk woke the next time to a nurse slapping his arm when it didn't yield to her needle.

"Goddammit," Patryk said, his voice prickly, his mouth dry.

"You're awake," the nurse said.

"'Course I'm awake. Yer needling me like a pin cushion."

"Grandpa Patryk." Owen entered the room. "You're awake."

"Oh, what a hospital full of geniuses. What the hell am I doing here?"

"Dehydration." Owen held up a paper cup. "Turns out drinking only coffee, Coke, and booze will take its toll when you're ninety-whatever age you are."

The nurse finished placing the IV and made a note on the chart. "No more pulling that out, Patryk. You'll never get out of here if you keep that up. I'll have some ice chips sent over now that you're awake."

"Pour some Jack Daniel's over it."

"That's cute, Mr. Rusek," the nurse said as she left the room.

He scowled, his mind clear now. He tried to sit up. "Get me the hell ahta here."

Owen pushed his great-grandfather's shoulders down. "Whoa, there. Not yet."

"Rule follower, are ya?"

Owen smiled. "Not usually, but this is different."

"Get me ahta here and there's more of my inheritance in it for ya."

Owen raised his eyebrows. "Oh please. I'm about twenty-fifth out of your friends and loved ones you're leaving things to. We're not even Facebook friends. Not that I'd be on Facebook, but you would . . . if you wanted to be. That's your age group's scene."

"My friends're all dead."

"So now I'm about number fourteen. Cool."

"Hey, jagoff," Patryk said. "Get me ahta here or I'll tell your mum about the pictures on that screen thing of yours."

Owen jerked back.

"Cat got your tongue?"

He shrugged, brow furrowed.

"I could see your screen from here. I have the far-sight of a teenager."

Owen shifted his feet. "Yeah, well, must have been a dream."

"It was a dream, all right. Get that picture up on the screen again. The girl in the pink bathing suit. I want a chance to see her."

Owen's face crumpled in disgust.

"Show or I tell."

"It's my girlfriend. That'd be totally gross. For all of us."

Patryk smacked his forehead. "Holy cow, your girlfriend? You just conjured that girl up on your screen like that?"

"She sent it to me."

Patryk crossed his arms. "Sent it?"

Owen shrugged. "I guess you didn't have this kind of thing when you were my age."

"We didn't need this shit. We just met up and talked. We had plenty of things."

"No, I mean the clothes. Everyone was covered head to toe, right?"

Patryk lay back against his pillow. "I'm not that old! Girls wore nice short dresses—around the knee, but still, not long. But you're right, there wasn't any way to send a boyfriend a nudie, no. Yet the girls were eager to get together with the boys just like now."

"In the olden days? Really? That's not how people tell it now."

Patryk felt a chill and pulled his blanket closer. It stuck on his feet. Owen adjusted it for him.

"It's true," Patryk told him. "People were discreet back then. Girls were less eager to get naked until they weren't, and then they were just like anyone ya might meet now. Thing was, once ya hopped in the sack or behind the hay bale, marriage was pretty close behind. That was the biggest difference. Not that people had sex, but that they had to be careful about it."

"Makes sense, what with women not having rights back then."

Patryk pointed at the electronic device. "You really like that girl?"

"I do."

"So why don't yinz get married? See her in person like that."

Owen laughed. "I'm *seventeen*."

"So was I. So was half the town when they married. Younger, often."

"Not these days."

Patryk's eyes went wide. "Where's my book?"

Owen held up the latest James Patterson.

"Not *that* bullshit. The book we were reading at home. *My* book."

Owen shook his head and moved his coat off the chair. "Right here. Mum thought you might want it to keep you busy until they spring you out of here."

"Well, she's right. Bring it here, big guy."

Owen opened it and pointed to a section of the book. "You were asleep when Mum and I finished reading about Lukasz's first year in Donora. But what's this? Some kind of summary notes. Mum said to ask you when you woke up."

Patryk wiggled his fingers. "Get me my cheaters. Can't see a damn thing close up. And let me see your pictures on your screen thingy. It's a trade."

Owen rolled his eyes. "Sure, sure, but I'm not showing you my girlfriend."

"Whose girlfriend are you going to show me?"

Owen puffed his cheeks and blew out his air. "Where do I start, Grandpa Patryk? What kind of girls do you like? Blondes, redheads, brunettes? Short hair, long hair, athletic girls, studious?"

Patryk shoved the cheaters onto his face and pointed at the iPad. "Holee shit, I like 'em all. That thingy can find me a girl to fit a hair color?"

"This thingy can find you anything you want in the whole world. Anything at all."

"I don't give a shit what the girl looks like, just show me."

Owen held up his finger. "One picture and then you tell me more about Lukasz and Mary. Mum'll kill me if we sit here looking at porn all day. And she'll know. She just looks at me and knows things like that."

Patryk stuck out his bent hand. "Deal."

Owen looked at Patryk's craggy fingers and a million questions leapt to mind. "What happened to your hand?"

"Pictures!" Patryk said.

And so they looked at pictures of lithe brunettes in aprons posed in vintage kitchens, sweeping, boiling water, wiping down countertops. "Your great-grandmother looked just like that," Patryk said.

Owen let out a little gag and put the iPad to sleep. "Well, that ruined vintage kitchens for me, Grandpa. Thanks."

"Humph," Patryk said.

"Now tell me about all of this."

Patryk pulled the book onto his lap and opened it. "Let me think. I remember when my sister wrote this part. She was yapping with Aunt Esther, who was telling stories and sucking down beer like she was tasked with draining the town of it."

Owen pulled his chair closer to the bed.

"Here. Oh yes, I remember. Esther couldn't recall all the details of 1911, probably because she was sauced. Always with the *Arn City Beer*. Let's see what I remember from this list."

Patryk ran his crooked finger down the page. "They said the year 1910 stopped like the line in the wireworks when a hot cobble broke free, flame-orange steel wire flying like a snake held by his tail. Oh yes, I remember." He tapped one line of writing. "Lukasz's engagement fell apart. And lucky for Donora, or there'd be no Stan Musial."

"Really?" Owen got onto his elbow to see better.

Patryk ran his finger along the sentence. "For Lukasz, 1911 limped in like his wounded heart. Aneta stopped coming to the Kowalks', and Zofia was wrought with fear of bad luck brought by the 1910 Wigilia. She wanted Lukasz to patch things up with Aneta, but he refused. Zofia repeatedly hatched plans to get Aneta down the haus for dinner or some such thing, but the girl never fell for it. Thankfully, Aneta was savvy enough to avoid the charade." He tapped his finger on the book. "That's right. She married that fella. Hawthorne. The clothing man. Sharp dresser, good businessman. But soft as shit. If Aneta was interested in *him*, she would never have been happy married to Lukasz Musial. No way."

"So a broken heart can be a good thing," Owen said.

"Story had it Lukasz's ego was stung by the Wigilia affair. Mortified, I imagine. You know, all he could do was work with his hands, and he thought that would be enough. Good Poles used their hands and backs to make money and a family. They were proud of that. But then it wasn't enough, and Lukasz had a hard time for a bit. Poles don't suffer humiliation well."

Owen shook the ice in the cup. "Who does?"

"True, true."

Owen nodded. "What about the Kowalks? Did they hook Lukasz up with another girl? Mary?"

Patryk shrugged. "Didn't work that way. Zofia, with her worry about bad luck, decided it would take a new life to counteract the bad luck and got pregnant again. Lukasz moved out of the Kowalk home. They needed the space and he needed room to nurse his wounds. And due to the shortage of housing in Donora, the hotels did their best to meet the needs of all the men in the mills. Not finding a boarding room,

Lukasz did what all the men did who came new to town—they slept in shifts. The hot bed method."

"Hot beds?" Owen asked.

"Yeah. A man rented a room to sleep in when off shift and then had to skedaddle when he woke so the next shift of fellas could sleep. On nights before or after a shift, when Lukasz was strong enough to avoid the Bucket of Blood, he'd sit by the river on Gilmore Docks, staring into the fog, watching for his mermaid, hoping she'd appear like she had in Poland.

Patryk read more. "Lukasz drank, just like everyone did, to burn the soot from his throat. He saved some money, keeping an eye on the land he wanted. Spent plenty of time working at Mark's forge, fixing those umbrellas that broke by the dozen. Sometimes he slept on the cot when it didn't interfere with Mark's work. Every so often, some man bought one of Lukasz's wire animals, and he used that extra money to bribe the foreman to look the other way so he could walk out of the mill with nails for his dream house. Sometimes Mark took nails in exchange for Lukasz using his forge and sleeping there when possible.

"Mary, on the other hand, found satisfaction working at the Dunns' once a week, pulling shifts at the mill, and attending dances. That's what everyone did back then. Summer dances under the stars at Eldora Park, the grove, Kennywood, all the towns up and down the riverside had places to dance. Winter dances at churches or ethnic clubs or halls on McKean.

"And Samuel continued to be obligated to take the daughters of friends of his family on the occasional date and sometimes took a sorority sister to a dance at the University of Pittsburgh. Mary's heart still pounded when he asked her to dance. As for Ralph and Mary's parents, they still pushed her to invite Ralph to dinner. And so when she was about fifteen and a half, she began to think more about having a serious boyfriend. No one seemed to be right for her, though. Or rather, she questioned whether she was a fit for any man in town."

"So Mary wasn't pretty like the other girls?" Owen asked.

Patryk looked upward. "It's not that. She was a head turner. Her confidence, the way she carried herself as if she were the one born of kings and queens instead of Aneta." Patryk scratched his chin. "Maybe that's what always set Aneta off about her—she saw it too. But Mary, she was so much more than pretty. That smile, pulled up to one side more than the other. And that laugh. The kind that made ya laugh if ya heard it even if you didn't know what she was laughin' about. But like other girls? No way, no how."

Chapter 42

Mary

May 6, 1912

On her sixteenth birthday, Mary woke to the squeals of Victoria and Ann as they brought fresh-baked cinnamon rolls and coffee into the bedroom. Bright light streamed through the space between the curtains, and she realized how deeply she must have slept the night before.

"We stirred in sweet milk too."

She sat up in bed and crossed her legs, accepting the plate of rolls. The girls set the coffee mug on the side table and smothered her with kisses. "Wait 'til you see what Matka got you," Ann said.

"Thank you for breakfast." Mary was thrilled to have this kind of attention. "My first breakfast in bed!"

Matka stepped into the bedroom.

"Show her, Matka," Ann said.

Victoria slapped her hands over her mouth as though trying to keep herself from revealing the secret.

John stepped into the room alongside their mother, and Matka gave Mary her present wrapped in white butcher paper and tied with pink organza ribbon.

"I think you'll like these," Mrs. Lancos said.

Mary handed her plate to her sister. She put the present in her lap and ran the pink organza ribbon through her fingers. She couldn't remember her mother bringing anything so pretty into their house.

"Mrs. Peters at the Accent Shop insisted she wrap it with that ribbon."

Mary pulled the bow loose. "I'll keep it forever, Matka. I love it. Thank you."

"Open it," Ann said, clearly not impressed with Mary's interest in the ribbon.

The ribbon fell away, puddling into her lap. She turned the soft package over and unwrapped it, savoring every fold as it opened. She splayed the paper, her breath catching at the sight. Stockings. Mary held them up and they unfolded, revealing tiny flowered embroidery. Pink, yellow, and blue flowers tumbled down the front of each stocking.

"Oh my. *Matka*," Mary said. "I've never seen such beautiful stockings, such beautiful anything."

"Stockings?" Johnny tossed himself onto the bed. "Worst present ever."

Mrs. Lancos smiled and shoveled him off so she could sit beside Mary. "Girls, take the boys and Rose and get breakfast while I talk to Mary."

Mary ran her finger over the dainty flowers—roses, tulips, and irises, each its own piece of art. She couldn't even imagine the great offense of putting such beautiful sewing on her feet and legs, of all things.

"So grown up," Matka said.

Mary nodded but didn't take her eyes from her new stockings. How had Matka even come to know what the most fashionable stockings of the season were? She imagined being at a dance with Samuel. She'd worked hard at toning down her athleticism in front of him after he ignored her at a few baseball games. When last autumn swept in and took baseball out, she found it easier to be a lady. With the new stockings, she could do the shoe dance without the embarrassment of removing her shoes, revealing gray mended stockings. Maybe her feet would appear smaller with all the attention on her ankles and the hint of shin that might show when she sat.

"Thank you, Matka. I'll thank Papa too."

Matka shifted on the bed and took the stockings from Mary, holding them up, folding again. "We thought these would do well when ya have dinner at Ralph's."

Mary's throat clenched. Ralph. Her mother hadn't mentioned him lately, and now she tossed this out as though it had been planned since birth.

Matka gently laid the stockings back on the paper and folded the top. "I told ya before, yinz two would be matched."

Mary's temples pulsed. This couldn't be right. "Ralph's been calling on Sally Dudova for months."

Matka waved her hand through the air. "Schoolyard attraction. Nothing more."

"They're courting, Matka. Just the other day, I heard Sally was planning a spring wedding."

"Not with him."

"Yes. With him."

"That's not what his parents say."

Mary thought of all the people she knew who'd married. Many of them had chosen their spouses. Fathers may have been asked for permission, but there'd been no matchmaking for many. "I'm not going to marry Ralph just because—"

"We say so. We'd keep ya with us forever, Mary. Ya do the work of the rest of the girls on yer own, plus bring in outside money. But ya need yer own home. Not now, but in two years' time. I was married at sixteen. This gives ya extra time. I see the value in waiting for this man. For Ralph."

Mary shook her head, disbelieving. "Don't you trust me to pick my own husband?" Her mind raced. She stared at the package in her lap. Her excitement at seeing their beauty and her surprise in being given such a generous gift paled now that she knew it was attached to Ralph. Were his parents having the same conversation with him?

"Other boys are interested in me."

"Mary." Matka's voice was patronizing.

"In fact, Samuel asked me to dinner with his family. They're eating down on the river after St. John's Eve. They're having a—"

"Mary Lancos. *Please.* Ya live in your head with these fairy-tale hopes. This Samuel's given no sign he wants to marry ya. In a blink, you'll be an old maid. And Ralph's parents insist he get engaged within the year then married in two. Forget Samuel. He's forgotten ya."

Mary couldn't breathe. Her throat tightened, hurt by Matka's words. "Why don't you think Samuel would marry me? Or someone like him?" Mary's eyes welled. "Why would you say such an awful thing? This is America. *I'm* American."

Matka smoothed Mary's hair back and tucked a lock behind her ear. "Someone has to say it, Mary."

Mary's mouth fell open, tears falling down her cheeks. "Mrs. Dunn thinks I can marry very well. She's impressed with me and says it all the time."

Matka stiffened, eyes narrowed. "*Mrs. Dunn?* She's not yer mother. You're not her kind."

"I am her kind. She's like us."

"Not anymore."

"But she—"

"Ya work for that woman, that's it. She doesn't care for ya like a mother. Works ya like a dog."

Mary tried to keep silent. She bit her tongue but the words spilled. "She's a better mother than you. She's *nice* to her kids."

Matka's eyes widened, and then it was as if a balloon exploded.

Mary wanted her words back. "Matka, I'm—"

Matka slapped Mary's face, stinging her skin. She couldn't breathe. Matka stopped breathing too, the two of them connected in their shock, staring at each other. Mary had crossed a line. She deserved the smack.

"Well," her mother said, her chest finally heaving again. She swallowed hard, looking so shaken that Mary thought she might actually apologize. Matka inhaled deeply, her breath quivering on the exhale.

"I've got to see to breakfast. Enjoy yer rolls and coffee."

Mary was dizzy. Her heart pounded, aching that her birthday dawned with a smack.

Matka was going back to what she always did, the previous order of things. Mary touched her face where she'd been hit. It didn't matter that they had fought or that Matka had slapped her; it was over, and Mary was back in her place.

"Thank you for breakfast," Mary said, trying to swallow her tears.

Matka stood, rubbing the palm of her hand against her apron as though the slap had hurt her as much as Mary. "This'll make sense someday, 'specially when ya have yer own children. You'll see."

Matka left the room as tears flowed down Mary's face from embarrassment she'd earned a slap on her sixteenth birthday. She closed off the part of her soul that recognized the pain. She told herself it barely even stung. It was just the way her mother did things. Mary shouldn't have pushed her.

Mary should enjoy the peace, the coffee, and a roll that someone else had made. She didn't have to fetch the water or coal that morning. The sugar and cinnamon coated her tongue then turned bitter making it impossible to swallow. The deep loneliness was monstrous that morning, so big she wondered if she'd ever be able to pray it away.

She would talk to Sally about Ralph. Mary needed to focus on Samuel or find someone else she liked as much.

She lifted her gaze to see Mr. Cermak in the hallway, leaning against the wall, watching her. She pulled the bedcover up to her collarbone. She wanted to leap up and slam the door shut, but she was frozen by his intense, awful stare. What had started as just an odd sensation of encroachment when he was around the house had turned to repulsion, and now fear.

His hand was down his pants. *Was* his hand in his pants? His eyes were half shut and a lazy smile covered his face. When Mary didn't move, he looked over his shoulder, then turned back to her, stepping farther into the light spilling out of her room into the hall. He fussed with his shirt.

Mary froze, her eyes following the movement of his hands. Before long she realized he'd undone his pants. Black pants, bright white skin, his hand sliding up and down. Confused and repulsed, not knowing what exactly she was seeing but feeling threatened and nauseated, she leapt from bed. She tore past him and into the kitchen.

She grabbed Matka's arm. "Mr. Cermak's got it out and he's … he's disgusting."

Her mother drew back. "What the hell're ya talking about?"

Mary dragged Matka down the hall. Mr. Cermak was coming toward them, shirt tucked in, smiling as though he'd just come out of the bedroom he shared with the other boarders.

"What?" Matka asked. "Got too much work waiting."

Mary pointed. "He was in my doorway, staring at me, and he took his shirt out and—"

He lifted his hands. "I just woke up."

Matka looked from one to the other. "What happened, Mr. Cermak?"

"I really have no idea, Mrs. Lancos. As I said, I was just getting up and about now." He smiled at Matka.

Mary searched his face for a flicker of the lie so she could convince her mother that he'd been exposing himself, that the disgusting look on his face made her want to peel off her skin.

But just thinking about saying any of that when he stood there, appearing as respectable as anyone else in the world, she found the words dissolving, unable to speak.

Matka nodded, believing him. "Honestly, Mary. This started out a wonderful day, didn't it?"

Matka's scolding came hot like the slap had been. Mary's insides twisted. Had she misunderstood what she saw Mr. Cermak doing? Had he been tucking his shirt in, not pulling it out?

"Apologize to Mr. Cermak. He's our most loyal boarder. Always pays on time. Pays extra expenses sometimes."

Mary swallowed rising vomit, forcing it away. She rushed past Mr. Cermak and Matka, heading to her room, where she dressed then snuck out of the house without saying goodbye or doing a single chore.

**

Mary had been at Mrs. Dunn's for several hours, minding the boys and cleaning while the youngest napped. Mrs. Dunn worked in her bedroom and dressing room. Eventually she summoned Mary and sat her down on a small bench in front of a table and mirror.

"I've been putting together some things for my niece's hope chest. She's marrying in a month. Anyway, I started to think about how grown up you are. I was married at your age. And I heard rumblings from Mrs. Harper the other day."

"Rumblings?"

"That perhaps you've been promised to someone. A Ralph somebody?"

Mary's shoulders slumped.

"I thought you had eyes for Samuel."

She nodded, then shrugged. "I . . . I suppose I still do."

"Your parents want you to marry someone else?"

Mary's inclination was to keep her family business to herself, but she needed Mrs. Dunn's encouragement, her kindness. Her boss wouldn't repeat what Mary confided. "I'm not officially matched, but they don't think Samuel will marry me, so they keep bringing up Ralph's name."

"What do you think about that?"

Mary thought of what Peggy had said to her about taking a match if one was offered. She shrugged.

Mrs. Dunn smoothed Mary's flyaways and adjusted her bun. "You're young, but eventually you'll be able to make choices of your own. I wish I had the answers for you and Samuel. Love is a funny thing."

Mary flinched at the word. Was this love? She let the feeling that came with thoughts of Samuel sit for a moment. The way other girls spoke of love, Mary was certain she wouldn't have to wonder about love if she'd been struck by it. "I don't love Samuel. He's tall and the only one who regularly asks me to dance. I suppose I like him more than anyone else. Yes."

"Well, no matter your immediate plans, I know you've been putting things away for when the time is right. In your hope chest."

Mary cringed.

"You do have one, right?"

Mary wanted to confide her secret to Mrs. Dunn. She could trust her. But something stopped her every time she tried to get the words out, to describe how she secreted most things behind the fireplace hearth and moved her gifted linens from hatbox to drawer to under the mattress, depending on the season. It was the height of shame. Saying the words aloud felt disloyal to her parents, increasing the weight of the lies she had already told. "Of course. I mean, it's small. Not really a chest, not like you mean. But my most precious things are safe."

Mrs. Dunn put her hand on Mary's and squeezed it. "Well, you're precious to me. And I want to add something more to your collection, if I may."

Mary inhaled deeply, sitting straighter when Mrs. Dunn pulled a small black velvet bag from inside a wooden chest, the sound of metal objects clinking together.

Mrs. Dunn loosened the pouch's strings and pulled out tiny silver objects two inches high. She held two between her forefingers and thumbs, and Mary saw an engraved letter on the front. "Salt and pepper shakers," Mrs. Dunn said, handing them to Mary.

The shaker was tiny, the same shape as a corseted woman. It took Mary's breath away. "So beautiful."

"Happy sweet sixteen, Mary."

Mrs. Dunn turned the bag over and emptied the rest of the shakers onto the dressing table behind Mary so she could look at all eight. "I wish I had twelve for you. I thought the engraved letter Ms were nice, even though it's for your first name and not your last, let alone the last name of the man you will marry someday. I mean, who knows, right? Your husband might be a Peter Sewald or a Theodore Ramey."

"I'll treasure these forever." Mary's eyes stung, touched by her generosity and that Mrs. Dunn remember her birthday. Mary pressed her hand to her cheek, Mrs. Dunn's softness bringing the sting of Matka's slap back to mind.

Mrs. Dunn took Mary's hand and squeezed it. "The idea is to have shakers for each person at your table. You can collect more over time and add to your collection. When you're engaged, people will buy you things. Silver pieces don't have to match to be used on the same table."

Mary thought of Mrs. Dunn's parties. She often set the table with various patterns of silver for each person, each gloriously heavy and ornate but all different.

Mrs. Dunn offered the wooden chest to Mary. "It goes with the salt shakers."

"Oh, no, no," Mary said. "I couldn't take this too."

"Please. It would make me happy for you to have it."

She looked at the box, wondering if Mrs. Dunn realized she'd been lying about having something that served as a hope chest. The swirled wood grain on its surface made it look painted. Mary thought back to when her father had sold her silver spoon to pay for the down payment on the house. Nothing she owned was viewed as hers. Her earnings, everything, was really her parents' property, and if they needed the money, they'd sell everything and anything.

"I would prefer to just take the pouch by itself if possible."

"Why?"

"Well . . . there are times . . ." Heat crawled up Mary's neck. "Sometimes when money's short we have to . . . well you know."

Mrs. Dunn furrowed her brow and hugged the box to her belly. "The spoon?"

Sweat burst out at Mary's hairline.

Mrs. Dunn took Mary's shoulder. "That's not just *your* story. It was once mine, too. It's been so long that I forget the way that some people . . . the way *I* used to live."

Mary felt loved, salved after the way Matka and she had fought earlier. She eased each shaker back into the bag, loving the sound they made, chiming against each other like tiny bells. She pulled the strings tight. "I'll never forget such a generous gift, that you see me as someone someday having dinner guests who expect to have their own set of shakers at the table."

Mrs. Dunn put down the chest and took Mary's hands. "Why, of course I see you that way, Mary. How else would I? Look at how you answered me then—polished language, soft, sure voice. You've come so far."

Mary inhaled deeply, honored that Mrs. Dunn thought of her life like this. It made Mary feel valued, that the life she dreamed about was possible.

"No matter who you choose to marry, *you'll* be special. You aren't like most girls. Oh, I wish I would have been more like you when I was younger."

Mary smiled. "What do you mean?"

"Confident, regal, spirited. Strong and intelligent."

Mary absorbed each sentiment. Every girl yearned to be called beautiful, graceful, and charming, but these words, Mrs. Dunn's words for Mary were different. Each a treasure as valuable as the things Mrs. Dunn had been gifting to Mary for years.

"I've seen you at baseball games laughing, heckling players, and catching fly balls."

Mary thought of Papa's orders to be more ladylike. "I'm too old to play now."

"Well, it's not that I think baseball should be in your future, Mary, but neither should marrying a man you don't love. I know it's none of my business, but don't lose the best parts of yourself. Don't *give them away* just because someone tells you you're supposed to."

"I won't." *Please, God,* she prayed, *let me keep these things that are mine. Don't let me give them away.*

Regal. She thinks I'm regal.

"Good. I'm sure you know full well what is prized about you. Keep those things safe in your heart, just like you keep the silver and linen in your hope chest. You're much too smart not to. Much too smart."

Chapter 43

Lucy and Owen

2019

Lucy and Owen opened as many windows as they could in the attic, dust causing each to sneeze so often they stopped blessing one another.

"I can't believe we're digging through all this," Lucy tossed an old felt hat aside, "crap."

Owen lifted a box and turned his head to sneeze. "It's not crap, Mum. You know it. We only got him to agree to stay that one extra night in the hospital if we vowed to do this for him."

"And his mind is a steel trap still, isn't it?" She shook her head, looking around.

Owen set the box down, nodding, surveying the space. A flash of yellow caught his eye. It was dull, but definitely yellow. He pointed. "There."

He stepped over trunks and boxes and stood on a single bed that had been slid against the wall. He reached for it and pulled the yellow object from the top of the wardrobe. He held it out to his mother, eyebrows raised. "A flower crown?" He shook it, releasing a plume of dust.

Lucy pinched her nose and took it from him. "Looks like the crown painted in the book." She moved to the book and opened it to the correct page. She shook her head. "Can't believe that thing didn't dissolve. My God, those girls made this over a hundred years ago."

Owen shook his head and hopped down. "Maybe not. That book jumps back and forth and maybe the crown was from 1950 or something."

She rubbed her nose. "I don't think."

Owen grabbed the book. "Gramps wants the blue-painted box with pink and yellow flowers. I don't see that anywhere. But here's that wire he said to bring down. Said Lukasz Musial used to make animals or objects or something."

"I don't see the box," Lucy said, looking back at the book. "Says Lukasz took a long time getting over Aneta, that the man she loved was American and . . . well, Lukasz had a hard time with not being able to declare for citizenship for years. So he worked hard, drank some, and Mary was busy working for the Dunns, in the mill, going to dances with someone named Samuel."

Lucy rubbed her eyes.

Owen leaned in to see. "Hmmm. Samuel? Not Lukasz?"

"I guess not."

Owen yawned.

"We better get you to bed," Lucy said. "We'll ask Gramps about it later. He was insistent about us bringing down the chest and wire, but . . . I wonder if it's even up here. And I'm gonna die if I stay up here one more second." Lucy took Owen's arm and pulled him. "We'll have plenty of time to look for that stuff later."

Owen skimmed the attic again. "Yeah. Sure. I guess if that book says Mary turned sixteen, then we must be getting close to her and Lukasz meeting, *really* meeting like husband and wife. Then Stan Musial. He'll be born soon, right?"

Lucy chuckled. "Always comes back to baseball for you, doesn't it?"

"I guess it does, Mum. But that's not news to you."

They headed down the stairs to the hallway below, finally able to breathe again.

Chapter 44

Mary

Thick, humid summer had come again and Mary was back at the riverside, helping her sisters with their St. John's Eve crowns. She settled Victoria's onto her head and brushed some loose hairs behind her ears before kissing her cheek.

Still disinterested in boys, Victoria was hesitant to offer her crown to the Monongahela and risk losing it, or worse—having it recovered by some disgusting boy. So instead, she kept hers safely on her head. Mary patted her sister's shoulder and ran off to help her friends finish their crowns.

Ann was ecstatic to send hers on its way, hoping Matthew Landover, the boy who sat next to her during cursive and civics classes, would pluck hers from the river. She snuck to the fire pit before tossing it into the river, certain he could identify hers by the row of pink peonies interspersed with violas, daylilies, sage leaves, and rosemary sprigs.

Mary didn't make a crown. Samuel had invited her to dinner with a flurry of romantic gestures to prove he was interested in dating her. She ignored her hesitations, her nervousness about eating with his family and said yes. She still heard about him and heaps of girls he took to dances. She saw them together. She wasn't stupid. But something still drew her to him. Something made her agree to his invitation, hoping the result of it would prove to Matka that Mary was worthy of someone wealthy and educated.

Mary was convinced Samuel would accept her family as well if the two of them grew closer. After all, everyone in America was an immigrant in some way.

When the time came for the girls to send their crowns into the water, Mary helped Ann and wished her good luck. They followed the candlelit crowns downriver, Mary checking over her shoulder for Samuel, who had said he'd come get her when the sun set and dinner was to be served.

There wasn't any sign of him, but a yelp came from the water. She heard panic in the voice, and it reminded her of when Papa had flipped his boat into the river. She scanned the river to see who was in distress, and finally her eyes settled on a place not far from where she stood. Two boys wrestled in the water and spit at each other.

"They're all right," a woman standing next to Mary said. She kept watching, wondering if the woman was right. The boys swam closer to shore, bickering about which had let the skiff flip over. One kicked at the other, soaking their mother but thankfully missing Mary's dress. The woman scolded the boys in Italian and smacked their behinds.

"Mary?"

She turned. Not only had Samuel come to meet her as planned, but he had brought his mother and sisters as well.

"You escaped the messy splashing, but I can see you need a lemonade, don't you?" Mrs. Blake said, her smile softening her sharp features and stiff posture.

Mary took deep breaths and reminded herself to speak the way Mrs. Dunn had taught her. "That would be lovely," Mary said. "Thank you."

Samuel put his hand at the small of Mary's back and escorted her to the table under the oak where the rest of his family waited. Mary thought of her birthday stockings, wishing she could show them to Samuel but knowing there was no way to even show her ankles at the moment. Perhaps when she lifted her hem to dance later.

The Blakes' maids had used wagons to transport prepared food to the riverside to serve.

Mary sat between Samuel and his brother, who picked his teeth the entire meal.

"So, Mary, tell us about your people," Mrs. Blake said.

"Well, my parents are Czech. My father works in the Ella Mine."

"Mary used to row him to work every single day before she got a job in the nail mill," Samuel said.

Mrs. Blake and Samuel's sisters stared at Samuel as if he'd just passed gas.

"A nail girl?" Samuel's sister Rachel asked. "Isn't that interesting."

"It's not really," Mary said. "It's hot and dirty. But it pays well."

"It's admirable," Mrs. Blake said. "Samuel told us how clever you were in school. It's too bad you had to give that up to work."

"Oh, no. I don't mind. I've been cleaning homes around town since I was eight and have worked for the Dunns since I was eleven." Mary sat straighter in her chair to convey her strength and pride. She worked to slow down her speech and pronounce each word clearly.

"Oh yes. Now I remember," Mrs. Blake said. "Mrs. Dunn told me you're a diamond in her household crown. She doesn't know how she'd manage without you. You put the whole house back to rights whenever you show up."

This gave Mary a shot of confidence and pride.

Mr. Blake slammed his hand on the table, causing all the crystal and silver to shiver against each other. "What in goddamn hell is happening here, Sadie?"

Mrs. Blake swallowed hard, looking frightened by her husband's outburst.

Samuel and his siblings froze.

"Damn girl," Mr. Blake said, gesturing toward a redheaded maid. "Brought the wrong drink again. *Again.* Can't a man enjoy the drink he wants every single goddamn day . . ." His words slurred once the anger had diminished. "Goddamn stupid hunky."

"Dad," Samuel said through clenched teeth.

Mrs. Blake finally snapped to attention. "Darling, Thomas, please. We have a guest."

Mary shifted her gaze to the family members at the table, trying to get a sense of what would happen next. Her parents had outbursts regularly, but usually in response to her mother hounding her father over money or him hounding her about not having his socks darned. But because the maid botched Mr. Blake's drink? Was there a correct way to prepare a drink? In her house, it was beer or whiskey or whiskey and beer; the only recipe was *open bottle and pour.*

Mary looked at Samuel, who appeared horrified. "*Dad.*"

"What? Don't goddamn give me lip. You and your parade of ladies, sizing up our value like we're on spec."

Mary narrowed her eyes at Mr. Blake. She didn't know him, but she hated him, as though he radiated aggression and she absorbed it. She was sorry for Samuel living with such a man. She reached for his hand but he snatched it away.

"Goddamn hunky help's unreliable." His words slurred and slipped into one another but his cruel intention was clear.

Mary grimaced and stole a look at Samuel. *She* was hunky help.

The maid returned with a new drink and set it in front of Mr. Blake, her hand shaking so badly she knocked it over drowning the food on his plate. Mr. Blake flew to his feet, took the girl by the shoulders, and bellowed in her face, "You're goddamn useless. You're fired. Go."

Mary couldn't breathe. It was as though she were the one being screamed at.

The family stared as the girl dashed away. Another came to blot up the spilled drink. The conversation resumed, the family discussing who was summering where that August.

Mary couldn't believe what she was seeing. Her stomach turned. It was as if she'd been struck in the belly, stunned by the way Mr. Blake behaved and how the family acted as though nothing had happened. She'd been able to ignore the pain it caused the day her mother had slapped her, the day the boarder stuck his hands in his pants as he stared at her. But this? It was an earthquake. *This* family wasn't supposed to be this way.

Samuel pushed his food around with his fork; his siblings did the same. Mary didn't want to do anything except run. The brutal berating, Mr. Blake's words, his tone, his body—she wondered what happened when the family was safely hidden at home. There wasn't a person in Donora who hadn't been smacked by parents, been yelled at, yelled for, or chased with a wooden spoon when patience wore thin, but this . . .

She'd put families like Samuel's above hers, thinking they were different. But they weren't. They were similar in ways that made her blood course cold.

Mr. Blake guzzled more drinks and was pulled away by a friend halfway through the meal. When he left, there was a collective exhale at the table. Mrs. Blake's shoulders relaxed and the girls began to talk amongst themselves about the dance they'd attend later.

Samuel leaned into Mary and took her hand in his, his lips near her ear. "I'm sorry about that. He's old-fashioned, I suppose. He's been in the bottle most of the day and—"

She crossed her arms. "Parade of ladies? Hunky?"

"It's nothing."

"Samuel." Mary eyed his mother and sisters to see they were engrossed in their own discussion. She knew Mr. Blake was used to having his life and work run in an orderly fashion, but to say aloud a slur meant to hurt for something so silly? Mary felt her heritage and her questionable standing with Samuel deeply at that moment.

"It's all the favors my mother has me doing for her club friends. Take this one's daughter with the fat ankles to this dance and that one to dinner and 'oh, Samuel, please, just one last time with the cross-eyed girl from Gary, Indiana.'"

Mary didn't like that he thought of the girls like that—the one with fat ankles . . . Hunky.

"Why'd you invite me tonight?"

"You know why."

"Tell me."

He glanced at his sisters and shifted, talking lower. "Mary, come on." His attention on her normally sent excited chills through her body, but this time, it did nothing.

She lowered her voice as well. "I know why I wanted you to invite me. Tell me."

"I don't know what you want to hear."

Mary looked away.

"Samuel?" Mrs. Blake said, making Mary and Samuel startle. "You'll make sure the girls are escorted home later?"

He nodded. "Of course."

Mrs. Blake narrowed her eyes at Mary for a moment, then went back to talking with her daughters.

Samuel grabbed Mary's hand. Mary shot a look at his mother. She didn't notice. Mary waited for a thrill to work through her body from his hand being on hers.

Nothing.

"I like you, I do," Samuel said. "You know that."

She nodded.

He squeezed her hand. "You sure you like *me*?"

Mrs. Blake pushed away from the table and Samuel stood to pull her chair out of her way.

Mary looked down at her dress and flicked lint away. She was drawn to Samuel, that's for sure. He was tall, smart, handsome, rich. What was not to like? Besides his kissing and dancing. There was that.

Mary stood and thanked Mrs. Blake for the meal, not sure she'd ever be invited to dine with them again. His sisters and mother went to freshen up in the ladies' tent and Samuel returned to Mary's side.

He took her hands. "Let's go dance." He started to pull her toward the music.

Mary didn't budge. She couldn't let this matter drop. "I do like you. But at least tell me you don't think of me as a hunky. Or that you don't see my family as less than yours."

"Mary. Of course not."

"Good. Because every stinking dime your father makes comes off the backs of Poles, and Italians, and Czechs . . . I'm only a little Hungarian," she mumbled as though that negated the slur in general.

"It's all the same to my father. You know that. That old crowd of men. The label's not meant to be mean. Just a way of grouping the people who work for him."

"Like I said, the mill, your house, runs off hunky backs. Crippling work. Dangerous."

"They're good jobs for uneducated people. They tell us all the time. They're grateful to be out from under royal dictates and utter . . . poverty."

They? She stared at Samuel, really studied him. She'd been stunned by his father's actions and words. She'd heard friends, even her own father, called hunkies a million times. It rarely caused someone to fight about it. It's just how it was. *But she was American.* She'd never felt the word *hunky* sink into her skin the way it had that night.

Mr. Blake was extremely drunk. Perhaps he didn't normally behave that way. She'd certainly seen plenty of drunk fathers, but she'd thought Samuel's family was different. Their home was organized, clean, big, welcoming, *lemony.* My God they changed furniture with the seasons! Mr. Blake shouldn't have been the kind of man who'd be sloppy drunk and cruel.

"What do *you* think?" Mary poked Samuel's shoulder. "Am I a hunky?"

He paused just long enough to make her breath catch.

"Of course not. You're Mary. You're wonderful."

Stunned, she didn't respond.

He grasped her hand. "You're marvelous and bold and I wouldn't have asked you to come if I didn't see how fantastic you are."

He tried to lead her toward the dancing again, the laughter of revelers ringing out again.

Mary resisted.

He tilted his head and smiled, his cowlick flopping in a warm breeze. "What do you say? The rest of the gang's waiting at the pavilion. Please."

Mary, still shocked by Mr. Blake's behavior, worried that Samuel's thinking might align too closely with his father's. Matka would say she warned Mary about exactly this. Mary would not allow herself to be grouped, to be made smaller for no reason but her heritage. She wouldn't allow the disgrace Mr. Blake assigned to those who worked in his mill and served his food to ever be how she saw herself or anyone she knew.

She reminded herself of Mrs. Dunn. She had bridged the gap between her past and present, living a beautiful life. Mary wasn't ready to just walk away from the idea of Samuel. There was a kernel of pity for him inside her at the way his father had humiliated him. He couldn't help the things his father had said or the way he treated people. Again, she thought of Mrs. Dunn, the way she'd been treated by her in-laws when they first married. Maybe it just took time for people to fully appreciate another's gifts, someone who was different.

"I really like you, Mary. Give me a chance to show you that I think of you in a million ways and none of them have hunky in the name."

She didn't argue the point that she was in fact of the heritage his father disparaged, that pretending she couldn't be called a hunky wasn't the same as accepting that she was, liking all of her, that part included.

Samuel rubbed the back of her hand with his thumb. "I'll show you, Mary."

She sighed and finally gave in to his tugging. She'd give him a chance. She lifted her chin and squared her shoulders. "Sure, Samuel. Let's go."

Chapter 45

Mary

Summer went quickly for Mary, busy with work and dances with Samuel. Only twice did they go together in a way that could have been considered a date. All the other times, they had met each other there. His dancing improved as Mary coached him, her mood lighter with his more facile footwork, even with more intricate dances like the bunny hug. She had to admit, though she loved how they felt together, dancing and kissing when they could, she wasn't confident in the possibility of them ending up together. She wanted him, what he had to offer, but didn't trust him.

The dinner at the river with his family still hovered around them. Mary was not sure she wanted him inside her heart, even if he came with apologies that felt sincere, a great deal of money, and position. Was this all a woman could expect in a marriage, even in a marriage she chose for herself? No love, just position? Was that all right with her?

At the wireworks, Mr. Dunn had approached her intermittently for information about people who might have been stealing nails, wire, or tools from the mill.

"Aside from my goodwill in wanting to help you support your family," Mr. Dunn reminded her, "I've asked you so many times, and you never see anyone stealing?"

Mary was irritated, not knowing until then how much her spying had played into her being given the coveted nail-girl position. She had thought that him mentioning how observant she was had been mostly offered as an aside meant to flatter her, not the reason she'd been given the job. "I'm sorry for not seeing people steal, but I'm just keeping up on the line. Do you want me to step away and watch for thieves?" She held her breath, unable to imagine her work if he said yes, that's what he wanted from her.

"No, no. Rumor has it that the mill is greased good. I'm hearing 'bout nails missing and . . . no. I want your eyes on your work. But I'm just surprised that after two years, you've only seen a couple kegs go missing."

She'd heard plenty of rumors too. Heck, she knew for sure that Peggy took nails. But she couldn't imagine fingering some man with a family or a woman supporting her parents when she had no solid proof besides gossip. She was sure they'd all pay for nails if they were paid better. But ideas like that were latched to organizing and mentioning that was a ticket to being fired. She was surprised that she'd not seen people steal too. She was less observant than she thought.

"If I see something—"

"If you *hear* or see. And union talk. You clue me in on that, Mary. We take care of you, so please remember to take care of Mrs. Dunn and me."

Mary clenched her jaw. She'd not thought of it that way. "I understand."

"Men have been running their traps about Jeb Turner, and how he's letting half his men leave with hundred-pound kegs of nails. And he's organizing."

Mary shook her head. "I haven't seen that."

"My wife said you are vigilant in your work, that the tiniest details are important to you, that you value us as a family . . ."

The threat inside these statements frightened Mary. "That's right. Mrs. Dunn means the world to me. I do value your family beyond any pay I receive." She quaked. Was she being clear enough? "If I see something, I will tell you. I don't want to put my job in the mill or your home at risk."

He patted her shoulder. "Show me the attention to detail my wife seems to think you possess in spades."

Now she worked extra hard to notice people leaving with things they shouldn't. But she was beginning to see that she was watched by her targets as much as she watched them. It made sense. It was never a secret that Mary worked for the Dunns. Of course her coworkers wouldn't be obvious about pilfering when she was there. How naïve of her not to realize any of this until that moment.

**

One day in October, Mary finished her work for Mrs. Dunn and was elbow deep in ironing at home, excited to head off to another dance. The basket of dirty boarders' clothing ballooned like an ice cream threatening to fall off its cone. She had one iron heating on the stove and the other she was using, her sisters poised to deliver pressed clothing to the proper recipients.

"I'm done," Ann said after she brought the finished garments to their owners. She lifted her hands in the air as if surrendering.

"No, you're not," Mary said.

"I'm getting picked up in thirty minutes."

"Picked up?"

"The Smiths are taking me to dinner and the show at the Carmichael."

"You're thirteen," Mary said. "Samuel's getting me in forty-five minutes for the dance tonight. Do you know how long it's been since he's escorted me to a dance instead of just meeting there?"

Ann shrugged. "Come with me, Victoria. Do my hair." Victoria tossed aside the shirt she was holding for Mary and trotted after Ann. Mary's blood pumped in her ears. No way was she going to miss this dance with Samuel just so her little sister could enjoy an expensive meal.

A voice came from behind Mary. "How about my drawers, little lady?"

Hair stood on the back of her neck. Mary turned to see Mr. Cermak standing two feet behind her. She went around the other side of the ironing board. He inched closer. "Big night tonight with Miss Candasera and I need to look my best."

She was relieved to hear he had a date. Perhaps he'd be down the aisle and in his own house soon.

"A bride for you, good," Mary said.

He looked her up and down. "If it's you, yes."

Mary stepped back from the ironing board and switched out the iron for a hot one. She held it, the hot side facing him.

"Your things are in your room." She spoke as taut as she could, keeping his gaze even as he conveyed his lust for her. How had it taken this long for her to put a word to what she saw in his eyes?

"Oh, how capable you are, sweet Mary. Someone will be very lucky to land you in his net."

"Sweet? Hadn't heard that one."

Please God, please God, make him go away. Mary held his gaze with a glare, thankful he wasn't moving toward her or disrobing in any way. She stepped toward the ironing board, still with the iron out. "I've work to finish."

"Before your dance?"

"Yes."

"I love to see you like this, your gaze so hard on me, as though you think you can control this situation. Inside, you're squirming. I can feel it. I only wish I could feel your body squirming underneath me. Wouldn't that be something?"

Mary pushed the iron forward, the metal clicking against his shirt buttons as she made contact.

He winced and pressed his hand against his chest. "What fun you are. Someday we'll have fun together."

She slammed the iron to a shirt, finishing each motion by sweeping the face of the iron toward him.

"Off to meet my lady for a show." He backed away, hesitant to go.

Mary gagged at the thought of being the lady waiting. Her mother's steps in the front hallway, her presence, got Mr. Cermak moving and Mary heard the front door close as he finally left. Mary shook the shirt she had finished and hung it on a hanger. Matka entered the kitchen. "We need to get rid of Mr. Cermak," Mary said.

"This again? He's our best boarder. Doesn't steal. Always pays on time."

Mary finished buttoning the shirt and hung it on the line. "He's *disgusting*."

"Mary!"

"He is."

"Stop it. The money tree out back hasn't gone leafy yet, if ya haven't noticed. Don't drive a good boarder away."

"He's always staring. Always touching—"

"You?" Mrs. Lancos asked.

"No. I told you before. Himself."

"An accident. We're packed in here like sardines."

Mary slammed down the iron. "*Not* an accident. He lurks." Mary mimicked how he stood, making his leering facial expressions, pushing her hand to her crotch.

"Enough. Why's he lookin' at ya that way if he is? What're you doing to make him do all that?"

Mary switched out the irons again. "Unless you consider slaving away with the wash and cooking to be doing something alluring, then nothing." Anger burned her insides. "I'd never do anything to make him pay a bit of mind to me. He's disgusting."

Matka shook her head.

Mary raised a fist. "I'll sock him in the jaw if he touches me. I swear to Jesus above." Mary crossed herself and asked forgiveness to God for bringing Jesus's name into it. "If he drops those pants even a little, I'll kick him between the legs."

Mrs. Lancos rubbed her temple. "A misunderstanding." Her voice was thin, troubled. "Haven't seen 'im do a thing to any of yinz. Yer sisters?"

"I keep an eye out for them. It's me he follows."

Matka's shoulders slumped, her exhaustion obvious. Talking about Victoria and Ann seemed to change her attitude. "Oh, so you're a better mother than me?"

Mary smoothed another shirt on the ironing board. "That's not what I meant."

Matka looked defeated. "I'll set 'im straight."

"Unless you're telling him to leave, don't say a word. I don't want him angry if he's going to be here with us."

"I watch over yinz girls, Mary. And if I saw a hint of shenanigans, I'd sock 'im myself."

Mary paused, unsure if her mother was serious. "Okay. One more shirt," she said. "Then I'm changing for the dance. Dinner's on the stove."

"Not eating?"

"I'm going dancing. Ann's apparently dining with the Smiths and going to a show."

Matka's face lit up. "Wonderful! Such good friends."

"Why do you see the Smiths as good friends for Ann and you say Samuel couldn't possibly be good for me?"

"Shit, Mary. Again?"

"Shit, is right," Mary said, slamming the iron onto the shirt.

Matka glared. "Young lady. Yer sass and disrespect. I've had it." Her chest heaved, jaw clenched. "Too many times. Go right to yer room when you're done. Stay put."

Mary stopped ironing and met Matka's furious gaze with her own. Her face flamed and she shook her head. She sprinkled starch on the shirt, and dragged the iron across the material, clicking against the buttons, the familiar scent filling her nose. She wouldn't argue with Matka anymore, but she wasn't going to listen to her either.

Chapter 46

Mary

With the ironing complete, Mary set her plan to sneak out for the dance in motion. She dug into the old dress box where she kept fabric scraps and fished out a cherry-flavored lollipop. "Victoria." She held up the candy.

Victoria was washing up to go to sleep. She sat up and licked her lips.

"You can have this if you promise not to tell Matka that I left."

Victoria's eyes went wide.

"It's strawberry."

Victoria nodded.

"I'll bring you something special after my shift tomorrow."

Victoria shoved the sucker into her mouth and her eyes closed in pleasure. "This is better than anything."

Matka had turned in for the evening with a headache, and Mary was confident she could get to and from the dance unnoticed. She put on her clean dress and brushed and recoiled her long hair at the nape of her neck. She washed her face at the bowl and dug through her canvas bag for toothpaste. Her toothbrush was missing. She ran her tongue over her teeth, feeling the grime. She searched her dresser, yanking a drawer open. Maybe she'd accidentally set it there.

Nothing. "Where'd I put that toothbrush? I'm losing my mind."

"It's ruined." Victoria said from the bed, smacking her lips.

"What is?"

Victoria removed the lolli from her mouth, clicking it against her teeth. "Johnny needed something to build his ramp to make his marbles jump through the air."

"So he took my toothbrush? I bought that with the money I had left from what I give to Matka."

"I know."

"Why didn't you stop him?"

Victoria popped the candy back into her mouth. "It was fun."

Mary stared at her eleven-year-old sister sucking on that lollipop, sheet pulled up to her chin, appearing content but worried.

Mary shook her head. Of course it was fun. It wasn't as if her siblings were given the circus toys, play guns, or even the white leather baseballs that the Dunn children always had. She sighed. She was the one who had taught them to make toys out of ordinary objects.

Mary sat beside Victoria and smoothed the sheet over her body. "It's all right, Victoria. I can brush my teeth with a hanky."

Victoria nodded, her face relaxing.

Tucking Victoria into bed made Mary think of the night she had spent at the Dunns' in the guest room. "And someday I'm going to marry a wonderful man and live in an enormous, beautiful house with fresh-smelling sheets, and every single child will have his own room, new toothbrushes each year, and toys from the store." She leaned against Victoria. "Oh, the hair ribbons we'll have!"

"And me? Bring me to live with you?"

Mary dotted Victoria's nose. "You'll have first pick of everything."

Victoria threw her arms around Mary's neck and squeezed.

Mary took the blood-stained hanky from her drawer, added paste to it, and scrubbed her teeth. Every time she touched the ruined hanky, she thought of the angel Lukasz Musial had given her that she had hidden away, how she had wrapped the angel ornament in this soiled hanky and couldn't wait to unwrap it to store it away in something clean, something worthy of such a beautiful creation.

Mary made Victoria promise again that she wouldn't tell anyone where she went. She popped open the window and slipped outside, careful to keep her freshly shined shoes from getting dusty in the backyard. She snuck around the front of the house to wait for Samuel to pick her up as planned.

**

Mary hoisted the hem of her dress and took the stairs up the front of the dance hall two at a time. Samuel had rarely promised anything to her, but he had promised to pick her up at her house and take her to the dance. They were to enter together as a couple. She told herself it didn't matter that he didn't show up, that meeting up with friends and dancing with him had always been fine with her.

Her breath heavy, she checked her coat, took the song list, and entered the hall, surveying the room. She smoothed her hair and calmed herself down. She told herself to act dignified. She thought of Mrs. Dunn's advice to remain poised and quiet in her interactions with men; certain types of men expected to be addressed with the same ease as gentle falling snow, even if what was said turned into ten feet of hard-packed fury.

Mary spotted Samuel, his head above the rest of the crowd. She beelined for him, torn between pitching a fit and acting forlorn, like so many girls did to get what they wanted from the men they liked. *Soft and gentle, hard-packed fury. Please God, let me do this with dignity.*

She touched his sleeve. "Samuel."

He nodded and looked away.

Mary crossed her arms. Her voice quivered. "I'm sure there's a reason that—"

"Yeah, yeah."

Mary's mouth went dry. What was happening? She hadn't imagined him asking her to the dance, so what was wrong? She steadied her voice, keeping it gentle but determined. "Next song's 'Carrie Furnace Waltz.'" She waved the list at him.

He nodded. "Okay, well . . ."

Her heart seized. The ability to control her emotions was dissolving. "What is it? Why didn't you—"

He snapped around, looking at her straight on. "I told you. It's that I need to—"

It was then the energy in the room transformed. The crowd quieted and shifted their attention in unison, turning in the same direction, gasping the same gasp. Mary turned slowly to see what everyone was gaping at.

A woman parted the sea of people, wading through the hall. Tall and slender, she was draped in a green beaded chiffon dress that swished along the floor with grace as she walked.

This dress wasn't just beautiful. It was different from anything Mary'd ever seen. Every curve of this woman's body was draped, obvious, alive, soft. The corsets all the girls she knew owned changed their body shapes, dictating appearance by pinching, rounding, lengthening or shrinking the body rather than it yielding to the natural shape of a woman. This dress allowed the woman to slink along like liquid mercury, making Mary think it was the first woman's body she'd ever seen even though she had one herself.

The woman cast an eye around the room, a small smile on her pink, slightly parted lips, her eyes sparkling. She nodded as everyone's eyes met hers, and finally, she saw someone who made her smile widen. She came nearer and nearer to Mary.

The woman glanced at her and nodded, then stopped in front of Samuel.

"You made it," Samuel said, his voice breathy.

"It took doing." She spread her arms. "But here I am."

"You look . . ." He ran his hand through his hair. "Beautiful," he whispered, his words floating, his whole body almost levitating toward her.

Mary's heart stopped, then fluttered, just barely remembering its job was to keep its beat. Her head swam, feeling as if it were lifting off her neck. Her hands grew hot and clammy.

Samuel and this woman talked, their bodies drawing close as she brushed his shoulder. He took her hand, kissing the back of it. Their words, the music, and the crowd noise all receded and Mary could only feel, only hear the drumbeat of her blood rushing past her ears.

"You all right?" Samuel asked.

Was he looking at her?

"Mary?" He took her by the arm, and the beautiful glistening woman watched too, her eyes wide. "You got my note?"

Mary barely gathered his words. "Note?"

"I left it at your house."

Mary shook her head, her cheeks flushed. The press of dozens of revelers' eyes fixed on her.

"I'm sorry." He backed away from her.

The band struck up again. The dancers coupled up, the mass of them enveloping Samuel and this woman, their heads moving above the rest.

His date was eye level with him, and they glided as one, Samuel's feet light and precise as they'd never been with Mary. She'd always worried Samuel would find an ideal partner in someone tiny, someone completely different from her. But this woman was so much like Mary that it pierced her, the woman's refinement an example of all the grace Mary had rarely seen beyond older, wealthy women. Yet here was this young woman, Mary's age, unrestrained by typical girlhood shyness or feigned coyness.

At one point, Samuel's feet did catch his partner's, but instead of irritation, her expression registered surprise, then delight as they fell together, laughing, their bodies conveying an intimacy that Mary could only imagine feeling with him. Seeing them like that just demonstrated how disconnected Mary and Samuel had been all along.

Could he at least pretend to feel something toward Mary? There wasn't even a smidgen of sadness, nothing that showed he'd ever been interested in her. Mary was the one who had let him trample her feet at every dance for two and a half years. He had used her, and she'd let him do it.

She clasped her chest. The pain. Her knees weak. Was she dying?

And he . . . he swept around the dance floor as if stepping on clouds with the most beautiful woman Mary'd ever seen laughing in his arms. How could he have not warned Mary? A note, he said? There'd been no note. He simply didn't care.

She finally found her legs again and turned to bolt out of the hall. One step forward and she smacked right into Lukasz Musial. She sidestepped him, but he latched onto her arms.

"No," he said.

"I have to go."

He gently shook her again, getting her attention. "Stay."

Her eyes burned and she avoided his gaze. She tried to wiggle out of his grip.

"Look," he said.

Slowly, her gaze met his, and the kindness in his eyes seeped into her. She looked away, Lukasz's sweetness enflaming her hurt even more.

"Stay. Dance."

He slid his hand down from her wrist, his fingers threading between hers. His palm was warm against hers.

She swallowed her sobs again and looked at Lukasz. His face conveyed warmth and understanding. A pair of dancers swept by them, brushing her arm. She looked over her shoulder to see Samuel with that woman pressed against him, her cheek against his, their eyes closed, moving as one.

Mary pulled away again but Lukasz held tight. "Stay. You are so . . . Stay, please."

An arm's length apart, they kept their hands clasped. His attentive gaze was full of concern, and something made her trust him.

He shifted his hand to hold hers in the proper dancing position. He warmed the small of her back with his touch, pulling her close. Finally, she laid her hand on his shoulder and let him guide her around the dance floor. The music lifted them, and she didn't mind in that moment that she was five inches taller. His shoulder was strong under her hand.

The music shifted to a slower tune and he pulled her closer, the heat of his body against hers.

Lukasz's dancing was skilled and delicate, and she was bolstered in his embrace. It made her think of the elegant Christmas angel he'd made, his ability to do delicate work with such strong hands.

When the song ended and the band announced a break, the lamps were turned up. Embarrassment flooded Mary again. She stepped away from Lukasz. He tried to keep her hand in his, but this time she wiggled away and ran for the cloakroom.

She pushed past the hatcheck girl and retrieved her own hat and coat. She shoved one arm in and dashed away with Peggy yelling her name as she exited the hall. The brisk fall night mixed with the heat of humiliation. She'd never been so upset, but it wasn't as though she hadn't been warned about the other girls he dated. She should be angry at herself the most. Matka had warned her and she refused to listen.

She ran home, turning her ankle on the way but ignoring the pain that shot up her leg. She burst through her front door to find her parents exiting the kitchen with cups of steaming coffee. They stopped dead at the sight of her.

Mary halted. Her punishment.

Dread settled over her as she realized the holy hell her parents were going to give her for sneaking out. She pressed her hand to her forehead, breathing heavy, full of rising tears.

"What the hell?" her mother asked.

"I just—"

"Oh." Mr. Cermak stepped out of the kitchen with his own steaming mug. He reached into his pocket, pulled out a piece of paper, and handed it to Mary's parents. "This came for Mary earlier. I forgot."

He stood behind Mary's parents, smirking. Matka unfolded the paper. "Read it, Mary." She held the paper out to her daughter.

Mary didn't take it at first, but then Papa growled something about respect. She said the words aloud for her parents, who couldn't read English. "*I can't take you to the dance, Mary. I've been asked to take another. You know how parents are.*"

Mary thought of Samuel's date at the dance.

"What does that mean?" Papa bellowed.

Mary jumped.

He gripped her shoulder and shook. "Answer me."

"I guess he couldn't take me to the dance." Mary glanced at Mr. Cermak, wanting to scratch his eyes out.

"Ralph? I'll beat the stinkin' hell ahta him."

Matka pulled Mary closer and pointed to the part of the letter signed by the writer. "Whose name is that? That's an S, right?"

Papa bent in closer. Mary drew her finger across the paper, wishing she didn't have to share her humiliation. "Samuel."

Papa turned his angry eyes on Mary. "Samuel? Who the hell is Samuel? I've been talking to Ralph's father."

Mary's breath caught as tears fell. "He doesn't want me, Papa. Even if I want him." *Neither of them want me.*

"Nonsense. A match is nearly complete."

Mr. Cermak leered.

Mary's anger expanded her chest, making it hard to breathe. She'd had enough of everyone pushing her, no one she liked wanting her. "I just left a dance where Ralph danced every single one with Sally. You and his father might have this big idea, but we're most certainly *not* matched. We can choose for ourselves."

"This isn't a democracy," Papa said.

Mary bit the inside of her cheek. "Yes, it is. Why live in America if I can't even choose a husband? You always said—"

"Well, not this Samuel," Papa said, glancing at Matka.

"It doesn't matter, Papa."

"What's this boy up to, muddying the waters for my daughter? Ruining her reputation? I'll kill him. What's his last name?"

Mary's eyes burned. "It doesn't *matter*, Papa." She thought of the grace and beauty of the woman who had come for Samuel at the dance. That was what Matka had known that Mary hadn't. Matka could envision this woman and had known someday she'd arrive to take Mary's place with Samuel.

Her parents continued to bicker about who Samuel was and what that meant for Mary's reputation, but all Mary wanted was the pain to go away. She repeated the words silently. *Samuel doesn't want me.* He found the woman who matched his dance steps, every single one. Mr. Cermak sneezed, drawing Mary's attention back to what was happening in front of her. She wanted him gone, didn't want him to witness more of her humiliation.

"Heaped over this Samuel business, I forbade ya to go dancin'," Matka said.

Mary couldn't hold it in anymore. "You'll be happy to know I've been punished good. Both boys are smitten with other people, so punish me all you want. Give me double ironing, the rest of the wash, why don't you just work me into the ground like I'm a dead dandelion?"

"Enough." Papa sipped from his cup. "No dances. You work, you come home, and you go to Mrs. Dunn. That is all."

"No dances?"

"Forever, if you keep it up," Papa said, his decision feeling like deep betrayal to Mary.

She stared at him wondering who exactly he was at that moment.

Chapter 47

Mary

Mary's world shrunk after the dance—home, the wireworks, the Dunns'. One night when her shift ended, Kasandra and Peggy rushed off to do their hair and go to the dance at the Miller's Hall. Mary considered begging her parents to reconsider her punishment, but with all of the work Matka had piled on her, she didn't even have a clean dress to wear.

The November night was brisk and she pulled the wool sweater tight against her. She'd have to start wearing her worn wool coat. It had been remade three times so far. Mary crossed the mill floor, passing shipping. Out of the corner of her eye, she saw Lukasz and Chaffy. She kept going, then thought about how kind Lukasz had been the night Samuel had humiliated her. It was as if Lukasz had known that she'd needed someone to hold her up, just for those few moments, even if insecurity had rushed right in the second the music had ended.

Mary retraced her steps back to Lukasz to thank him. She waved and called his name. The grinding conveyor squealed and covered her voice. "Lukasz." She waved wildly, then stopped, not wanting to seem silly. She drew closer. The two men were at the end of the nail belt, filling wooden kegs with fresh, perfect American Steel and Wire nails.

She stopped, stunned. Maybe they were just helping the girls get organized, or maybe they were helping move the product to the next bin. She drew closer, waving again. No one noticed her. All eyes were on Lukasz and Chaffy. Lukasz put the keg under one arm and yanked his coat around it. Chaffy did the same, though he had more trouble carrying his. He went back to dump nails out, then ran after Lukasz, who was already moving toward the back of the mill. He pulled back the loose metal siding and let Chaffy pass through before he followed behind, the metal sliding back into place.

Sweat formed on her forehead. What should she do? Report them? Lukasz?

The door to the men's locker room slammed. Mr. Halcott strode toward her, wiping his hands with a towel. His gaze fell on the space where Lukasz and Chaffy had slipped through, and he focused on Mary.

Her throat tightened. Had he seen the two men steal the nails? She knew it was her job to report such things. But Lukasz? His kindness, his quiet smile, his gentle embrace as they danced . . . he had kept her from collapsing. She couldn't report him.

Mrs. Dunn. If Mary disappointed Mr. Dunn, he would make her fire Mary. She shivered at the thought.

"Good evening, Mr. Halcott," she said as he neared her, straightening her shoulders, acting calm, normal.

"Mary." He nodded. "What is it? You look frightened."

She cringed. "No. Not at all."

"Your shift's over, isn't it?"

She nodded.

"Then?"

"Nothing. It's . . . I went back for my sweater. I forgot it."

Mr. Halcott lifted his chin and continued on, surveying the mill floor like a wolf hunting prey.

Mary moved toward the exit, glancing up at the offices where Mr. Dunn worked, where all the higher-ups kept watch. Movement in one window caught her eye and she waved at the form, unable to see who it was but hoping for dear life that no one else had seen Lukasz and Chaffy sneaking nails out, thieves in clear view if only someone noticed.

Chapter 48

Lukasz

Cold November wind cut through the skin of the wireworks, making the heat inside worse because of the contrast in temperatures. Sweat dripped from Lukasz's hair as he finished loading a set of wire bundles. Waiting for the next load, he rubbed his shoulder and slogged to the pipe that sent water into the mill for the men to drink. Someone grabbed his shoulder as he bent in to get a sip. He spun around to see Chaffy.

"Stop it with the nails for a while," Chaffy said.

"I paid," Lukasz said.

"White shirts wouldn't agree with that."

"So I pay, then don't get them?"

Chaffy elbowed Lukasz out of the way and took a long swig. He wiped his mouth. "I'm in the same pickle. Broke my back last summer hauling lumber for goddamn Rosco's room n' at. I git it. But no more for now."

Lukasz thought of all the nails he was storing at Mark's shed. Every week, he tucked money into the same tin box that held the rings he'd made for Aneta, proud he was getting closer to a down payment on the property where he would build a home with the nails he'd traded his bosses for labor.

Lukasz bent over and cupped his hands to drink more before pulling out his hanky and wiping down his face.

"I'm serious," Chaffy said. "Dunn's got a nail girl watching. Last week when we took that haul and I had to dump half of mine on account of my sore hand? She was watching, writing something down. This week? I get told to cut it out until the dust settles."

"Same girl's probably taking nails home to her father. She'll make sure no one knows," Lukasz said in slow English, even though he wasn't fluent as he wanted to be.

Chaffy pulled Lukasz's collar. "This is different. This girl works for the Dunn family at home. The tall one. Mary."

Could it be Mary? He'd spoken to her many times and he had danced with her, but he didn't really know her. Maybe she was the sort who followed rules right down to the last word.

Lukasz glanced at the offices overhead. "You're right. I'll go easy," Lukasz said as he stretched his back, walking back to position himself to receive the wire bundles. They began their tandem throwing, Lukasz tossing two for every one of Chaffy's. When they finished, they stumbled to the water pipe and were met by the foreman, his boss, and Mr. Dunn.

"Musial. My office. Now," Mr. Dunn said.

Three other workers were in the office, their faces sooty, eyes wide.

But Mary was standing with Mr. Dunn, her arms crossed and her jaw clenched. Lukasz made eye contact and she nodded, sliding her gaze away.

"Now, Mary. Which of these men did it?" Mr. Dunn asked.

Mary straightened and stared at each one of them.

Lukasz knew he'd taken nails, that many people did, but he had no idea if these particular men had.

Mr. Dunn pointed. "Go on closer, Mary. Get a good look."

She inched toward the men. Lukasz was frightened, but he couldn't help studying Mary. Her dress was relatively clean, so she must not have been working a shift. She must have come in specifically for this. Her hair was combed and neatly braided at the base of her neck. Her nails were clean, her cheeks were pink, and her lips were apple red—not painted, just natural. A fresh citrus scent lifted off her when she walked past Lukasz and back toward him again.

When she got to Lukasz, she paused, staring at him, her thick black eyelashes flagging large brown eyes. She bowed her head slightly as though listening for the answer she was to give. Her chest rose and fell in deep breaths. He wanted to take her hand the way he had the night they'd danced.

"Him?" Mr. Dunn stood beside Lukasz.

Mary jumped. The foreman raised his eyebrows, and Mr. Dunn stepped closer. "Don't be afraid. You stopped when you got near him."

"I'm not afraid," Mary said.

She moved down the line, full of confidence, making eye contact with each man. She finally turned. "I'm sorry, Mr. Dunn, but it's not any of these men. It must have been that fella that you let go last week for coming in drunk. But these men? No. I spoke with Mr. Palmer the day he asked what I saw. I told him then who I thought it was."

Mr. Dunn leveled his gaze on Lukasz, then surveyed the rest. "You're sure, Mary?"

She looked at each man again.

"It means your job, Mary."

Lukasz guessed Mr. Dunn meant she'd lose more than her job at the mill. If Lukasz was understanding, it was Mary's position at his home he was dangling in front of her. This sent fear right to Lukasz's heart. Had she seen him take the nails?

Mary looked at the men again, staring at Lukasz once more. He held his breath.

Mr. Dunn pulled Mary aside and each said something too quiet for Lukasz to make out. His heart beat so hard, it shook his insides. Mary was a fine girl, but if she'd seen him steal, she would tell. She was a good person, and good people followed rules.

Mary turned back to the men yet again. She inhaled deeply and straightened to her full height. She shook her head and gestured with her hand in a way that reinforced what Lukasz hoped she said. "None of these men."

"None?"

Mary grimaced and she spoke through clenched teeth. "I'm sorry, but no."

Mr. Dunn took Mary by the elbow. "Well, keep an eye out."

She nodded.

"Go on then. You're free."

Mary strode out of the room, her graceful strides reminding Lukasz of how she looked when she danced or caught a foul ball.

Mr. Dunn crossed his arms, widened his stance and stared down each man. "I trust Mary Lancos with my life and my children's lives, and if she says none of you hunkies stole my nails, I'm inclined to believe her. But we'll be watching. Someone's taking shit and I mean to discern exactly who it is."

Chapter 49

Mary

Mary left Mr. Dunn's office and stomped back to his home. She was pushing the kitchen door open when she realized she had forgotten to bring the lunch pail back. She untied her hat, angry and scared. She jammed it on the rack and removed her coat.

It can mean your job as well as theirs. She knew what he meant. She couldn't imagine having to endure a disappointed Mrs. Dunn.

She was angry at Mr. Dunn for putting her in the position of tattling. And Lukasz and the others. Peggy had told Mary about people taking things from the mill in trade for favors to bosses, but now it was her problem. When she dropped the lunch pail at Mr. Dunn's office, she hadn't been expecting to be asked to participate in a lineup of men accused of stealing. She'd almost choked at the sight of Lukasz. She'd already decided not to report him back when she had seen him with the keg, but to have to lie right to Mr. Dunn? It wasn't right. None of it was.

"What's wrong, Mary?" Mrs. Dunn asked as Mary poured water into a glass.

Mary couldn't confide this. "I forgot Mr. Dunn's lunch pail."

Mrs. Dunn shrugged. "We have others. What's the matter, really?"

Mary sighed, wondering what to say. She patted the sides of her hair. "I'm a mess. Later, the dance and—"

"Nonsense. We'll freshen you right up. It's Samuel that's bothering you, what you told me about the girl he brought to the dance? That's still sitting heavy with you, isn't it?"

That wasn't untrue. It had shaken Mary. "Yes. But as you know, I'm determined to go to this dance—"

Mrs. Dunn asked Mrs. Harper to make them tea, and she guided Mary upstairs to her dressing room. "I've got Katya to watch the children today," Mrs. Dunn said.

Mary was confused.

"Come along."

Mrs. Dunn sat Mary down at her dressing table and undid her hair, brushing it one hundred times. She told Mary about Bartholomew, the boy her parents had matched her with. It had turned out very well for her and Mr. Dunn that she had disobeyed and followed her heart, and she knew the same was certain for Mary. Mrs. Dunn coaxed Mary to tell the stories about her and Samuel's courtship and their dinner on St. John's Eve. And in the end, they both realized Samuel was not trustworthy with his affection and his family was ghastly.

Mrs. Dunn made an upturned claw with one of her hands and flexed her fingers. "You know, I hadn't thought of this in ages, but your story reminded me. One time at the Blakes', I passed Mr. Blake in the back hall headed toward the powder room."

Mary wasn't sure what she was saying.

Mrs. Dunn made the claw gesture again. "Samuel's father. Grabbed me as I passed by him." She pointed to her right buttock. "And I socked him right in the jaw."

Mary's mouth gaped.

"I never told anyone." Her voice was barely above a whisper. "I can't believe I just told you."

Mary held up her right hand. "I won't repeat that."

"So you see, sometimes things happen in a way that is unexpected and awful, but it turns for the greater good. If Mr. Blake is like that, perhaps Samuel'll be that way too." She paused. "I'm so sorry, Mary. Here I was pushing you toward Samuel, and he's not worthy of you at all."

Mary loved that Mrs. Dunn talked to her this way— like a friend, almost. Samuel wasn't right for Mary, but she still wanted him to want her. She wanted him to yearn so she could turn him away.

"I'm glad you're permitted to go to this dance. You need to get out with friends and have fun."

Mary fingered the silver comb on the dressing table. She wanted to explain that she was coming to see herself as unmoored, in between being a true American girl and the immigrant world her parents had left behind. She'd never imagined that would influence who she married until recently. Her papa had once thought she could marry anyone in the world, but now he and Matka were pushing Mary toward a match with a Czech-American just because he owned a store and his parents were off the same boat as them. Matka's belief that only someone exactly like them would understand them confused Mary.

It was America. She had gone to school with children of all nationalities. They worked together, and they all put their might behind the mills and every blessed business in town. Yet Old-World traditions were gradually seeping into her parents' plans for her. Mary thought Mrs. Dunn might understand but didn't want to make her parents look bad to her.

"It's been weeks since I went to a dance. I'm still humiliated when I think about it. Everyone watching me watch Samuel and his date. Maybe I shouldn't go tonight. Seeing Samuel waltz around the room with the most desirable woman in the world all night doesn't inspire me to go. Phoebe . . . even her name is special."

Mrs. Dunn chuckled. "You're named for the Blessed Mother. Can't get more special than that."

"Lots of Marys in the world." Mary thought of Matka telling her she was actually named for someone she'd only heard mentioned once in her life.

"But only one you. What makes you say this Phoebe's the most desirable woman in the world?"

Mary cocked her head, remembering. "Well, her hair, perfectly finished. Her pompadour was *enormous*, but somehow at the same time it appeared . . ." Mary held her hands to show Mrs. Dunn how the girl's hair had swept up and out the front of her head.

"Effortless?"

"Yes," Mary said. "As though she just woke up looking like that every day, yes. And I was the complete opposite. Unprepared, unsophisticated, uneverything." Mary turned in her seat to face Mrs. Dunn. "I don't even know what I was looking at with her dress. It was as if she wasn't corseted; the dress clung to her in a way that just stopped my breath. She had to have been wearing a corset. But I could see her shape instead of her *being shaped* by something under the dress. I don't know . . . she was soft and curvy not stiff."

Mrs. Dunn turned Mary back around and took another section of her hair to brush. "It sounds like she was quite unique."

Mary nodded.

"What'd you do when you realized she was with Samuel?"

Mary cleared her throat. "I tried to leave, run out, but one boy, he took my hand and we danced and . . ."

"See. So many men to meet."

Mary closed her eyes, enjoying Mrs. Dunn brushing her hair, thinking no one in the world was right for her.

"You said your two friends are engaged now and it took them a while."

Mary nodded but wasn't in the mood to go to the dance anymore, not really. Seeing Lukasz steal the nails, being put in the position of lying by Mr. Dunn, Mr. Cermak, Papa, who endlessly made Matka angry . . . she wasn't so sure men were worth it.

"How about we create a different hairstyle for you? Something that's more you—effortless. You are that, Mary. You really don't see it?"

Mary shook her head.

"I think I have the perfect dress for you."

"Oh, no I—"

"Yes."

The idea excited Mary and she smiled.

"Let's get you freshened up, then we'll finish." Mrs. Dunn took Mary to the bathroom, pointing out the items to use to wash up before dressing. When Mary came out of the bathroom, Mrs. Dunn took her back to the dressing table.

Mrs. Dunn lifted and secured sections of Mary's hair. "Do you want Samuel? Despite what you know about him?"

Mary rubbed her arm. "Dunno. I love certain things about him, but . . ." Revealing such things made Mary self-concious.

Mrs. Dunn led Mary by the hand to her closet. "All the more reason to go to the dance. It's nearly Thanksgiving. There'll be plenty of men from out of town. It's just what you need."

Mary marveled at Mrs. Dunn's closet. Each and every dress was perfectly pressed. Mrs. Dunn pulled an ice-blue brocade gown from the closet and draped it over her arm.

Mary wasn't so sure she should wear it. "I don't have the right shoes and—"

"One thing at a time, Mary. This suits your grand nature. It's been so long since I've seen you smile and laugh, and you're even slouching a bit. You're not a stooper. That's not who you are."

Mary's spine straightened. "I hadn't realized."

"We're going to get you back to normal, starting tonight." She ran her hand down a champagne-hued beaded gown. "Oh, I remember this one. Maybe this is it for you tonight?" They went through Mrs. Dunn's entire closet, and she explained the ball or party or dinner she had attended when she'd worn each dress in her closet. Mary was lost in yards of taffeta, heavy and light wools, chiffons, and silks. She couldn't imagine owning a closet like this, but she'd be dreaming of it for the rest of her days.

Mrs. Dunn held the ice-blue dress up again. "This is it for sure, Mary. Just like we thought earlier."

"Too fancy."

"Not too fancy for you. And it's French. I think it will look like the dress you described."

Mary shook her head, disbelieving.

"They'll have the shoe dance, right?" Mrs. Dunn asked.

"Yes."

"A special night, then. Even if you don't want Samuel, you'll feel better seeing him want you. And there're so many others. This dress is what you need tonight."

Mary hesitated.

"Remember, I sent Mrs. Harper with a message to your parents earlier. It's taken care of and this is important. The Mary I know is bright and shiny, and this dress will draw Samuel back. And if you don't want him, it'll lure all the rest too."

"Sounds simple." Mary tried to see herself as Mrs. Dunn had described.

"It is simple. Fashion can do so much for a person. Here. Let's try it." Mrs. Dunn turned Mary away from the mirror. "So you can see it all at once." Mary stretched her arms up, and Mrs. Dunn slid the frock over her head, the silk lining shimmering down her body, tickling. She'd smoothed the fabric against her hips, understanding instantly, finally, exactly what luxurious fabric was and why it mattered.

Mrs. Dunn pulled the strings on the cotton corset that was sewn into the dress. "The integrated corset has soft boning that gives with the shape of your body instead of having bones that create the shape. It's all the rage in France. Not every woman can wear this type of gown, just tall, thin girls like you."

Mary tried to turn to see herself in the mirror, but Mrs. Dunn kept her facing away. "Not yet."

"I'm offending the dress by putting it over my dingy underthings."

Mrs. Dunn giggled. "Rarely does a woman's underthings match the fashion she shows the world." Mrs. Dunn fastened the dress, explaining every inch of the gown. "My cousin had this made in France but never wore it because she got too big, and there was no one her mother thought deserved it more than me. Well, I can't fit into it either."

"You could wear this easily," Mary said, running her hands over her hips.

"No, no. I couldn't. Not anytime soon. Not for months."

Mary glanced over her shoulder but didn't ask the rude question.

Mrs. Dunn continued to fasten the dress. "Yes, I'm expecting."

Mary was excited for her but could tell by her reaction that Mrs. Dunn was not. "Congratulations."

"Thank you, Mary." Her voice was low and formal.

Mrs. Dunn went to her closet and rolled out a dolly with cubes and hooks that held over a dozen pair of shoes. She pulled a pair out and set them in front of Mary.

Mary pushed her foot into the satin shoe, narrowing her toes to try to make it fit. "It's wide enough but way too short."

Mrs. Dunn stepped back, deliberating. "I would have sworn we wore the same size shoe with me being nearly your height."

"It's all right." Mary shrugged. "The hem hits right when I stand, and when I lift it to dance, everyone will be too busy to notice my shoes."

"You can't wear your boots." Mrs. Dunn turned to her shoe cubby. "Let's try these."

And so they crammed and stuffed Mary's feet into each pair as hard as they could, but it was no use.

Mrs. Dunn grabbed her hips. "On second thought, you're right. You're dazzling enough. Not one soul will notice what's on your feet."

Mary grimaced.

Mrs. Dunn's eyes widened. "I know you're worried about the shoe dance. By the time they do that dance, you'll abstain."

Mary chuckled. "Abstain?"

"Say no! If by some very strange happening you're not yet dancing with the man of your dreams, whomever that is, you'll amaze them all by standing back, not participating in that specific dance. Like a queen watching her subjects."

Mary sighed. She couldn't believe the time and effort Mrs. Dunn was taking on her behalf.

She grabbed Mary's arm. "You'll stun them with quiet mystery."

There was *no way* Mary was removing her shoes at that dance. She smiled. Her mother's responses to everything were always short orders. No nuance, no "maybe this, maybe that." Just do it. But Mrs. Dunn was wonderful with her conspiratorial advice.

Mrs. Dunn looked her up and down, taking Mary's hands in hers. "Time for you to see." She took Mary toward the mirror. "You are enchanting."

Standing in front of the mirror, Mary's mouth fell open. The opulent dress with its moody blue beading, chiffon, and silk changed colors when she moved, clinging to her curves, curves she didn't know she had. She ran her hands down the dress. She'd never known that her body was so womanly yet slim. When had she changed? She touched her hair. Like one of those Gibson girls. Her lips were a rich red, not bright or garish. The sweep of charcoal across her lids made her eyes smoky and stand out at the same time. She'd never seen herself as beautiful before, but she would have said she was in that moment.

"Feel your beauty, deep in your bones. Who cares what shoes you've on? As a matter of fact, I believe the day I made Mr. Dunn fall in love with me, I wore work boots and muddy coveralls. *Matter of fact*, it's better to wear the shoes you're comfortable in to fully be yourself." Mrs. Dunn was gleeful as she led Mary downstairs to the keeping room, where she unveiled a velvet and fur cloak.

Mary drew back. "I can't. This is too much. What if something happens to these beautiful things?"

Mrs. Dunn slung her arm around Mary's shoulder, walked her to Mr. Dunn's Roadster, and tucked her inside. "What could happen?"

Mary laughed. "I don't know, but that's the thing with me. You never know."

Mrs. Dunn got behind the wheel and fiddled with Mary's hair. "Wear the dress and cloak in exchange for a day's pay. I trust you completely."

"Four days' pay." Mary bit her tongue, thinking of her mother.

"No, no. I don't want *anything*, but I understand pride, so I'm humoring you by taking one. Maybe. We'll see. You worry about having some fun."

Mary looked down, lifting her hem to her brown boots. She remembered how she'd looked in the mirror, the way the dress and hair had made her feel like a queen. She could do this.

"Your suitors await."

Mary closed her eyes and a Hail Mary came to her lips. She prayed that the night would live up to the exquisite clothes, sad that Matka couldn't share in the moment, and feeling as though she'd betrayed her again.

Chapter 50

Mary

Mary drew a deep breath and stepped into the lobby of the hall. Toby Horowitz glanced her way, then looked again, tapping Henry Gresheki, who looked Mary's way, with wide eyes. She looked over her shoulder to see what was drawing all the attention. Nothing was behind her. No one. A thrill tumbled through her, then insecurity then excitement again. One by one, people turned in her direction. She removed her hat and gloves and smiled, basking in the energy.

Mary stepped carefully toward the cloakroom, using tiny strides to keep her boots hidden under the hem of the dress until everyone was busy dancing. She exchanged the magnificent cloak and hat for a coat-check ticket and entered the ballroom, the band and couples in full swing. Couples did the bunny hug and the grizzly bear before chaperones forced them back into a series of hesitation waltzes.

Mary spotted Samuel and Phoebe across the room. Phoebe's feline movements and self-satisfied expression were amplified by the silver beaded dress that glimmered under the soft lights as though it were a skin. Mary reminded herself that the gown she wore rivaled Phoebe's, a French dream as well. In that moment, Mary herself rivaled Phoebe.

"Holy Cane and Abel, where'd you get that dress?" Weira asked.

"You look like a princess. A sexy princess," Peggy said and touched the dress. "Where's the corset?"

Mary whispered in her ear, "Sewn into the dress with this soft . . ." She shrugged. "I don't know, but it's amazing, isn't it?"

"*Stunning*," Kasandra said from behind. "I'm green as grass over this gown."

Gasps and double takes came from all directions, causing Mary's confidence to swell. "Thank you, Kasandra. Mrs. Dunn dressed me. Isn't it a dream?"

Samuel and Phoebe separated at the end of the turkey trot, and she strolled, breathless, fanning herself, giggling with some other girls, comfortably slipping into conversation with people Mary had known all her life. Phoebe fit into Donora with the same effortlessness she fit into her stunning dresses. Samuel took off for the punch table, not looking Mary's way once. Not once.

Her throat tightened. She was angry, not hurt. He had carelessly let her go. His father's treatment of their help had been an abomination, but now, feeling like she did, she realized that seeing Mr. Blake's behavior had been a gift. It made clear that there were differences between daughters of Czech immigrants and sons of Irish mill managers. This trapped her between her American promises and her immigrant beginnings, but now that she knew, she could prepare for such things.

Besides Samuel's family being as awful as any family she could name, he'd made no effort to court her properly. That hurt the most. That he never really did care at all. She didn't want someone who didn't exert himself to win her affections. She thought of the last dance she had attended, when Phoebe had arrived for the first time. Mortification had spread through Mary like molasses, sticking to every inch of her.

She pulled up to her full five foot ten inches, awash in the admiration of her peers. She thought of Lukasz, how he'd held her up when she could barely stand. Short Lukasz, the shy Pole, was more a man than Samuel with all his suave ways and breeding.

The waltz ended and an announcement was made for the dancers to pile their shoes in the center of the floor.

Mary craned to see if Lukasz was around or if there was anyone else she might like to dance with. There were plenty of boys she didn't know, and it would be nice to meet other people, to dance with someone who didn't know what she normally looked like and that most of her clothes were threadbare and patched.

Mary lifted her hem to get a quick glance at her shabby boots. She stepped toward the growing mountain, gauging the shoe styles, conditions, and sizes. All seemed to represent at least their Sunday best. Mary backed away, ready to be mysterious, aloof, too sophisticated for a silly shoe dance.

Growing enthusiasm gripped the room, energy ramping up. The bandleader called for the last of the shoes to be tossed in. So many people, so many opportunities, people still glancing Mary's way. Who cared what Samuel and Phoebe were up to? Who cared what Mary's shoes looked like? She should just do it. She edged closer to the shoes.

She *wasn't* mysterious. She was the exact opposite. What did she care if she didn't have beautiful shoes to match her ethereal dress? She was going to play along, and she had a feeling tonight was the night she would meet her prince.

She bent down to lift her hem and untie her shoe when someone tapped her on the back.

"What on earth? Johnny?"

Her little brother rubbed his arms, shivering. "Matka's sick. Ann and Victoria can't stop puking. You gotta get Papa."

That was supposed to be Ann's job tonight. Mary looked her brother up and down. He was nine. A bit younger than Mary had been the first time she'd rowed her father back and forth. But it was night and Johnny had never done it, so she couldn't send him. She looked down at her dress.

"Matka says now," Johnny said. "Get his pay even if he doesn't come home. They're short on mortgage."

Her stomach clenched. She put the back of her hand against Johnny's forehead. "Where's your coat?"

"Lost it after school."

"Oh, Johnny. Matka's going to—"

He rubbed his bottom. "Already did. And I'm not sick," he said. "Just cold."

She looked at her gown. She should stop back to change it before getting her father.

"Hurry," Johnny said. "Matka caught wind of Papa's friends meeting at the Hole-in-the-Wall."

Mary looked back at the dancers and the grins that lit their faces as they drew shoes to partner up. Johnny broke into a jog, and Mary followed suit to catch up, taking him by the shoulder. "Go to Mrs. Dunn's on your way back home. Tell her I'll be up just as soon as I can. I'll be very careful with the dress. But don't tell Matka any of that."

He nodded, grabbed Mary around the waist, and hugged her tight. Mary rubbed her hands over his back and on his arms to warm him up. "Go on." He ran off.

Mary sighed. Her eyes naturally went to Samuel as they'd been doing for the last two years. He lifted a dainty silver strappy shoe above his head as Phoebe sashayed toward him, their eyes locking. Mary inhaled deeply, waiting for that painful twisting of her heart that always came with thoughts of him not wanting her, but nothing came.

She exhaled. Loneliness remained. Not sorrow for Samuel, for something he'd never promised her anyway. Now her disappointment was for the chance she was missing, all the men standing there who might be her one true love.

Chapter 51

Lukasz

Working daylight shift, Lukasz wandered the night streets. He'd ignored the call to drink even as it lured him still. Halfway up the Fifth Street stairs, he ran into Aneta and Tytus Hawthorne. He nearly passed them by, but Tytus grabbed Lukasz's arm and pulled him aside.

"Lukasz," he said, a giant smile on his face. "Look, Aneta. Lukasz."

"Hi, Lukasz." Aneta's eyes darted away but Tytus gave her a nod and she turned back to Lukasz, warm and friendly. She stepped toward him and hugged him, squeezing him tight before Lukasz even knew what was happening. "I'm so happy to see you." She pulled away. "You look wonderful."

Aneta's greeting made Lukasz happy, surprised. From the nod he had seen Tytus give, Lukasz got the feeling that Aneta must have confided in him about her marriage match to Lukasz when they had first arrived in America. Tytus seemed to understand Lukasz was probably never a threat to Aneta's affection.

"Good to see you," Tytus said.

"Yes," Lukasz said, still feeling awkward.

Tytus took Aneta's elbow. "Aneta's not feeling great. She's expecting, you know."

Lukasz raised his eyebrows. Aneta glanced at him with a smile.

"Congratulations," Lukasz said, his throat going dry.

"Listen," Tytus said, "you never stopped by for that hat. It's 1913. What're you waiting for?"

Lukasz smiled. He wanted to say he was never stopping by, but Tytus—his openness, his utter likability—kept Lukasz from blaming him for the direction his life had taken. Still, hearing Aneta was expecting startled Lukasz, intensifying his loneliness, reminding him how long it had been since he'd stopped by the Kowalks' to catch up with all the news, how long it had been since he'd kissed a woman.

"We bought a house," Tytus said. "And we'd love if you stopped by sometime. For a drink."

Lukasz nodded.

"Thompson Avenue. Just up from St. Dominic's. Fifth house. Near the Dunns'."

He knew the place. Could have been the one on the postcard he still carried with him. Beautiful lawn in summer, white fence and expansive two-story home that peered down over the street. "Sure," Lukasz said. "Congratulations, Tytus, Aneta. I wish you luck."

Tytus looked Lukasz up and down. "You're just off shift. You need sleep. Here I am, talking your ear off."

Lukasz stuck his hand out. "See you."

"Stop by. At the shop *and* the house." He gripped Lukasz's hand and swung it. "Good man." Tytus slung his arm around Aneta's waist, helping her down the stairs and into the settling fog.

After that, Lukasz thought about numbing his mood with drink. But so far, he'd gotten through the day without it. He'd spent the time after his shift making wire bears for Mark's brother-in-law, who lived in the woods of Washington County. He fixed three umbrellas and soldered a hammer that had its head knocked askew. He decided to try his luck at the shoe dance.

He told himself he didn't need the flask, but he pocketed it anyhow. When he arrived at the dance, the shoe dance was finished and his chance to find someone special—someone who might be the woman he was looking for, who was looking for him—was finished too.

He uncorked his flask, sniffed it, and put it to his lips. No. It was time for him to take charge of his life. He turned the flask, drizzling the vodka over the cobblestones. Better that he'd missed his chance. He didn't want to take his shoes off anyway. Zofia no longer darned his socks, now that he moved out. When he had any free time, he chose to make wire animals over clothing repairs.

He recorked the empty flask and took off for the riverside, where he found his peace, even in the cold. The scent of river filled his nose. Maybe he should just walk right into the water, let the cold water lap over his feet, creep up his shins, sting his thighs, and ice his stomach. A few steps more and he'd lose the shore under his feet, and the Monongahela would freeze his chest and stop his heart.

He drew deep breaths of smoky air as the fog settled around him, displacing the black air with new, fresher air that filled his lungs.

As he reached the crest of the riverbank, he thought maybe he'd end his life. He stood there looking over the dark curving river, the crush of the mill noise punctuated by a belching train whistle. Somehow, the repetitive, saturating noise had become silence to him. Inside that peaceful numbing, a snowflake landed on his coat sleeve, intricate pristine threads sitting beautifully on the dark wool for two heartbeats before turning watery and disappearing into the fabric.

He looked upward. A full moon, pink and blazing through the clouds, shocked him. Its rays reflected off the newly fallen snow as if the heavens had laid down a winter blanket over the dark, barren ground. Blue light reflected off the snow, a pink haze circled the moon, and he felt as if he'd been dropped into another world.

Chapter 52

Mary

The water was rough, making Mary question whether she should venture across, but she'd learned years before that defaulting on the mortgage was not an option. When she was a little girl, Mary's parents sold a silver mirror Matka'd been given by her mother back home. At the time Mary didn't understand how they hadn't found another way to pay and keep the mirror, too. Witnessing her mother's sadness in trading away something she loved made Mary work harder and always pay her share at home. She only kept back the funds and treasures that were extra.

Mary assuaged any guilt by telling herself that in the long run, this would ease any burden on her parents when Mary married. They wouldn't have to send her to her wedding having bought a chest full of treasure. Mary told herself the things and little bits of money she hid away could always be used in a dire emergency. So far, she hadn't had to resort to selling the treasure. She rationalized that Ann contributed to the household and so did the boarders. Her parents worked until their bodies and souls turned raw, yet there was always something putting their mortgage in jeopardy. Someday, her secret stash would save them in a way that Mary could not yet envision, but she trusted that it was so.

Mary had no choice but to go across in the gown, even if the winter water was choppy. She considered taking off her cloak and hanging it on a tree branch or folding it and laying it at the bottom of the boat, but in the end, keeping the cloak on her body was her best chance to keep it dry and clean.

She lifted the hem and stepped into the boat, sloshing water over the side, wetting her boots. Thank goodness she couldn't fit into any of Mrs. Dunn's beautiful shoes. She removed the special gloves Mrs. Dunn had given her, folded them, tucked them into the cloak pocket, and rowed, surging through the fog with every pull. When she reached the dock across the way, she tossed the rope around the piling and climbed out, cringing every time her gown made contact with the wood dock. She walked into the street and headed south to the tiny bar where she and her mother had found her father the last time.

Mary entered the bar, holding the gown up and tight against her legs. The smell of cigarettes, yeasty beer, halupki, and body odor hit her nose. She wiped at it with the back of her hand and breathed through her mouth. She spotted her father sitting on the far side of the bar.

She approached him slowly, not wanting to convey the same hostility her mother had the day she had humiliated him. She pressed her hand against his shoulder. "Papa?"

He puffed out his cheeks and blew out his air. She scanned the bar, looking for a sign that he'd already spent all his money.

"No, Mary. I'm not drinking my week's pay."

She squinted at him and shook her head, sorry that he knew exactly what she was thinking, that her mission was that clear.

"It's my cough. Barely made it up the hill. They saw me struggling and sent another fella in there right in front of me. Bastard needed work, but I need it more. The mortgage . . .

They kept my entire week's wages, Mary. Like my work ain't worth nothin'." He dropped his head in his hands.

She looked closer at the glass in front of him. She sniffed it. Water. She pulled him close with one arm, wanting to comfort him, absorbing his desperation. "Come home. Please."

He wouldn't budge.

She pulled him again. "Please. Don't sit here alone."

He gave in to her tugging, facing her. He leaned his head on her shoulder, shocking her. She first thought to push him away, to not let him embarrass himself. But he slung his arm around her and she patted his back, comforting him. "Papa," she whispered. "Come home. Don't stay here alone." If she could coax him home, that would be an enormous household victory. She wanted him safe and warm, not risking his health in a bar.

He sat up and swung his arm out. "Not alone, Mar. Look at these fellows. Good men, every one."

She patted his back and sized up the bar. Men hunched over drinks, staring into space with half-shut eyes, their cheeks and noses inflamed with drink. Every once in a while, one grunted at another. When a shift had first let out, the group must have been livelier, but the remaining few who had decided not to make their way home were falling away. Sadness filled her at the sight. Not the anger that shook Matka like an earthquake, just deep sadness that these men found their homes less appealing than the stinking bar.

So it was with the men who did back-breaking, black-lung work. She'd heard countless times how shots and beers were the only things to clear their throats, yet many times the drinks weren't near enough to do the job, and there was the matter of the lungs—shots and beer didn't flush those out a bit.

"Can't go home to Matka. Not until I get her money."

"But how?"

"Don't worry 'bout that. Go on home, my good Mary. Thank you for being good to me. I just . . . thank you." He shrugged.

"You're my papa. Of course I'd—"

He looked at her, eyes drooping and resigned. He didn't know the hell she'd catch for going home without him.

His eyes suddenly lit up. "Look at you. That frock. You're an angel."

Mary shook her head.

He gripped her shoulder. "I told you not to do that. Know your worth."

"But you and Matka want me to marry Ralph. You're not letting me know my worth."

Papa's eyes saddened and Mary stopped herself. Now was not the time to argue. She wrapped herself in Papa's sweet words, the truth he seemed to only tell when the two of them were across the river from home. She lifted the hem of her gown.

Papa snorted. "A smart angel. Sturdy shoes."

She looked away. One of the men collapsed onto the bar, sending his beer glass flying off, shattering as it hit the floor. The wasted night lay heavy on her heart. She pictured everyone dancing, the laughter and joy. The hem of the gown had browned. She should have known it was useless to think a piece of clothing would change the course of her night, her life.

She hated this feeling, this pity for herself. But now that Peggy and Kasandra were engaged, it was as though she was being left further and further behind. Just sixteen years old, but she felt like an old woman, heartbroken and hopeless. So that was why all those women were bitter. Maybe Matka was right all along.

She hooked her father's neck with her arm and lured him close, his scratchy stubble pricking her cheek. "Love you, Papa. I love you."

He jerked, the declaration seeming to startle him. He nodded and patted her back.

Outside the tavern, Mary pulled the cloak tight. Snow tumbled down in large flakes. The road was coated. At the dock, she stepped into the boat and sat, letting the snowflakes land on her, some dissolving when they hit her exposed arms, others melting slowly. She stared into the dark smoky sky, the thick lacy flakes light as feathers.

The still air seemed almost warm despite the evidence it was cold enough to snow. The full moon was so bright, its rays broke through the snowy canopy of fat flakes. She squinted. Pink. She'd seen pink and orange summer moons, but never in winter, never a cold pink moon that poured snow like granulated sugar. If not for how terrible the night had gone, Mary would have thought the pink moon was magic.

She gripped the oars. "Please God, help me. Tell me what to do." She imagined her mother's anger when she arrived home. Same old story.

Hopelessness grew, enveloping her as she rowed. How quickly Samuel had gone from having Mary on his list of dances to only Phoebe. It was as though Mary had never existed. The way he'd thought a simple note left at her house was enough to sever ties when Phoebe came the first time. Just like his father, she supposed. Her insides lit with anger. Her spirit was fragile and cracked but somehow still holding. She let the feelings of vulnerability take hold.

What if this was it? What if her one chance to be with someone who could give her a lemony house, a lemony life had passed her by?

Chapter 53

Lukasz

Under the sweet pink moon haze, Lukasz squinted into the distance over the water. The tingling he got when he saw his mermaid on the water rushed over his skin. Had something caused it? He strained to hear, to see.

There, movement off to his left. Memories of his Wisloka Mermaid—the dreams, the sightings—returned. He rubbed his forehead. Was he ready for Morganza, home for the insane and delinquent? He couldn't blame the sighting on booze this time.

He stumbled farther along the top of the banks, concentrating, telling himself to wake up, wake up, wake up. He looked into the night sky and held his palms out. Snow dropped, thick white flakes draping everything in sight, filling him with wonder. He'd kept his promise for no more drinks. Not one until he recovered enough money for the property he wanted to buy. He consoled himself with this achievement. His lonesomeness was strong but tinged with hope. If he built a house, he could present himself better to eligible women. The pink moon shined down, reassuring him with its odd appearance. Anything was possible. Anything.

Movement on the water drew his attention again. Something, someone was out there. Closer, closer, closer, the object came. He got up on his toes to see nothing. He moved along the banks.

There. He stopped. A voice. He wasn't crazy. He thought of all the nights he'd seen something in the fog—his elusive mermaid.

He raised his hand. "Hello," he yelled. Nothing. Maybe calling out chased her away.

An oar splashed, cutting into the water. He watched the shoreline, waiting, rubbing his arms, talking to himself to be sure he was awake. A boat came into sight, knocking into the dock, the hollow sound of wood against wood ringing out.

"Hello!" he yelled again.

A pause in the noise on the water came.

"Hey there! Howdy there!" Two men stood in a boat waving their arms. "A welcoming committee! Donora *is* the best town next to ours," one man said. They fell against each other, laughing. Lukasz was embarrassed by his insanity. *Mermaid.* It was two drunks from Webster. Lukasz moved quickly along the bank, instantly feeling the tug of the flask in his pocket, grateful he'd dumped it out. From a distance, he watched the men cresting the bank, heading over the tracks and into town.

It was coming up on December, January soon after, then his three-year anniversary of arriving in Donora. What had he achieved? Aneta had secured her future with a wealthy American with nothing more than her good looks. His stomach churned. He'd drunk too much and gambled at times, losing some of the money he'd been saving for property. But in America, he could start again. He rubbed his back, sore from an awkward toss of a wire bundle when he'd gone to work hungover.

He could change. He *was* changing. He was standing there wrapped in loneliness and not drinking. He told himself to stop the sorrowful thinking. He was strong—he had won his job the very first time he'd set foot in the wireworks. He was tireless. He was worthy. Aneta's choice of Tytus didn't mean Lukasz wasn't a worthy man. With his anniversary coming, he was just beginning to feel his wholeness, his Americanness. In two years, he could declare his intention to become an American citizen.

He vowed again. No more drinking. No more anything but work.

He looked up. The pink moon hush laid a calm over him, stilling Lukasz's fears. He didn't need drunken hallucinations and mermaid dreams to propel him. Not anymore. He was strong all by himself. And he knew—this was what it felt like to be American.

Chapter 54

Mary

A tugboat moaned. Mary glanced over her shoulder to see a massive barge bearing down, masked by darkness and the crush of mill noise. She dug her oars deep to stop, to keep from drifting too close. It passed with an eerie whoosh. She held her breath, bracing for the wake.

The turbulence lifted her boat and dropped it. She squeezed her eyes shut, hanging on tight. When the wake settled, she pulled Mrs. Dunn's cloak tight around her neck. Beads of sweat sprouted at her hairline and she swatted them away with the back of her hand.

She was a little past halfway across the river when movement drew her eye. Another barge. This time, she had to keep rowing to stay out of its way. She gripped the oars and rowed as hard and fast as she could. She was far enough past it not to be hit, but she was practically inside the wake. It would dump her into the river for sure. The cold water would freeze her quickly, and the heavy cloak and gown would wrap her feet as she kicked. She heaved for breath and her shoulders burned with pain. Her hands, raw against the wood.

Pull, pull, pull.

She looked over her shoulder to see that she was nearing the dock. Relief swept over her and she lifted the oars to glide. She slumped forward for a moment. *Thank you, sweet Mother of God.*

Her rowboat lifted. Her eyes flew open. Another shot of wake. She grabbed the sides of the boat, but it was too late. She dumped into the river, cold water biting her legs and snatching her breath.

Her feet found the shoreline. The water drenched her from the thighs down, a million cold pinpricks over her skin. The cloak was half soaked. She fumbled with the button at her throat, shedding it as fast as she could. She couldn't breathe. She held the cloak high, but part still dragged through the water. Everything was ruined.

Move. Get out of the water.

She trudged forward, sucking back the tears threatening to burst. Her throat went raw.

The coat. The gown.

She looked down as she pressed on. On the shore, she bent over, clutched the cloak around her midsection, and sobbed.

Chapter 55

Lukasz

Still struck by the grapefruit moon that hung above, dumping snow like rain, Lukasz shivered. A tugboat moaned, pushing a coal barge through, practically silent despite its size. Lukasz had a long shift the next day, a double if Chaffy was still sick. He eased himself up, backing away from the river, the bank obscuring the water the farther he went.

And then he heard it. A yelp?

A splash. Another yelp.

He paused, pinning his ears back. Could he trust his hearing, a man who talked to mermaids?

A splash again.

Another pair of drunken men? He cocked an ear. Nothing. He shrugged and turned.

Another yelp, splashing. He froze. *Move away*, he told himself.

More splashing.

This time he was sure. He inched toward the bank, just to prove he wasn't crazy.

One more crash of water. He looked down the bank to begin his descent and saw a figure rising out of the water.

He rubbed his eyes. A woman.

She moved up the bank, over the freshly fallen snow.

Lack of good sleep must have been doing him in. Was he passed out like the night on the Wisloka? Was he dreaming? Lukasz moved down the bank toward her. She glistened in the pink moonlight, her body shimmering in blues and greens. A woman rising out of the river? His mermaid? He rubbed his eyes again.

He was close enough to hear her gasping for breath, crying. She focused on her feet, trudging through the snow. A crying mermaid, holding a flimsy skin above her head with one hand as she came forward. Her tail? Her body gleamed, sharing its reflection with the dazzling snow. He looked up at the pink moon, the shifting clouds giving space for even more light, enough for him to see that this was no dream.

His gaze back on the mermaid, the flickering shine of beads and gems made him question reality again. *What in hell?* His gaze finally swept upward settling on her face just as she stopped and saw him. Her arms flew outward to steady herself, dropping her wrap. She was as stunned to see him as he was to see her.

Mary?

She froze in place. They stared. His heart lurched.

The dress she wore was the color of ice, and the wetness caused it to drape each curve. She looked every bit a mermaid, ascending out of the river.

Her shivering and teeth chattering snapped him out of his daze. He took a few more steps down the bank, standing a little bit above her. He shook out of his coat and put it around her. He picked up her wet cloak and put it over his arm.

"Thank you," she said through trembling lips. Her hair was matted around her face. Her hat! Hands to her head she realized it was gone, hidden by the dark river.

Lukasz brushed her hair behind her ears and took off his hat. He held it up to offer it to her. She hesitated, then bent forward and let him push it down tight over her head.

"Co jest nie tak?"

She shook her head. "Nothing." When she could hold back her crying no longer, she dropped her face into her hands and shuddered.

His heart ached, but he hesitated to touch her, not wanting to scare her or make whatever was wrong worse. "*Dom*, home."

She shook her head and cried harder.

He couldn't stop himself any longer. He couldn't stand to see her cry, to feel her unnamed desperation. He wrapped her in his arms. "Mary, Mary, Mary."

She sobbed, melding into him, her body jerking as he squeezed tighter, his embrace holding her together. He held her for some time, heat building between them. But she still quaked. "You're so cold." He pulled away. "Home."

She finally lifted her eyes, but he didn't know what she wanted.

He looked at her glittering dress and thought of the way she had risen up the bank like the mermaid he'd dreamed about so many times. It was as if he'd always known her, connected in ways he couldn't name.

Before he could think better of it, he found his whispered words. "*Moja syrenka.*"

She shook her head, not understanding.

He searched for the words in English. He didn't know how to say *mermaid.* He searched for what the mermaid meant to him, that the beautiful mermaid he'd seen while drunk in Poland had given him direction, the motivation he'd needed.

He struggled for the words. "*Piękny.*"

He could tell she was searching her mind in the same way he'd been. Finally, her eyes lit up just as he found the English too. "Beautiful," they said at the same time.

She stepped back down the hill as though she needed space to fully absorb what he'd said. He hoped he hadn't frightened her.

Her eyes filled. Her expression turned questioning. "Beautiful?"

He nodded. "*Bardzo dużo.*"

Her chest heaved as she stepped up the slope. "I don't know what the hell that means."

"Very beautiful," he said as he stepped toward her.

She grasped his arms and held his gaze, their breathing synchronized. He'd never been so glad to be sober, to fully absorb something happening to him. It wasn't until a train whistle blasted behind them that they startled and disconnected.

She shook, still cold, and he knew he needed to get her warm with more than an embrace. He took her elbow and jerked his head up toward the top of the bank. She followed him up. When they crested the bank, he looked up at her, taking in her full height. She was a good four or five inches taller. He wondered if she considered him small, not enough, as Aneta had.

She grabbed his hand and held tight. Without words, she conveyed something about him that he hadn't known—he was as tall as he needed to be.

He wrapped his arm around her waist. "Home," he said, guiding her toward Meldon.

On the way, she stopped to catch her breath. She coughed into her closed fist and looked down, opening Lukasz's coat as if she had just remembered she was wearing an evening gown. She covered her mouth, gasping. She held his shoulder, steadying herself as tears came again.

He pulled a hanky from his pocket. "Luckily, I didn't lose this one. I lose them all the time."

He dabbed under her eyes.

Her teeth chattered. "Tonight started like a dream. The gown's ruined. It's all ruined."

He knew what she meant about the dress, but she couldn't have been more wrong. "My dream was of *syrena*. Not ruined. Not at all."

She pressed the handkerchief into his palm and cocked her head as his fingers closed around hers. "*Syrena?*"

He looked deeply into her eyes, their hands clasped. Icy crystals formed on her lashes, her coal-black eyes shining like the sky that held the pink moon.

He'd been dreaming of Mary all along.

Chapter 56

Mary

Everywhere Lukasz's body touched Mary's was warm—her waist where his arm was looped, her stomach where his hand was pressed, the length of her left side against his right. Her heart was the warmest of all.

"Up to Marelda," she said through numb lips. She shuffled, her wet feet deadened, her toes icy. The burning cold was too much. She gasped and stopped. Without hesitation, Lukasz slipped his arm behind her knees and lifted, carrying her easily up the stairs as if she were made of downy feathers.

She burrowed her face into his shoulder, the scent of soap, of him, filling her nose. Up to McKean, then scaling the Fourteenth Street stairs, they finally reached Mary's front porch. He fumbled for the knob and booted the door fully open, stepping inside the home.

Mary squeezed her eyes tight, unwilling to let him go. The fire crackled and the scent of cinnamon mixed with sauerkraut filled her nose. She didn't attempt to stand, and Lukasz didn't put her down.

"*Dom.* You're home," he whispered in her ear, his whiskers tickling her cheek, thrills spiraling through her. He brushed his lips over hers, and she gripped tighter around his neck.

He finally tipped her upright, her feet on the ground. She reluctantly released her arms, the indoor warmth stinging her thawing skin.

He rubbed her back, moving her toward the blazing fire. He set his hat on the mantel, hung her cloak on a hook, and stooped to untie her boots. Mary steadied herself by holding onto the top of his head. He was on his knees when her mother entered the room with a gasp.

Matka pulled her robe sash tight, tying it in a bow.

"Matka," Mary said. "I'm—"

"Christ Almighty," she said.

Lukasz removed Mary's boots and set them near the fire. He put his hand out and moved toward Matka. "Lukasz Musial."

Matka stared at his hand before taking it.

"She dumped in water," he said. "The boat . . ." He mimed the action of something tipping over. "I saw her coming up the riverbank like a . . ."

Matka gasped again. "Papa?" Her face paled. Mary was reminded that Matka was sick, but knew her coloring was due to fear of not making the house payment.

Mary's warming skin tingled as if it'd been set aflame. She didn't want to tell her mother the truth, but she had no choice. She glanced at Lukasz and decided it didn't matter if he was there. He wouldn't understand everything, and her mother would most likely hold back any outburst. "His cough. It kept him out of the mine, and he didn't get paid."

Matka put her hand against her forehead. "Lost a day's pay?"

Mary looked away.

"Tell me," Matka said. "Look at me."

Mary glanced at Lukasz, who was studying them both. "The week."

"The whole week's pay?"

Mary nodded. This was how things worked. If the mine owners could stiff a fella, they would.

Matka paced, planting a fist on her hip. She mumbled, stalking across the rug. Mary knew she was adding numbers; there was no illness too great to stamp out her figuring of costs and household revenue.

"He'll get the money," Mary said.

Matka stopped flat. She pursed her lips and leveled her gaze on Lukasz. "Who's this again?"

"Lukasz Musial," Mary said.

She looked Lukasz up and down, scowling.

"He saved me."

"*Saved* ya?"

Lukasz nodded.

"Wake from a barge flipped me. He helped me home."

Matka straightened, hardening every plane and angle in her body. "Well. Thanks, Mr. Musial."

He nodded.

"Work in the mill?" Matka asked.

He nodded again.

"Damn quiet," Matka said.

Lukasz widened his stance. It was then Mary really absorbed how short he was. Funny how she hadn't thought about his size when he'd carried her like dandelion seed up the winding hills that led her home.

Lukasz gestured to Mary. "She's safe."

Mary held her hands near the flames. "Thanks to you, Lukasz."

He faced Mary, locking into her gaze, his eyes holding her as steady as his arms had.

Matka shoved his hat into his chest. "Thanks."

He put on the hat but didn't move his gaze from Mary. She shook out of his coat. "Stay for coffee," Mary said.

"No," Lukasz and Matka said at the same time.

Mary held the inside of his coat toward the flames, warming it. "Stay," she said over her shoulder. "You brought me home and it's so cold. You're freezing."

"I'm fine," he said, glancing at Matka.

Under his penetrating gaze, Mary's heart caught with each beat. She wanted his arms around her again. She peeked at her mother, who was watching him. Matka's tacit disapproval billowed across the room like when she unleashed the folds of a quilt over a bed with just one snap.

Mary shook his coat again. "Get into it while it's warm, then." She slid the coat onto his arms, brushing her hands over his shoulders, adjusting the coat's fit.

Matka stepped closer, looming. "Go on."

He nodded. "Stay warm," he said to Mary. He backed toward the door, not taking his eyes from her until he closed it.

**

The door clicked shut and Matka exhaled. She grabbed Mary's arm. "What the hell're ya doin'?"

Mary wiggled out of Matka's grip, moving closer to the fire. "I told you."

"Are ya seeing this Lukasz behind our backs?"

"'Course not. I almost drowned. I'm lucky he was there."

"Oh no, no. There's more than *that* goin' on. I saw how he looked at ya. How *you* looked at him."

"I was being polite. That's all." Lukasz had taken nails from the mill, and her devotion to Mrs. Dunn made it impossible for Mary to be with a man who'd done such a thing.

Matka frowned. "Who're his people?"

"The Kowalks? I think?"

"Ya do know him."

"I've seen him at the mill and at church and—what does it matter? I'm not interested."

Matka crept closer. "When'd ya meet him?"

Mary thought of when and where she had run into him—Candlemas Day Mass, the mill, St. John's Eve, Christmas Eve, a few dances—but it was when he'd danced with her the night Phoebe had made her magical entrance, when Lukasz held Mary close, showing her she should stay instead of running off, ashamed. They met at a dance. "That's when our hearts met."

Matka tossed a log on the fire. "What'd ya just say?"

Mary almost laughed at the silliness of it. Matka wouldn't understand. "A dance. We met at a dance."

"What about Samuel and Ralph? Are ya tarting around town? How many boys that we don't know about? I knew all that baseball ya played would haunt us in the long run."

Mary spun around. "Stop it, Matka. You're ruining it."

"Ruining what?"

"My five minutes of having someone care for me. Take care of me as though I was delicate."

Matka scoffed. "Ya get plenty of care." She looked Mary up and down. "And what the hell're you doing in that dress?" Mrs. Lancos ran her fingers over the beading, inhaling. "It's beautiful. It's expensive. It's *not* yours."

"It's Mrs. Dunn's."

Matka put her hand to her throat, her face turning deep red. "It's ruined."

Mary looked down. A dirty, scalloped watermark showed where the water had lapped at her legs, the fabric stiffened by river mud. Frightened at what her mother would do, her breath caught in her throat. "I'll clean it. I will."

"You'll lose your pay for a year. Why'd she let ya have this?"

Mary shrugged, wondering the same thing. They should have trusted Mary's instincts that all would not be well.

"Why?"

"She thought I deserved to wear this dress. She believes I am smart and pretty and . . . and she doesn't use it anymore."

Mrs. Lancos flung her hand to the side. "And she just gave it away? Like it would change something to wear it, Cinderella?"

Cinderella. The word stabbed. "Why don't you think I'm good enough?" Mary's voice cracked. "Why don't you see me like Mrs. Dunn does?"

Matka balled her fists at her sides. "Why don't ya think *we're* good enough? We're yer family. Not her."

"She just lent it to me."

"Lent it."

Mary hesitated. Wasn't that better than giving it?

Matka crossed her arms. "You're quiet. You're hiding something." She shook her finger. "How much?"

It was as if Matka understood every single thing Mary did, inferring entire stories and truths from just a kernel of information. "I'll stop at the Dunns' and ask myself," Matka said.

Mary grumbled at the threat, taking it seriously. This was why she had to hide her special things in the fireplace hearth instead of out in the open, in a beautiful chest like other girls. "One day's pay."

Matka covered her mouth. "And yer father's lost a week's wages." Her hand quaked and Mary's stomach burned.

What had she done? Her mother had every right to be mad. "I just wanted something pretty, just for one night. I didn't know Papa would lose pay. I didn't know. I'm so sorry."

Mr. Cermak stepped into the room, turning Mary's blood as cold as her feet.

"I can help," he said.

Matka turned. Mary glared at him over her mother's shoulder.

"Help?" Matka glanced at Mary, then put her attention back on Mr. Cermak. "What do ya mean?"

"Let me pay the mortgage. You're like family." He pulled a money clip from his pocket and licked his finger before flipping through his bills.

Mary rubbed her aching temples, not wanting anything from that man.

He waved the bills. "I've come into some extra cash. How about a loan, dear Susan? You've been so good to me. Always wonderful food, your family so kind . . ." He kept his gaze on Matka though Mary knew who he was talking about.

He took Matka's hand and pressed the money into her palm. "And especially after the misunderstanding with Mary, the matter you discussed with me. It would be my honor to make it up to the family."

Matka stared at the bills, spreading her fingers wide as though she was afraid to grip the money. "We can't. No."

He folded her fingers over the cash. "I insist. I've had the pleasure of your family for years now, and I would love to help. I feel like family."

Matka smoothed her hair. "I just don't think it's . . ." Mary could see her softening to the idea.

He took her by the elbow. "How about we talk it over in the kitchen. It means a lot to be able to help."

"I really don't think so, Mr. Cermak. I can't say when exactly we could repay you, and it's bad to have this kind of thing between us."

"Oh, I insist. A talk. What's the harm in that?"

Matka shrugged. "No harm, I suppose."

They entered the kitchen, leaving Mary alone, hoping for no deal but feeling as though her mother could easily be talked into one.

Victoria wakened when Mary entered their room. She helped Mary out of her dress and into warm underthings and a flannel nightgown. Though Victoria was young, she understood Mary's need for help that night. She fetched extra wood for the fireplace. The two sisters pushed Ann to the far edge of the bed and climbed under the covers.

Even though Mary yearned to have her own bed, always irritated by kicks to the back and pushes off the bed's edge, that night, snug between her sisters, Mary was safe from Mr. Cermak. In the tangle of her sisters' limbs, she found comfort, and it reminded her of times she'd forgotten until that moment, before they'd grown older and apart.

Even with the coziness, she was unable to sleep. She thought of Lukasz, back to the dance when he'd stopped her from leaving, the way he'd rescued her from the river, scooping her up and whisking her home. *Strong* was how she thought of him. Protective.

Her eyes flew open, remembering. He'd brushed his lips over hers so gently, she'd nearly forgotten he had. He was rough around the edges, with his jagged English, his serious expressions, and his shyness that softened all the rest.

But he was strong in the way Donora's silent hillside held everything built into it tight, safe from falling into the noisy valley below. And Lukasz was there for Mary. All those times he'd arrived when she'd needed someone before she even knew it . . .

She looked out the window through the space between the curtains. The night was black. Was it? She got up on her elbow and squinted to see better. No sign of the pink moon glow that had drawn her eyes to the river. Had Lukasz seen it? Had it been there at all?

She touched her lips and sighed. It was too bad she couldn't be with him, to have him wrap her in his calm strength again. She thought of Matka's searing stare, all the things she hadn't said aloud, but Mary knew she was thinking. Lukasz was too short, too foreign, too Polish, and simply not Ralph. There was no reason to entertain thoughts of Lukasz Musial beyond being grateful for all the times he'd caught her when she was falling. That would have to be enough.

Chapter 57

Mary

Papa didn't return that night or the next, so Matka grew surly, nearly every task punctuated with slamming spatulas on tables or children's bottoms. Even baby Rose couldn't escape their mother's ire. Mary took charge of watching Rose to shield her from rough handling. Matka snapped at boarders, ordering them to help clear the table.

Except for Mr. Cermak. Since he'd supplied the mortgage payment, he'd been elevated to a position that Mary described as "special lazy ass."

With the help of her sisters, Mary used every spare moment to clean Mrs. Dunn's evening gown. With toothpicks and cotton, they swabbed each bead, embroidery thread, and sequin. Eventually, Mary had no choice but to return the gown. She had been petrified that Mrs. Dunn might stop by the Lancos house, asking for it. She was miserable, wondering what Mrs. Dunn would do when she saw it.

The next Wednesday, Mary went to work. She covered Mrs. Dunn's gown in a clean linen sheet. Panicked, she nearly dumped the gown on the porch and ran. She forced herself to open the door, rehearsing her apology.

She hadn't expected to see Mr. Dunn standing in front of her, arms crossed. It was bad enough to confess to Mrs. Dunn, but Mister too?

"Mary," he said. "Come in."

She entered. "Hello, Mr. Dunn."

He gestured at the bundle in her arms. "What've you got there?"

"Nothing. Well, just . . ." Mary looked down. Though the gown's ruinous state implied carelessness, she hoped that her efforts to clean and return it indicated that she hadn't purposely been inconsiderate. "It's for Mrs. Dunn."

"Madeline's up with the children. I can take that."

She stepped back. "I'd like to give it to her."

He stepped aside. "All right, then."

Mary nodded and entered.

"Say, Mary? I looked into Darrel Lupka as the possible thief you suggested."

Her throat tightened.

"You sure it wasn't Musial or Holmes or Chaffy? Because the records of when each was working and the missing nails don't match up."

Mary dizzied. The fear tasted metallic. Or was that just the usual taste she'd grown accustomed to? Why was Mr. Dunn still asking about that night?

"I know you said it wasn't the others, but I've just been thinking. Since that day in my office, I haven't gotten reports about nails going missing."

Mary gripped the dress. "Maybe I didn't see anyone at all. Maybe it was the night the line went down and we had to scrap those mangled nails. I just . . . no, I don't have any other information for you."

"And you're sure?"

Mary thought of Lukasz, how kind he'd been to her, but sensing what might be coming.

"Mary?" Mrs. Dunn entered the kitchen with baby Clara on her hip.

Mary exhaled, relieved at the interruption.

"You're here. How's your family? Your sisters still ill?"

Mary couldn't speak. She shook her head. "Better now."

She wanted Mr. Dunn to leave so she could explain about the dress without him hearing. Mrs. Dunn would understand that she hadn't been reckless, but Mr. Dunn?

"I'll take that." Mrs. Dunn held out her arm for Mary to lay the dress over.

"You have the baby. I'll take it to your dressing room."

Mrs. Dunn handed Clara to Mary. "I have to run up for my hat anyway."

Mary handed it over, willing Mr. Dunn away. The edge of the dress hung below the linen sheet, glinting in the light. He squinted at it. "What's that?"

"It's that old dress that—" Mrs. Dunn uncovered the dress and held it up, the brown hem no longer muddy but stained. She pulled the sheet back quickly to hide it. "It's nothing."

"What's that, darling? On the bottom?" He pulled the sheet away again, staring. Finally, he looked at Mary. "What happened to that dress?"

Mary forced a swallow. "My mother was sick, and I had to get my Papa's pay, and a barge went by and swept my boat up and dumped me . . . and . . ."

"You were in a boat in that dress?" He stared at his wife. "How much was that dress?"

The wooziness expanded in Mary's chest. Her neck flushed hot as she thought of how he'd reacted about the Staffordshire dogs, about anything that cost money.

"It's from my sister, Bessie. You remember. A hand-me-down. It's nothing. It was an accident. She wouldn't be careless."

"I wouldn't," Mary said. "I took off the gloves to row and everything."

Mr. Dunn scratched his cheek and studied Mrs. Dunn. "Maybe you're one of those people who's too trusting, dear wife. Too giving for your own good?"

Mary's hands shook. She couldn't help thinking he was talking about himself being too trusting of her at the mill.

Mary glanced at Mrs. Dunn, who patted the dress over her arm.

"Why don't you start the bottle for Clara, Mary?" Mrs. Dunn said. "Darling, the boys want to show you the airplanes they made." She shooed Mr. Dunn away.

He didn't move. "If Mary's family just suffered illness, I think perhaps she shouldn't be here. All that flu ripping through town. They bring disease to the mill, and I don't want it in my home."

"Michael." Mrs. Dunn looked as though she was struggling to breathe. Her face conveyed a mix of disappointment and worry. After hesitating, she patted Mary on the back and took baby Clara. "Perhaps you're right, darling."

Mary's stomach lurched with fear. She searched Mrs. Dunn's face for a clue as to whether she was being asked to leave due to the possibility of spreading illness or it was the end for her working for the Dunns for good.

"Take care of yourself, Mary. It's best not to spread anything," Mrs. Dunn said. The casual distance in her demeanor chilled Mary. She wanted to argue and defend herself and find out just who he meant by "they." She wasn't a "they."

She glanced at Mrs. Dunn, who was fussing with Clara, not noticing. In a moment's time, Mary became estranged from the future that she and Mrs. Dunn had fashioned and alienated from her family, who had shaped her past. She'd been holding the baby, so if she was going to spread something, she would have already.

But with Mr. Dunn there, Mary understood something else was happening, something she didn't want to force Mrs. Dunn to express. Mary had never imagined it, but she now wondered if Mrs. Dunn's affection for her was a secret from her husband. Perhaps all those things that she'd given Mary, all the time she'd spent with her, was information never shared with Mr. Dunn.

"Besides, a nail girl needs to be well rested to complete her tasks," he said. "Can't have defective *materials* slip by you, right, Mary?"

She nodded, feeling as if she'd been dangled from a cliff, left to hang and wonder if she would even still have a job at the mill. Mary stepped into the cold, pulling her coat tight against the wind, pondering if she'd lost two jobs in one day.

**

When Mary went to work at the mill on Thursday, all was normal. Mr. Dunn waved from above. She waved in return, crossed herself, and prayed no one took anything. She was afraid she was being observed to monitor whether she was watching the others. She knew she would have to turn in the very next person she saw steal just to keep her job safe. With lost pay for the dress coupled with her father's loss of a week's wages, she could not afford to lose her job.

Seeing Lukasz at work confused Mary. She prayed he didn't steal anything while she was on shift. Just thinking about his touch, the thrill at being held by him, distracted her. Excitement spun through Mary when he was on the same shift. On break, she'd saunter past him, slow as possible, her breath catching as he tossed hundred-pound wire bundles into rail trucks like they were two ounces of embroidery floss. But she was also angry that she'd had to lie for him, feeling pressure from Mr. Dunn to catch someone stealing.

"Mary?" Lukasz followed her to the mill exit one night.

She glanced up at the windowed balcony to see if any white shirts were watching. She kept on until she was out of the mill.

Lukasz pulled her arm.

"Oh, Lukasz. How are you?"

He stepped in front of her, making her stop. "Dinner. Please come with me. Or dance or . . . something."

Mary was flattered but looked away. She'd been thinking of him endlessly, watching him not for Mr. Dunn but for herself. Spending time with him wasn't smart. Not with her job at risk. His too.

"I can't."

"You can."

She laughed, surprised at him saying that. "I can't thank you enough for getting me home and—"

"I see you noticing me."

Mary flinched. "It's not what you think."

"What?" A glint sparked his eyes. "That you find me handsome and want to spend time with me?"

She giggled, surprised at his sense of humor. He couldn't have forgotten what had happened in Mr. Dunn's office. "I have to notice you. I'm paid to notice."

His face twisted. He pushed his hand through his hair. She could see he was considering what she'd said.

"I mean it, though. Thank you. *Dziękuję Ci.*"

He grinned and she knew she'd slaughtered the Polish.

"For getting me"—she mimed picking something up—"*dom.*"

He smiled and nodded. He bent forward and rubbed his back, moaning. "Back is broke."

She laughed and wanted to tell him yes, she wanted to see him.

But she shook her head. "I don't think either of us should go to dinner or a dance. Not like you mean."

Lukasz rubbed his chin. "This is about Mr. Dunn, but you didn't tell. You *chroniony.*" He looked up as though the English words he was searching for were written in the clouds. "Protect me," he said. "You didn't tell him."

"Tell him what?" Mary backed away from Lukasz. She opened her arms. "I didn't see a thing."

Uncertainty flashed over his face, replacing his confidence. There was nothing else to discuss. She walked on, leaving him behind.

**

Lukasz repeatedly asked Mary out. Each time, she said no. Yet she thought of him constantly—his strength carrying her home from the river, the warmth when he was close, the gentle way Lukasz's lips had brushed hers had replaced the memory of Samuel's probing kisses. Finally, she understood what her girlfriends had been yammering about.

And yet, thinking of Lukasz that way was as useless as thinking of Samuel. She wasn't good enough for Samuel, and Lukasz wasn't good enough for her. No, she wouldn't admit that. Because he was good enough in many ways—just not the ways she'd dreamed about. He wasn't the man she and Mrs. Dunn had been planning for all these years with the ways and means to give her a lemony house and the life that went with it.

Two Wednesdays in a row, Mrs. Dunn was already gone when Mary arrived to work. Though Mary was sure her connection to Mrs. Dunn had been marred, she still had a job, and for that she was grateful.

And Mr. Dunn . . . she'd managed to avoid him in the mill since he'd told her to be better at finding out who might be stealing nails. Her distance from the Dunns provided a cushion for her to soften toward Lukasz. She hated that people stole from the mill, but she understood why. Still, it could cost her job. Was a date with a man worth all that? *No* was the answer that came to her every time.

Once when Mary was on break, Lukasz and Chaffy finished loading the rail car and stepped away. They headed toward the spigot for water. Lukasz scrubbed his hands, used them to cup water into his mouth, then rubbed his face down. He stood up and shook his head, water splashing in every direction. He reached into his pockets and pulled the lining out of each. When he dried his face with his shirt, Mary realized he must have forgotten his hanky. She smiled, remembering that he had mentioned he had a habit of losing them.

He noticed Mary watching him. He wiped his forehead with his arm and smiled. Mary waved. He nodded and went back to work. What was she doing? She couldn't expect him to stop asking her out if she kept waving to him.

When she opened her locker that night, something winked near her hat. She removed a shiny object and a scrap of paper. The shiny thing was a mermaid made of wire, glistening with pools of blue, green, gold, and white. The thin metal scales were sewn loosely with wire so that the torso and tail moved, almost like she was alive. She recognized Lukasz's work immediately, remembering the angel.

Mary tried to read the note. "Mary, *piękna syrena*." *Syrena.* He'd said that the night he had taken her home from the river.

"Whatcha got there?" Kasandara came up behind Mary.

Mary showed her.

Kasandra let out a whistle. "Someone's smitten."

"What's it say?"

Kasandra shook her head. "What I would do for my fiancé to write this way."

Mary pulled her friend's arm. "Stop teasing me. What's it say?"

"Sweet as honey, all right."

"Please. You have to."

Kasandra looked at the note again. "*Beautiful mermaid.*"

Mary ran her fingers over the fine enamel. Obviously it was a beautiful mermaid he'd made for her. "That's it?"

"Out of water and dreams, a mermaid came. From the great Mon river, a watery angel. Lukasz."

Mary raised her eyebrows.

"Looks like *someone* knows how much you love the water, Mary."

Mary nodded, the beautiful words swirling through her. She was still confused but taken with what Lukasz had written, that he'd thought of making her something. "Is Lukasz still staying with his sponsor family? Kowalks?"

Kasandra squinted, then a smile lit her lips. "Boy-oh-boy-oh-boy. What are you up to?"

Mary chuckled. "Nothing. I just want to thank him."

Kasandra shrugged. "He's hot-bedding at Donora Hotel."

Mary touched her lips. Hot-bedding wasn't great. He'd only be at the hotel long enough to sleep, and Mary wouldn't dream of intruding or hanging around a hotel lobby. She leaned against the lockers.

Kasandra pulled on Mary's sleeve. "Sometimes he sleeps at the forge on the hill."

Mary pulled on her coat, unsure of what Kasandra meant.

"You know. What's his name, the Pole, the blacksmith off of Short Street. His shed's set back in the woods behind and sort of below his house. Lukasz stays there sometimes when he's making mermaids for girls."

**

Mary didn't go to the shed right away. She wanted to give Lukasz something in return for the mermaid.

At her house, she tucked the mermaid inside the hearth, near the edge where she could get to it when she wanted. With the bricks removed, she dug through her fabric scraps, finding two plaid flannel pieces that were stain free and big enough to cut into two. Perfect for handkerchiefs that Lukasz could use on shifts to wipe his face.

She turned the edges, quickly stitched around the squares and slipped them into her pocket, hoping he would like them and find them useful.

Mary was tying on her hat when Mr. Cermak came in the front door. He and the cold wind chilled her.

"Stay, Mary. Let's chat."

She grimaced. "I've got . . . somewhere to go."

"You are a puzzle." He took off his coat. "I'm not an ogre."

She forced herself to look at him. His gaze made her feel dirty. It was as if she could see his thoughts since the time he told her he wanted to feel her under him.

Mr. Cermak stepped closer and brushed a tendril of her hair away from her face. She slapped his hand away.

"Be grateful for gifts from friends, Mary. Receiving gracefully is as important as giving."

She pursed her lips, wondering how he knew about the gift from Lukasz. She realized he was talking about the money he'd loaned her mother for the mortgage.

Perhaps she should have been more grateful for that. But she wasn't and wouldn't stay with him a second longer. "I have an errand." She rushed past him, breathing heavily even before she started running to the shed.

"I'll be waiting," Mr. Cermak said to her back.

Every stride through the strong wind peeled away the filth his presence had left on her skin.

**

It took Mary a couple times to locate the path to the blacksmith's shed. When she finally approached the building, smoke curled out of the chimney along with the scent of coffee.

She hoped it was Lukasz inside and not the blacksmith. She knocked. No answer. She opened the door and stuck her head inside. Lukasz stood across the room at a workbench, his back to her.

She stepped inside unnoticed. The space was warm, coffee was on the stovetop, and there were some biscuits in a basket. A blue-and-white-checked curtain closed off the window light.

With the fireplace roaring and the forge fired up, sweat beaded at her hairline. Lukasz was dressed in his pants and an undershirt, his pants belted with a rope. His shoulders were broad, his back V-shaped.

Lukasz was putting objects into tins, his wiry muscles contracting and releasing, stirring something new inside Mary. Dizzying, tingling sensations spread through her. She thought of Samuel and the flickers of attraction to him. The magnetism to Lukasz was different. It started deep in her bones then spread throughout, prompting her to move toward a half-dressed man, to reach out and touch his shoulder.

He spun around, face full of shock. His breath was heavy, arms tense as though he was readying to protect himself. Seeing her, he sighed and smiled. He didn't have to say a word; his expression told her all she needed to know.

"Hi," she said.

"Hi. What . . ." he fumbled for words, so Mary jumped in to explain what she was doing there.

She pulled two handkerchiefs from her pocket. "I made them."

He reached for them, then pulled his hands away, holding them up in surrender. "Dirty."

Mary nodded. "They're hankies. Simple cloth. Hemmed. I saw you needed one today, and I wanted to thank you for the beautiful mermaid you made. And to tell you we're even now. You don't have to make me anything else. You don't have to thank me for anything at all."

He grabbed a rag and wiped his hands, staring at Mary, his brow furrowed.

She'd walked in on him without a shirt. She realized he was uncomfortable. He hadn't asked her to stay. Perhaps he hadn't wanted to see her. Maybe he was being nice, asking her on dates. Her present was a good idea. They were even now.

"Sit?" He gestured toward a cot set against the wall near the fireplace.

Mary didn't move. "Do you understand what I said?"

He tossed the rag onto the bench and leaned against it. "You make me beautiful present to tell me not to make you any more presents."

She nodded. It sounded illogical when he said it. "I'm grateful for what you did the other night and for the mermaid and for . . . the note." The wording of it had made her stomach flutter. "It's so kind. But you can stop asking me out now. We're even." She wondered if she was speaking too fast for him to understand.

He washed his hands at a faucet in the far corner of the forge and slipped into his shirt but didn't button it.

He was dismissing her. And rightly so. They were even, after all. "It sounds strange now that I'm saying it," she said.

"You don't want to stay? To sit?"

She wanted to stay more than anything, but it would be wrong. What was happening to her? "Why'd you take the nails?"

He spread his hands. "I pay and take. Like everyone."

She looked away. "Who? Who'd you pay?"

"Foreman, line boss." He shrugged. "Depends."

"But not Mr. Dunn," she said.

Lukasz laughed. "He gets plenty." He put one hand high above the other. "Mountains of pay."

Mary felt better hearing that he'd paid for the nails, even if it wasn't a sanctioned purchase at a store. Those men lost much in the mills, as much as they gained in wages. But still, she was conflicted.

He rubbed his chin. "So . . . stay?"

Little shivers coursed through her, his gaze penetrating her. Go. She should go. She wanted to stay. If she were honest, it was why she'd come there in the first place.

She untied the ribbon that held her hat on. He took it and set it on the workbench. She unbuttoned her coat, and he hung it on a hook near the front door. He studied her. Mary's heart thumped, realizing she was filthy from work. Somehow, it didn't matter. He looked handsome, his carriage so proud.

All she wanted was his arms around her. She stepped toward him tentatively, as if approaching open fire. *Please,* she thought, *please want me too.*

And as though he'd heard her thoughts, he moved toward her. His arms lifted her in an embrace, giving her the sense of flying. He set her down, and they clung to each other. He dug his fingers into her hair, every caress sending new sparks over his skin. She traced his jaw, his heart thumped against her. She pulled away and touched his chest. "I can feel your heartbeat."

Their breath deepened, synchronized. The intensity snapped them apart. Mary struggled for air.

He stepped close again and drew his finger across her collarbone, his gaze following the trail down her neck and arm. He touched her lips, then followed it with a kiss, his gentleness as shocking as Samuel's aggression, making her kiss back. She tingled the way she'd heard she should, and it startled her.

"I should go," she said, her lips still against his.

He pulled back, and she lowered her forehead against his. "I should go." She forced the words through shallow, staccato breath.

He stepped away, arms spread wide.

She couldn't go. She didn't want to go.

He wiped his hands on his pants. The spell was broken for him, she could tell.

But it was too late. She couldn't leave. She took his hand. "I'm not leaving."

His shy smile appeared again. "Coffee?"

She nodded and sat on the cot.

He set the coffeepot on the grate inside the fireplace, then sat, his leg against hers. She brushed her skirt with one hand, and he slid his over hers. When sitting, they were the same height. He turned her hand over and drew circles in her palm, threading his fingers through hers, his fingertips fluttering up her wrist. Her insides trembled and heat spread to every hidden spot in her body.

The sound of boiling coffee drew their attention. He went to the stove and brought each of them a cup.

She sipped. "You didn't marry Aneta."

"You don't like Samuel."

She shook her head. "He chose another."

"Aneta, same."

"I didn't want him anyway." She sipped. "I decided."

"I didn't want her." He sipped.

"I heard Aneta broke your heart."

He narrowed his eyes on her. "No," he said, then chuckled. "I had dreams of a *syrena* and other things. Stupid."

"*Syrena?* Dreams?"

"A beautiful woman of the river. Rising out of the water." He gestured toward Mary's legs. "Like a *ryba* . . ." He looked to the ceiling, trying out English words, miming movement with his hands. He put his palms together and pushed them forward as though swishing through water. "A beautiful woman fish."

"A mermaid. Kasandra told me," she said, laughing at the image. "The note. And what you said that night you found me at the river."

"Funny? Why?"

He looked hurt even though he too was chuckling. Mary sipped her coffee, loving the way his eyes crinkled with even a hint of a laugh, loving the regal seriousness in the way he looked at her, the way he held himself. "I don't mean to laugh at you, Lukasz. It's just . . ." She looked into her cup, not knowing how to explain her nervous laughter, that it was bubbling out of her and stemmed from excitement she couldn't describe.

"I've been dreaming of you," he said.

His words jolted her. She forced another sip down and told herself she should leave. Mary thought of Matka, mad about everything, and Mr. Cermak's ugly stare, how his presence cast a cold shadow, and she knew she wouldn't leave.

"Me?"

"I didn't know it was you until the other night at the river."

Strains of music began to filter into the shed, easing her apprehension. "What's that?"

Lukasz jerked his head toward the door. "Mark. Family for big wedding. Full celebration. Dinner, dancing."

"At his house?"

Lukasz nodded and stared at the door. He started to pull away as though the mood had been broken by her question.

She grabbed his arm. "It's all right," she said.

He exhaled a deep breath and strode to his workbench, his back to her again. "Go, Mary. You should go."

There was nothing she wanted more than to be close to him, to dance to the distant sound of music. She knew it was risky, wrong, and confusing, but suddenly she didn't care what trouble she got into for wanting such things.

She went to him. "Dance," she said. "Like that night when . . ."

He shook his head.

She held out her hand. "It's just a dance."

He looked away.

She gestured toward the door. "Music's free tonight."

He chuckled.

She saw that if she wanted him to dance with her, she needed to be clear, to lift any veil of uncertainty that their language differences might create. He was too respectful to trespass. She took his hand and stepped into him. He turned his gaze back to her and she nodded.

He slid his hand around her waist, his touch shocking her all over again.

Their bodies brushed up against each other, hands clasped between them as he led her in a very slow hesitation waltz. They circled the space, their feet falling in sync. When they'd spun around the room several times, he dipped her, his breath against her neck. He lifted her upright and put his head against the spot where her neck met her shoulder, his lips electrifying her as they brushed her skin. They continued to sway against one another, their breath the only sound against the faint music. She backed away from him toward the cot, pulling his hand.

He let go of her hand. A voice sounded outside, coming down the path, yelling for Lukasz. Lukasz's eyes went wide. Mary covered her mouth.

Lukasz pointed. "I forgot. The tools."

"Tools?"

"It's Jed Handleman. He needs them for his new nursery." Lukasz grabbed a satchel from under the window and put his finger to his lips. Mary flattened her back against the wall so she'd be behind the door when it opened.

Lukasz swung the door open and shoved the bag out.

"Ouch, hey, Musial, good to see you. This is heavy as shit."

"Yes, yes, there you go," he said.

There was a pause. "Oh, okay . . . I thought I'd see you up the *haus* at Mark's party," the man said.

Lukasz began to shut the door. "No. Busy. You know, work."

Handleman pushed his foot to block the door closing. "Oh, I see. Ohhhh. I get it. You're *busy*." Lukasz blocked Handleman from coming in farther. Handleman was quiet for a moment. "All right. Your work's wearing a dress, right? Good man."

Mary wondered if Lukasz had led a trail of women through the shed, like Samuel had a parade though his house. The thought dampened her mood.

Handleman cleared his throat. "Oh. Here."

Mary heard rustling.

"Mark said you'd do them. Simple fixes. Mighty windy the other day."

Lukasz mumbled and shoved a bundle behind the door, near Mary's legs. "See you, see you. Good evening." Lukasz shut the door and leaned his forehead against it.

When he finally righted himself, Mary pulled on her hat and coat, laughing again.

"This isn't funny."

Mary secured the ribbons under her chin. "Kinda funny."

"No, no, no. Not right."

"Lukasz." Mary shrugged. She wanted to ask him if it was common for him to invite girls to the shed. Not that he'd invited her. She'd barged in. "Jed Handleman doesn't know anything."

"He knows something."

"He doesn't know it's me."

Lukasz went to his workbench and leaned against it, one ankle crossed over the other.

"If he tells . . . People might think . . ."

She thought of her father's words about Berta, who had gotten "lost in the rice." Mary should have been petrified at the thought that she was in a situation that could be mistaken for something untoward. But she wasn't. Her heart thudded at the idea of being near him, alone with him. Still, the lack of fear told her it was all the more important to leave. She noticed the handkerchiefs by his hand and she pointed. "I hope you like them."

He held them up. "Thank you, but—"

"We're even. Yes."

And out the door she went.

**

For the entire week, Mary thought of Lukasz nearly every waking moment. She replayed the collection of moments she'd had with him since they'd met, especially those in the shed.

Chores flew by as she relived their private dance, bodies pressed together, strains of music curling through the woods, filling the shed, the gentle notes mirroring Lukasz's touch. She trembled remembering the way he'd dipped her, his head in the crook of her neck, breath soft against her skin, his lips following his fingers along her collarbone giving her the most tender, intimate experience of her life.

She took extra trips to the locker room, passing shipping, and noticed Lukasz wiping his brow with a plaid handkerchief. She glanced upward to see if she was being watched. She shot a thumbs-up to Mr. Dunn, hoping he took that to mean she was watching the men, trying to catch them stealing. She was certain there was no way for Mr. Dunn to know that Lukasz had stolen her heart.

A week after she'd gone to the shed, Mary was the reason the line shut down. She had been so lost in thoughts of Lukasz that she missed a minute of nails coursing by, the burrs going unsanded, then spent another five attempting to retrieve and fix them to no avail. This rattled her. She'd never been the cause of anything shutting down, least of all an entire line at the mill. She pretended to be ill and left work early, heading straight up the hill to the shed. She told herself if she just saw Lukasz one more time, she could see that the way she remembered he made her feel was all wrong and she'd be finished with her endless mooning and daydreaming.

Already dark but still two hours before her shift would have normally ended, she bypassed the path to her house and flew into the shed. Lukasz spun around from his bench.

"Mary," he said. He registered surprise, then joy, rushing toward her, stopping inches from her. "Oh, Mary."

He took her face in his hands and brushed his lips over hers. She let out a moan and softened into him, their kisses desperate, probing. She pulled out of the kiss and took his hand, guiding him toward the cot. She was moving as if her body wasn't hers. She lay on the cot, shifting her back to the wall. She patted the thin mattress. "It's all right."

"Too small," he said.

"My sisters kick me all night. Plenty of room here."

He smiled. "Like me at the Kowalks'."

"I won't kick you in the back. I promise."

He shook his head. "Mary."

Hearing him say her name, his accent lifting the R away and replacing it with a hint of a D, made her feel as if her name had never been spoken aloud before. She sat up on her elbow. "I'm not leaving."

He sat on the cot and pulled her hand tight against his chest. She ran her fingers up and down his back. Lukasz spoke in his lovely, hobbled English, and told her of his cold, empty life in Poland, how he had lent his ticket-to-America money to a friend, lost a contest to Waldemar then won it back, finally making his trip to America. Finally he laid beside her.

"I have these memories of my parents in front of the fire after dinner and . . . I don't remember them talking so much as the sweetness between them. I have that same dream, to hold someone close with love. To have a home together."

It thrilled her that his idea of home mirrored hers. His English was choppy and her Polish was worse, but Mary understood every story he told, and knew he grasped every word she said as well. "Bursting with children?"

"Boys," he said, threading his fingers in and out of hers. "Many boys."

"You better have some girls."

"Girls?"

"Daughters will keep you in your old age," she said.

"Ahhh. Smart."

"Well, first the girls need to go when they marry, then they need to be there for when their parents are too old. Some girls never leave home."

He looked deep in her eyes. "You?"

She looked at the ceiling. "If it comes to it, I'll buy my own house. I bring home quite a lot of money between the mill and the Dunns'. It goes to keep our household upright. But I think I could actually man my own home at this point. If I could keep all my pay."

"Don't you want someone to protect you? To keep you and give you all the children you want?"

This question made her think of Mrs. Dunn and her life, the expansive guestroom and bath. When had Mary's dreams shifted from being the mistress of a household, leading a lemon-scented life, to being the breadwinner? She thought of Mr. Dunn and his coldness when she had returned the dress, Papa's failings, and Mr. Cermak's revolting intrusions. She thought of the things she'd hidden in the fireplace hearth for the day she got married and moved away. Perhaps she'd been hiding them away for herself, not for her entrée into a marriage with a man who would control her purse, but hid the things to fund her complete independence.

Lukasz shifted and brushed the back of his fingers along her cheek. "Mary?"

She wasn't sure how to express the feeling that had swept in. Her excitement at being with him was tinged with melancholy. She wanted to be with him more than anything in the world, their limbs laced together in perfect calm, but . . .

for the rest of her life? Could he give her what she wanted, what she'd dreamed of?

"Protect?" She almost mentioned the way she was protecting herself from Mr. Cermak. "I've worked since I was eight. And I've even managed to save some things for my dowry—treasure, special things . . ." She'd never told anyone about her treasures. Not even Mrs. Dunn, who'd given her so much, who believed in her so much. Yet with Lukasz, the words flowed. Maybe the language barrier bridged them somehow.

He rolled onto his back and slid his arm behind her head. She rested her head on his chest, his heartbeat swishing in her ear.

"Treasure?" he asked.

She shifted and put her chin on his shoulder so she could see him. No matter what, she was compelled to confide in him. She didn't know how it was possible, but it was as if they'd been tethered with invisible wires their whole lives. "I've hidden away small gifts over the years. Like a dowry. You know, for when a woman marries—her family gives the husband's family money or things."

"You're the treasure."

She buried her face in his chest, feeling his heart pound, overwhelmed.

"Your parents are old country? Your mother's accent—Czech?"

Mary nodded. "They want me to marry this boy Ralph, but we don't want each other."

"So you hide your treasure?"

"My parents don't have things saved for when I marry. They sell everything we can spare to pay the mortgage and taxes. So I hide the things away, waiting for the day I marry and make a home."

"But they own a home?"

Mary expanded with pride. "They do."

"The American Dream," Lukasz said.

"But no extras. And it can be a stretch. Oh boy, do we stretch, I'll tell you. But the things that Mrs. Dunn gives me, I hide them, I keep them so my parents won't have to worry when I finally marry. They'll thank me then. I know it. But now, I can't . . . I have to hide them."

"Ah, so you have secrets too? Like my nails from the mill."

"I hadn't thought of it that way."

"You're strong, smart," he said. "You'll have everything you want in life. I can see that."

She snuggled into him, her eyes growing heavy. "A clean lemony home, a husband who loves me and saves his pennies, and children."

"Lemon home?" he asked.

"Clean and fresh like the Dunns'. Everything there is . . . perfect."

"It's America, and a lemon home you should have," he said as Mary fell into the deepest sleep she'd ever had.

Chapter 58

Lukasz

Lukasz woke to find that Mary had disappeared sometime in the night. The fire was low and a chill had settled in the shed. The spot where Mary had lain was cool to the touch. He was relieved. Perhaps she had made it back into her house without her parents having to question where she'd been.

He used the outhouse, washed his face and under his arms, tidied his hair, and put on a fresh shirt. He wasn't sure what exactly was happening between Mary and him. She was adventurous; he'd always seen that in her—when she had saved him from the bosses at the mill, when she had caught a foul ball or dove into the river to save her father in a capsized boat. Perhaps her coming to the smithy and sharing her secrets was nothing but another adventure for her.

But then he remembered her prayer just before they'd fallen asleep. She whispered it, barely louder than her breath. He had wondered if she was even awake when she had recited her Hail Mary. But when he nudged her, she'd already tumbled into deep sleep, and he just held her tighter.

Even if he was partly an adventure for her, a girl who prayed before falling asleep was still anchored to something greater than her acts of rebellion. He couldn't explain why he took such a risk, letting her stay the night, even though he'd wanted her to. He had considered dragging her home and depositing her on the porch so her parents could see what a wonderful, respectable man he was. But he didn't do that. His need to keep her beside him had been too much. In the morning light, he berated himself. How stupid of him to have risked her honor. But he had to admit it was the deepest sleep he'd had since coming to America. To him, that confirmed their connection.

There were so many little details he couldn't name about Mary, yet their souls understood, their hearts knew everything. They were meant for each other. Ridiculous, but that knowing kept returning like the moon returned each night. What else could explain this, their attraction, the fullness of *knowing* each other without really knowing each other at all?

He started on the umbrella repairs and thought of Aneta, the Polish language they shared yet had nothing to say, their awkward embraces. One sweet kiss stood above all the forced ones. It wasn't until he replayed the way Mary had lain with him, staring into his eyes for hours, that he realized Aneta had only given him passing glances or scowls. Never once had they been suspended in one another's gaze, electricity coursing between them. No one, not one other woman, had ever made Lukasz feel like that.

He was starting night turn that evening, and he wanted to see Mary at her home, meet her parents again, and court her properly. Yes. Every thought since waking had been about her. Every revisited sensation was rooted in her breath against his cheek, her sweet smell, infectious smile, her eyes squeezed shut when she laughed hard. Everything had been recorded through his fingertips and skin, cataloged for when she was no longer near. He had no choice but to go see Mary, to be sure she knew he wanted her.

**

Lukasz drew a deep breath and let it out. Through the window, he could see the Lancos family in the front room. All five children and Mary's parents were either cleaning up the table, playing marbles, or reading. He yearned to be part of them. He repeated the names Mary had told him—Ann, Victoria, Johnny, George, and Rose.

He knocked at the door and the noise level dropped. The door swung open. A man stood there, his face weathered. "No rooms. No board. We're full." He began to close the door.

Lukasz jammed his foot against it before it could shut. "Mr. Lancos?"

He shoved the door again, but it didn't budge past Lukasz's foot. He peered at Lukasz through the slice of open door. "Mortgage is paid." He leaned closer to the hole but still didn't invite Lukasz inside. "And I haven't gambled in years. Not years."

Lukasz couldn't process all the English coming at him so quickly, but he understood that Mr. Lancos thought he was someone he wasn't.

"I'm here about Mary. I'm Lukasz Musial."

Mr. Lancos drew back. Lukasz pressed the door and it gave a little before it was shoved back on his foot.

Mr. Lancos's face reappeared, and he held up his forefinger. He brushed his hand through the air, signaling for Lukasz to move his foot. "Be right back."

Lukasz pulled his foot away and the door slammed. He paced the porch, waiting, hoping, yearning for Mary to appear. When the door finally opened, Mr. Lancos stood with his wife. The younger children clustered on a settee along the back wall, Mary stood beside the fireplace. The boys poked at each other and one sister, probably Ann, pulled one of them across her lap to separate them. The scent of cabbage and potato filled Lukasz's nose, and he saw that the dinner table was only half cleared.

He was unnerved, rethinking his boldness. But then realized he had no choice. Action was nearly always the answer.

Mr. Lancos loomed, arms crossed, frowning. He and Lukasz formed two sides of the valley's mountain walls, Mary, the river in between. Mrs. Lancos glowered, her expression like granite, her apron smeared with kitchen waste. Lukasz glanced at Mary, who grinned and nodded, giving him confidence to proceed.

Lukasz removed his hat and shook Mr. and Mrs. Lancos's hands. He used his best English, clear as he could. "I'd like to sit with Mary, to court her."

Mary's face lit up even more and bounced on her toes.

Mr. Lancos glanced at his wife. "No."

Mary's face fell. "Papa, please. Remember that Christmas Eve—"

"Shhh, Mary." He focused on Lukasz. "You're new here."

Lukasz shook his head. "Almost time to declare my intention to be American."

Mr. Lancos shook his fist. "No. Mary's American. She's promised to another."

"That's not true," Mary said.

Mr. Lancos swung around and faced his daughter, fists clenched. Mary's eyes widened. Lukasz stepped toward her, reaching.

Mr. Lancos put his hand against Lukasz's chest. "No."

Mary's face indicated she wanted to know why. Victoria slid to the edge of her seat. Ann looked frightened. The boys reached past their sister to bat at each other and ended up rolling onto the floor, wrestling. Lukasz wouldn't lower himself to ask why not, not in front of the whole family. But he wouldn't give up.

"I will ask again. Soon."

Mary smiled again. Victoria straightened and grinned at her sister.

"She's not to go aht," Mr. Lancos said. "Girl's been aht enough."

Lukasz suspected that had to do with her being gone the night before, though clearly they weren't aware she'd been with him.

"I'll be back," he said, and he turned and left.

Chapter 59

Mary

Mary watched the door close and heard Lukasz's feet beat a path down her front stairs, disappearing along with her hope. She tensed, waiting for what was to come.

Her father turned, teeth clenched. He snapped his fingers at the row of Mary's siblings. "Your sister's gotten herself into trouble, keeping secrets, and I won't have it. I trusted you to behave, Mary. Told your mother not to worry. That my Mary was smart and kept us first in her mind and actions. She told me she took care of it, so I kept quiet."

Mary's blood rushed, loud in her ears. What did her father know? She thought of Mr. Handleman.

"But now I must speak."

Mary was positive Handleman hadn't seen her, but if he had and told her father, she would already know that. She thought of the hidey-hole, her treasures. She glanced toward the fireplace. Nothing was disturbed.

"You're obstinate and rebellious."

Her father's words stung. How many times had she stuck up for him when her mother was angry? How many times had she helped him when his cough was too much? All those trips back and forth across the river, their talks. She'd always been special to Papa. He knew her better than Matka, saw Mary as a whole person rather than someone merely to do chores and watch over siblings.

"Of course I'm obstinate and rebellious. I'm American. You love that about me."

She didn't like this side of him, siding with Matka against her. Papa needed to get back into Matka's good graces after losing his pay and then staying away for days. Mary'd seen it a thousand times, just not with something that mattered to her so much.

He pointed. "Matka told me. You gave away pay to wear some dress. Got ruined? The one you were wearing that night you came for me in Webster."

She exhaled, relieved at least he didn't know about the shed. "I did. But Mrs. Dunn hasn't said anything more about taking pay since the night she let me wear it. She cares about me."

"We owe interest and principle to Mr. Cermak, who was paying us until a week ago. Now we owe him, and you give away money as though our money tree's in full bloom." Mary recognized Matka's wording and knew Papa'd been given his orders.

Mary nodded. *That's your fault that we owe him money*, she silently screamed, her heart cracking open that Papa blamed her.

Her mother looked on, quieter than Mary had ever seen her. This was an act, all for Papa to please Matka after losing pay.

"Think about Lukasz, at least. Please. He's nice."

"He's foreign." Papa pulled himself up to his full six feet of height.

So are you. Mary bit her tongue. Could Papa really say that with malice against Lukasz with any sincerity? She glanced at Matka, who busied herself with a loose thread on the cuff of her sleeve.

"You had your fun with Kasandra last night, staying at her house for half the night," Papa said. "Next week you work, you come home."

"But it's nearly Christmas. We have Mass and—"

Papa shook his head. "This year, your sisters get the tree with me."

Mary's jaw dropped. Her favorite part of Christmas Eve was choosing just the right tree to bring home and decorate.

Matka nodded. "As soon as Christmas is over, Papa will meet with Ralph's parents again."

"The time has come," Papa said. "With this Lukasz sniffing around . . . Matka was married at sixteen. It's time before—"

"But Papa—"

"And don't bring up that Samuel again. That's not how these things work."

Mary wasn't looking to argue for Samuel. "I won't marry Ralph."

Her father snorted, irritated the conversation continued.

"And Lukasz didn't ask to marry me, just to court."

Papa stared at Mary as though something she'd said was causing him to consider something different. "You marry Lukasz, you lose citizenship. He's Polish, right?"

Mary nodded.

"My daughter the Pole? I don't think so."

"It's all the same in America, if you haven't noticed. Ralph's a hunky. We are, Lukasz is. They don't care which exact part of over there we're from. We're all the same to them. Breaking our backs in the mills. Same schools. Neighbors. What difference does it really make?"

"Pfft. US law is the difference. Marriage is the difference. Working together is one thing. You will *not* give away what your mother and I sacrificed to give you. We left our homeland to make better lives. American lives."

Mary crossed her arms. "He just wants to visit, take me to a dance."

Papa dug his hands into his pockets. Matka stepped closer to him as if to support him. "Ralph it will be."

Mary pushed her chin in the air, pulling up to her full height. "I won't marry *anybody* if Ralph is my match. An old maid, giving you my pay, is better than that." She could save her treasures and her extra money and surprise them all when she bought her independence with a little house wedged into the hillside, even one room to call her own. She was beginning to see why her parents would have sold their silver, gifts given to Mary as a baby in order to secure independence. Having hidden things that she might use as a nest egg was more important than ever. Anything was better than being forced into a marriage.

Papa coughed that whole-body cough, his chest rattling like an earthquake, the argument taking its toll. Matka rubbed his back, softer with him than Mary could ever remember her being, their alliance suddenly wrapped in steel wire, keeping Mary out. Papa recovered steadier breath. "Ann's old enough to do more. You eat as much as a man. It'll be better for you to have your own household. With Ralph. He's American but Czech. Like you."

Mary flung herself on the settee. "Ralph doesn't want me. And I don't want him."

"That doesn't matter, my daughter. He'll inherit his father's store, the house. You'll live well."

She slung her arm over her forehead and considered it. A large home. Lemon-scented? She didn't know if Ralph's was, but guessed it wasn't. They were wealthier than the Lancoses, their home bigger, probably flush with more cabbage than imaginable, the smell of it infiltrating every inch. She was sure they didn't care a lick about lemon-fresh cleanliness. "I'll live in misery."

"Just like the rest of us," Matka said.

Mary rushed to stand. Perhaps this comment pointed at Papa would push him back to Mary's side of things.

But no, they held hands, her father's giant paw swallowing Matka's smaller one, the two of them joined in thought and body, something Mary couldn't remember seeing ever. "To pay back Mr. Cermak, you'll need to pick up more houses to clean," Papa said. He looked at Matka, who nodded to encourage him to go on. "And demand Mrs. Dunn pay you for anything extra you've done."

Mary stood frozen, the trust between her and Papa torn completely, the closeness they'd shared on their river travels shattered.

"More work, less time to think of Poles."

A sob rose in Mary's throat, her breath sucked away from her chest.

Matka elbowed Papa.

"And no more secrets," Papa said. "No more Lukasz Musial. He offers nothing. There's weakness in his eyes. I hear it in his voice. I see it in his small clothes. You'll marry a big, established man, someone who can take care of you, not someone with nothing, not even his papers, waiting to drag you down."

Mary dug her fingers into her skirt, enraged at her foreign father despising a fellow foreigner as if they were somehow different, as if Papa was somehow better.

Chapter 60

Lukasz

Lukasz dug his hands into his pockets and stalked away from the Lancos's home. He ached for Mary. Each beat of his heart carried a sense of love and pain, fear that he might not hold her in his arms again. But he wasn't giving up. He would prove to the Lancoses and Mary that he was worthy.

He knew Mary was interested in him, but that didn't mean she would disobey her parents again. One thing gave him hope—Aneta. She had disappointed her family for love, for the life she wanted. Perhaps Mary would do the same. Perhaps he could win her parents over. It wasn't so long ago that they were new to America. Surely they remembered what that meant.

"Lukasz," came a voice from behind.

He stopped and turned. Through the fog, a figure came closer. Zofia, her arms loaded with parcels.

"You walked right past me," she said.

"I'm sorry. I didn't see you. I was—"

"*Pogrążony w myślach,*" she said in perfect, comforting Polish. How he loved when he didn't have to force his thoughts to fit a language that wasn't his.

"Lost in my own head, yes."

She smiled at him, and suddenly he wanted to walk with her, to talk, to feel like he belonged to a family again, as he had when he'd first arrived. He took her packages from her.

She smoothed her hair and adjusted her hat. "It's been a long time, Lukasz. I would have thought you'd moved out of town if folks hadn't reported on your attendance at work."

"I'm sorry about not visiting more. I just couldn't think about having to face Aneta and all her happiness and . . ."

Zofia put her hand on Lukasz's arm. "I understand."

They stood in silence for a moment, awkwardly shifting and shrugging.

"So, umbrellas! You've been busy. Everyone I know has an umbrella you've fixed."

He blushed, knowing that was an exaggeration, but it was a sweet one all the same. "You make it sound noble."

She smiled that pinched smile. He'd missed her fondness for him. "We've missed you."

"I've missed you too," Lukasz said. He couldn't believe he hadn't sought Zofia out for council. She must have forgiven him for not pressing Aneta to marry him. "Everyone."

Suddenly he needed the warmth of family; he needed the Kowalks. "Let me get you home," he said. He walked toward her house, both yammering about the time that had passed, feeling as if they'd seen each other just the day before. Inside Zofia's, he set the bags on her table, noticing that the sightline to the back of the house had changed. "Another addition?"

She nodded. The house smelled savory and sweet with her wonderful holiday baking. Lukasz's mouth watered.

"Come to Wigilia. I mean, unless you're having dinner at a girl's house?"

He smiled.

"There's a girl, isn't there? Lost in thought about a girl?" She crossed her arms.

"Sort of."

She gasped, and he was reminded of how devout she was about Poles marrying Poles, even in America. "Polish?"

He looked at his feet. "Bohemian. Parents are."

She smiled. "She's American?"

"Yes."

"You're going there for dinner?"

He shook his head. "No, I . . ."

"They want her to marry their own kind?"

"I get that feeling. I see her at work, though. She's a nail girl."

Zofia exhaled. "That doesn't sound like good luck, her parents' disapproval. But things will work out, won't they? Some years are awful. This year was better. Next will be grand."

"I hope so," he said, marveling at her unusual comfort with the idea of bad luck.

"So come for Wigilia. Please. The children would love to see you. Let's start the year off well."

He nodded and hugged her tight, warmed by her invitation but unsure. Would Aneta and Tytus be there? He didn't know if he could take that, even though he was surer than ever that he and Aneta had been a bad match. But Tytus reminded Lukasz of all he didn't have. He thought of his tin box in the shed loaded with cash. Still, it wasn't what Tytus Hawthorne had.

"Please," Zofia said. "Nathan was asking about you the other day."

Lukasz agreed for the moment, pleased he'd run into Zofia but not sure he would attend Wigilia, even though it was exactly what he needed.

Chapter 61

Mary

On Christmas Eve, Mary moved through her home like a ghost. Her parents barked orders, even knowing Mary knew what to cook, bake, and clean better than they did. When Papa rounded up Ann, Victoria, and Johnny to go cut down the tree, the stab at being shunned hobbled Mary. It was as if she'd committed a horrible crime.

How could she have known that Papa would lose a week's pay at the precise time she gave away a day's? The fact that Mrs. Dunn still hadn't withheld it from her salary or even brought it up didn't make anything better, even though it should have.

It wasn't as though Mary's missing pay could have filled in the gap that her father's had left. The Christmas preparations did nothing to soothe her parents' anger, and it taxed their cash even more. They were joyless, deepening Mary's sadness. She didn't care if they had no money for gifts, but to not give a smile or sweet touch to their children or each other, or even a cheerful hello to the boarders, made Mary wish she lived somewhere else.

She dusted the front room, cleaning away as much of the daily soot as she could. She swiped the wood moldings above the windows, yearning to sing her Christmas carols at church, to go to confession, to be where golden candle glow lit the space and would lighten her heart.

When she finished with the windows, she moved to dust the fireplace. A stoneware jar held a fireplace poker, pan, brush, and some umbrellas. She wiped those handles down, less concerned with cleaning them than the rest of the room, hoping her father would notice it fresh and sparkling when he returned.

She tossed another log and some pine boughs on the fire, sending sparkling embers up, the fragrant scent of Christmas pine filling her nose. She brushed away the embers from her skirt and used the poker to adjust the logs, reminding her of the fireplace at the shed, the thrill of spending time alone with Lukasz.

Mary dusted the mantel, shifting the pieces of crèche to wipe between them, admiring baby Jesus, Mary, who watched over him, full of contentment, and Joseph, who watched over both.

Mary leaned her forehead against the stone mantel, remembering the thrill of Lukasz molded against her, the feeling that had flowered when they lay together.

Love.

She shook her head. Was she crazy? She barely knew him.

The feel of a hand pressing against her bottom made Mary whip around, her skirt twirling into the fireplace flames. She gasped and recoiled, batting at the flames with the help of Mr. Cermak.

When the fire was out, she breathed heavily, anger consuming her like the flames that had just eaten away at her skirt.

She smacked his shoulder with all her might. He jerked back, a wicked grin coming as he rubbed his arm. "Feisty as hell," he said. "Nimble, magnificent."

His words turned her stomach. Every nerve stood at attention.

"Go away," she said.

He pulled her arm. "I'm going to ask your parents to court you."

She yanked her arm away. "No."

"I've a lot to offer. I've a bundle of cash, and I feel like we know each other so well."

He lunged for her again. She hopped away, backing toward the side of the fireplace, careful to avoid the hearth and flames. He came toward her again. She reached behind her, her hands making contact with the tools in the stoneware jar.

"Stay away," she said.

He shook his head and stepped closer. She latched onto whatever tool was behind her and swung it at him.

He leapt out of the way and she smacked the fireplace. An umbrella, now bent. Hopefully it was enough to keep him back. "We don't know each other at all."

"I know your secrets," he said, menacing, coming closer but moving back when she poked the umbrella at him.

Mary's blood turned cold, grateful she'd learned to swing a baseball bat along with the boys on the street. She held the umbrella toward him. "I don't have secrets."

"All girls do. But yours are special. You've more than most. You're wily and smart and . . ." He moved past her outstretched umbrella to the fireplace where the mantel ended, running his hand along the very bricks that hid her hidey-hole.

He couldn't possibly know about her things. She was careful not to let anyone see her move the bricks. Still, she panicked, the umbrella quivering in her hands.

He dragged his finger along, stopping at the exact brick she had to wiggle first to reveal her treasures. "You rebel and choose your own men even when your parents push in another direction. There's plenty of room in your life for me."

"Stop it," Mary said. "You're too old."

"Not any older than that man you've been visiting. I've seen him around the Bucket of Blood, fistfighting circus strongmen for an extra bit of coin. What's his name again? Luke? Luka? Something ugly."

She couldn't breathe. Fear paralyzed her as she realized he'd been following them. "You don't know him."

He lurched toward her. "But you do, don't you? I agree with your mother. I saw how he looked at you when he rescued you from the river; he knows you and you know him in a way that your parents would surely disapprove of. I'll tell them."

"You weren't there when he brought me back. Not right then; I know you weren't. Where are you getting all this?" Her mother might have favored Mr. Cermak, but Mary was quite sure she wouldn't have confided in him.

"I was there. Out of sight, but I heard it all. So sweet. Him coming to ask permission to date you. Your father won't allow it. An immigrant for his American daughter? Lose your citizenship? Your father's no dummy. I'll tell them what you're up to."

Mary clenched her skirt, trying to keep calm, to hide her fear that Mr. Cermak would do such a thing. She straightened and squared her shoulders. "There's nothing to tell."

"I saw you go into the shed. I saw you with him."

She clenched her jaw but fought against showing the surprise that wracked her. "I don't know what you're talking about." Her voice quivered.

"I'll tell them." He grinned.

Had he been following her regularly? Distracted, Mary lowered the umbrella. He lurched again, knocking it away, and grabbed her tight against him, his lips hard on hers, his tongue snaking into her mouth. She twisted and rammed her knee into his crotch.

He buckled and stumbled back. "That's how you want it to be, huh? Okay. I like it best this way."

The front door flew open. Papa and the children burst through, pine tree first, laughing as they shoved it inside, following behind, singing Christmas carols. Mr. Cermak was doubled over, trying to straighten and act as though nothing was wrong.

"You're disgusting," Mary said, snatching the umbrella from the floor and pointing it at him to keep him back.

Papa and the children quieted. He whipped off his snow-dusted hat and looked from Mary to Mr. Cermak. "What the hell?"

Mr. Cermak shrugged, glaring at Mary.

"He's an awful, filthy man, and I want him gone."

Her father tossed his coat on a chair, then stepped over the tree, coughing into his bent arm.

Mr. Cermak straightened and appeared relieved. "Your daughter doesn't understand how the world works. When someone pays your mortgage, he should be treated kindly."

Mary's papa stared at his daughter, then eyed the bent umbrella.

"He—"

"I found her treasure trove, and she attacked me when I said I wouldn't lie for her."

Mary gasped, and her siblings gathered around her. George held onto her skirts. Her face burned. "That's not true. He . . ." Her words trailed off as she watched Mr. Cermak wiggle one brick, then another.

Papa glanced at Mary, then joined Mr. Cermak at the wall. The man dug his hand deep inside and pulled out small bags jingling with the bounty. Next came the silver Mrs. Dunn had given her on various occasions and the box with the canvas wrapping ribbon and linens. Mary was stunned at how much she'd hidden away, at the sight of it splayed on the floor like no more than junk at a second-hand store. The fire reflected on the beautiful silver, her silver.

Papa took one of the sacks from Mr. Cermak and dug his coal-stained finger into the cinched neck. He opened it and turned it over in his palm, the monogramed silver salt shakers clinking into his hand along with the angel and the mermaid. Mary's heart stopped at the sight of her precious treasure. She reached for the angel and mermaid, not wanting anyone to defile them with ugly anger.

Papa blocked her hand and picked up one of the bell-shaped salt shakers, and turned it into the firelight. "Ms? Someone made these for you?"

Mary shook her head. "Mrs. Dunn had them from her family and didn't want them. She wanted me to have a hope chest to have things for when I got married."

"So you did hide these away?"

Mary nodded.

"These are silver. We needed money. You—"

He opened another sack, turning it out on a side table near the settee. Pennies, dimes, and quarters tumbled onto the table, glistening in the firelight, all her ugly secrets.

"You could have helped us," Papa said.

Mr. Cermak smirked. This lit something in Mary, and she couldn't control her anger.

"I help you every minute of my life, Papa. I rowed you to and from work for years. I keep houses, work at the wire mill, and cook and clean here. What else can I do? Shed my skin and make a coat for this revolting man to wear this winter? What else can I possibly do?"

Papa took her arm and gripped it so hard, her hand went numb. "Don't disrespect me this way."

"I just want to have something for my home when I marry. That's it."

"You declined the match we made."

"There was no match made. He wants Sally and—"

"I'll marry her," Mr. Cermak said.

This silenced them all. Only George sniffling into his sleeve cut the quiet.

"That would even us up. What with this armed assault—"

"It's an umbrella." Mary shook it at him.

Mr. Cermak ignored her, facing her father dead-on. "For her assaulting me and for the mortgage."

Papa glanced at Mary, breathing heavy. He pushed his hand through his hair. She could see he was considering the offer. "That would erase my debt?"

"That and her little treasure trove here," Mr. Cermak said. "A dowry as Mary intended it to be."

Mary went to Papa, who was lining the salt shakers up and stacking the coins into towers.

"No. Papa. Take all of it, pay him back with it."

"I don't want that shit," Mr. Cermak said. "Not without Mary."

Papa ignored them both, stacking coins.

"Tell him no, Papa," Mary said. "I won't."

Papa stopped with the treasure. "I need to think. I need to talk to Matka."

Mary's anger boiled up again, knowing what Matka would say. Mary'd been wrong not to hand over her treasures, to withhold money. But for Papa to consider marrying her to this lecherous man? "You have to think about it? He attacked me."

Papa shook his head.

"You *believe* him?"

Papa looked away.

Mary straightened and backed away. Mr. Cermak stared at her, his sly smile cutting her from across the room.

He moved toward her. Mary held up the umbrella. "One step closer and I'll shove this right through you. Ann, get my coat."

Ann did as she was told. "Don't go, Mary."

Mary inched toward the door, grabbing her hat and scarf.

She eyed Papa, wanting him to make her stay, to tell her he believed her, that he wouldn't even consider her marrying Mr. Cermak.

Papa turned his back to Mary, taking the last of her breath with him.

**

Mary tried to keep from breaking down as she darted away from her house, her long legs carrying her halfway across town in no time. Her mind tangled around thoughts of betrayal, Christmas Eve, her future, and the sadness and anger in Papa's eyes when he saw all that she'd hidden away. Her emotions twisted, interwoven with threads of sadness and ire. When her legs grew tired after walking the length of town several times, she found herself in front of St. Dominic's.

Father Kroupal was heading into the front door with his arms loaded with poinsettias. Mary ascended the stairs two at a time, putting the bent umbrella under her arm and taking one pot from the priest.

"Thank you, dear Mary."

She followed him into the sanctuary, and they each dipped a hand into the holy water, crossing themselves.

"These will be beautiful at Mass."

They walked up the aisle, genuflecting and making the sign of the cross as they reached the altar. He pointed to the left. "That one goes there."

Mary set the pot down and turned it to show off the best leaves.

"It's lovely, Father."

"Ready for Midnight Mass," he said, wiping his palms. "I haven't seen you much lately, Mary. You used to be our very best parishioner. Pious."

"I've been working a lot. But I say my prayers. Always."

"See you tonight, then," he said. "Whole family, I hope. I'll have confession in an hour or so. You should come."

Mary inhaled sharply and let out a sob before she even knew it was rising out of her.

He led her to the front pew. "What is it? What's the matter?" He glanced at her bent umbrella.

She struggled to swallow, her throat hurting from dryness.

"Trouble at home?"

She nodded.

"Well, Christmas can do that. Christ's birth can dredge up all the best and worst in us."

She couldn't imagine telling him all that had been happening in her life.

"Would you like to confess now?"

She shook her head.

"Sometimes it's nice to just sit here and absorb all the goodness, isn't it?"

She nodded.

They sat for a long time, both of them kneeling to pray at some point. Mary clasped her hands below her chin and squeezed her eyes shut, begging God to tell her what to do next. She silently recited Hail Marys and Our Fathers and begged good and hard for an answer. Eventually Father Kroupal slid back to sit, and Mary stood.

"I can see you're pained, Mary. When you're ready to confess, I'll be here. But sometimes the best thing to do is to help someone else when you feel so bad about life."

Mary fought to keep from rolling her eyes.

"I have some parcels that need to be delivered to new arrivals in town. I have three baskets, and if you took them for me, it would give you time to clear your mind and me time to clean up before going to the Lipinski's for dinner before Mass. Maybe you'll return for confession after some fresh air."

Before she knew it, she had two baskets slung over one arm and the third over her other. He scribbled on a piece of paper and handed it to her, but he was already explaining what he'd written. "Start with the Marshalls on Murray Avenue, then Allen Avenue where the . . ." He kept talking, but Mary just wanted to get out of there.

"The Oreliks live in the first block of Allen, but that's not . . ." On and on he went until he tugged on Mary's coat. "Mary? Then the Dubinskys . . ." On and on.

Though uninterested in the errands at first, Mary found peace in delivering the parcels. When she got to the end of the list she realized she'd stopped listening to Father Kroupal's directions at one point so she dug the paper out of her pocket to get the correct address for the last home.

On her way again, she looked into the sky, the sun silvery, disappearing behind the hills, further darkening the smoky, foggy evening.

Sorry to have her errand nearly finished, Mary vowed again she wouldn't go home no matter how heavy the loneliness grew. No. She was still too angry, betrayed by Papa again.

Mary'd always been proud of her capabilities, but now it was like none of that mattered. Her parents looked at her in a way she just could not live with. She was an employee to them, no more important than the unrelated boarders. Something as special as Christmas shouldn't be wasted on them, no matter how sad she was, missing her siblings.

The silver sun slipped away, dropping the temperature almost immediately. With it came icy rain and Mary scoffed at her broken umbrella. She opened it anyway, needing to keep the remaining basket dry. She headed for the last stop on her list of good deeds, thinking if she walked slowly enough, she might walk back into a life she actually wanted.

Chapter 62

Lukasz

Lukasz dressed in his cleanest and newest underthings, pants, and shirt. He scrubbed and freshened up under his arms and everywhere else that rarely caught a breeze and never saw the sun. He combed his hair and opened the box that held his latest creations. He'd already dropped off the cat he'd made for Vacek Verba to give his daughter and stowed away the coins he'd been paid. He paged through the dollar bills and change, pleased that he had been responsible in saving, that again he could seriously plan to buy property. Just before leaving for the Kowalks', he organized the materials he'd selected to make something for Mary later, but he was almost late for dinner.

When Lukasz reached their home, Nathan and the other kids tackled him at the door, dragging him in to show him the Christmas tree they'd already decorated. At the top was the angel Lukasz had made for Zofia. It glimmered and winked in the soft candlelight, making Lukasz proud and confident. He wondered if the one he'd given Mary at the dock years before was at the top of her tree. He would have given anything to be invited to the Lancos home, but her family needed time to reconsider him and his request to court Mary. He understood.

Zofia's kitchen was hot, her stovetop covered with pots and pans, the air filled with decadent Wigilia foods. The table was set in full regalia, with pieces of straw peeking out from under the delicate white linen tablecloth. Lukasz imagined Mary decorating her family's tree, humming "Joy to the World," sitting down to dinner, and heading to Midnight Mass afterward. He understood a father's desire to protect his daughter and was willing to work to convince her family that he was worthy, that even though he was not yet an American citizen, Lukasz Musial deserved a chance to get to know Mary better.

He handed Zofia her present. Her eyes welled.

"Open it," he said.

She unwrapped it and held it into the light. "Oh, Lukasz. Simply beautiful. Exactly like our house." She rubbed her fingers over each section.

"I even added the new room off the back. Luckily I saw it earlier this week."

"Thank goodness for nails from the mill, right?" Zofia said, laughing. "And the door. It's blue. I would know this anywhere."

Lukasz smiled and looked at his feet, thinking about Mary and how she'd been watching people to see if they stole. Zofia pulled his chin up. "We are so glad you're here, Lukasz."

Alexander entered the house. When he saw Lukasz, he shoved his hands into the air, whiskey bottles clinking. "Lukasz Musial!" He slung one arm around Lukasz and jostled him. "So glad you made it."

"Me too, Alexander. Thank you." Another rush of belonging filled Lukasz.

He poured Lukasz a glass. "Anything else, Zofia?"

She studied the table in the same way she had that first year Lukasz was in Donora, when Zofia was pregnant and bickering with Alexander. She counted seats, shifted a chair at the children's table, and added another glass to one place setting.

"Unlucky thirteen," Alexander said.

She grumbled, but her tone was soft. She turned to Lukasz. "Lukasz is here again. That's lucky anytime."

Lukasz sipped his drink as a knock came at the door. Zofia answered it and guided Aneta and Tytus Hawthorne into the room. Behind them was one of Hawthorne's brothers. Zofia hadn't said for sure they were coming, and the earlier comfort disappeared. Lukasz downed the rest of his drink and filled his glass to the brim with Alexander's special brew, ignoring his roiling stomach.

"Hey, Lukasz." Tytus ambled toward him, arms full of parcels. He set them down, taking Lukasz's hand in both of his, shaking it and smiling. He lifted a hatbox from one of the bags. "This time, I'm prepared."

Lukasz drew back. Aneta joined them, threading her fingers through her husband's, her loose dress hinting at the baby inside. "I think this is perfect for you," she said.

Lukasz hadn't brought them gifts and was mortified.

"Seriously. I owe you," Tytus said.

Lukasz narrowed his eyes at Tytus. He didn't understand.

"You gave your blessing to Aneta and me when we first got together. It meant the world to her."

Lukasz started to protest, but Aneta's warm smile made him stop. He would let Tytus think he'd been a bigger man than he was. He was grateful to Aneta.

The hat was beautiful—a black derby.

"Easy fitting," Tytus said, holding it up. "*Rousing Gentleman* is what it said in the catalog."

Lukasz was struck by its handsomeness and the gesture. "They name hats?"

Joseph Hawthorne, Tytus's brother, introduced himself, studying the hat and Lukasz. "Oh yes. The Braden, the Rambler, the Armon. On and on. But this one . . ." He put it on Lukasz's head. "Perfect choice for this gent, Aneta."

Everyone gathered around, agreeing. Lukasz's mood lifted, but the awkwardness remained. He'd brought no gift for them. "Thank you," he said, shaking Tytus's hand firmly and, for once, with true goodwill. He was grateful for the magnanimous gesture. The only thing unlikable about Tytus and his brother was that they were utterly likeable.

Lukasz's loneliness didn't dissolve, remaining solid, a mass, but it was obscured by the good feelings that developed by Aneta's and the Hawthornes' thoughtfulness.

When the children returned from spotting the first star of the night, it was time to pass the wafer, state what they were grateful for, and eat.

Lukasz was most grateful for everyone speaking Polish and that he understood each word and didn't have to search for translations, but the Hawthornes struggled, as both were learning Polish after a lifetime of ignoring their heritage.

Zofia was serving the first course when a knock came at the door.

Everyone froze, spoons halfway to mouths, baskets of bread held midair between them.

Alexander cleared his throat, his eyes widening.

Zofia grabbed his hand and shook her head. "We determine our luck this year."

Alexander studied his wife for a moment, confused, then pleased. He nodded and went to the door. Relief flooded the room. They remained quiet as breadbaskets were passed, and soup was slurped. Still, they strained to hear what was happening around the corner at the front door.

Alexander stuck his head into the room and gestured to his wife. "A girl's here. Has our address as the Lipinskis'. Some basket for them." He waved a scrap of paper over his head. "Come read this."

Zofia stood, pushing past Alexander.

Alexander sat again. "Eat, eat, everyone. Zofia will be a minute." Conversation turned jovial and loud again as the Hawthorne men asked the children what they wanted from Santa, teasing them about naughty and nice behavior.

Zofia reentered the room, holding a bent umbrella toward Lukasz. "I know it's an imposition, but when I saw this and the icy rain, I couldn't let her go."

Lukasz nodded, knowing that might give him a reason to avoid church that night. "I'll fix. Tonight." He dug back into his meal. "So good, Zofia."

A hush came over the room. Lukasz finally looked up. Zofia was talking to someone still out of sight, their words muffled by the boot room wall.

Zofia leaned into the boot room, pulling someone by the hand. A young woman came into view, struggling to smooth her wind-blown hair. She pushed a lock of hair behind her ear and smiled at Zofia.

Lukasz dropped his fork. Everyone including Zofia and the woman turned to him.

His face flooded with heat.

Was it really her?

He stood, unable to believe his eyes. "Mary."

She drew back, appearing as surprised as he. She looked down at her dress and smoothed it before looking back at him, only him, a broad grin lighting her eyes. "Lukasz."

Alexander lifted his glass. "Lucky thirteen!"

The Hawthornes and children toasted. "Lucky thirteen."

Lukasz stood slowly, feeling like he was floating. He went to the thirteenth chair and pulled it out.

She sat. Lukasz patted her shoulder, keeping himself from swallowing her in his arms, and went back to his seat. The chatter in the room, the laughter, Mary being there—the warmth from it all flooded him, and the loneliness inside him shrank with every beat of his heart.

**

Lukasz and Mary left the Kowalks', walking at a polite distance from each other in case anyone was watching. They dropped the basket at the proper address, figuring out that Father Kroupal had transposed one digit, causing Mary's confusion but bringing her right to Lukasz.

The icy rain had ended, but they stepped carefully due to slick patches. Mary swung the bent umbrella between them.

"I'll walk you home, then fix that and return it to you by morning," he said.

She shook her head.

"It's easy. I fix them all the time."

"Not going home."

He reached for the umbrella. "Let me?"

She nodded and handed it to him. Within a few more steps, their hands had found each other. She leaned into him as they walked. Lukasz thought he misunderstood what she said about going home. "What does that mean about home?"

She squeezed his hand. "The shed. Take me there."

He started to shake his head, but she was already tugging him in that direction. When they reached the gravel path that snaked past Mark's house and into the woods, Mary glanced over each shoulder as though worried someone would notice them.

They entered the cold shed. Mary slid the bolt to lock. He glanced at it but didn't ask why. He lit a lamp and started a fire in the fireplace. He walked toward the forge to heat it and she pulled his arm. "I don't care about the umbrella."

"What happened?" he asked.

"No. Just talk." Mary removed her hat. "About anything. In Polish, in English, I don't care."

He used the bellows on the fire, unsure what Mary wanted, what rambling about nothing might do to help her. He set the bellows down and turned to her, wracking his mind for a topic he could easily talk about in English. A moan from a tugboat echoed up the hills.

He eased closer to her. "Ever wonder how loud that boat would sound if all the mills went away?"

She unbuttoned her coat. "Can't happen. This place only exists because of the mills. They'll thread our veins through the wire mill before they shut any of it down."

He slid her coat off her shoulders and tossed it behind them onto the cot.

"You're right," he said.

They moved closer to each other, the outside mill noises pulsing against the silence in the shed.

"I argued with Papa."

Lukasz tilted his head. "On Christmas Eve. I'm so sorry."

"Mr. Cermak, our one boarder, told him about my hidden things, my treasure. He saw me hide them away. Papa's angry because they needed to make the mortgage and I could have sold those things. Then we wouldn't have had to borrow money from a boarder, from that horrible rat of a man." Her voice cracked.

"Did he do something?"

Mary shifted her feet. "I took care of it."

Lukasz looked her over, searching her skin for any sign of bruising or harm. She looked intact except for her hair, which was sprouting every which way from its pins.

Her eyes filled. "My parents needed the money and I just kept quiet about having these things. They could have sold them then. Silver salt shakers. I have some silver from Mrs. Dunn. *Repoussé* it's called. Imagine they name silver patterns like they're children. It's silver, covered in flowers of every kind. It's lovely. It's something my parents never could have given me if I lived there another twenty years. Mr. Cermak saw me hide things. He watched me."

Lukasz gripped her arms, not understanding most of what she was saying but getting the gist of it. "I'll go and . . ." He clenched his fists. "*Zmiażdżę go.*"

She grasped his hands and loosened his fists so her fingers could slide between his. "No. Please. Stay with me."

All he knew was that he wanted to make her safe, keep her safe, hold her heart. Finally, she was asking him for something, something he could deliver.

She looked at the cot and back at him. "I was cleaning and cooking when . . ." She spread her hands and let them drop. "Look at me in this messy dress."

"You're magnificent. Just like that. In that dress."

She looked down. “It has holes.” She smoothed her hair as though she had just then realized it might be mussed.

“It has you.” He wanted to take her in his arms and kiss her, take her to the cot, to lay with her, to make love to her.

She stepped toward him and brushed his shoulder, then cupped his cheek. She was everything he’d never expected he’d find in a woman; charming but straightforward, steely, and never glum even when her smile was tinged with sadness he only partly understood.

He should have felt small in her presence. Her towering height should have tied his tongue, but when they were together, he found the words he needed. Everything, despite their language barrier, was understood. She already saw it all, saw right into him. Yet he was hesitant to push her. His body tingled. She stepped against him, playing with the hair at the nape of his neck. She smelled like flowers even though she’d said her dress wasn’t clean. His body tensed with desire.

He leaned into her, his lips grazing her neck, his fingers tracing downward. She tasted salty and sweet.

She ran her hands over his shoulders, pulling him close, her breath hot against his ear. He tightened his arms around her waist and she arched into his caresses with a moan.

He exhaled and released her. He had to stop what was happening or soon it would be too late. He pulled away. “I’ll take you to Peggy or Kasandra if you don’t want to go home.”

Her breath quickened, her lips parted, red. “I’m staying.”

He didn’t want to make her leave. “Don’t say that.”

She put her hands on his chest and backed him up to the cot, the edge against the back of his legs. He grasped her wrists.

She pressed him, forcing him to sit, and stepped back. She slid her fingers up her shirtwaist undoing each button as she went, his breath catching each time a mother of pearl orb slipped through its opening. She shook out of the shirtwaist and tossed it aside. She undid her skirt and stepped out of it, sauntering to Lukasz, never taking her eyes from him. He rubbed his chest, wondering if she might stop his heart without even touching him. She turned her back to him, sitting on his lap. "Loosen me," she said.

He could barely catch his breath. He fumbled with her corset strings, releasing them. She unhooked the front hooks and slipped the garment off, leaning back against him. He slid his hands around the front of her, kissing her neck, cupping her, feeling her breath quicken as his fingers brushed over her belly. He told himself to move slow, to savor every sensation, to let her decide everything they did.

He caressed her, pulling the hem of her chemise upward, his fingers lighting on her garters, untying each with one hand. He stroked her thighs, rolling the stockings past her knees, then mapping upward again, her skin softer than anything he'd ever touched.

Every bit of her held his attention, and he could have lingered on each square inch for a day. She pushed away and stood, looking at him over her shoulder. He gasped for breath, bracing himself as she slid the chemise straps over her shoulders, dropping it to the floor, her beautiful back exposed to her drawers.

She faced him and lowered herself onto his lap.

He almost passed out. She took his face in her hands, her thumbs stroking his cheekbones. "I want to be clear, Lukasz." She nodded. "Understand what I mean?"

He inhaled and kissed her, frantically, forcefully, and she returned his kiss without hesitation. She slipped his shirt off him and undid his fly allowing him to get his pants off. She moved against him and he spun her onto her back, convinced of her desire.

Lying on his side, he drew along the length of her body, fingers sweeping over her hip, into the dip of her waist, fluttering over her stomach, her breasts, and her legs, removing her drawers.

She ran her hands along his back, pulling him close. He buried his face in her neck, moving with her, exploring, always waiting for her to give before he took. Mary's touch grew more urgent and firm, lingering, dizzying him.

"Mary, Mary, Mary," he said as he kissed her.

She shifted and pulled him onto her. He paused above her, their eyes locked. "Be with me forever."

He smoothed her hair, waiting for her response.

"Mary?"

And she pulled him into her, answering with quiet taking, letting him know that she wasn't surrendering anything to him, but rather they were sharing. They had grown into full love, unexpected and pure, their breath, their very being in unison.

Chapter 63

Mary

Mary woke in the shed and kept the lamp flame low as she got ready to leave. Lukasz's breath fell deep and even as he slept, his face soft, unworried. Mary hoped she had something to do with the peacefulness, that when he'd asked her to be with him forever, he'd meant it.

She smoothed his hair, kissed his forehead, and closed her eyes. Was this what she wanted? What had she done? She exhaled. No, no regrets. She couldn't fathom how it was possible that she had these strong feelings for Lukasz, but they seemed to have been there all along, put there fully developed as if by magic.

Mary told herself to get moving. She would try to approach her parents in a way that wouldn't antagonize them. Most importantly she wanted to make things right with Papa, to at least get rid of the regret that lay heavy in her chest because of their fight. She wasn't sure it was possible, but she had to try.

She took the bent umbrella, smiling at how Zofia Kowalk had insisted that she come inside, that a man who routinely fixed them just happened to be there for dinner.

Walking home, it hit her fully. She stopped and pressed her hand to her chest. She *loved* him. The realization expanded. Impossible, except that it was true. *Hail Mary, full of grace* . . . God must have been coaxing Mary and Lukasz toward each other all along. How else could she explain their coupling—so strong, so fast?

The Christmas star, still shining above, comforted her as she finished her walk home. Not one light was burning when she entered the house, and she gripped the bent umbrella in case Mr. Cermak lurked.

She snuck into her bedroom, changed into her nightgown, and slipped into bed beside Ann. Thinking of Lukasz, she marveled at what she was experiencing. Finally she knew exactly what women meant when they said a man made them safe, protected. She pulled the quilt tight, recalling Lukasz's strength wrapped around her. She knew right then how her adulthood would start. A good, strong man. How magical it was to be in love with him.

Ann shifted, flopping her arm over Mary's waist. The day Mrs. Dunn asked her if she loved Samuel, Mary had struggled to name her feelings. How silly that seemed in light of what had sprouted between her and Lukasz in mere days. Love—the only word that came to her when she thought of Lukasz.

How was it possible?

God? Mary, mother of Jesus? A magical pink moon?

All of them.

What else could explain such a thing?

**

Mary woke later than usual after getting home from the shed so late, donned her robe and shoes, and went into the family room, where all her siblings were sitting around the Christmas tree digging into presents.

Her parents turned to Mary and nodded but didn't indicate they knew anything about her had changed or that they cared she'd been gone since the scene with Mr. Cermak and Papa.

Johnny looked up, gift in his lap. "Mary! You slept so late! I wanted to sit with you at Mass."

Mary felt tears rising and she shot a glance at her parents not knowing how to respond.

"Open it." Ann started to pull on the ribbon that tied Johnny's stocking closed, drawing attention away from where Mary had been the night before.

They all laughed as Johnny opened his stocking filled with oranges he didn't want, but he loved the shotgun he received. With whooping, oohs and awwws, the family opened gifts, smiling like no other day of the year. Rose received a doll and a remade dress and resoled shoes. George opened a used baseball mitt and brand-new baseball. Ann and Victoria were given new summer dresses and winter hats, scarves, and mittens. And Mary was given a new coat. Her breath left her at the sight. She could feel the way her remade, little girl coat pulled across her back when she moved. "This is so . . . I can't take this. Not after everything—"

"You'll take it," Matka said. "My daughter needs a nice coat."

They silently agreed not to discuss the hidden things for the moment and Mary was grateful. It was the best part of being a family, the letting go of trouble until a better time came to address it.

Mary knew Matka stowed Christmas presents away all year long so even in lean years, the children had things to open. Her guilt bore deep. She hoped her parents took everything from her hiding place to pay the mortgage. That might help alleviate her sorrow.

When the children finished opening presents, Mary went to her parents and started to explain how sorry she was to have been dishonest with them about her hidden hope chest items.

They accepted her apology.

"We gave everything over to Mr. Cermak," her father said. "Only way he'd leave. Had to kick him in the ass. I believe that he . . . attacked you. He admitted as much. He lies, and I won't stand for hearing such things said about my daughter."

Mary wondered if he meant Mr. Cermak had told them she'd been to the blacksmith's shed, but she wasn't going to ask.

"Ann told us," Matka said. "He bothered her, too."

Mary covered her mouth. Had she failed to protect her sister?

"We didn't know how much he fancied ya, that he'd try to force ya to . . . whatever he did. He admitted it. Only once turned to Ann, and she told us after ya left," Matka said.

"Told him no discussion." Papa glared at his wife, who looked down. "Took advantage of my working so much." He took Matka's hand and pulled her close. Mary felt a great release at this news, at what she was seeing. Matka nodded.

Her mother held up a loaf of bread. "To thank Kasandra, her family. Take it later."

Mary was confused but didn't ask what they were thanking Kasandra's family for.

"Passed her parents walking home after Mass," Matka said. "Said ya were helping finish up Christmas dresses for Kasandra's little sisters and you'd be late with 'em. That was nice of ya. Nice of Kasandra to include ya after…"

Mary sighed with relief that her friend had somehow known to cover for her the night before.

There was a knock at the door. Mary's heart seized, thinking Mr. Cermak might return. Papa answered. There was a long pause, and Mary assumed it was Mrs. Pierce dropping off her annual fruitcake.

Papa's voice grew loud. Mary and Matka went to the door.

Lukasz? Mary's heart pounded.

Papa pressed Lukasz's chest, backing him out the door.

"Papa!"

He spun around.

Mary went to Lukasz and pulled him into the house, taking his hat.

"What's he doin' here?" Matka asked.

Mary threaded her arm through his, pulling him close. He looked at Mary, then approached her parents.

"I'm here again to ask . . ." He pushed his hand through his hair. "No. This time I'm . . . I ask for beautiful Mary's hand to marry."

Mary couldn't stop smiling. She willed her parents to agree, to see her excitement and understand.

Matka stared Lukasz up and down. Papa scowled.

Mary couldn't take her eyes off of Lukasz. She was so proud.

Papa paced, shaking his head.

"Please, Papa," Mary said.

He clenched his jaw. "He's got nothing to offer. Nothing."

Lukasz flinched. Mary nodded at him, wanting to encourage him. He straightened, exuding the strength she'd witnessed so many times before she'd fallen in love with him. It didn't matter that Lukasz was so much shorter than her father, than she. Lukasz embodied all the grit and brawn she needed in a man. And more. She thought of his hands making delicate wire sculptures, his fingers flitting over her skin.

"He's got plenty to offer. More than enough."

Papa grabbed the poker and stabbed at the dying fire.

Mary went to him. "He's strong as anything. He's got a good job." Papa shook off her hand. She put it back on his shoulder. "He's like you, Papa. I want to marry a man like you."

Papa turned, pushing his broad shoulders back, stretching to his full height. His lip curled like a dog. "Jobs come and go. Men get sick and bodies break when you work with your hands," he said. "Ask Matka."

Mary added a log to the fire, knowing Papa and Matka needed to hear more, different arguments. "He's put away nearly enough for a home."

Papa growled and shook his head.

"Yinz don't know each other," Matka said.

Mary laughed. "You're ready to marry me to Ralph. I don't know him."

"I planned for her to marry an American," Papa said. "She won't be American if she marries you. It's the law. No."

"I'm American." Lukasz pressed his chest. "In here."

"Not the same," Mrs. Lancos told him.

Mary wanted to scream that her father still hadn't applied for citizenship and he'd been here for nearly two decades.

"As soon as I can," Lukasz said. "I'll declare my intent to be American. Just two years."

Papa gestured at Lukasz. "And he's small. Look at him."

Mary and Lukasz looked at each other. Mary recalled being in his arms, in his bed, under him. "He's not."

Lukasz smiled.

"Look at him," Papa said. "Really look. Because once something like this is done, it's done."

A smile came to Mary, turning into what felt like a silly grin. "He's brave and strong. And he's always there when I need him. And he's good with his hands."

Papa dug his hand through his hair. "What the hell's that mean?"

Mary didn't know what to say to explain what she meant, thinking of the delicate wire animals and angels he made.

"Crazy," Papa said. "A match made for economics is reasonable. All this other shit is useless. You don't know him." He pointed at Lukasz. "And you don't know her."

Lukasz looked at Mary, still smiling. There were no right words to explain. But the two of them understood. She'd never felt so connected to another human being.

Mary and Lukasz reached for each other's hands.

"He wants a nice home and a mess of kids and . . . me."

"We have dreams. We have love," Lukasz said in slow, precise English.

Papa shook his head. "Love. *Christ.* Love is nothing." He stepped closer to Lukasz, pushing his chest out. "All this dreaming and ideas, and yet I don't see that you have a house or anything solid to offer my daughter. Just last night, I kicked a man out of here who had more to give her."

Mary could see Lukasz considering what Papa said. He would remember what Mary had said about Mr. Cermak.

"What about the big lemon-smelling house ya want?" Matka asked. "What about all that stuff Mrs. Dunn put into yer head about life? What about how she thinks ya deserve a king?" Mary flinched with every word, knowing Matka had chosen them to wound Lukasz, but he kept his gaze steady on Mary, holding her up.

Mary thought about what an Irish home, lemony and sweet, had meant to her for so long, the bathroom attached to a bedroom for guests, the bathtub. She could still smell the oils and lotions when she thought of them.

Then she remembered the night before in the shed, the dingy cot, the chill and smoky scent in the air, her body charting his, all of it. Never once in that time did she think she wanted something other than those moments in that run-down shed.

Mary pushed her chin up and squeezed Lukasz's hand. "I don't need any of that. Not when we're together."

Her parents choked as if they'd been kicked in the belly at the same exact time. Matka tossed her hands in the air.

"Not good enough. I won't agree to less than she deserves," Papa said. "So I'll ask again. What do you have to offer my daughter?"

Lukasz narrowed his gaze on Papa.

So much, Mary thought. *Tell him about the money you've saved, about how you could build the house yourself, about the tiny animals you make, and the way you earned your job by throwing hundred-pound wire bundles faster than two men at a time.*

Lukasz inhaled and stepped toward Papa. "What do *you* have for her to take into marriage to someone else?"

Papa's eyes blazed and he balled his fists. "What did you say?"

The two men stared at each other. Papa's breath went wild and the scratch in his chest that always brought his cough was building. Lukasz stood tree still against Papa's silent threat, his massive looming.

Mary stepped toward Papa to calm him, but before she got near, he charged Lukasz, throwing a punch.

Lukasz whipped his hand into the air. He caught Papa's fist, stopping him midpunch.

"Fucking Polak," Papa grunted.

Lukasz twisted Papa's arm behind his back, bending him over. Mary and Matka froze. Even with Papa's health problems, Mary'd never seen him as vulnerable to another man, to anything besides illness.

"I *love* her." Lukasz leaned on Papa's bent back. "I love Mary with more than mountainsides. Strong as steel, I feel for her."

Lukasz's garbled comparisons charmed what was left of Mary to charm.

Papa struggled for a few pitiful moments then gave up, going to his knees. Lukasz released him. Mary and Matka rushed to help Papa up, but he swatted their hands away. He staggered upright and crossed the room, clutching his arm. Matka went to him, asking if he was all right.

He shook his wife's hands off again and glared at Mary, then Lukasz. "Can't live on love."

"But Papa—"

"Just ask my wife."

Lukasz put his hand to his chest. "I don't plan to buy a home with love."

The four of them stood in the room, shifting their weight, unsure of what should happen next. Papa was cowed and Mary was proud. Lukasz, his shy gaze going to the floor, reminded her nothing had been settled. The tension had only lessened.

Matka shook her head. "This matter can't be settled right now. Not before Christmas breakfast."

Lukasz glanced at Mary and then her father.

Papa's eyes bore a despondency that was different from what Mary had seen in him before. He waved his hand through the air, a lion giving over his pride to the next generation. *Was* he surrendering? Papa's frailty hit her hard. She'd humiliated him by bringing an unwelcome male, a stronger, quicker one, into the house. She felt as though she'd embarrassed him as Matka had in that tavern, even if Mary wasn't screaming at him in front of fifty friends.

Mary'd never wanted to dishonor Papa. But for once, someone thought of her well-being. Well, for the second time. An astonishing sense of love washed over her in knowing that Lukasz stood up for her, protected her, and she couldn't have guessed what that would feel like until that very moment.

"Go ahead," Papa said to Matka. "Feed the strongman. Must be starving, an animal like him."

Papa left the room, Matka glancing over her shoulder in utter confusion as she followed him into the kitchen. Mary ran to Lukasz. He wrapped her in his arms, holding tight.

She cupped his face and kissed him hard before latching her arms around his neck.

"Mary, Mary, Mary," his words unfurled into her ear.

"My strongman."

"My mermaid," he said, rubbing her back.

"My love," she said wishing they could steal away to the shed.

"Everything is fine," Lukasz whispered, his breath against her ear sending thrills over her skin.

Mary was drawn back to reality. She pulled away from Lukasz. She looked toward the kitchen, thinking her mother had changed her mind a little too quickly.

"I don't know, Lukasz. I just don't know."

Chapter 64

Mary

After Christmas, Mary invited Lukasz to dinner a couple times a week. She worked extra hard at stretching the food so her mother wouldn't use that as a case against him. Mr. Cermak was out of the house, and she was relieved not to have to look over her shoulder for him.

Though her parents allowed Lukasz to attend dinner, they weren't particularly warm to him. Still, it was a beginning in Mary's eyes, and she worked doubly hard to be cheerful and productive at all times.

The nights Lukasz visited were pleasurable not only for Mary but her siblings, with all the handstand contests, somersault races, and arm wrestling—which he often pretended to lose. But it was the other nights, the ones when her parents thought she'd gone with friends after work, that Mary lived for.

She and Lukasz would leave the mill separately, and no matter the route each took, they ended up in the little blacksmith shed in the woods. It was late enough that Mark was done with his work and they had it to themselves.

Whoever got there first stoked the fire. It took only moments before their clothes were off and they were nestled on the cot, snug under a wool blanket, legs and arms intertwined, finding the path into each other's hearts by way of their bodies, defying everything she had ever heard about the order of things when falling in love.

They lay next to each other in the firelight, fingers doubling back on the skin they'd already explored, each time feeling new.

Lukasz gasped when he rolled onto his side, his rib aching. Chaffy had lost his grip on his bundle and grazed Lukasz with it as it flew across the mill. Mary caressed oil into his skin, his wiry muscles relaxing under her touch.

She massaged up his chest and into his shoulders. "Be careful," she said. "Can't have you injured, can we?"

"Right there, dig in there," he said.

She kneaded the top of his shoulder. "You'll bounce back nicely."

"If only I was as resilient as you, Mary."

"Me?"

"You're strong and resilient, like steel itself."

She smiled at the way he used the word, resilient. "Like you too, iron strong."

He turned on his back and pulled her near him, her head on his chest. "I'm iron, yes. I won't break easy, but I can't flex like steel, like you. I see it clear. Nothing turns you too hard. You feel sadness and then let it move through you. I feel sadness and hold it like those whiskers you shave off the nails and stick to magnets."

She held him tight. "That's the loveliest thing I've ever heard."

He kissed the top of her head. "I meant it when I said I wanted to be together forever. I can't live like this, hiding."

She rolled onto her back, arm flung over her head. He kissed her breast, the hollow of her stomach, and back up. "Soon," she said. "My parents are warming to the idea of you and me."

Lukasz got on one elbow, brushing her hair from her eyes. "Sometimes you just have to act. The Mary I fell in love with doesn't worry about what people think."

Mary thought of Mrs. Dunn and how much she wanted her approval. She couldn't imagine telling Mrs. Dunn about Lukasz, even though she wanted to so much. But after all Mary and her mentor had discussed about homes and hope chests and the way that Mrs. Dunn's life had been transformed because of the man she married, Mary knew Lukasz would be deemed beneath her. A tug of shame came with the thought. Because it wasn't just that she thought Mrs. Dunn would be disappointed, it was that Mary worried *she* might be, too. Was Lukasz less than the dream she'd been wanting to fulfill or just a different shape of it? Who exactly was Mary disappointing more?

She shrugged and rolled away from him. He spooned her and slipped his arm around her waist. "What's wrong?"

"I don't know when my parents will say yes. And they aren't just *people*, I don't want to disrespect them. They're my family. All of them. And Mrs. Dunn . . . I can't even explain what she's meant to me."

He kissed her cheek. "This is America, Mary. The greatest country on earth. I came here knowing that people can make any decision they want. Aneta chose another man even though we were matched. Surely you can choose who you want."

She nodded but said nothing, a gap widening between them like every time she snuck out of their nest to leave for home. She understood Papa's concern that she would lose her citizenship if she married Lukasz. On the cusp of agreeing to marriage, Mary felt her Americanness deeper than before, as much as her breath or heartbeat or bone. The thought of abandoning it made her resist the sensations that filled her heart and body, that lured her toward Lukasz. "But I'll lose my citizenship if we marry. With vows spoken and a couple of signatures, I'll be Polish, as though I swore an oath to a king I never even heard of."

He squeezed her tight. "Two more years and I can declare my intentions to become a citizen. Then you get your citizenship back. I want that. That's why I came here."

She thought of her parents again. "Maybe we should wait. Once you declare, we can marry. Like you said, it's just two years away. By then, my parents will adore you as much as I do. And—"

He tilted her chin toward him. "Wait? When I think of you, my heart stops. For just the length of my breath, but long enough that I notice it, just enough to remind me you are everything. If my heart stops that many times between now and when you say yes to me, I might drop dead. You stop and start my heart with just one thought, one touch, one kiss. I don't ever want to leave America. I'll never leave you, Mary. As long as you want me, that's all I need. I want to be your American husband."

She thought again of Papa and Matka. Her father had been in America since 1890, and he still hadn't declared his intention for citizenship. That ridiculous fact jarred her. She kissed Lukasz, then pulled back. "And you don't want to go back to Myscowa?"

"Not for anything."

"Ever?"

"Never."

"And you'll apply for citizenship the minute you can?"

He nodded, brushing her lips with his fingers. "Mary Lancos, I promise you I'll be the best American and take care of you every minute we breathe. I know what you want—your lemon house. I can give that to you. I can."

He buried his head into her neck. "I've never felt like this before. This . . ." His lips moved against her skin, sending chills throughout her body. "Love. It's so strong, my heart hurts. It's the dream we both had."

Her eyes burned. She heard his words, felt them against her skin. His intentions seared into her soul the same as if he'd sworn them in court. She believed him to her very core. She believed that he would protect her, love her, provide for her.

In nearly every way she barely knew him, yet she felt as if they'd lived one thousand lives together. She ran her finger along his jaw. "I feel it too, Lukasz. I do."

He pulled her on top of him, and they explored the innermost parts of each other. After, they dozed, and Mary told herself she'd have to leave soon to finish her chores at home, that she'd just close her eyes for a moment.

Chapter 65

Mary

Mary woke naked and bleary-eyed, and she realized she was still at the shed. She scrambled off the cot in a panic. She yanked on her stockings, chemise, dress, and boots. Lukasz got up and took her by the shoulders. "It's all right. Let's tell them. Right now. I'm begging you—"

"What time is it?"

He kissed her and looked out the curtain while she smoothed and tied her hair into a knot at the nape of her neck.

"Eight thirty, I'd say."

She exhaled. "I should have been at Mrs. Dunn's a half hour ago." She slapped her hands over her mouth. "My chores at home. Matka's going to kill me."

"It's time. Tonight. We'll tell your parents we're going to get married."

"We can't just tell them." Mary sat on the cot and tied the laces. "They have to give me permission. I'm not old enough. And they won't if I don't handle this right."

"It's America."

"I know, I know. But in this America, I still have parents telling me what to do."

"Parents you had to keep secrets from, that wanted you to marry a man you didn't want. They need you but give nothing."

His words crushed her. "They're just trying to survive."

"You deserve a home, a husband, children."

"I know. But just . . . not yet."

He pulled her into him, kissing her hard. They laid their foreheads against each other. "I love you, Mary. More than anything in this entire universe. Last night, we were one. We are married as much as any paper would say. My *syrena.* My dream come to life."

This made her smile. "And you are mine."

"I'm your mermaid?"

She wiggled away, backing toward the door. "My dream come to life. You are that, Lukasz. The dream I didn't know I had."

"Go on, then. But tonight we talk to your parents. Tonight we begin our life together."

**

When she entered Mrs. Dunn's kitchen, she found her sitting at the kitchen table with her face in her hands, weeping.

Mrs. Harper banged her spoon on a pot. "Oh, thank God you're here."

Mary kneeled in front of Mrs. Dunn. "I'm so sorry I'm late. I didn't mean to be so inconsiderate. I was just—"

Mrs. Dunn dropped her hands from her face and gripped Mary's wrists. "You didn't do anything, Mary. It's not that at all."

"Here come the waterworks again. Get your waders on."

Mary glanced at Mrs. Harper, whose back was to them as she stirred her pot.

"The kids?" Mary stood and looked for any sign of any one of them.

"They're fine."

"Better'n fine," Mrs. Harper said. "I nearly took my spoon to the lot of 'em. Sent the whole squalling pack of 'em into the streets for the day."

Mrs. Dunn pushed the chair across from her back with her foot. "Sit."

Mary removed her hat and coat.

"We have to leave," Mrs. Dunn said.

"Here it comes," Mrs. Harper said.

"Please, Mrs. Harper. Allow me my sorrows."

"Just tryin' to help."

Mary looked around. "Leave?"

Mrs. Dunn smiled through tears. "Indiana."

"The Gary Works?" Mary had heard how large and important they were to the United States Steel Company.

"One and only," Mrs. Harper said.

Mrs. Dunn nodded. "It's quite the promotion. He'll run the whole damn thing." She pulled a balled-up handkerchief from her sleeve and dabbed her eyes.

Mary's head pounded. She swallowed hard at the thought of not seeing Mrs. Dunn regularly. "Wow."

"Wow's right. But it's not what I want. Apparently, I have as much say in the move as the kitchen sink."

"This ain't the first time, Mrs. Dunn," Mrs. Harper said.

Mary thought of the other families who'd lived in the Dunns' house before. Irish, Scottish, and Irish again. She couldn't imagine another family in this house now, no matter what their nationality. "I never thought of you moving."

Mrs. Dunn blew her nose into her hanky.

"Maybe you'll be back," Mary said.

Mrs. Harper scoffed.

Mary ignored the commentary and slid to the edge of her seat. "They want to build that zinc mill, and they're building all those homes in Cement City for the families of management. Donora's only getting bigger. I bet they send you back lickety-split."

Mrs. Dunn cupped Mary's cheek. "Oh, Mary. I do love your optimism. There've been times I've fed off it, your energy and smile and ease. It's almost as though you were teaching me, not the other way around."

Mary wanted to tell Mrs. Dunn what had happened at her house with her treasures. But she was too embarrassed, especially with Mrs. Harper butting into their conversation.

"Life never goes as expected," Mrs. Dunn said.

"Sure as shit right," Mrs. Harper said under her breath.

"Please, Mrs. Harper. Go tidy up the front rooms. Mary and I are talking."

Mrs. Harper adjusted the flame on the stovetop and waltzed past them, tears filling her eyes. "I know my opinions aren't wanted here."

Mrs. Dunn sighed. "I wouldn't have believed I'd feel this way about leaving here seven years ago. What difference does it make if the home I keep's in Donora or Gary? It's all the same."

Mrs. Dunn took Mary's hand and squeezed. "I can't think of anything more miserable than starting this same life over somewhere else, without anyone I know . . . Mrs. Harper, that old python. You. Especially you."

Mary tried to keep her composure and be the mature woman Mrs. Dunn had taught her to be. But holding her hands, sitting in the kitchen with nothing but the tick of the clock, her emotions bubbled. She leapt up and hugged Mrs. Dunn. "I don't want you to go. I can't live without you. I can't."

Chapter 66

Lukasz

After his shift, Lukasz washed up, put on a clean shirt, and headed up the street toward Mary's. He wished he'd finished the ring already. He'd made one and then melted it back down when he realized it was far too much like the ones he'd made for Aneta years before. Mary needed something special, something he couldn't really even imagine yet. He considered taking some of his savings for the house and buying a ring, but he decided it would be more important and meaningful to prove his worth in property than in store-bought jewelry.

Still, he didn't want to wait to talk to Mary's parents. He'd thought about it all day, rehearsing how he would explain his intentions, imagining every objection he might hear from the Lancoses and his responses. Maybe it was simply a matter of them seeing him and Mary together again to understand how much he loved her.

Like Mary, he was surprised by the intensity and speed of the love that had developed between them. He was prepared to explain that while he knew it was fast, that didn't lessen the depth of his love. He understood giving Mary a life took more than just love. He would protect their daughter and give her a life bigger and better than any other man could, even if he started with less, even without being American. Yet.

He worked on his English with Chaffy all day long, shouting over the machinery and talking on breaks. No Polish.

He arrived at Mary's home, taking deep breaths. He tucked in his shirt and brushed lint from his coat. Victoria answered the door, her eyes full of tears.

Lukasz looked over her shoulder. No one else was there. "What's wrong?"

"They're in the bedroom," she said, stepping aside to let him in. "Papa's sick."

Lukasz looked toward the hallway that led to the bedrooms. Had he understood that right? "Sick?"

Victoria gripped her chest and made a coughing noise. "Really bad."

"Let me help. What do you need?"

Victoria disappeared down the hall.

Lukasz strained to hear what was being said.

Victoria returned, shaking her head. "Mary said go on. She'll find you when she can leave. Stay healthy." Victoria pushed him toward the door. "She said to force you out."

He turned and took her hand, patting it. "I can do something."

"No. No. Go on."

Another knock came and Victoria opened the door, letting in a man with a leather bag. He shook Lukasz's hand, probably thinking he belonged to the family.

Victoria gestured toward the hallway. "Back room." She dropped her face into her hands and sobbed.

Lukasz didn't think it was his place to hug her, but he couldn't stand to see her cry. He patted her shoulder and her back. Once he did, Victoria fell into Lukasz, grasping at him.

He held her tight, still patting her. "The doctor's here. Your papa'll get better now."

Her sobs slowed and she backed away, rubbing her nose with the back of her hand.

He handed her a handkerchief from his pocket, relieved that he'd picked up a clean one after changing his clothes. "He's going to be all right. He's a strong man. I see that every time I'm here."

She smiled through tears. "Thank you."

"I'll check back. If there's anything you need at all, Mary knows where to find me." He started toward the door.

"Here, Lukasz," Victoria said. She held the handkerchief toward him.

He shook his head. "You need it." He wanted a concrete reason to have to return, even as little a reason as retrieving a hanky. "Tell Mary . . ." His voice dropped off. He wanted to say to tell Mary he loved her and longed for her, longed to experience the way he saw the world with new eyes every time they were together. "Tell her I'll be back. That I have something for her."

"I will," Victoria said.

He left, feeling as though his great plans to make his dream with Mary a reality were obscured again, like Donora's cloud-covered skies and the cottony gray fog that hid away the golden sun nearly every day.

Chapter 67

Mary

Mary helped her mother explain to the doctor how her father's coughing came in tides, growing stronger and deeper, swallowing him, then weakening his breath to panting until it deepened, consuming him all over again. Only vomiting interrupted his coughing intervals.

The doctor shooed Mary out of the room to give her father privacy. She held back sobs for her father's ravaged body, for the lost opportunity for her and Lukasz to talk to her parents that night, and for Mrs. Dunn moving out of Donora.

Voices drew Mary to the end of the hallway. Lukasz and Victoria were talking, and he comforted her with the gentle kindness Mary had come to know.

Mary started to move toward them, but the bedroom door whined open behind her and the doctor waved Mary toward him.

He asked her to warm some water and bring it, and as she started toward the kitchen, Victoria entered the hall and stopped at the sight of her. She touched her sister's cheek. "You're crying."

"I am?"

Victoria handed her a handkerchief. "Here."

"Thank you." Mary dabbed her nose and folded it, noticing the embroidery at the edge. Curlicue paisley swirls.

"Mary!" Matka said from the bedroom.

Mary stuffed the handkerchief back into Victoria's hand. "Put the water on," Mary said over her shoulder as she ran toward Matka's voice, ready to help in any way she could.

Chapter 68

Mary

Despite Mary picking up a mild strain of Papa's sickness, she went to work regularly for the next week. Victoria stayed home from school to help their mother, while Ann and Rose fell ill too. The family couldn't afford to lose Mary's wages on top of Papa's and Mr. Cermak's board.

Papa had been diagnosed with a complicated strain of the flu, every major part of him experiencing some bit of awful ill—vomiting, diarrhea, and a cough made worse by chronic lung issues. Mary worked the day shift with Lukasz working night turn.

Her work was mindless enough, at times too mindless, and her thoughts wandered to the way Lukasz made her feel. A pang would come in her chest when she thought of him, and she realized it was yearning. The sensation would sink into her bones, taking her breath away. Love. She'd never imagined that a person could be utterly saturated by thoughts, sensations, and scents of the one they loved.

She exited the mill and heard Lukasz calling her. He caught up with her, grabbed her arm, and led her off to the side. They fell into an embrace and separated quickly. He pulled her into the shadow and hugged her again. She pushed him away.

"No, no, the flu's tearing through the house. If you get it, you'll never forgive me. It's a nightmare come to life."

"You're sick?"

She nodded.

He palmed her forehead, his eyes worried. "Not warm."

"I'm getting past it now. Everyone but Matka and Victoria has spent the last week running to the outhouse."

"You should have sent word. I would have helped. I knew you were coming to work and just thought you were all right."

"I was well enough to work and quick enough to the breakroom when needed. We need the money."

"I'll help pay what's missing to your household, your father's wages."

Overwhelmed, she let go of all she'd been holding inside. She collapsed into him, forgetting she didn't want to make him sick.

He caressed her back and whispered, "I'll take care of you, Mary. Anyone you love, I'll love. I'll take care of all of you. But we need to tell your parents."

She couldn't imagine talking to her papa about this, especially not after he'd been so sick. The time was wrong. Yet there was that yearning.

She buried her face in Lukasz's shoulder, never wanting him to let her go. She wished he could scoop her up and take her home the way he had the night she went into the river. She wished her parents would have loved Lukasz right from the start and that they'd view him as a valuable addition to the family, not someone beneath them all.

"I've missed you so much, Mary. I can't sleep, thinking of you."

A siren sounded to signal the mill shift had started. She pushed away from him. "You can't be late. None of us will have money if they dock your pay or fire you."

He nodded and kissed her.

They separated, Lukasz running into the mill just as the final screech of the shift siren sounded. Mary leaned against the mill wall, her stomach agitating, the flu still threatening. The nausea swirled and finally demanded to be released. She steadied herself with a hand on the wall and threw up. She wiped her mouth and trekked home, up the winding hills and steep stairs, wanting to do nothing but crawl into bed, to feel Lukasz's strength beside her.

Chapter 69

Lukasz

Lukasz stopped by the Lancos home after night turn with a dozen doughnuts he'd bought from Millie Utinski's bakery on the way up the hill. Mary was gone, working at Mrs. Dunn's. Lukasz offered money to Mrs. Lancos. She looked as if she might accept, but she refused it, taking the doughnuts instead.

"We're fine without any help. Fine." She shut the door on Lukasz.

Glad she had at least taken the doughnuts, feeling like that meant progress in getting her to accept him, he descended the front porch stairs. Johnny approached with a pail. "Treasure, Lukasz!" he said, raising it over his head. Lukasz laughed, remembering when he and his friends used to hope and search for treasure buried near their bend in the Wisloka River.

Johnny held the bucket up and Lukasz dug his hand into the rocky stash to go along with Johnny's dream. He brushed dirt aside and pulled out some of the rocks, blowing on them.

Lukasz almost didn't look closely at what was in the boy's hand, but Johnny's gasp make him pay attention. "See?"

Lukasz leaned in.

"A clear stone . . . and a pink and a blue," Johnny said.

They were rough, but Lukasz could see their beauty. "Where'd you find these?" he asked.

"Docks on Webster side." Johnny puffed his chest out. "Been rowing Papa across like Mary used to. Well, he kept me waiting, and a shiny bit of somethin' caught my eye so I started digging. Mary once told me about a pink moon she saw on the river. Said it was dropping snow like rain, but it looked pink, jewels from above . . . pink ones, she told me."

Pink moon? Lukasz had seen a pink moon once—the night his mermaid had come up the riverbank. Had Mary seen it too?

"And look," Johnny said, proud. He picked up more stones, pink and clear, covered with dirt. The small pink rock looked as if it could have been chipped from the moon that night.

"Mary said I'm doing a good job."

Lukasz smiled at the mention of her. He'd begun to feel her absence more fiercely than he'd felt her presence; the thumping in his chest was a confluence of loss and love.

"Can I have one of the pink ones?"

Johnny cocked his head, keeping his eyes on his bounty.

"Please? It's perfect for something I'm doing for Mary."

Johnny bent closer to Lukasz's hand and shuffled the stones back and forth. He plucked one up and gave it to Lukasz. "That's the best one. Pinkest one of all."

Lukasz gently squeezed the back of Johnny's neck. "It's perfect, Johnny. Thank you." He reached into his pocket and drew two pennies out.

Johnny's face lit up. "Wow."

"Take them." Lukasz pressed them into Johnny's hand. "You earned them."

Johnny stuffed the coins into his pocket. "My own money." He threw his arms around Lukasz's waist. Lukasz patted his back then Johnny dashed away, taking the stairs by two.

**

Lukasz finally knew exactly what he needed to do for Mary's ring. He ran his finger over the stone in his pocket, its rough pink moon edges. He took it out and studied it, nearly walking into a tree. It was pink, all right. He'd seen plenty of clear quartz before, had found it on riverbanks, in mines, or tossed aside from the mill's coal hauls that were needed to make the coke. He had never paid much attention to it until now, until Johnny had unearthed some pink in just the spot that it might have fallen from the very moon he and Mary had stood under the night she'd come rising out of the river. But before he worked on it, he wanted to see Mary. Just for one second to know she was all right.

He turned back toward Thompson Avenue, asking a man headed to work which house was Mr. Dunn's.

When he was sure which house was correct, he went up to the porch and knocked on the front door. The door opened to Mary, a baby on her hip.

She jolted. "Lukasz."

"I needed to see you to make sure you're all right. You feel better?"

She glanced over her shoulder. "I do."

A figure came into shadow behind Mary.

"Everything all right?" It was a woman's voice. Mrs. Dunn? The Mrs. Harper Mary had mentioned?

Mary stepped toward Lukasz, pulling the door closed a bit. "I have a lot left to do, Lukasz."

"I'll meet you after to walk you home."

She shook her head. "I'm staying here tonight."

"Mary?" a woman said, opening the door fully.

He immediately knew it was Mrs. Dunn from her fine pale blue dress, coiffed hair with jeweled combs, and sparkling necklace.

The woman took the baby from Mary. "Do you need help, Mary?"

She shook her head. "No. This is Lukasz. My friend."

"Oh. Well, Lukasz, it's nice to meet you. When you're ready, Mary, the boys need help with shoes."

Mary nodded. Mrs. Dunn smiled at them both and entered the house.

Mary backed away from Lukasz. "I have to go."

He stuck his hand out to keep the door open. "I tried to give your mother money, but she didn't want it."

"We'll talk tomorrow."

"Mrs. Dunn said you could talk now."

Mary looked over her shoulder. "I can't. Really, I have to go."

A male voice came from behind Mary. It was muffled, but Lukasz would know it anywhere. Mr. Dunn. Why wasn't he at work?

Mary's face whitened and she slammed the door.

Lukasz hesitated, his pride smarting at being shoved away. But he knew it was risky, that Mr. Dunn might fire one of them if seeing Lukasz at his house caused him to think Mary had lied for him.

He tore down the stairs and ran to the next corner before turning back just as someone shut the Dunn's front door.

Chapter 70

Mary

Mary held it in as long as she could. She bolted to the mill locker room to throw up. Kasandra, on her last shift before quitting since her wedding date was near, had done much of Mary's work that day. When she returned to the line, Kasandra stared, pointing at her.

"You're in trouble," she said.

Mary cringed as if she'd been hit in the belly. Her father's words came to her. "Berta's ruined. She's in the rice."

Kasandra took Mary's shoulder. "*You are.*"

Mary shook her head.

"I suspected, but you just confirmed it."

Mary began sorting nails again, keeping her gaze there. It had entered her mind, but there was so much illness in the house, it was easy to dismiss the thought. "I didn't confirm a thing."

"Oh yes, you did. You're white as a ghost. Even if your mind doesn't admit it, your body knows."

Mary shook her head.

"Listen. No one knows but me. I saw you and Lukasz together outside the mill last week, and I just added it all up." Kasandra put her fingers to her lips and turned them as if she was locking something away. "I won't say a word. But if you're this sick, someone else will notice eventually. And then . . . well, you know."

Panic swept Mary. She worked faster and faster, trying to ignore what all of that meant. She'd been stupid, so lost in love that she didn't even worry it might happen. She'd done such a fine job of ignoring the possibility she hadn't even prayed about the matter. She swallowed her nausea. Too in love with Lukasz, too lost in the terrain of the couple they were becoming. No. It wasn't happening. It just wasn't.

**

Mary ran home, hoping she might shake the baby right out of her body if she ran hard enough. Plenty of women saw their pregnancies end early, too early, and they were told they'd been doing too much and needed rest.

She went directly home, thinking it wasn't true. And if it was, how would she tell Lukasz? He wanted to marry her more than anything. She believed that, but this changed it all. Her salary was always figured into their talks about buying property, building a home. And Papa. She imagined his face, Matka's too. She couldn't think of a good way to set this truth free.

What if she'd been wrong? What if she'd chosen Lukasz in a moment of weakness, out of her desire to leave her house, wanting to feel loved, wanting to love but not caring who the person was, just wanting out of the life she'd been given?

She took the dried laundry to the kitchen. She waited for the irons to heat up. *Keep moving*, she told herself. She put the laundry in piles of like items. What if Papa was right? What if losing her citizenship meant losing her family? What if it kept Lukasz and Mary from their dreams?

The laundry had piled up when they were all sick. Shirtwaists, chemises, skirts, handkerchiefs. She cringed at the sight of the blood-stained handkerchief from Andrzejki. Aneta had been so mean to her that night, but at the Kowalks' on Christmas Eve, she was perfectly polite. Mary set the stained handkerchief aside. It was time to throw it out.

She piled one hanky on top of another, and she noticed that the last one had the same blue paisley swirls as the bloodied one. She stared at it, then dug the stained one back out and set the two beside each other.

When did they get this one? She searched her mind for when they had acquired a matching set of handkerchiefs that weren't even theirs.

Victoria bounded into the kitchen. "Oh, thank God. I was about to cut up undershirts to make hankies."

"You could wash and iron, too. It should be your job by now," Mary said, still staring at the two handkerchiefs.

Victoria leaned on her elbows and ran her finger along the paisley embroidery. "Lukasz lent us two handkerchiefs?"

"Lukasz?"

"Well, they're a match. Look." Victoria drew her finger along the swirl.

Mary shrugged. "Sure looks like it, but no. That one's from that night I got the bloody nose. Aneta gave it to me. Well, threw it at me. But Lukasz never gave me a hanky. Always losing his . . ."

Victoria held the unstained one up. "He gave me this one the night he came when Papa was first sick. I was crying, then the doctor came, and you were crying and you used it."

"Lukasz gave you this?" Mary said, remembering, trying to string thoughts together that didn't quite fit. "You're sure? Lukasz?"

Victoria held them up. "'Course I'm sure." She turned them back and forth. "They're exactly the same. You must not remember him giving you that stained one."

"Oh, I remember exactly when I got that hanky, believe me. But it doesn't make sense. They can't be exactly the same."

Victoria turned them over. "You know what Matka always says."

"The back of a woman's embroidery tells you everything you need to know about her. Don't even need to add initials." Mary said. "Pull out the iris hankies the three of us made for Matka."

Victoria found them. The front looked exactly the same. They turned them over. Victoria's stitching was as neat on the back as on the front. Ann's was a mess, strings crossing back and forth over each other like she was making it up as she went. Mary's was neat, but the telltale mark of her getting bored while stitching, distracted by playing ball with her brothers, was evident. Same exact pattern on the front, but the back told the tale of three separate embroiderers.

"Now look at the paisley ones." The sisters studied the front. A small pretty design in rich blues, both the same. But when they turned them over, the backs looked like crossed railroad tracks; someone as sloppy as Ann had made them. Or as rushed. But the sloppiness was identical on the back of each.

"So we're sure," Mary said. "This hanky's the one Lukasz gave you that night Papa was sick."

"Positive."

"Then . . ."

Victoria leaned in to Mary. "What?"

"I slept with the stained handkerchief the night of Andrzejki." The words were out before Mary could stop them.

"Oh my goodness." Victoria covered mouth with both hands, eyes wide.

"Holy mother of Pete. It worked?" Mary traced the embroidery on each. They matched. Lukasz and Mary were meant to be. "That crazy wives' tale worked?"

Victoria shook her head. "Thank God you got Ralph's shirt out of the bed. That's all I have to say."

It was silly. Mary followed so many traditions to bring luck and blessings throughout the year that she half believed them, teasing her mother when she didn't follow them. But this . . .

Victoria brushed Mary's arm. "What's wrong?"

Mary shook her head.

"You look like that death flu just returned right to you."

Mary shook her head again. "Just . . . It's nothing. But don't tell anyone this. All right?"

"Forgot already," Victoria said flouncing away.

Mary's doubts about Lukasz filtered through her again. She pressed her stomach. Lukasz was strong and determined, but he wasn't a god. Had she chosen wrong, driven by the invisible mandate of some bloody handkerchief? She smiled at the thought. Ridiculous. Yet, perhaps none of this, nothing that developed between her and Lukasz had been her choice at all.

Chapter 71

Mary

It was true. No, it couldn't be. But it was. No, God wouldn't let something like this happen to Mary. Would he? Of course he would. It was the way things worked. She'd been lax with her prayers, broken commandments, fallen deeply in unsanctioned love.

Mary searched her mind for the pattern of her monthlies. They didn't come regularly, but they always eventually came. When was the last? August, she had been at the Eldora Park dance after a baseball game. September, she had skipped swimming because of it. October, she never got it. November? Those months didn't matter anyway. She hadn't had sex with Lukasz until Christmas Eve. January? Nothing. February? Illness. Now mid-March . . .

She exhaled, her hands shaking. She'd no idea when exactly it happened. Maybe she wasn't expecting. So she threw up too much. The flu was lingering in Donora, circling back on entire households.

She stopped. What was she doing? Why was she taking Kasandra's word for it? She shook her head. She didn't want to be with child, but she was satisfied Lukasz was the man for her.

She hadn't told him her suspicions. She thought of how she had shoved him away when he had come to see her at Mrs. Dunn's. Was he angry at her? Should she have talked to him like she'd been given permission to? She couldn't risk Mr. Dunn seeing them together like that.

Again, she luxuriated in the thought that she wasn't having a baby, that she was simply irregular. It was ridiculous to think this could happen so quickly.

Destiny. She knew the handkerchief thing was silly, but she loved it, loved that it had happened.

Still, a dark thread had been sewn into her feelings about good luck. What about all her dreams? All her conversations with Mrs. Dunn? Her own family's dreams for her? If she was having a baby, she'd have to stop working at the mill. Her fate would be tied to a man who couldn't provide all the things she'd imagined for her life. At least not in the way she'd planned—he had nothing to offer but himself and his affection for her. She wanted Lukasz very much, but the loose thread of regret gave her pause every time she thought of her life dreams going away.

She entered Mrs. Dunn's house and started the dishes that Mrs. Harper had left for her. With the Dunns moving soon, Mrs. Harper had to find a new job and had gone for an interview at the O'Malleys' on Norman. There were no other written instructions in the kitchen, so Mary went to find Mrs. Dunn. She ran into her in the foyer, heading toward the kitchen, working lotion into her hands. "This winter's been so rough on my skin." She looked up at Mary. "Listen, I have something very important to ask you."

"Okay."

"Well, I want to ask—Mr. Dunn and I want to ask you to move to Gary with us."

Mary couldn't have been more stunned, even with her current list of surprises.

"You can take care of the children and keep house full time. There's a young man there studying to be a teacher, and he could tutor you and the boys, and before long, you'll be ready to meet some people. Our friends there will have children your age. Of marrying age, is what I mean. People you should know. You've some edges that still need to be refined—like the nail whiskers, easily sanded away—but that's it, Mary. I think you'd meet someone worthy of you if you came with us. A nice fresh start."

Mary couldn't believe what she was hearing, the timing, what it would mean for her . . . if only things were different.

Mrs. Dunn grinned. "I can see how happy you are, Mary. We are too."

She embraced Mary, who was overwhelmed by the offer. The scent of Mrs. Dunn's lotion was too strong and turned Mary's stomach. She broke away and ran to the powder room, making it to the toilet just before it was too late.

She washed her mouth and left the bathroom, one hand over her mouth, the other on her belly.

Mrs. Dunn watched from down the hall, her gaze going from Mary's belly to her face and back again.

Mary drew closer.

"Oh, Mary. No."

Mary swallowed the bile rising in her throat.

"It couldn't be that," Mrs. Dunn said. She looked at the rose-scented lotion in her hand and then back to Mary. "You *are*, aren't you?"

Mary shook her head.

"You're having . . . no . . . a baby?"

Mary couldn't speak. Her hands shook both from throwing up and from Mrs. Dunn knowing what she'd done.

Mrs. Dunn paused, her face sad, eyes watering. Then she took Mary into her arms and led her into the study to the leather settee near the desk. She shut the door and poured her water, letting Mary drink.

Mary looked at the floor, ashamed.

"That rose-scented lotion . . . every blessed time I'm with child, the first sign is that one sniff sends me flying to the bathroom. Like you just did. And you're a peculiar shade of gray. I wore it for half of my babies."

Mary cleared her throat.

Mrs. Dunn put her hand on Mary's. "Do your parents know?"

She shook her head.

"Well."

Mary found the courage to look Mrs. Dunn in the eye. "I'm so sorry I disappointed you."

She cocked her head and smiled. "Do you love him?"

Mary nodded.

"You know, you could still come with us. You could have the baby in Gary—no, Chicago—and then you'll live with us. No one will know. You can continue on the path you planned."

Mary looked away, her face tensing with held-back tears.

"You can," Mrs. Dunn said. "This happens to girls all the time. And they move on. And most of them have none of the inner strength you do or the potential or . . . well, I see you doing so many different things. Running a large household, women's club meetings, helping others who aren't so lucky . . . so many wonderful things."

Mary was dazed by Mrs. Dunn's view of her—the possibilities she saw, and the fact that Mary would never fulfill any of them. Hearing Mrs. Dunn's solutions floated Mary for a moment, made her think that maybe she should just leave with the Dunns, start over where no one expected her to be anything other than what Mrs. Dunn said she was. Imagine starting life that way, people expecting big things from her, believing she'd achieve them.

Mrs. Dunn touched Mary's shoulder. "It happens to many girls, Mary."

If she was to believe all these wonderful things that Mrs. Dunn thought about her, Mary had to tell her the truth.

"It didn't happen *to* me, Mrs. Dunn. I'm so sorry to tell you this, but it's the truth. I wanted it to happen. I love Lukasz."

"The man from the other day. At the door?"

She nodded.

"Mr. Dunn said he thought that was him. He said he suspected . . . well . . ."

"I know he's not the kind of man you wanted for me, the kind *I* thought I wanted . . ."

Mrs. Dunn put her arm around Mary, pulling her close.

"I'm not who you thought I was," Mary said. "I'm not who I thought I was."

Mrs. Dunn patted Mary's head as she laid it on her shoulder. "Oh, Mary. Don't ever say that. A woman like you, a woman who claims her decisions—that's exactly what I thought about you. You're *exactly* who I knew you were."

"But I won't be any of those things that you said. I won't even be American if I marry him. Not until he applies for citizenship. I can't even breathe, thinking of all the things I won't be anymore. Not if I . . . well, what choice do I have? Truly."

"You can choose. But all those things I mentioned take many forms, Mary. Your life will be hard in some ways and easier in others. But that'll be the case even if you come with us. What you need to hold dear, like all the things in your hope chest, is the knowledge that you are magnificent."

Mary sighed, tears streaming her cheeks. The words to the Our Father came to mind . . . trespasses, trespasser . . . Mary had fallen in faith, she was awful—as far from magnificent as a girl could be. The lost hope chest items proved that to her.

"You are, Mary. You are." Mrs. Dunn answered as though she knew the very thing Mary was thinking. "I'm sure Lukasz will give you all the things he's promised and more. I know you wouldn't choose him if that wasn't the case."

Mary exhaled and crossed herself. She wanted to believe in herself as much as Mrs. Dunn did. She had to. If she was going to marry Lukasz, she'd have to trust him, believe that she'd chosen right. And if she had to force it to be right, she would.

Chapter 72

Lukasz

After Lukasz saw Mary at the Dunns' home, a wave of insecurity hit him, taking him back to when Aneta had decided she wanted someone else. The way Mary had referred to him as a friend to Mrs. Dunn hurt him. Mary's refusal to talk to him even when she'd been given permission, stung. Had Mr. Dunn seen the two of them together? Only going to work and not getting fired soothed his mind about that part. But seeing Mary in that grand house, with its heavenly lemon scent that tumbled out when she opened the door, made him question whether he was indeed the best man for her.

Once he sat with his insecurity, he went over all the other things that had pointed Mary and him in the same direction, toward the same house in Donora.

Many times he'd close his eyes and reimagine the scent of the Dunns' home, the one Mary had described with such affection. He didn't have much money, not what he wanted to have before marrying, but with Mary's paycheck, they could do it. He would give her what she wanted, even if not all at the same time.

He'd finished her ring. Jahn, the stonecutter, had helped him shape the rough pink stone to make it fit the ring he'd made, smoothing its roughest parts but keeping little peaks and valleys of pink and clear stone, like the moon that had dropped its rays over the snow the night he'd carried her home from the river.

Lukasz would show her in a million different ways that he understood the sort of life she wanted, that he could give it to her, that what they shared when they lay on the cot and made love was what they'd share every second of the rest of their lives.

He'd heard her father was recovering nicely from his illness. It was time to have their talk. He and Mary deserved to make their way in the world together.

He finished his shift and was heading up the hill to her house when he ran right into her. Her face was red and splotchy, eyes swollen, and she dabbed at them with a hanky, a hanky with blue-embroidered swirls.

She froze when she saw him. He rushed toward her and wrapped her in his arms, lifting her off the ground, not caring who saw. He was going to give her the ring and they would convince her parents once and for all that they belonged together.

She let him hold her, and when he released her, he saw the tears running down her face. "Your father's sick again?"

She shook her head.

"Then what?"

"Can we go to the shed?"

He nodded and took her hand. They ran the whole way there, as darkness was descending. He lit the lantern and started the fire, the March weather still chilly. He looked over his shoulder.

"Sit, Mary. What is it?"

She looked away from him.

Lukasz patted the ring in his pocket. "Come, sit." He realized she wasn't going to rip her clothes off like she often did when they reached the privacy of the shed.

They sat beside each other, and she pulled another hanky from her coat pocket and lined it up with the one Lukasz had given Victoria.

Lukasz stared at the two hankies, one of them with dark splotchy stains. It didn't make sense.

Mary turned them over and traced the messy strings on the back. "It's exact."

He thought of how Adam's mother described her work on the back of the ones she made. "The exact same mess."

"Exactly the same. Both of them." She held up the unstained one. "The one you gave my sister." She held up the stained one. "And this one."

He squinted at them, realizing that she was saying they were both his. "But how . . ."

"At Andrzejki two years ago. I was bending down, Aneta was standing up, and we smacked heads. I bled all over the place, and Aneta threw this at me."

He leaned back against the wall, replaying what he could remember of that evening. Aneta had come to the shed. He'd forgotten to help set up at the church. He walked her to St. Dominic's. She was angry, and then she cried. "That's right. I gave it to Aneta right before she went in . . . I guess. I think." He leaned forward again, looking at the hankies. "They are the same. I see."

She took his hand in hers. "That Andrzejki night I took the hanky to bed to keep it against my nose, and I was so mad when I woke up not having dreamt of my husband, not having dreamt of anything at all." She laughed. "My mother tried to stuff Ralph's shirt in my bed so I'd sleep with it. It was so stupid. All of it, but then . . . Today, I ironed and saw the two hankies together for the first time. I thought that maybe it was meant to be. This dumb little thing everyone hopes is true. Sleeping with clothing, melting wax, a shoe game. I can't believe I'm saying this, but . . ."

Lukasz wiped her tears. "We *are* meant to be. I told you of my silly mermaid dreams. And then I found you."

She nodded.

He pulled her tight. "We are meant to be."

She exhaled, her breath hot against his ear. She was stiff, not yielding or taking like normal, not even a little.

"What is it?"

He heard her force a swallow down.

He froze. "What?"

She pushed away from him. "I need to see your face."

"What is it?"

"A baby."

He raised his eyebrows. Baby. The word spooled through his mind until it spilled out into the room. "You? A baby?"

"Us," she said.

He wondered if he looked as shocked as he felt. He shouldn't have been. It wasn't as though he didn't know how these things happened. But he never wanted to linger on the thought, not even when it had crossed his mind a few times.

"Lukasz?"

He looked at her stomach. It appeared as flat as ever. "A baby."

She nodded and pulled his hand.

His mind reeled. Everything was in the wrong order. He dropped to his knees making Mary gasp. She grabbed his shoulders. "Are you sick? Are you going to throw up? Oh God, I knew I should have . . ."

He dug into his pocket and held up the rusted tin box he'd been carrying around.

Her mouth fell open as she pulled it from him and popped open the lid. He held his breath, watching her fish the ring out. She shook her head. "Oh, Lukasz." She ran her finger over the pink, oval quartz, the steel wire accommodating the stone's imperfect shape.

"I wanted it to be round, but it wanted to be oval. And slightly off, but . . ."

Mary cupped his cheek. He turned into her palm, kissing it.

"It took its own shape?"

He nodded.

"Like us," she said.

"Like us."

He stood and kissed her, his feelings overwhelming him. All the things he could never say to anyone else came spilling out, his English sentences tangling and catching on wrong words. "That night on the river, you rising out of water, shiny dress like mermaid skin, when your father broke your heart or when you dance, even with clumsy Samuel, with me, when you dive for a baseball and we all duck, when your face goes dark with deep sadness or lit by great joy, you're pure. Always true."

Tears began to fall down her cheeks and she looked like she was having trouble breathing. Was he being clear enough?

"No pretend with you," he said, shaking his head, searching for more words. "We look like we don't belong together, but we do. I should feel small, like nothing with no education, no good English, almost nothing to give you, not even American, but when we're together, I am ten feet tall. With you, I can do anything. I *am* everything." He had no idea if what he said made any sense. "Mary?"

He reached to wipe her tears at the same time she did, their hands joining. He kissed her fingers, pulling her closer. Wanting her to say something, anything.

She cocked her head looking like she was carefully choosing what to say. "You saved me, Lukasz. Again and again."

His chest filled at hearing this. Someone needed him. He hadn't felt this sense of belonging since his family splintered all those years before. *Love.* That's what it was, Mary loved him and he could feel it like his breath. He had purpose. "Marry me. Please."

She swallowed hard making his heart stop. But then she broke into a smile, her tears coming again. "Yes, yes, yes, I will."

He slipped the ring onto her finger and she laughed. The joy he'd seen her exude at various times was now just for him, for this moment.

She wiggled the ring around her finger. "It fits. It's … perfect." She looked at him, questioning. "How'd you get it right?"

"I just knew."

She nodded and latched her arms around his neck, pulling him close.

They kissed and caressed, shedding clothes along with every doubt. Together, each breath and touch felt right, and he knew, no matter what they'd face, they trusted each other. They were meant to be together. And so it would be.

Chapter 73

Mary

They left the shed, walking hand in hand to Mary's home, a skater lantern lighting their way that March night. Mary's stomach flipped from excitement, her nerves, their baby. They walked on the raised sidewalk on Heslep Avenue, large porched homes overlooking them.

Lukasz stopped. "Hold up the lantern."

Mary lifted it toward two homes, each with stone steps leading to welcoming entrances.

"You know I've been saving, Mary." Lukasz held his hands slightly apart, angled them so they pointed between the two homes. "See right there—that piece of land, slim like sliced bread?"

Mary nodded.

"Two warring brothers own those houses. They want something—someone—between them. We'll buy it, and we'll build a home. It'll be small, but someday . . ."

"You'll have a room for every child, and it will be beautiful. A beautiful life."

Mary exhaled. A home they would build and make the exact way they wanted. She rubbed her stomach. A baby! She envisioned them for the first time with a child in a little house wedged between warring brothers. The calm it would bring, her life settling as it should, soothing her worries. She crossed herself and said a Hail Mary, thanking God for the way her life had turned down a new path. A baby, an unexpected gift.

**

A baby. By the time Mary and Lukasz reached her home, all of Lukasz's reassurances had dissolved and Mary was choked with fear. Maybe they should just apply for a marriage license and lie about her age, then tell her parents everything at once. Plenty of girls did it that way. But Mary didn't want that; she wanted approval. A tiny wedding at St. Dominic's, her girlfriends gathered, Matka excited that Mary was finally a homemaker herself. They wouldn't have to confide the baby to anyone if they moved fast.

Mary quaked, her hand on the doorknob.

Lukasz put his hand on hers. "Together."

She nodded. "Forever and ever."

They turned the knob and entered. Papa was slumped in a chair across from the fireplace, staring into the flames. His long legs stretched outward, his cheek resting on his fist. Matka was darning socks across from him. They turned in unison, each of their faces growing dark when they noticed Mary and Lukasz's entwined fingers.

Papa pushed to his feet, his legs shaky after such a long illness. Mary immediately regretted their decision to tell her parents before getting married. Begging forgiveness would have been better.

Lukasz removed his hat. Mary put it on the rack. Her mother dropped her face in her hands as though she knew what was coming.

Lukasz walked forward. "Mr. and Mrs. Lancos, I'm glad you're well." He slowed his words, finishing each one at the end as best he could. "Mr. Lancos."

Her father gave a half nod, suspicion sweeping over his face.

Lukasz straightened, and Mary remembered when he had caught her father's flying fist on Christmas morning. *"Feed the strongman,"* Papa had grumbled, humbled by Lukasz's physical domination. Mary didn't want another wrestling match. She wanted them to like each other and realize they both loved her and should want the best for her.

As for Matka . . . Mary wasn't sure exactly what man would have suited her for Mary if not Ralph. Someone better than the Lancoses, but not too much better, like the Blakes were. Her parents should know that in America anything was possible. Papa had told her that since she was a child. Yet here she was jammed solidly between two worlds—American, yet not American enough.

"Mr. Lancos, I want to ask your permission," Lukasz said, stumbling over the word *permission* several times, "to marry your daughter. Your beautiful daughter. We are in love. We . . . I *love* her. I've saved money. I put my eye on a property, and we've planned—"

"No." Papa crossed his arms and glared. "The match is bad."

Mary stepped forward.

Papa put his hand up to stop her. "He's best suited for a mine. He wouldn't even have to bend over to work in one. His size is . . . his . . . he's not good enough for you, Mary. He'll end up in a mine, tire of it, take you to Poland, and you'll never come back. You'll lose your citizenship, and they won't let you back in. You won't be our daughter anymore, just some Polish peasant. And you're too young."

Mary couldn't believe what she was hearing. It sounded as though he'd rehearsed the list of reasons a million times. "Stop it. Matka was married already at my age, so I'm not too young. And Lukasz has work in the mill. He's not suited for the mine."

Papa bristled. "What's wrong with the mine?"

Mary flinched. “Nothing. I didn’t say that.” The next words caught in her throat. She was irate at Papa and his derision of Lukasz. She didn’t want to shame Papa, but she needed him to see the truth, the silliness in what he suggested. She drew herself up but made sure to soften what she said. “It’s that *you* don’t even have your citizenship, Papa. Lukasz wants his. He’ll apply in two years when he can. But you . . .” She shook her head slowly, not wanting to hurt him. “You’re a good man, a good American, even if you don’t have a paper that says so. Lukasz’s the same.”

Matka stood by Papa. “We forbid the union. No more Lukasz.” She swung her hand, palm out. “We thought if yinz had the chance to see each other clear, it’d end. Mistake. But now yinz are done. Stop thinking of each other.” She gestured to Lukasz. “Respect our wishes. Our family has decided.”

A flash of movement near the end of the hall forced Mary to look. Victoria and Ann leaned around the corner, crossing their fingers. Mary smiled. It wasn’t a matter of her family not approving. She needed to explain if Lukasz couldn’t.

He glanced at Mary. She took his hand and squeezed. “We do respect you. That’s why we’re here and not just running off.”

“Running off?” Papa scoffed.

“She’s hidden things before,” Matka said.

“No, it’s that—”

“Enough.” Papa stepped forward. “Enough games and playing with your choices. You’re my daughter. I’ll pick your husband. You’ve asked. I said no, so it’s no. Not another word.”

“You’ll see. I’m good for Mary,” Lukasz said.

“Get aht,” Papa yelled then started coughing into his hand.

“Yinz’ll make him sick with all this shit,” Matka said. “Cruel. Bringing this when he’s still fighting that flu.”

“He’s always sick, Matka. You say so yourself.”

Papa looked wounded.

“*Mary Lancos!*” Matka said.

"Always sick?" Papa glared at his wife.

"That damn Ella Mine," Matka said. "I could dig coal aht of yer lungs."

"I'm not weak!"

"We didn't mean that, Papa. It's just your cough, and it would make things easier if I'm out of the house. One less mouth to feed. Matka said so herself when I turned sixteen."

"Goddamn it, Mary, stop," Papa said. "You're purposely trying to make us angry, and it's sinful." His cough took hold again.

Mary and Lukasz looked at each other. "Why would I do that?" she asked, feeling wounded. She just wanted their blessing to go forward with the man she loved.

The baby.

Lukasz nodded at Mary. They had no choice. The baby would convince her parents, would change the way they viewed their request.

She squeezed Lukasz's hand tight. Her heart pounded. Her mouth went dry as she licked her lips. "There's a baby."

Her parents went from anger to shock, mouths dropping. Mary braced for the deluge. Matka'd been calm during this discussion, and Mary could envision the swirling outrage she'd been holding in. It would explode now if she couldn't understand that this was right. Mary braced. She was ready for the torrent.

Lukasz tensed, probably waiting to defend himself when Papa leapt at him.

Matka's lips quivered. Crying didn't come easily to her mother, and she appeared fragile and broken with the few words Mary had spoken. Papa stepped forward. Mary and Lukasz held their breath. Papa's cough returned midstride and he stopped.

Mary stepped back, waiting for his fists to fly at Lukasz, but Papa froze. He lifted a fist and shook it, then dropped it, leveling his gaze on Mary. He shook his head. "All these years." He cleared his throat, eyes welling, the expression much too similar to what Mary had witnessed when Matka had dragged him from the bar in Webster. "We talked about dreams on the boat, and you and . . ."

Mary wanted Papa to scream. She wanted Matka to throw something, wanted them to fight with her so she could convince them that Lukasz was exactly the kind of man she needed.

Papa looked at Mary's belly and flinched as though the very sight, the notion that she was carrying a baby, pained him.

"It'll be a boy, Papa. You'll see. We'll name him John after you and . . . you'll see."

He looked down with barely a shake of his head. Mary had never seen her parents bruised by something—not by the loss of pay, a roof that threatened the mortgage, her father's drinking binges that threatened the taxes, or all the mouths to feed.

"I forbid it," he said calmly. "I won't forgive you. You've made your choice. You chose to leave your family, your country." He covered his mouth with his shaking hand.

Mary stared at her parents, eyes darting from one to the other. Her life had been a roaring tornado of their forceful language and orders accompanied by swats or smacks, but now… this soft fuming, the quiet spreading of horror through the room, suffocated her slowly, gently. "That's it?" How could they just end things? Was it even possible to end things with one's daughter?

Papa turned and shuffled down the hall toward the bedrooms. Matka hadn't stopped staring. She stepped closer to Mary. She waited for a slap, left her cheek open to it. "You ain't learned nothin' from me, from that Mrs. Dunn. *Nothin'*." Her voice was frighteningly clear and steady, her hands clasped at her waist.

"Matka," Mary reached for her.

Matka brushed Mary's hand away and followed Papa without another word, her strong back slumped from all the anger she wouldn't let out.

The sudden still in the room was crushing, only the crackle of the fire in Mary's ears. Mary breathed deep to stave off the sadness, the fear. A spark landed on her dress. Lukasz swatted the fabric, extinguishing the ember.

He took her hands and pulled her to him, roping his arms tight around her, his lips at her ear. "It's all right, Mary. I am here."

**

Mary and Lukasz spent the night in the shed comforting each other, soothing the fears that alternately rose up in each of them. Their limbs tangled and they found comfort and love in that little shed on a half-sized cot, with reassuring words that they didn't need another single person. They had their strength, their goals, and their ambition. And now a baby.

"You'll have a special life, Mary. Do not worry. You'll have the home you dream of, the children, all of it. I was born under a lucky star. It demands a special life."

"I know, I know, I know," she breathed the words into her kiss, and they fell into sleep, waking to greater resolution. They had a plan, and there was no time to look back.

**

Mary and Lukasz set off to speak to Father Kroupal at St. Dominic's. He'd been kind to Mary many times, and when she approached, his face lit up as it always did. When he saw Mary holding hands with a man, his expression darkened. He rushed toward them with his hands up as though stopping them from entering.

"Hello, Father Kroupal."

He clasped his hands at his waist. "Hello, Mary."

"Can we talk to you?"

He tilted his head, glancing at Lukasz. "Oh, Mary. Your parents told me you might be coming."

Mary flinched. "Coming?"

"She worried you might have . . . well, who is this? Your young man? The man who . . ."

Mary nodded, introducing Lukasz to the priest. "He's Catholic. He's made all his sacraments in Poland."

Father Kroupal shook his head. "Your mother was so worried, concerned about your soul and purgatory—"

"Matka said the word *purgatory*? I'm the one who drags her to church most of the time. Did she mention her own purgatory?"

Father Kroupal narrowed his eyes. "Oh, Mary. I agree with them. Respect their wishes, and when they get to know Lukasz better, perhaps things may change. You know. I was pleased to see her and accept her donation to help save your soul, and for that, I must respect her wishes. You're too young. There's a home for young mothers you could go to, and your family will take you back afterward."

Donation? Her mother barely spared two dimes for the collection in Mass when money was tight, and now she solicited the help of a priest to keep them apart? Home for young mothers? "So that's it? You won't help us?"

The priest shook his head. "I am helping you."

Mary tugged Lukasz's hand and they trodded out of the church.

**

Mary waited for the tears to fill her as they left church, practically running. She was propelled by practical action. She was going to be a mother, and to do that, she needed to be a wife. No more time for sentimental musings about crushed dreams.

Lukasz quickened his pace to keep up with her long strides. "Let's go back, Mary. We'll give the priest a donation bigger than your mother's."

Mary shook her head. "No."

"Then what?"

"We go to the justice of the peace, get the application, and then we see. But we can't wait anymore. I don't want anyone to see my stomach before we're married, and we need my pay to have enough for a house."

They stopped and Lukasz held both her hands. "Oh, Mary. When we're not together and I imagine you, one of the things I think of is how you walk."

Mary cocked her head, surprised that of all the things he would catalog about her, how she walked would be one of them. "I don't know what that has to do with—"

"You're so sure of yourself. It's clear in your long, pretty walk. Proud."

She squinted. "Thank you, but we have to—"

"I know. I just wanted to tell you that no matter what, you're strong enough for anything, beautiful enough to be a princess, smart enough for . . ." He kissed her forehead. "For anything."

She smiled and leaned into him to whisper as people flooded past them heading to work or to shop. "Lukasz. We need to get married now. We have about three minutes before everyone in town can see I'm going to have a baby."

He nodded. "We'll go to St. Mary's. The Poles won't let us down." He shrugged. "But we'll have to lie."

She searched her mind for something Katya had said about her sister years before. Something about a license. "The priest won't question us if we go to the judge and have the marriage license for the priest beforehand. He'll assume I'm old enough to marry, and he'll do it for us. And Father Shivinsky doesn't know me. Other than to see me in passing."

Mary and Lukasz turned down the hill to go to the trolley. "We have just enough time to get to the courthouse in Washington and back to work. I need to work as long as possible."

Lukasz lifted his shoulders and let them drop. "So we just say to the judge we want to marry?"

"Yes. And that I'm—how old should I say? Seventeen?"

They boarded the trolley and sat in the back where it was empty, their heads pressed together. He scratched his chin. "No. Say twenty-three. That way they don't look twice at you."

"You're right. Every underage girl goes there saying she's just the right legal age."

"No. We'll say twenty," Lukasz said. "You looked twenty when I first saw you all those years back. On Candlemas Day."

Mary's eyes brightened. "Candlemas Day Mass. That's right . . . the candles."

"The judge won't question."

They sighed in unison and Lukasz kissed her forehead. "Your father will forgive you. I know it. He loves you more than anything. I can see."

She looked away, not wanting to consider that he might not. "I hope you're right, Lukasz. I hope you're right."

Chapter 74

Mary

On April 14th, 1913, Mary and Lukasz stood in St. Mary's Church in front of Father Orziemaxeuski. To Mary's left was Zofia, who'd lent her a white dress that no longer fit her. She held Mary's bouquet of lily of the valley and one pink rose with some greens. Alexander stood for Lukasz, a tear glistening down his cheek, making Mary smile despite the sadness that no one in her family attended the wedding.

The baby stirred inside her, thrilling Mary. Lukasz put a second ring he'd made for Mary on her finger and added the engagement ring, making Zofia swoon. As the couple walked down the aisle with Zofia and Alexander trailing behind, Mary saw something out of the corner of her eye—a person ducking into the confessional.

Matka?

The woman was the right height, the right build, and had the right hair. Mary stopped.

"What is it?" Lukasz asked. "Are you all right?"

She stared at the thick confessional door. Something inside told Mary it was her mother. She was there, even if hidden.

Lukasz pulled Mary's elbow. "Come on. Zofia made us wonderful lunch."

Mary's throat tightened, wanting her family to have been there. Zofia and Alexander came closer. "Let's go, beautiful bride," Alexander said.

Mary nodded, willing the person who'd gone into the confessional to come out and show herself.

But maybe it was best if Mary didn't know for sure. She could pretend it was Matka, that deep down she was happy for Mary and saw that Lukasz would be a wonderful husband.

Lukasz wrapped his arm around Mary, guiding her toward the exit. "I love you, Mary Musial."

She looked at him close, his soulful gray eyes hiding blue same as the Donora sky, conveying more love than she imagined possible for two people to feel.

Love.

It was enough for them. It was going to have to be.

Chapter 75

Patryk

2019

In the hospital—or still jailed, as he thought of it—Patryk sat up and snuck a cigarette and a lone match from his wallet. The nurses would give him hell, but no worse than what his granddaughter would do if she caught him. Just one drag, maybe three, would do.

Owen walked out of the bathroom and saw what Patryk was doing. "Whoa, whoa, whoa, Gramps." He loped across the room, yanked the cigarette out of Patryk's hand, and stomped it out. "Gramps, seriously. You trying to get us kicked out?"

"What do you think?"

Owen clutched his chest. "You could have blown us all up. There's oxygen."

"Where?" Patryk asked, turning a page in his book.

"Everywhere. It's a hospital."

"I goddamn know that. We were supposed to be sprung hours ago."

Owen sighed just as his mother walked into the room, waving papers over her head.

"We're outta here."

"Mercy. Thank you, Jesus." Patryk swung his legs over the edge of the bed and then got woozy.

Owen and his mother swooped in and supported him while his senses returned.

His book slipped off his lap, smacking the floor. "My book."

Owen scooped the book off the floor and cradled it. "Can't wait for more of that story."

"You like it?"

"We love it," Lucy said.

"So Lukasz and Mary got married?" Owen asked. "And that's for real?"

"'Course. We wouldn't have Stan Musial without Mary and Lukasz Musial."

"But the mermaid stuff, the strongman?"

Patryk jammed his thumb toward Owen. "Were you snoozing for half the story?"

Lucy smiled at Owen. "Those myths stick around for a reason."

"Oh, Mom, come on. No such thing."

"Well, Lukasz was a strongman for sure," Patryk said. "Mary was practically a mermaid. But it doesn't really matter, does it? The story is as it should be."

"Well, sort of. Her dad forgave her, right? Did he like Lukasz once the baby was born?"

Patryk sighed. "Well, Owen, my boy, that's all folded into Stan's story. When we're back at my kitchen table with beers and shots and chipped ham sandwiches, I'll tell you all of that. *That's* a story for tomorrow."

The End . . .
For now . . .

Also by Kathleen Shoop

Historical Fiction:

The Letter Series:
The Last Letter—Book One
The Road Home—Book Two
The Kitchen Mistress—Book Three
The Thief's Heart—Book Four
The River Jewel—A prequel

The Donora Story Collection
After the Fog—Book One
The Strongman and the Mermaid—Book Two
The Magician—Book Three

Romance:

Endless Love Series:
Home Again—Book One
Return to Love—Book Two
Tending Her Heart—Book Three

Women's Fiction:

Love and Other Subjects

Bridal Shop Series:
Puff of Silk—Book One

Holiday:

The Christmas Coat
The Tin Whistle